"The reason you've never read a book like *Appleseed* is that there's never been a book like *Appleseed*. The scary thing, though, is this is a world you might recognize. This premise, this content, this form, this language—only Matt Bell could have given us this novel."

—Stephen Graham Jones, author of *The Only Good Indians*

"A meditative thriller with an ethical heart." —NPR.org

"Woven together out of the strands of myth, science fiction, and ecological warning, Matt Bell's *Appleseed* is as urgent as it is audacious."

—Kelly Link, author of *Get in Trouble*

"There's a particular thrill reading a book that has such certainty of vision, one that guides every page and allows us to truly picture the connections between our past and our future. We see the naturalist's mind placed in the realm of the imagination as a way to try to grasp what's happening to our planet right now. It's a beautiful tribute to what fiction can do, and these characters and their visceral struggles will remain with me for a long time."

—Aimee Bender, author of *The Butterfly Lampshade*

"[An] ambitious speculative epic and striking take on climate change." —*USA Today*, Summer's Hottest Books

"Myth meets science; fable confronts existential crisis. In its bountiful prose, gleeful genre-hopping, and the sheer scope of its storytelling, *Appleseed* points toward hopeful futures for literature—and the planet."

—Sam J. Miller, Nebula Award–winning author of *Blackfish City*

"Matt Bell's *Appleseed* expands in the most entrancing manner to encompass everything from the hidden hoofs of fauns to the pending doom of the planet. What a sui generis feat of imagination and scope this novel is."

—Idra Novey, author of *Those Who Knew*

"Part tech thriller and part reimagined legend, *Appleseed* is a thought-provoking and mysterious read that explores climate change, manifest destiny, and corporate versus family responsibility. One of those books where every time you try to put it down, you inevitably say, 'Okay, just one more chapter.'"

—*Fort Worth Magazine*

"In *Appleseed*, magic and science aren't integrated but simply juxtaposed; the juxtaposition suggests that mythologies of hybrid human beasts have been transferred over time into imaginings of robot beasts, genetically modified creatures and people who can exist outside their bodies. It proposes a fungibility of matter and consciousness that's both horrific and transcendent."

—*Los Angeles Times*

"This ambitious work of climate fiction weaves together three timelines to depict the myriad ways that humans destroy their environments. . . . This fascinating novel is rich in thought-provoking ideas and world-building."

—Buzzfeed

"With Bell's inventive incorporation of myths and legends, this is an unparalleled and unforgettable examination of the effects of climate change."

—Book Riot

"Thought-provoking and accomplished, [Bell's] new novel acknowledges its debts to climate fiction and demands that readers examine the implications of humanity's relationship with the natural world. In *Appleseed*, Bell asks a new set of intriguing questions about what might constitute the future of the world—and who or what will be left to experience it."

—*Sierra*

APPLESEED

APPLESEED

A NOVEL

MATT BELL

MARINER BOOKS

New York   Boston

P.S.™ is a trademark of HarperCollins Publishers.

HarperCollins books may be purchased for educational, business, or sales promotional use. For information, please email the Special Markets Department at SPsales @harpercollins.com.

A hardcover edition of this book was published in 2021 by Custom House, an imprint of William Morrow.

FIRST MARINER BOOKS PAPERBACK EDITION PUBLISHED 2022.

Designed by Angela Boutin

Frontispiece & part titles © starostov/stock.adobe.com

Library of Congress Cataloging-in-Publication Data

Names: Bell, Matt, 1980- author.
Title: Appleseed : a novel / Matt Bell.
Description: First edition. | New York, NY : Custom House, [2021]
Identifiers: LCCN 2020050897 (print) | LCCN 2020050898 (ebook) | ISBN 9780063040144 (hardcover) | ISBN 9780063040151 (trade paperback) | ISBN 9780063090385 | ISBN 9780063040168 (ebook)
Classification: LCC PS3602.E64548 A86 2021 (print) | LCC PS3602.E64548 (ebook) | DDC 813/.6—dc23
LC record available at https://lccn.loc.gov/2020050897
LC ebook record available at https://lccn.loc.gov/2020050898

ISBN 978-0-06-304015-1

22 23 24 25 26 LSC 10 9 8 7 6 5 4 3 2 1

For Jessica

Where now can one find the certainty that the world is a machine since in so many respects it resembles a tree?

—Magdalena Tulli, *Dreams and Stones*

When I added the dimension of time to the landscape of the world, I saw how freedom grew the beauties and horrors from the same live branch.

—Annie Dillard, *Pilgrim at Tinker Creek*

A man is ruled by appetite and remorse, and I swallowed what I could.

—Elise Blackwell, *Hunger*

APPLESEED

I n the faun's clawed and calloused hands the pomace comes
out rich and sweet, a treasure of crushed cores and waxy skins
and pulped flesh, a dozen colors of apples distinct in the gap
between the cider mill's grindstone and its wheel. He squeezes
his fingers into the trough—if the wheel slips, he'll lose his
hairy hand—and jerks free a handful of mash, dumping it onto
a stretch of cheesecloth spread across the floor. He hops side to
side, his hooves sliding on the slick boards, his claws' sharpness speeding the pomace's recovery from the circular groove.
Occasionally he lifts his horned head to nervously watch the
millhouse door: if he strains he can hear his half brother's voice
outside, still negotiating for seeds already freely given.

The faun hurries to finish before his brother loses the miller's attention: his brother has many gifts, but a penchant for entrancing gab is not one. Every seed he pries from the mill comes
up wet, each black kernel is coated in mottled skin, browning
flesh, strands of core—all moisture and fertilizer for the long
walk ahead. The room is thick with apple-drunk wasps, but the

faun ignores their buzzing and the prickling welts their stings raise along his forearms.

Despite the irritation, he harbors the wasps no ill will: What else should a wasp be except a wasp?

The faun digs and sorts, pushing more seeds inside his leathern bag, filling it to bursting, then tamping down the mash to make room for more seeds. The moisture of the pressed pomace seeps through the tanned skin; by the time the brothers reach the Territory, a musk of sickly rot and sweet fermentation will have worked its way deep into the faun's fur.

Ten years into this apple planter's life, the faun has come to crave this clinging, cloying smell: the smell of the future he and his brother are making, all their orchards to be, the smell of his truest hope, that the Tree he seeks waits inside these seeds— although even if this is the year he plants it, then still ten more impatient years must pass before the Tree the seed contains might deliver its first ripe apple, revealing itself—and as always whenever the faun makes himself sick with hope, it's because the pomace's rotted drunken scent promises him something else, something more than mere trees, and yes, as he lifts the next fistful of crushed apple to his nose and breathes in its ferment, there it is, that hoped-for future beyond smell, beyond taste, beyond want, where one day this faun must go, forgotten and forgetting.

PART ONE

CHAPMAN

THE INVINCIBLE EARTH

Chapman wakes in the cold and the dark and the wet pre-dawn slush to the sound of his brother, Nathaniel, already up and tending to the sputtering ashes of last night's fire, cursing and shivering, huddled beneath his only blanket; despite Nathaniel's ministrations, the coals beneath the ashes stay dead, the gathered wood wet, breakfast impossible. Shelling himself out from his bedroll, Chapman rises too, offering his brother a grunted good morning before stamping his cloven hooves against the frigid ground, trying to quicken blood sluggish with sleep. As first light breaks, he stalks silently away from their campsite, climbing the last ridgeline of this Pennsylvanian mountain pass to watch the night's rainfall trickle off into morning mist, admiring the fine accidental melody of clean water falling branch to branch; a moment later dutiful

Nathaniel follows along, dragging their bags and tools to where Chapman waits upon his outcropping of rock, one clawed hand raised to shield his golden eyes as he surveys the forest they'll cross today, snowpack still jamming the forest's shadows, sparkling ice coating its swampy glacial kettles and its irregular lakes, all this waiting beauty backlit now by the red shroud of sunrise, the new day's dawn setting aglow a vast world not yet fully explored.

"This, brother," Nathaniel says, placing one calloused hand on taller Chapman's bare brown shoulder, waving the other out over the Territory below, "this is where we'll make our fortune." Pointing out the first landmarks they're due to pass today, he traces a path out of this mountain gap and down through the slim strand of tilled earth that gives entrance to the Ohio Territory, then the way beyond into the unsettled, unmapped forest swamps of the interior, past the river bottomlands and sheltered ravines where they sowed last year's nurseries, toward the next uninhabited acres where they'll aim to plant this year's seeds.

As Nathaniel happily details his plans, Chapman smiles his much-practiced smile, his sharp teeth slipping from behind his broad lips. "Look, brother," he interrupts, pointing out dim campfires barely visible through the morning mist, flickers of flame and smoke rising in far-off sheltered dales. "There are so many more of us this year."

Every year, these fires move deeper into the landscape, each one a distant sign of strangers come to expand the human mark, to put the land to what Nathaniel has taught Chapman are its rightful uses: here are settlers hunting and trapping and gathering wild foodstuffs, cutting down trees and tearing up rocks to make room for placeholder farms, making way for the

towns to come, while others tap trees for sap and hang tin sug-
aring buckets over hot coals, sometimes passing the time with
amateur fiddling, the inviting sounds of their instruments carrying across even the most desolate starless, moonless nights.

Together the brothers measure again the increasingly be-
lievable potential of this Territory, its wilderness cleared by war
then emptied by treaty; as he has at the start of every other
year's journey, Nathaniel tells Chapman again how this taken
land can now be brought to heel by industrious men, how by
many hands the foundations of a new civilization will be laid
here, the land year by year made ready for the coming of more
people, until one day the uncultivated earth gives way to what
he says will surely be the grandest of cities, each graced by
the tallest buildings and the widest avenues, all populated by
an endless parade of hardy settlers planting horizon-busting
fields of wind-tilted golden grain, harvesting fruitful orchards
planted by these two forward-thinking brothers.

Chapman and Nathaniel and these others gathered around
their distant fires are only the first to come, he says. "Even if our
industries should fail entirely," Nathaniel concludes, "surely we
will not be the last."

Nathaniel has said this for ten years now, the same lines recited from the same mountain pass at the outset of each year's
venture. "It's time to go," Chapman says, suddenly impatient
with his brother's story. He ties his bedroll and his tools over
one bare shoulder, slings his leathern seed bag around the
other. The morning air is chilled and damp, but the bark of
his skin keeps him warm enough that even in winter he wears
no shirt or coat, only a pair of trousers hacked off above his
inhuman knees. He dusts the last of the night's frost from his
flanks, then whinnies lowly, stretching tall to rub the smooth

shells of his curved horns with his clawed hands, first his broken horn and then its intact twin, for luck. Nathaniel laughs, then mimics his brother's superstitions, rubbing his own bare temples, where just recently a few gray hairs have started creeping through the brown.

"Meet you at the river," Nathaniel teases, sidestepping onto the narrow trace path leading down the ridgeline, "if you can catch me." He rushes to build his slim head start, but his advantage doesn't last long. A moment later Chapman surges past him to drop down the steep plunge of the mountainside, his hooves sliding precariously on loose scree as he picks up speed, the joy of moving fast filling him from the inside out, his fur standing on end, his heart leaping with happy effort. He quickens his pace with every step until a barking cry rips free of him, the sound of his voice foreign enough to this Territory and every other to frighten all the nearby roosting birds into sudden startled flight, the gray sky filling with their black silhouettes, their many cries joining the whooping of this one faun, returned at last to wildest lands.

AS MANY YEARS AS CHAPMAN'S MADE THIS PASSAGE OUT OF PENN-sylvania, the thrill of arriving in the Territory has never ceased to provoke his fullest wonder. Propelled by joy, he runs dangerously this morning, his furred legs taking leaping, straining steps, his splayed hooves seeking purchase on sharp juttings of quivering rock, on old-growth roots thrust through black earth and slushy snow, other obstacles threatening to trip him and send him sprawling. When his descent smooths onto more level ground, he increases his speed again, his few possessions banging rhythmically against his muscular torso as all around him the forest deepens. The sun has only a pale power beneath these trees, where the frontier's every shaded feature is a fresh barrier to progress. Searching for the way forward, Chapman follows a trail trampled by first peoples or fur trappers or single-file processions of deer, the path a barely visible scrawl plotting the way forward, then crosses dry strands of seasonal creeks strewn with the lacy bones of trout, an unremembered stream quickening with snowmelt; he encounters a thicket impassible except by hacking out each halting step with his tomahawk. He leaps fallen columns of oak and maple, vaults lichen-stung trunks maybe giving shelter to squirming snakes, the only animals he can't abide; his movements scatter squirrels and chipmunks playing amid rotted leaves, forest mice leaping hungrily over melting snow. Once an explosion of foxes appears, a half-dozen pups running through the flattened grass of a meadow once purpled with loosestrife, yellowed with goldenrod; in the moist underbrush he spies the year's first warty toads hopping hungrily through the moldings of mud rattlers and the pellets of horned owls.

Abundance everywhere, everywhere gathering and joy and predation and sorrow: amid all this untamed splendor, every acre of forest is an empire in the shape of the world.

Wherever Chapman ventures next there waits some unnamed waterway or unexplored meadow, some ridge never described, never made anyone's landmark. Or so he once believed, come late to this landscape cleared of its most recent inhabitants. Now he just as frequently exits untouched woods to find newly planted lands, the forest's brambles burned back, its glacier-spilled stones stacked into makeshift garden walls, so many trees felled to make rough-sawn boards, boards nailed into unsound houses held upright by mortar and tar and hope.

New construction makes Chapman nervous; long inhabitation doubly so. From his youngest days, he could follow a wooded trail haphazardly stamped flat but couldn't abide a road cleared by men with picks and shovels and mules; he could skirt the edges of farms but couldn't cross their fenced-in fields without his skin aching with hives, his bones burning in their sockets.

Only after Nathaniel hit on the idea of planting frontier orchards did Chapman begin to better acculturate himself, their nurseries tucked amid their wilder cousins easing his flesh toward the idea of the domesticated, Nathaniel's stands of apple trees wild enough for Chapman to pass among them as long as the trees are planted from seeds, never grafted.

By midday he reaches the river he seeks, the sun emerging over its clear, fast course, its waterline raised by snowmelt and spring rains. He squats over his hooves to scan the sparkling water for signs of trout coming up to feed on the gathering insects, hungry for their pleasurable slap and splash, then picks a tick from his fur, squeezing the pin of its head with clawed fingers, the pressure not enough to kill it but certainly to make it release. Half wild as he is, he doesn't count himself as one of the forest creatures, but anything afflicting them might afflict him too, a lesson painfully learned his first wet season in the Territory, when he caught a hoof rot that Nathaniel treated as he would any common goat's: with dreadful cuttings, then the application of stinking herbal salves.

Waiting for Nathaniel, Chapman swings his bag around his bare frame, rests it above his bony knees. He pulls it open even though he shouldn't—the seeds could easily dry out despite the moist pomace and pulp—and then he plunges his head into the bag's opening, breathes deep the wet ferment inside. Around him are a thousand fresher scents, all the Territory's perfumes and poisons, promises and provocations, but Chapman's favorite is the one he carries lashed to his chest, kept contained within his satchel: not the attractive smell of apples ready to be picked, not the smell becoming taste of an apple bitten, but this rotten stinking hope, the intoxicating promise of *what next*.

The Tree, the Tree, the Tree: taste and smell are almost the same sense, even in memory, even in dream; with his face buried in the leathern bag, Chapman imagines the taste-smell of the apple of the Tree he tells himself it's possible to plant, to grow, to harvest one glowing apple from, one apple all he'll need to change his life.

Let Nathaniel make his fortune, if he can. All Chapman wants is one particular apple.

The faun sneezes, snorts, and shakes. He removes his head from the bag, gives his attention back to the phenomenal world at hand, the light already different, the shadows slightly shifted in a moment, then more so by the time Nathaniel arrives an hour later, huffing down the narrow riverbank.

"Brother," Nathaniel says, revealing a shirt wet with perspiration as he unshoulders his burden. He takes a knee, tries to catch his breath. "You waited for me this time."

"Yes, brother," Chapman happily replies, both of them grinning now, both glad to be back in the Territory, to be here together. Nathaniel has the steadiest step in the Territory, his stride is swift and sure; he is a man sure of his place, a plower of fields, a planter of seeds, a man charged to bring order to the wild chaos—but without Chapman he'd soon be lost. There are no reliable maps of the Territory and the brothers carry no compasses, relying instead on Chapman's wilder parts to suss out wild ways for them to travel: as they leave the riverbank, he kneels, puts his nose to the wet ground.

"What is it?" Nathaniel asks, but Chapman only shushes him.

"Quiet," he says, stretching low against the fragrant earth. He sucks in a deep breath through flared nostrils, finds his own smells intruding: sweat and dirt, tobacco, apple flesh; the wind within the skin, his trap of bark and fur. He filters himself out, tries again. This is trail as a container for sign, visual, auditory, olfactory: the stamped mud and broken twigs, the kicked-away pine straw and haphazard middens of fur-laced feces and owl pellets; the sounds of birds pecking at exposed seeds; the smell of decaying matter being carted away by ants or beetles. This is trail as time travel: to be able to read the signs is to know this place as it was hours or days before. In the dirt it is written: the last time it rained, the last time it snowed, flooding the landscape, burying it beneath white powder; how long since there was lightning overhead, bright danger sparking low above the tinder.

"This way," Chapman says, leading Nathaniel through narrow bands of grass gently trampled by deer and moose, then along routes traveled by the wolves and coyotes and bobcats the brothers sometimes believe they see stalking black slates of dark slashed between the trees. Hours later, they make their first camp, their hearts glad for the smooth progress of their first day back in the Territory; tonight and every night they will sleep bared beneath the naked stars, without even a tent to spare them from the weather. Always they travel light, then endeavor to travel lighter. They can't leave behind their bags of seeds, but much they believed they could not live without in Pennsylvania will be discarded in the wilder Territory, unnecessary weight left in the ruins of some minimal campsite, near a blackened splotch of earth where they burned a fire, a matted stretch of grass where they lay down to sleep upon what will soon be threadbare blankets.

As their westerly journey continues, the spring sun shines warmer every day, but in the shadows beneath the trees the snow often persists and the damp heavies their lungs, producing phlegmy coughs that leave Nathaniel racked in his bedroll but barely inconvenience hardy Chapman. Despite their hunting and gathering they are often underdressed and underfed, their bodies thinning as they grow irritated with each other's constant presence, each other's tics and habits; they squabble and bicker, but nonetheless there is laughter too, nonetheless there are moments of beauty beneath the great trees. The penumbra hemming the light of their campfire. The way yesterday's rain trickles through the canopy of pine and oak. The deep moist loam pungent beneath their feet. The distant cries of coyotes, the happy snuffling of a nearby bear whose feeding goes unperturbed by their passage; few sounds are better than the bright tinkling of running water somewhere ahead, a chance to refill their waterskins.

Time and miles pass. To ease the hours as they walk, they sing together, their voices forming rough harmonies over snatches of half-remembered hymns, bawdy folk tunes; at night they crowd beside their campfire to dry their bones, lighting their pipes and talking of the nurseries they'll plant every year forever, of the matured orchards they'll revisit this autumn. "I believe in the promise of the wilderness," Nathaniel says, staring into the firelight, as nightly he repeats his self-made creed. "I believe this continent's far territories, each equally dense and foreboding and unpathed, await only the bravery of good men. And I believe in the taming of those wilds, how any acre not put to use is an acre wasted."

The good earth, the invincible earth, the earth that can only be improved, made more useful, better suited for Christian inhabitation; an earth giving up its treasure for the good of mankind, a race of which Chapman is at least partly a part.

Mostly this future waits its distant turn. In the present, there is the dark forest to navigate, there are nurseries to plant and land to claim with trees, trees they'll one year sell to settlers surely following behind them. Every morning Chapman and Nathaniel roll their dew-soaked bedrolls, pack their one pot, Nathaniel complaining his clothes will never dry from the forest's damp, Chapman leading his shivering brother onward, his hooves following the trails of other hooved beasts. Unlike Nathaniel, who slinks off to hunt whenever the opportunity presents itself, Chapman never eats the flesh of these animals. But neither does he fear starvation, not here in the bountiful Territory, its lands filled with bright bunches of berries, with undomesticated fruits and wild corn, with pale tubers hidden beneath the rich dirt.

Despite the ever-present chill beneath the canopy's shade, sometimes a bright shaft of sunlight beams through wherever some tree has fallen beneath the weight of winter snow or the sharp crack of spring lightning. Weeks into their journey, the brothers stand in one such pillar of light, clapping each other's shoulders affectionately, this man and half-man united by their journey and by the destiny Nathaniel has designed for them to earn.

"I believe, brother," he says, his face flush with the sunbeam's warmth, "that you and I can put this place to its right uses, that you know best what might grow where, what land might take our seeds and make them thrive."

In this Nathaniel is correct: whatever else Chapman is, his wildness is a boon, his faunish body a living dowser for good earth. By his guidance the brothers soon arrive at a sharp bend in a river's creased arc, fertile soil holding a stand of tall trees tucked inside its watery curve, some of them healthy and whole, some recently lightning burned and therefore easier to remove.

"Here," Chapman says, "right here," he repeats, pointing at the level stretch of riverbank that surrounds them.

"Yes, brother," Nathaniel agrees, rubbing his hands together. Even with the land waiting to be cleared, it's possible to imagine a humble house appearing here, a home where a man and his wife and his children might grow some crops and raise some stock and even catch fish for dinner, brown trout leaping over a manageable rapid, their mouths hungry for the hook.

Chapman is one of a kind; he'll build no house nor plant any garden, he accepts he'll have no wife and raise no children, not like this, not as a species of one, half wild and half man, alone in the world except for his human brother. *Later*, Nathaniel says of his own prospects, deferring any pursuit of his desired family until he's made his fortune in apple trees. For now only today exists, and today they'll plant a nursery so some other man might come here and finish the work, all that must be done to settle this land as Nathaniel's Lord intends: to the good life of husbandry and stewardship, to the total dominion promised all righteous men willing to put to profitable use every square inch of this God-gifted earth.

JOHN

THE MANIFEST EARTH

John squeezes sideways through a slim slot in the Utahn stone, his shirt rasping against the rough surface of the red rock canyon, its walls baking with the desert summer's heat; he emerges covered in rust-colored dust, dust worn free by burning winds over tens of thousands of scorching days. On the other side of the slot waits a high-walled cul-de-sac of stone, a roofless chamber gaped toward the sun and the wind, its floor piled with hundreds of sun-bleached bones, startlingly white femurs and skinny ribs and cracked skulls, other joints and struts of the many shattered skeletons cast into this pit. A bone might last forever in the desert, but it's not the bones John has come to see. Painted across the chamber's red rock walls are varnished figures, tall black smears of charcoal, once colorful inks blanched gray by time. Nearly every figure is male, each is an exaggeration of a man: men running, men hunting, men worshipping, raising lanky arms to a distended sun, their torsos overly long, limbs stretched and unarticulated.

Giants of a vanished earth, giving praise to a world now gone. John's come to stand among them, to confront their remains. He traces the black lines of the petroglyphs, their meanings opaque, untranslatable. Perhaps this one a bird. Perhaps this one a fox. Perhaps this one an ancient bear, more dangerous than the recently extinct grizzlies. Whatever the original intent, eventually the mode of every sign becomes elegy, even ink scraped into timeless rock. John kneels, scattering bones and stones, then runs his hands through the dust. He smears the cooling smatter over his face in hot white streaks, inhaling a deep breath of bone and rock; he matches a set of ancient antlers, rattling the bleached bones, their knotty knobs cackling as he raises the horns. When the bones touch his forehead, he starts, surprised at the feeling of bone on skin, his face flushing with shame or fear or both.

John throws the antlers away, lets them clatter forgotten to the canyon floor. In the quiet that follows, he stands, wiping his hands on his jeans, then turns in a circle to take in the paint and the bones one more time: intellectually he understands what he sees, but as always the feeling eludes him. Maybe it's too late for him to feel what he thinks the people who worshipped here must've felt: to be of the world, not against it; to live with the plants and the animals, not apart or above them. It's not so easy to shake off his culture, his fading but still omnipresent civilization, despite all it ruined and wasted, despite knowing all he knows about what it's cost, what it will continue to cost; maybe he won't ever be able to feel at peace with the world or at home in it, not as he desires.

Maybe not. But what he does next doesn't have to be for him. Maybe all he can do is keep trying to give the world back to itself, to continue to free whatever he can from the long damage of human want.

DESPITE THE DISAPPOINTMENT IN THE CANYONLANDS, JOHN'S PILgrimage continues. The next morning, he drives north into Wyoming, through the Grand Tetons toward what was once Yellowstone. At the park's southern entrance, he retrieves his bolt cutters from the truck's bed, then clips the chains sealing the gate. His presence here is a crime unlikely to be punished, the Park Service already shuttered ten years, but still he notes the solar panels powering roadside wireless readers, there to record his ID and report his trespass, a sure danger if he hadn't already disabled the pebble buried in his right hand, that inescapable bit of Earthtrust tech embedded now in nearly every American body.

Earthtrust. After the catastrophic California earthquake finally struck, it was Earthtrust that pushed an emergency funding bill through the last true Congress in Washington, a rushed order seizing all lands west of the Mississippi; then using eminent domain and the president's emergency powers to create the Western Sacrifice Zone, a long-planned takeover waiting only for the right shock: half the country abdicated and sold to Earthtrust for dollars an acre by a weakened government busy fleeing to dryer land in Syracuse.

"We hoped these days would never come. We promised to be prepared for when they did," Eury Mirov had said then, the Earthtrust director's broad smile flashing from the country's every telescreen. "Now we are ready. Now we are coming to the rescue." Two weeks later, unmarked convoys of soldiers and squadrons of lifter drones swarmed the West Coast, rescuing whoever they could—whether or not the victims wanted rescuing—and evacuating them to resettlement camps hastily erected in the Mojave, then to Ohio, where the first Volunteer Agricultural Community was being built even as Oregon and Washington seceded.

In those days, John had been in Ohio too, with Earthtrust, with Eury. He'd known her since childhood, but in those first months of the country's collapse he'd felt constantly off-balance, unable to understand how Eury had moved so fast, carrying out previously unspoken plans with a brutal tactical efficiency he hadn't realized she'd possessed. When he left her company, years after his first misgivings, he fled into the Sacrifice Zone with Cal and the others also quitting Earthtrust, all of them together promising to somehow one day push back. He hadn't wanted to meet violence with more violence, like Cal had; he'd simply wanted to atone for his part in what had happened, for the world he'd help bring into being.

Today he arrives at Yellowstone's Lamar Valley by noon, driving a browning landscape whose mountains no longer promise any hint of snowpack, only burned trees cascading down the slopes. John parks his truck at the top of a narrow ridge, leaving the unmaintained park road to walk into the valley on foot. Thirty years ago, John's father had brought his son here to share his awe of this greatest of America's preserves, the size of its wild-enough herds of buffalo and elk and bighorn sheep, the promise of spotting wolves at dawn; as a child of ten, John had stood shoulder to shoulder with other tourists to

watch the last pristine bison herd, the Lamar Valley bison the
only such animals never interbred with cattle to make them
tamer, more amenable to human contact.

Now the Lamar Valley's previous beauty has become a stark-
ness unbroken by movement, its emptiness a bleak power. John
takes in the eerie near-silence of the valley, no sound except
the wind rustling dry plants, the river trickling down below;
at the river's edge, he momentarily closes his eyes to listen to
the water's gentle rush whispering over worn rocks, breathing
deep the elusive scents of the dry grass and the sparse plants
along the riverbank. Before he opens his eyes, he tries to picture that long-ago day spent at some similar part of this river
with his father, when the hundreds of bison roaming the prairie
had been entirely uninterested in the encroaching crowds. He's
come today hoping for any sign of the old magic he'd sensed
then, so different from what he'd felt amid the fields of his father's farm. If he could only see that something of the wild
majesty that was had returned to this place, to these parklands
emptied of people with the rest of the Sacrifice—but when he
scans the opposing bank's tree line, his gaze meets not the bison he craves but instead the narrow wedge of a wolf's curious
face, impassively peering from the pines.

John startles. He knows he shouldn't approach—the wolf's
a hundred meters away, atop a steep embankment on the opposite side of the river—but he can't help himself. How lonely
he's been, how devastated he's become by his aloneness in the
months since he last saw Cal or any of the others he'd come west
with; now his loneliness colors every empty landscape, anywhere once home to more bountiful life. He fords the river,
splashing loudly, the wolf already backing away from the tree
line. Slowed by his sloshing boots, John clambers atop the

ridge, pulling himself up by the fracturing branches of the dry pines; he's soon out of breath, breathlessly hopeless. Likely the wolf was never there. Just more wishful thinking, in a world quick to punish such thoughts.

But then he finds it again, twenty meters away: gray furred, steel eyed, healthy enough, with no sign of mange or malnutrition.

The wolf permits John's gaze, gazes back. Then it begins to nose through the grass at something John at first can't quite see, then can't look away from: surrounding the wolf are the corpses of dead bison, erratic boulders of shaggy fur.

John approaches slowly, wary of the wolf and its snuffling progress. He counts a dozen giant bodies, then glimpses more hidden by the rustling grass: here a powerful leg ending in a strangely dainty hoof, there a horn curving through the stalks. Through the tall cover, he sees an unnervingly large yellow eye, open and staring, jaundiced and bloodshot; it's all he can see of a massive head except for the curve of one broken horn, the rest of its bulk obscured. The eye is cloudy, staring at nothing—and then it moves, rolls crazily in the broad black-furred face.

John cries out, unnerved; the wolf continues to pace nearby, unperturbed, its tongue lolling loose between its teeth. Watching John inch toward the injured bison, the wolf's face is blank, its mask that of every wild mammal, full of nuances John's never learned to read, but when he gets too close, it barks with a high-pitched yip, then barks again, the sound sharper now. At this second yip, the bison cries out too, its mournful groan shivering John's skin. He carefully pushes back the grass to reveal the unbelievable bulk of the injured animal, its hooves jerking dreamily, its body rocking in the dusty earth as it tries and fails to stand. It's a last juvenile, orphaned and alone, its stout ribs pressing through stretched skin and matted fur, its bold shoulders too atrophied to lift its heavy skull.

John kneels, rests his hand on the bison's bony crown. The bison snuffles, presses back against his touch—or so John imagines. Not everything in the world exists for him, and certainly not this futureless herd. The wolf lingers nearby, packless in this valley where the most successful reintroduction program in the country once thrived. It stalks uncannily from corpse to corpse, nosing each of the dead bison in turn, sniffing and prodding but not eating. Something's wrong, John realizes: a wolf alone wouldn't ordinarily pass up such an easy meal. He stands, determined to shoo it away from the juvenile, but as he rises, he hears, distant but closing fast, the telltale sound of approaching rotors.

John flees, quick as he can go, back the way he came, sliding down the slope, feet clumsy in wet boots; he hits the river fast, slipping into the shallow water, crashing over loose rocks. Only when his scramble reaches the other bank does he risk a look back. Above the ridge a dozen drones fly, heavy lifter quadcopters with bright yellow claws dangling underneath, arrayed in formation around a cargo drone the ungainly size of a dump truck. John should keep running, but curiosity and duty override his caution. He reverses direction, heads back across the cold river, then crawls up the bank to pause among the pines at the rise's lip. The noise from above is incredible, the downward thrust of the drones' rotors flattening the prairie to expose more corpses alongside the barely breathing juvenile and the improbably calm wolf. The heavy lifters descend, belly-mounted winches dropping claws on high-tension cables, their serrated jaws opening to dig into deadweight. One by one they ferry the bison into the cargo drone's open hatch, its bulk swaying and dipping with each catch, until one final drone lowers itself over the last living Yellowstone bison.

John forces himself to watch. The juvenile bellows a sustained cry, guttural and grieving as it struggles against the steel claw; its legs kick with late strength as it's lifted from the brown grass, its hooves running futilely on air until the drone deposits it among the massed dead of its herd.

John hears the creaking cargo doors closing, then the heavy rushing wind of the drones turning in formation. Soon the sky is empty, not even a cloud remaining to color the sunset. Once again the voice of the world reduces to the howl of hot wind crossing the lonely expanse of the Lamar Valley, rasping the thrashed and flattened grasses where the bison lay down to die. Only the wolf remains, sitting on its haunches, staring at John, its expression blank but its eyes alive, watching.

As the wolf finally rises and trots away, headed in the same direction the drones flew, John begins to shiver, his skin goose-fleshing. It's one hundred degrees in Yellowstone today, one hundred degrees at least—but once John begins shivering he can't stop, not for a long time, not until his anger once again overtakes his fear.

FROM THAT ANGER, JOHN KNOWS: SOONER OR LATER HE'LL HAVE TO plant a bomb.

For five years he's done this. Wherever he travels, he looks for chances to blow holes in dams over dry riverbeds, to use the truck's winch to tear down anti-erosion embankments bolstering curves of freeway, to rip free chain-link fences from litter-strewn roadsides. The gutted cities, the thousands of kilometers of empty concrete claiming the earth for no one there—John's task is endless and likely futile; he tries anyway, believing nature can reclaim what humans have taken, as long as you give it somewhere to start.

This is what John wants, what he followed Cal to try to make real: a rewilding of the West, beginning with a dismantling of the human ruins.

The highway leading south from Yellowstone is officially closed and theoretically vacated, the asphalt in disrepair but serviceable enough, its flaws jolting the truck without slowing its passage. The truck's bed holds the makings for improvised weaponry: bags of ammonium nitrate fertilizer, canisters of gasoline, left-behind blast caps, and pilfered sticks of Tovex. Fossil fuel explosives to undo a fossil fuel economy, to break the infrastructure left behind when everything west of the Mississippi became the Sacrifice Zone, half a country forcefully evacuated so American lives might flourish elsewhere.

Whatever might be reused, John wants destroyed. If the steel was left to be recycled, it would only be made into something else, some new construction, some other machine. John doesn't want more machines, doesn't want more telephone poles and wind turbines stabbed into the landscape. He wants precious minerals and untapped oil left in the ground, he wants water to flow only where it wants to flow. No more unregulated, unrestrained extraction; no more conservation in one place making expansion possible somewhere else.

He flees across Wyoming, through Pinedale, Boulder, Farson, Eden, Reliance: empty, empty, empty, empty, empty. Wherever he passes a closed gas station, he ensures the underground tanks are off, then noisily pushes the pumps over with his truck; otherwise he lets the truck's electric engine run solar, avoiding confrontation with any twitchy populations who might remain, anyone refusing to leave the Sacrifice Zone, anyone sneaking back in.

By late afternoon, he idles through the outskirts of Rock Springs, trawling between dust bowl fields and unpowered fast-food signs until he spies a signal he'd pretended he hadn't been seeking, a direction and a number spray-painted in bright orange on the side of a burned-out diner. He pulls the truck into the trash-strewn back lot, kills the ignition, lets the engine tick to a stop. Window rolled down, he listens: no insects, no human voices, no sound but the hot wind. How many months has it been since he's seen a blaze this fresh? He rubs his eyes, rolls shoulders sore from the road, opens the door, and steps out for a closer look. He'd recognize the graffiti's hand style anywhere, the orange numerals two meters high obviously Cal's, the arrow slashed below them making for a clear enough message pointing John forty-five kilometers east, even though the arrow points west instead: as Cal always says, sometimes the slightest, simplest misdirection is enough.

Tapping his foot, John scans the nearby buildings, the distant horizon. He listens again: nothing and no one, only the blowing dust, a distant creaking of rusting metal. No one now, but Cal was here, not so long ago. Cal wanting to see him, calling him back to her.

He drives, faster now, the dry ground along the roadside cracked as the concrete; following the blaze's directions, he leaves the highway for surface roads, concrete giving way to dirt as he crosses more dead farmlands, fields of what was once barley and wheat and corn, now only hard clay punctured by toppled wind turbines, most of their masts felled not by human hands but by unpredictably violent weather. The kilometers tick by, and then there it is: another set of orange numerals and another misdirecting arrow, this time high on a fallen turbine's bent blade.

He finds the next blaze twenty kilometers northeast, exactly as directed, and follows its order past more recently scorched splotches of infrastructure, bulldozed chain-link fences, a stretch of highway jackhammered vulnerable to erosion. The spray-painted distances keep going down, the blazes get smaller then disappear as the sun begins to set. Close now. He knows what to look for, even with less light left to find it: he turns onto a gravel road beckoning north, then follows a dirt road veering east toward a husk of a farmhouse beside an intact barn. He pulls in, parks beneath a leafless oak; he runs his fingers through his hair, scrubs his sunburned face with filthy hands. This time, when he rolls down the window, he hears clanging coming from the other side of the paint-stripped barn, a sound he follows to find Cal bent beneath the hood of her gray Jeep, her broad shoulders bunching with muscle.

Cal pauses her work, sets her wrench down carefully atop the oily mass of the engine. Even at rest she exudes an unruled energy: a violence in fatigue pants and a sleeveless undershirt. "Hello, old goat," she says without turning.

It's been months since John last saw her, longer since he was sure how she'd react to his affection, how he'd react to hers. He moves behind her, mirrors her posture, placing his hands beside hers on the lip of the hood, their hips close but not touching. Cal's body coils beneath his, poised, tensioned but not tense; John smells motor oil and trace explosives, her sweat, his own. He shifts his hands to overlap hers, knows she'll already have moved before he touches her. She twists beneath his leanness, her muscles rippling, and puts her mouth on his, mashing his lips beneath her teeth, then drives him to the ground, abruptly straddling him, her solid weight pinning his lean body to the clay exactly as he'd hoped she would.

C-432

THE EARTH RESET

C-432 urges the translucent photovoltaic bubble forward with a thought, moving the craft out of the crawler's darkened hangar to drop onto the frozen crust of the Ice. Once outside, he shields his eyes against the sunlight, its pale glow reflected and doubled by every meter of the monotonous landscape, the glittery white flatness stretching endlessly beneath the low blanket of the heavy white sky, all this whiteness all he's ever known, his every remembered life having been lived upon this high glacial shelf.

Emerging from the crawler's shadow, he taps his right temple twice, just below the first tight spiral of his right horn: at his touch, an overlay tints the bubble's curved glass hull, bright-colored flags winking into view to augment his vision. Each flag marks an entrance to the Below, some place where another C descended, while inside C-432's skull the voices of the remainder enumerate what those predecessors found there, down in that deep zone continually covered over and crumpled and only sometimes exposed again by the always-advancing glacier, its massive moving weight having long since buried beneath itself the world that was, now battered and bent into a slowly dispersing layer of rubbled wreckage.

The Ice moves as one mass but the mass is not homogenous. Its surface is shaped by precipitation and ablation, but underneath it's made of many frozen planes, shelves exerting incredible pressures against one another, a tectonics of ice causing stress fractures and sheer cleavings to continually open new crevasses to the air, their jagged breaks sometimes plummeting deep into the interior. As the bubble zips across this changeable landscape, C watches through the bubble's shell, the virtual flags whizzing by as the frictionless craft zooms onward, following a path relayed instantly from the rung at the base of his neck to the unseen repulsors keeping the craft afloat. Thirty kilometers out from the crawler, an alert arrives from the bubble's sensor array: there's a newly opened crevasse several kilometers away, offering a possibly stable access. As the bubble closes the distance, C checks the remainder's memories, then scans the bubble's records of other descents in this area: just because this crevasse opened recently doesn't mean there wasn't once another nearby, where some other C descended via some passage since collapsed. A new entrance to the Below is a welcome discovery, but he can't afford to chance exploring some previously spelunked wreckage.

There are no mundane descents beneath the Ice, every minute C spends Below too potentially deadly to risk death for the promise of nothing. The recombinant remainder is a cowardly voice in C's head: it urges caution, safety, restraint, cowardice, though individual cycles haven't always been so circumspect. Today it gets no argument from C-432. He's lived a long cycle, longer than most, but he's not stronger or smarter than his most recent predecessors, only more risk-averse.

However successful C-432 has been, he must know he's a diminishment: cycle after cycle, the mind goes on but the body grows fallible. The remainder dimly recalls other, better bodies, capable of traveling the bitter landscape on foot, C's then brown fur caking with dirty slush, the skin below blackening with frostbite but always replaceable, even before C's epidermis became polymer and plastic, neither susceptible to pain like proper skin nor recovering from damage as real skin might have. Now, with his blue fur so thinned it no longer fully protects him from the cold, he dons a heavy cloak, faded with use and age; he covers his furred face with protective goggles, then tugs on scavenged gloves that snag over his plastinate claws.

Exiting the bubble's quiet, C listens to the kilometers-high sheet of the Ice shifting and settling: beneath him lies the secret movements of cold against cold, so much frozen water compacted and crackling, creating both the icefalls breaking up the landscape and the passages leading through the glacial crust, toward the pitch-blue dark of the Below. Approaching this newest entrance, he tests the crevasse's stability before dragging his portable winch from the bubble to a spot mere meters from the lip of the drop, securing the machine with a whir of gear-driven screws.

So far, C has survived every expedition below the Ice, depending on how precisely you define *survive*, on how precisely you define *C*. He remembers more descents than any one life could contain, discrete experiences crushed together by sheer volume, a conglomerate dream of all the lost places he's been.

He has hundreds of cycles' worth of memories already; if he brings back only more memories, it will not be enough.

C DESCENDS. SECURE IN HIS HARNESS, HE WORKS THE OVERSIZED buttons of the winch's control dongle, setting himself dropping steadily upon the cable, kicking his hooves gently against the crevasse wall. After he falls below the last of the sunlight, he allows himself a moment's blindness in the glacier's dark interior before he reaches up to click on his headlamp, its narrow beam failing to illuminate much past his gloved hand steadying the cable, his dangling hooves, the harness straps digging into his furred thighs.

C presses the dongle's down button again; above him, the winch whirs. His hooves continue their slow tracking down the near wall of the crevasse even as the one behind him falls away, disappears into the dark: after another thirty meters, turning his head reveals no other surfaces close enough to reflect the headlamp's beam. This is the rarest and best kind of crevasse, one opening as C falls, offering a deeper descent than others. A lucky find, these days, and necessary too. In the past, C could sometimes avoid entering the glacier: despite the static appearance of its flatness, the massive moving pressures under the Ice frequently surfaced crushed boulders and frozen dirt, whole acres of concrete rubble and shattered plastic and the occasional bent wreck of crumpled steel, and occasionally even some rarer, better finds, once even the shriveled corpse of some unidentifiable creature, its thin skin mummified brown, peeling like paper when that cycle's C unstuck it from the cold. But in recent years—in recent decades—he's had no such luck: the surface of the Ice appears unchanged, but the once rich reserves beneath his crawler have undeniably begun running dry.

The winch's spool contains five hundred meters of cable, but from his end C can't measure how far he's dropped. In the lamplit crevasse, distance becomes ever more impossible to judge, sight reduced to a single beam of light, sound to his scrabbling hooves on the rocky ice, the huffing echoes of his breathing, the free water coursing inside the glacier, its gurgling trickle moving below the frozen surface. He descends until the wall slopes suddenly away from him, leaving him dangling free, spinning in his harness straps. C panics, yelps out, the sound echoing off the invisible ice. With his free hand, he grips the cable until his harness stops spinning; then he continues his descent, dropping meter by meter into the freezing unknown.

How long before his hooves touch any surface? C can't guess the likely span of his descent, he can only await its end; some time later there's a surface reflecting his light back up at him, then solid frozen ground beneath his grateful hooves. He slips off his harness one leg at a time, stepping away from the cable before fully considering the chamber he's found, this pocket of stale air carried along unbroken underneath the Ice.

The cave is cramped and low, but as C explores the contours of its walls he feels it funneling to one side, elongating toward a cramped tunnel. He hesitates at the tunnel's lip, listens for how fast the nervous clicking of his hooves comes echoing back, the sound dulled by the passage's uncertain length. On the surface, there is only the flatness of the Ice, novelty reduced nearly to zero, even its dangers long known; down here, beneath the great weight of the glacier, C knows he might find anything at all buried and frozen, much of it unnamable, unrecognizable, all of it the end of a world crushed and graveled and dispersed, ground down to finest grains.

There are many kinds of fears in C's heart but only one that rules: if the *tunnel* becomes *tunnels*, then C might easily become lost; if he becomes lost and can't make his way back to the cable, then he'll die Below.

No matter what happens, no matter how badly he's hurt, he must never die anywhere but in the crawler.

C's headlamp barely cuts the darkness, rendering everything a flat grayscale except the occasional glimmering glitters of trapped particulate. As he proceeds, the tunnel slants down and away in a crooked, uneven break, evidence of some obstacle farther in, a stubborn obstruction the Ice couldn't shove aside. He carries his ice axe in one hand, occasionally breaking his light beam with the other, because seeing his glove is better than seeing only more dark. The cold within the tunnel is an immense force; his breath fogs and freezes, his skin aches then burns, a painful tingling digging ever deeper into his muscles and bones.

Despite taking care, C finds the first sign of buried biomass not with his eyes but with his hooves, its surprise sending him tripping down the tunnel. He turns back to find a series of black roots wormed up from the floor, some as thick as his forearm, clutching in their wooden grips broken rocks and stuck gravel, captured dirt. It's not so much a tree as an inverted stump, but near it C sees the sign of more buried wood, frozen hard as stone. He circles the exposed root ball, then sends his light back the way he came. How far is he from the cable, the winch, the free air above? It's never easy to tell, once he's stepped away.

To strike the ice is to court further danger—chancing the tunnel's cave-in, the collapse of the crevasse—but if C wants to go on he needs to take as much of the buried tree with him as he can. He swings his axe at the root's base. His shoulders shudder from the impact, but the ice is unmoved. He waits, listens. When nothing happens he strikes again. The risk is enormous but the possible reward great, if he can dig free this root ball, if he can discover more tree beneath it, if he can extract its entirety back to the crawler. While he works, the remainder remembers: years ago another C found a field of such stumps at the bottom of a recently opened crevasse, a long-lasting breakage wide enough that its contents could be cataloged from the surface. The best find in a dozen cycles, enough biomass that the next C was an improvement on his predecessor, a rare reversal of the entropy of their many stacked lives.

The roots are stubbornly resilient, surprisingly fragile: at first solidly stuck, then crumbling free. Every scrap is useful, every splinter worth retrieving. C removes a tarp from his backpack, loads whatever he can pry from the ice onto the plastic sheet. He hacks a depression around the root ball, unearthing more trunk farther down, more tree, possibly more *trees*. The glacier is capable of gathering anything in its path, and if it's gathered a forest—

Greed clumps in C's gut, churns him dumb. The ice beneath his hooves melts slightly, body heat and the friction of his steps leaving a scrim of water, making each movement more treacherous than the one before. When the tarp is nearly too heavy to drag, C wraps the edges over the precious wood, then loops nylon cord through the tarp's stainless steel eyelets.

So much is left behind, the remainder complains, but there's danger in being away from the crawler after the sun sets, the temperature at night far lower than during the day, the translucent photovoltaic bubble unable to run far without sunlight.

C hurries, the heavy load compressing his spine, his hooves scrabbling for leverage. By the time he reaches the chamber where the cable waits, C's back is hunched, his breath comes in wheezes. His hands shake as he regathers the four corners of the tarp and secures them into a bulky pouch, attaching the tarp's eyelets to a carabiner dangling from the bottom of the safety harness.

He straps himself in next, then clutches the dongle, pressing the button to begin his ascent. His cargo follows, the tarp's weight spinning in the open air. On reaching the high wall of the crevasse, relief washes through C, the icy chill against his scrabbling hooves an improvement over the uncertainty of floating free—but then the cargo tarp snags a lone outcropping set in the smooth wall, one of the bony roots within catching beneath an unseen ledge.

C curses, jams the up button to try to force the tarp free. When that fails, he plants his hooves on the ice, then leans back and pulls at the tarp, lifting with his legs. When the tarp slides from his gloved fingers, he wipes steam from inside his goggles, then pockets his gloves. He digs his claws into the tarp, regathers the loose plastic into his fists. He squats and kicks away from the wall, leveraging his flailing weight: if he can yank hard enough the frozen root might shatter and free the rest.

He pries, he pulls, he kicks, he jumps again, senses the frozen wood starting to break—and then the whole tarp comes loose at once while C is at the farthest point of a leap away from the wall. The momentum throws him, he loses control, the tarp slips from his grip as its weight jerks him sideways; when he swings back toward the wall he strikes it horns first. Dazed, he barely has time to register the spiderweb of cracks spiraling out before the loaded tarp hits too, the second impact shattering the already cracking wall, the ice above coming apart fast, loosing a hail of fist-sized chunks and razor-sharp spikes.

Afterward, there's only the sound of his terrified huffing, of the cable's friction against the slowly spinning safety harness; C's face bleeds, his knee aches, he's covered in cuts and contusions. He reaches up to stop the cable's rotation, twisting himself toward the collapsed wall, its tentatively solid surface now impossible to reach until he climbs another twenty meters.

C secures the cargo tarp, then restarts the winch's spinning. *Almost there,* he thinks, *just a little higher.* But he rises only another five meters before the next loud crack sounds above him. In a panic, he aims his headlamp upward just in time to see more ice collapsing, not the wall before him this time but the one behind, its weight falling not in broken chunks but in one solid pillar that slams him face-first against the fractured wall, a vast expanse of blue-white ice solid enough to knock him dumb.

CHAPMAN

What makes an orchard? Nothing more than apple seeds and dank, dark earth, plus the labors and hopes of men: every seed the brothers plant is a dream of a tree grown, every completed nursery a belief in a more productive future. Upon their chosen plot, they drag the horizontal blade of their two-man saw through an oak's stubborn heart, the steel passing from faun to man and back again. They make the cut close to the ground, aiming to leave as little stump as possible, even though the brothers will abandon the stumps to rot, their roots softening until more permanent settlers arrive to pull them. Whenever he pauses to wipe sweat from his sunburned brow, Nathaniel resumes again his endlessly repeated cant, the ever-evolving speech Chapman has heard beginning to end countless times. "The wilderness must be pushed back," he says, before decrying the unruly contours of the Territory's fish-rich lakes and malaria-ridden swamps, its many waterways waiting to be straightened and smoothed. He details the surveyor's grid being laid down over the future shape of each of this new country's settlements, each plot platted out, the first footholds for future states to be divided into holdings fit to be owned by new American men, each a kingdom exactly equal to the quality of the man's efforts. Everywhere there will be newly productive farms and innovative industries, new concerns for timbering and the mining of coal and copper amid pastures cut from the forests, fruiting orchards replacing uninhabitable swamplands.

"It's by our ingenuity that our civilization is produced," Nathaniel says. "Other men have lived here for a thousand years, but wasn't the country we found nearly as wild as the day they first strode it? Where was their imagination for right uses? Where are their fences, their domesticated herds, their smart households making useful goods, ready for market? Why did they lack brick and mortar, steel saw and iron axe, the long reach of the musket? Could these first men not hear the voice of God here, as we do? We followed them to this Territory less than two hundred years ago, and already we have named it better, this America; already we've set out to properly parcel and sell its splendor, to make ready the state to be."

Chapman doesn't drop his end of the saw, he needs neither his brother's break nor his brother's nation-building tall tale, this aspirational mythologizing, its many erasures of war and disease. "You wish to be like a god," he says quietly, letting slip only this bland objection. He knows better than to argue his brother's points more voraciously, when the only reward for doing so will be a day of Nathaniel's stubborn anger in the fields or else his sullenness around the night's cookfire.

"If we are all made in God's image, why not act like Him as well?" Nathaniel asks, and Chapman lifts his horned head to object, *Not all, not me*—but before he can speak his brother says, "Now pull, and let us put this ground to right."

Their clear-cutting is slow, the centuries-old trees terribly dense from bark to bark: it takes an hour to cut an oak, another to limb it, a third to saw the trunk into logs ready to be rolled and stacked at the river's edge. Finally the oak crashes, half its branches breaking beneath its bouncing weight; afterward each brother works his tomahawk methodically up the tree's length, hacking the rest of the branches free. Soon their hands and forearms are slick with fresh sap, soon the sap is riddled with flies and bees and other hungry insects; their labors litter the ground with bright tan sawdust, with cut wood ready to be dried for kindling. Chapman aims to hurt no other creature, but every fallen tree spills birds' nests, squirrel hovels, spiderwebs, and wasps' nests. Everywhere the brothers make a home for an apple tree is somewhere something else no longer lives, and surely it's not only the saw that diminishes the world. What about every booted or hooved footprint stomping a stand of moss? Or the sparkling trout taken out of the river rapids by Nathaniel's fishhook, its belly filled with roe? Or every honeycomb broken and licked clean, every handful of berries Chapman snacks on whose absence deprives a bright bird, a nosing doe, a lost cub—

"Yes, brother, yes, a tree must die so a man might heat his house," Nathaniel says, "but surely there will never be any shortage of trees."

It's impossible to do no harm, but how much harm is permitted? Chapman has asked this question since he was old enough to wonder after his mother, to hear how in the birthing of his hooved body she met her end. Nathaniel tells him it wasn't his fault, but if not his, then whose?

Chapman works through the afternoon rain, he does a settler's work while settling nothing. He cuts and clears and hoes, he takes his turn dragging their makeshift plow through the rock-pitted ground until the brothers have turned this narrow plot of earth alongside the bright-sparkling river into quick-carved furrows of blackest dirt, their rows as straight as the stump-ridden earth will allow. After the rain trickles off, Chapman begins moving down each row, leaving behind cloven footprints in the soft turn of the soil. Unlike his faunish feet, his hands are human enough: fingers clawed, yes, backs furred, but all the rest commonly dull. He takes a handful of seeds from his leathern bag, he presses the seeds one by one into the black soil. Each seed is a bitter pill of wax and wood and cyanide-laced prophecy, leafed future: a tree in embryo, its nature impossible to know before it grows. It'll be ten years before these trees bear fruit, but as he plants Chapman imagines them already past their flowering, each tree's apples offering fresh wonders of touch and scent, texture and flavor: the skins might be red or yellow or green, dark-mottled matte or shined clear as glaze; the flesh moon pale, jaundiced, browned as if rotten. Only a few seed-grown apples are ever sweet; the others are destined to be peppery spicy or puckeringly sour, some repulsively bitter spitters.

Chapman plants another apple seed. By day's end, he will have planted two hundred seeds in neat rows, each stringy with pulp and pomace, each given its own hole, each hole mounded over by a scooped handful of black dirt. It's such a simple act, producing such a complex being, sprout and root, trunk and branch, leaf and flower and fruit unfolding. An apple seed becoming an apple tree is as much a function of time as of space, the years to come as necessary as rich soil and plentiful rainfall across the thousands of days it takes to make a tree fruit, for a tree to make fruit containing seeds of its own.

For the next stretch of nursery, Nathaniel hacks down more pines and maples while Chapman lifts moss-covered rocks from where glaciers let them lie, carrying them into the remaining forest or casting them into the sparkling river, where their accumulation forces free water into swirling rapids. From many a fallen tree there spills a nest of eggs or hatchlings, beneath every rock there is a wealth of worms. Chapman studies the riverbed hemming his nursery, how its new rapids also form a nearby pool of calm water that trout might find fit for spawning. When a bird's nest falls to the ground he stops his work to carry it intact to a stretch of trees past the bounds of his planned nursery, despite Nathaniel's scoffing, his entreaties for efficiency and haste, productivity above all else.

Wherever Chapman does not plant or plow, native abundance persists. Hundreds of miles of virgin forest lie in every direction—surely enough free woods will always exist for every displaced creature to find a new home. Surely the world Nathaniel aims to build can coexist alongside the world given and grown. Or so Chapman hopes. From these seeds will grow enough seedlings for Nathaniel to supply six families, six ruddy husbands and their brave wives and whatever squalling children are already born, the first of the many each man and woman might wish to have, the multitudes necessary to settle the continent. Thirty trees for each family, bought from enterprising Nathaniel and used to better secure their legal claim to whatever plot of cleared land each family has chosen to build a cabin, over whose door they might hang an oil lamp to light the unbearable dark of the Ohioan woods.

To plant an orchard takes a certain amount of time; hours pass, the sun flings itself high in the sky before falling fast. The temperature drops, the humidity becomes more bearable, a different hum of insects asserts itself. Chapman plants a seed, and whatever tree grows from it will create no exact copies, not without the art of grafting, unpracticed by the brothers. No matter how many trees they plant, they might produce any particular tree only once, and its uniqueness might easily be lost to weather or predation, to human whim. As the day at last dims, Chapman dreams again of re-creating one such unique specimen, the one he believes is the oldest fruit of the species, lost long ago but still hidden in the potential within each new apple tree, possible to grow from any particular payload of seeds.

This is the story he tells himself, his way of making sense of his years of labor.

But still, sometimes Chapman reflects on the backbreak of a day's work and thinks, *All this for an apple. All this for the only apple I want to eat.* And what else might his apple cost?

THE SUN SETS AND THOUGH THE WORK ISN'T DONE IT IS DONE FOR today. The brothers make camp at one end of the nursery, Nathaniel shaking out his bedroll on a stretch of trampled grass, Chapman using a hoof to dredge a shallow depression to house tonight's fire. Nathaniel stacks chopped wood over gathered kindling while Chapman bounds off to find dinner, gathering fistfuls of acorns, filling one pocket with wild blackberries and another with narrow tubers clawed from the dirt. He moves fast, reaching a gait he indulges only when assured he's alone: preternatural, beastly, unnerving even to familiar Nathaniel. Running wildly through wild lands, reveling in sore joints loosened by his quickness, with every step he shakes off more of the afternoon's efforts, his aches worked pleasurably free, thorny brambles scratching soothingly at his furred flanks. Birds squawk and flee the low branches at his approach; he frightens a doe and her young from a blackberry thicket, watching the white flags of their tails retreat into deeper woods—everywhere there is motion, every inch of the forest is alive at every scale.

Chapman's half a man and half a beast, but with Nathaniel he lives only a man's life, does a man's work for a man's reason: possession and enrichment, dominion and control. For Nathaniel, there's no other life worth living. But lately Chapman has wondered if without Nathaniel he might have become something else: a wilder creature, unbound from human wants. How much ego would have to be given up? How much belief in singular destiny, individual experience?

Chapman isn't gone long, but he returns to a slim cookfire already stoked, the brothers' one pot hung over the flames and the pleasurable sound of water rapidly boiling. Sitting on a mossy boulder beside the fire, happy and slow in his evening reveries, Nathaniel smokes his pipe, a plume of fragrant tobacco smoke rising from his beard as Chapman spreads his gathered foodstuffs on the grass. He cracks the acorns and peels the tubers, then flourishes a hand over the slender bounty until Nathaniel laughs. Together the brothers share the cooking, together they dine: Nathaniel sits cross-legged on his bedroll while Chapman crouches near the fire, eating a steaming potato out of his bare hands, sucking bitter acorn broth from his battered tin cup, picking blackberry seeds from between his sharp teeth. Gnats and flies and mosquitoes fall from the sky, their mass a swarming anger until Nathaniel throws greener wood on the fire, letting the smoke drive them off. There are gray wolves and black bears and blacker panthers in the woods, but there's little danger in the camp, at least while the fire blazes high, with Chapman's odd shadow looming and his faunish smell upon the air: garlic and clove, musk and sweat and man, the sweet rot of damp moss, a forest growing beneath the fur.

After dinner, Nathaniel takes their tin cups down to the water's edge to rinse away the last of the broth. The river isn't far, but Chapman can barely see Nathaniel past the firelight's glow, his brother's image reduced in the far darkness to the winking cherry of his pipe. Dishes done, Nathaniel returns to his bedroll, then casts his eyes to the shell of stars above. Lying back, he recites for Chapman stories remembered from a Bible whose weight he no longer carries: the warrior whose strength lives in the tangles of his hair, the fierce queen who beheads her enemies to set free her people, the Christ multiplying the fishes and the loaves, offering his followers food made as endlessly plentiful as his platitudes. A beggar is healed, then a blind man or a lame man; a dead man is raised living from a tomb of quarried stone, a story Chapman has never believed, not even as a child.

"No," Chapman says, turning restlessly. "The dead stay dead. And there's nothing any god will do about it."

Nathaniel knows who prompts this objection: their mother, whom Chapman never knew, whom Nathaniel speaks of only rarely. Instead he tells more stories, though there's only one Chapman truly loves: the Garden of Eden and its endless bounty, every animal and every plant waiting to be named and put to their right uses by the first humans, the Tree of Knowledge from which they were forbidden to eat, an apple tree like the ones the brothers have come to the Territory to plant.

Chapman loves this story, but he quibbles at its telling, nitpicks the story's shape to better fit his desires. "What good could a Tree of Knowledge do for immortals not yet cursed to die? Maybe they needed something else. Not a Tree of Knowledge but a Tree of Forgetting." He gestures grandly, his clawed movement lost to black air. He says, "A way to become new. Apple as untrod dream, from whose taste you could awake fresh as a babe, freed from all your years, all your decisions, all your compromises."

"All your triumphs," says Nathaniel. "All your loves."

"How few those are," says Chapman. "Too few. A slight sacrifice."

You wouldn't have to know your crimes either, he doesn't say. The dead stay dead, but at least you wouldn't know what you did to make them so, wouldn't know how it was what you were that had doomed them; such a fruit might even allow his body to forget itself, might let him become someone else, as ordinary as his brother. As a teenager, Chapman had once tried to cut his horns free of his forehead; after Nathaniel found him howling in bloody pain, their handsaw in one hand and half a broken horn in the other, Chapman explained what he'd hoped: that without his horns, he might have ceased being a faun.

Magical thinking, Nathaniel had scoffed then—*Would you have kept going*, he'd mocked, *cutting off hooves and tail, filing your teeth and claws, shaving your fur?*—but failure hadn't stopped Chapman's wanting. Fifteen years later, he again relates the tale he's been telling himself, a dream of his own making, born of his brother's retold scriptures: if a Tree of Forgetting has grown even once, then Chapman might plant it anew, might find in its fruit a magic by which a faun could forget he was ever any-thing but a man, surely a fate better than being both man and animal, torn between two worlds and forever home in none—

"Go to sleep, brother," Nathaniel interrupts, then rolls over, putting his back to Chapman.

The faun falls quiet, restlessly awake as his brother begins to snore. Despite their differences, here in the Territory at the turn of the century they form a partnership of two, their goals parallel enough: for Chapman, his Tree; for Nathaniel, a for-tune made speculating, by taming the land. But even *tame* is too strong a word: the brothers plant their seeds in fields plowed from wild riverbanks, but they build no proper fences, carve no passable roads, erect no sturdy houses. All they grow are barely domesticated trees, arboreal squatters planted on un-claimed land, destined to be sold to better settlers at passable profit. Even what grows in their nurseries will forever be unruly and ungrafted, each tree as twisted as the hairs atop Chapman's horned head, each utterly as unique.

JOHN

Inside the barn, Cal shows John the rare refuge she's found, hidden by a steel hatch concealed under a dusty layer of hay and chaff. At the bottom of a narrow ladder waits a spare concrete room, an emergency shelter with a bunkbed, a store of nonperishable food and medical supplies, a tank of potable water. John's immediately claustrophobic, but Cal shushes him, pushes him toward the corner shower. The water is rusty, stale, magnificent, stinging John's sunburned skin, streaming over Cal's stout musculature. The concrete muddies, the mud clogs the drain, they kick to clear the flow with their toes, playfully at ease as if they'd never parted, as if they'd parted on better terms. Afterward, John goes naked to his truck, enjoying the hot wind wicking away the shower's moisture, his body dry by the time he returns to the barn in clothes at least marginally less dirty than the ones discarded below.

Instead of returning to the bunker, they sit at a plastic folding table Cal's dragged into the moonlight near the barn's
entrance. Famished, John devours the simple meal Cal offers
him, the first hot food he's had in weeks. He sighs at the honest
pleasure of rehydrated beans and rice heavy with preservatives
and salt, a tumbler of cool clear water tasting of the tank, all
of it a joy after the austerity of protein bars and boiled water.
"How did you find this place?" he asks, sporking a second bite
into his already-full mouth.

"I was working my way down the Dakota fracking fields, dis-
rupting pipelines and breaking whatever I could," says Cal, stir-
ring her own food but not yet taking a bite. "You can probably
guess what there was to see. Fleets of oil company trucks left behind when the wells went dry, office buildings filled with recent
enough computers, already junk. Kilometers of server cables,
electrical wires, leaking pipes. I found a bulldozer and used it
to topple telephone poles, push over fence lines, break up the
roads."

"More *terrorism,*" interrupts John, making air quotes with
his hands. That's what the federal government in Syracuse calls
it, unwilling to recognize rewilders as separate from the rebel
groups roaming Wyoming and Montana, locals or new arrivals kicked out of the free Northwest: Bundyists with automatic
weapons claiming swaths of land as patriot preserves, driving
smokestacked pickups across the broken clay; bands of polyga-
mists unwilling to be taken east, clinging to the strip of waste-
land between what was once Arizona and Utah; the Navajo
Nation and the other rightful owners of the Southwest, sovereign peoples refusing to be moved from their lands, to ever
be relocated again. If Cal and John are terrorists, they aren't
the kind of terrorists who'd burned Reno to char, they weren't

the sort who'd detonated the crude oil tanks outside Houston, who'd set fire to the reserves stored below, setting off an inextinguishable underground blaze that had hastened the city's evacuation.

Despite John's occasional bombs, Houston burning forever wasn't what he'd wanted—but now that the city was empty, he did want it gone, as if it'd never been.

"I stopped to dismantle a fuel station in South Dakota," Cal continues, "taking apart the pumps and sealing the tanks before spending the night inside. In the morning, I woke to a truckful of Bundys parked outside, going through my Jeep. I saw one holding up my clothes, watched them figure out what they'd found. A woman, traveling alone." She smiles, leans back, crosses her muscular arms. Cal, no damsel. Cal, a fighter who quit the country's wars only to end up in this new one instead. "I knew it wouldn't take them long to figure out where I was. I snuck to the nearest ledge, lifted my rifle into position."

"Cal," John says softly, "I don't need to hear this."

"You asked how I found this place. This is how I found it." Cal mimes firing her rifle, three-round bursts taking each of the four men surrounding her Jeep in order, Cal working left to right, only the last man reacting in time to reach for his weapon. "There was a map in the truck's glovebox. They were scouts, sent from Nevada to look for supplies, possible outposts. They'd marked this bunker in pencil, so I figured it was a new discovery: if they never made it back to base no one else would know it existed. That afternoon I started working my way here, looping the long way around in case I was followed." She smiles again, her big teeth shining in the dark. "And also so I could leave a path for you."

Finished eating, they sit quietly, John rapping his knuckles on the table, knocking to open a door inside himself. "How'd you know where I was?" he asks, which is not quite the question he meant to ask. *What do you want?* he might've said.

Cal laughs, husky, deep-throated. "You didn't want to find me, old goat?"

"You know I did," John says, flushing, moving away as she leans forward, her hands pushing across the table. "But what if I hadn't seen your blazes?"

"Then I'd be fed and showered and unfucked, and you'd be as dirty and stinking and sad as ever." She pushes her scraped food tin away. "But you're right. There's more. It's time to go back east, John. Time to go see your girl."

Eury Mirov, Cal's enemy; John's too, if he believes what he's supposed to believe. Defending Eury to Cal has always been pointless, the anger she put in Cal permanent, scarring; Cal fought for Earthtrust too long, did too much she regrets. John's woken her from screaming nightmares that left them both gasping and terrified in their tent pitched on some windswept plain, the back of John's truck beside an empty highway, a dusty bed in an abandoned motel, some cramped room swept free of the carapaces of starved cockroaches.

Earthtrust—it's always Earthtrust. John tells Cal about Yellowstone, about the strange wolf he saw there and about the drones taking away the dead bison, the last living juvenile heaving in the dirt. "What were they doing?" he asks. "What could they possibly have wanted?"

Cal unrolls a laminated topographical map of the West, its mountains and rivers bounded by the borders of political divisions now defunct. "I don't know," she says, gesturing at the reset country marked with fresh scribblings of permanent marker, colored pen. "But I met Noor in Montana a month ago.

She reported seeing Earthtrust dronedozers gathering up fallen trees draped in tents of invasive moths in one place, dredging dry lakes in another, the machines moving right down the middle of empty riverbeds. Everywhere she went, everything dead or dying was being gathered up, taken away."

"For what? What do they want with dead, stricken trees? Earthtrust barely even builds with wood. Almost every building in the VACs is printed concrete, extruded plastic."

Cal throws up her hands. What good are his questions, which they can't possibly answer?

"At least Noor's all right," John says. "Where are Mai and Julie?"

Cal fills him in: Mai is back at Earthtrust, returned to the Ohio VAC's medical clinics, the only one of them who never directly resisted the company, the only one who'll be a citizen of the United States the next time they all meet. As for Julie—"You heard about the Cochiti Dam explosion?" Cal asks, rising from the table to pull back a tarp tacked to the wall, revealing a stack of crates—supplies or weapons or both.

The Cochiti Dam: forty-eight million cubic meters of earth and rock, almost nine thousand meters across the Rio Grande, just north of vacated Albuquerque. A month ago, someone set enough charges to blow the dam open, freeing what little river was left. It wasn't supposed to be easy to crack an earthen dam that size, but in the end all it took was effort and time, plus explosives.

"That was Julie?" John asks, already knowing the answer. Before the dam was built, the nearby banks of the Rio Grande had been inhabited by the Pueblo; the land the dam flooded was sacred, tended for generations, then abruptly *condemned* by bureaucratic language deployed to commit government-sponsored

crime. This was land Julie's ancestors had stewarded and protected; blowing up the dam couldn't restore what they'd lost, but
at least Julie could set free what remained.

"Good for her," John says, and means it. His family's land
had been stolen from someone else, further back than he could
feel. Now it's lost to him too, all its soil blown away, that once
fertile earth that gave generations of humans purchase. "What
are we doing here, Cal?" he asks, exhausted. He runs his hand
through his unkempt beard, its embarrassing tangle. He'll shave
in the morning, indulging in one more shower before they
leave, after he unloads the explosives and the rest of his tools
from the truck. "What's changed?"

Cal returns with a tablet computer, a scanner wand trailing
a fraying plastic cable gone yellow with age. At her touch, the
tablet begins its slow boot-up process, its software burdened by
a series of hacks and backdoor workarounds, bypassing security checks to keep the device from pinging home. "When we
left Earthtrust, the Secession was ended, the Sacrifice had long
since cleared Congress. I'd dragged people out of their houses,
loaded them into trucks and buses heading east; you'd made
sure the VAC in Ohio was up and running, putting your supertrees and your nanobees to work." Cal's face leans over the
tablet, her profile lit electric by the screen's glow: her chopped
hair, the hard angle of her soldier's jaw, the twice-broken nose
hung above the toothy glint of her smile. "But we both knew
the VACs weren't the end goal, that Eury Mirov wouldn't stop
there. We decided we didn't want the world she was bringing
into being."

John nods, agreeing, but was that all he'd wanted? Was it
always so simple as that? "I chose you," he says. "Me and Julie
and Mai and Noor, we all did. The others too."

"And because of that," Cal says, "I've had to take responsibility for everything that happened. For everyone we lost." And they had lost: a half dozen men and women who'd come west with them, then all the others who'd joined in the Sacrifice Zone, people who loved the land and wouldn't be removed. The first year had been spent running from Earthtrust security forces intent on emptying the West, the next dealing with the ever-harsher conditions post-Secession, post-Sacrifice, amid the forever drought spreading beyond the Southwest. But as the community of rewilders swelled, caravanning in four-wheel-drive trucks and SUVs, it eventually became easier to protect each other and to do their work, everyone working together to dismantle larger infrastructure projects, to effectively scavenge abandoned city blocks. For a while, everything had gone right, or at least right enough. And then it hadn't, not ever again.

"I know, Cal. I'm not—" John pauses, not because he doesn't know what to say but because he's surprised to find out he means it this time. "I'm not angry anymore. We were always going to despair at the futility of it. And something was bound to go wrong, sooner or later." One summer there were algae blooms on every reservoir, so that the water couldn't be safely filtered or boiled away; always there was unbearable heat baking their tents into ovens, never mind their hotbox RVs, whose solar air conditioners kept freezing from overuse. Three men drowned in a flash flood that washed away a camp in northern Arizona's red rock canyons, an unfortunate accident; it was so easy to die of exposure, it was so easy to fall and break a leg no one knew how to set, to succumb to a burst appendix no one dared remove. When the group was half its largest size, it started being preyed on by bands of preppers and survivalists, attackers they could repel but not without cost. A family was separated by an Earthtrust raid that captured the mother and daughter, sending the father and son rushing after by motorcycle: better to be caught together than be free apart. A suicide set off a run of copycats until they were all watching each other warily, talking gingerly, trying not to fight as their health worsened, as their sunburns flaked, as their teeth loosened against the hard nubs of expired protein bars.

Everything west of the Mississippi was desert, and those who stayed became desert creatures, stronger, tougher, leatherskinned. Years of struggle eroded their community down to its core: Cal and Julie, ex-military, ex–Earthtrust security, veterans who'd served together for years; Noor, a white hat hacker from California who'd gotten stuck on the wrong side of the Secession, having been in Dearborn visiting family when the big one hit; Mai, their doctor, an obstetrician from Great Bend, an adventurer, one of the last to hike the Appalachian Trail in those impossible-to-recall years when voluntarily living in the elements was something people did for fun.

And then there was John. Supposedly a brilliant programmer, an equally accomplished microbiologist. Not that he'd ever felt brilliant or accomplished, not while standing next to Eury, the only true genius he'd known.

Now it's Cal's turn to look away. "It doesn't matter if you forgive me," she says. "I need you even if you're angry. We knew some of what Eury had planned, knew what to watch for."

"You knew because I told you. Because I betrayed her."

"If you hadn't, we wouldn't know what's about to happen." Cal pauses, sets her jaw. "Pinatubo, John. Eury Mirov's actually going to do it."

John's been waiting for Cal to say this, but still he doesn't quite believe it. "There's no way the government will ever sign off—"

"Don't be naive. She administers half the country. The cities would starve without Earthtrust, and most of the rural areas too. The same is true abroad now. With VACs everywhere, she owns the only crops anyone can make grow. Who can stop her, if she decides to go forward? You said once that however Pinatubo turned out, it'd need a delivery system capable of reaching the stratosphere. Mai says Earthtrust's built a huge facility at the Farm's center, a tower topped by a twenty-story needle aimed at the sky. An injection point, just like you said."

"But Pinatubo was supposed to be a last resort," he says, visualizing how Cal had gotten the news from Mai: from her post in the Ohio VAC, Mai sometimes passed messages to a sympathetic Earthtrust train engineer, who left them in a dead drop at the magrail terminus in Cheyenne. It was always Cal who risked going to look for Mai's packages, never knowing when there might be a new one. What had Mai seen, back in Ohio? What did Cal know that she wasn't saying? "We know Eury's had the idea for the Tower for years. But that can't be the most efficient way to—" Geoengineering on a global scale, locking the rising temperature in place for a generation, making a respite in which humanity could transition to a new economy and a new culture, then beginning the long work of repairing the planet. A future intended to start on the Ohio VAC, built on the land where he and Eury grew up.

Despite Eury's assurances, he'd never once believed Earthtrust would amass enough power to pull it off.

Cal raises her hands in mock retreat. "Earthtrust doesn't have to be an evil company. The Sacrifice Zone didn't have to happen, the Secession didn't have to be a bloodbath, the VACs don't have to be surveillance states, they don't have to force you to give up your citizenship to gain entrance. But all that happened on Eury Mirov's watch. Maybe there's reason enough to geoengineer the stratosphere too, but can we trust Earthtrust to do it right, for the right reasons?"

Only now does John realize he's the last one Cal needs to convince. Mai already in place. Noor and Julie meeting up, heading east together. The five of them made their plans for getting back into the Ohio VAC years ago. All they have to do now is carry them out.

Cal leans forward, holding John's gaze. "Are you in, John, as you promised you would be?"

Her radiant intensity, her unwavering conviction—all of it overwhelms him. He has to look away so he can think his own thoughts, make his own decisions. "I'm tired," he says quietly, after a moment's pause. "But yes, I still believe."

"Good," Cal says, as she wakes the tablet's screen again, picking up the scanner wand. Maybe there's nothing else to say, maybe she already knows all she needs to know about John, about what he's good for, about plans he'll agree to carry out. "Are you ready to reenter the world of the living?" she asks, then reaches for his right hand, splays it palm down on the table: every Volunteer, every Earthtrust employee, every refugee or prisoner, has an ID pebble embedded in the loose skin between their right thumb and forefinger. Before they'd broken their fellowship and gone their separate ways, Noor had crafted new identities in anticipation of this moment. John was to become Joseph, shortened to Joe, because keeping the first letter and syllable count ensured you'd react to your fake name when you heard it spoken aloud. Single, no children, a birth certificate and a national ID number that wouldn't have held up to scrutiny ten years ago but probably would now, when there were so many refugees there wasn't time for the processing centers to verify every last bit of information.

Cal taps the tablet screen a few more times, reactivating John's pebble before installing the rest of Noor's hack, a deep-seated series of hidden subroutines John can summon with the right sequence of hand movements and purposeful blinks. A row of dim white lights winks on beneath the skin, each light the size of a pinhead: indicators barely visible through the epidermis, used to communicate basic notifications. John squeezes his thumb against the palm of his hand until four of the lights flash: orange, purple, green, blue; Cal, Julie, Mai, Noor.

Only the five of them left, out of all those who'd gone west.

During his retreat in the parklands, after he'd last left Cal, John had been alone, responsible to no one, or so he'd told himself: a sleepwalker, dreaming in the desert, despite the bombs and the makeshift bulldozing. Now, thanks to Cal, he's awake again, his solitude broken, his connection to her and the others restored; now he's ready, despite everything they'd done and everything that had already gone wrong, to do whatever it takes to try to make the world they want instead of the world they have.

John squeezes his fist to watch the lights scroll their colors again; he opens his hand, then looks up to catch Cal's stare, finally able to match the determination he sees there.

Whatever else had happened, John had never wanted to abandon the world.

C-432

C-432 is unconscious, C is injured, C is dying, this C is going to die, and soon. Waking for the last time, tangled in his harness, the tarp full of frozen wood still spinning below him, he throws back his head and howls with pain, then regains his wits: too much noise might further unsteady the already tenuous crevasse. He's battered and bleeding and his ribs are bruised or broken, but the worst danger is his right arm, pinned between the immovable wall before him and the fallen pillar that fell from behind, a slab that must still weigh thousands of kilograms. Every attempt to pull his shattered forearm free twists the stuck elbow, the pain producing a new scream he has to choke back before it can escape his chattering lips. He reaches with his good arm, his sharp teeth stilling his tongue against the pain as he slides the ice axe from its loops— thankfully he's left-handed, or else he wouldn't have been able to reach—and then strikes it awkwardly at the wall, just above where his elbow is pinned.

The ice doesn't budge, at least not where the pick end of the axe bites the surface. But from above, C hears another ominous creaking. It's impossible to predict the effect of striking the ice here, to know all the ways the reverberations might move through the crevasse wall above.

C-432 is dazed and afraid, but the remainder has been mortally wounded many times. Now it instructs with calm, lucid brutality. If he cannot strike the ice, then the only other way to free himself is to turn the axe around, to switch from the pick end to the blade, then to put the blade to flesh and bone.

He queries the remainder, begging for some other option.

The remainder acknowledges his pain, but it will not offer false comfort.

The remainder doesn't care about C-432 any more than it did any of his predecessors.

The remainder wants only to go on, in this body or any other.

C-432 HAS LIVED LONGER THAN ANY OTHER RECENT CYCLE, BUT that doesn't mean he's ready to die. After his escape, he drags himself away from the crevasse, one arm amputated below the elbow, the other dragging the heavy tarp, its plastic shot through with sharp shards of frozen wood and slick with steaming blood leaving a bright red trail brushed across the snow. His movements are awkward and pained, his vision swims and his legs wobble, but he can't abandon the prize that cost him his forearm. The translucent photovoltaic bubble dips low at his approach, ready to ease his entrance; once aboard, he struggles to pull the tarp up after him, its weight nearly too heavy to heave one-handed into the bubble's cramped space. There's blood everywhere, so much spilled material he'll have to replace, but that's a problem for later. For now he has to concentrate at least enough to pilot back to the crawler. He steadies his severed limb in his good hand, holds the throbbing pulse above a makeshift tourniquet: how hot the skin is, how swollen the flesh, how much worse it will soon be. The AR command console swims in his blurring vision, but the craft sputters and starts to float; outside the winch remains secured to the ice, but C has no choice but to abandon it, hoping the crevasse won't swallow it before he can return.

Not that it'll be exactly him who comes back.

The rung backs up the mind; the Loom reboots the body. The remainder is a combinatory self, minds stacked one atop the other; each C has a body reprinted as closely as possible to the one before, but often a lack of biomass necessitates certain replacements, polymer and plastinate extrusions filling in the gaps. The Loom rarely reverses these permutations, no matter how it's refueled: once a body part has been replaced with an inorganic substitute, every future C will bear the same replacement. Sometimes the replacement is an improvement, some part made less susceptible to injury, but each is also a diminishment of the real. If a polymer hoof can't be as easily injured, it's also less sensate, less aware of the surfaces the creature navigates. In recent years more drastic modifications have forced C to have to relearn how to walk or to perform other simple motor functions, like the one cycle when his left leg was made ever so slightly shorter, its bones lightened and augmented with inflexible plastic.

Among the remainder are those who believe that whoever became C must once have been a better being, fierce of claw and tooth, fleet of hoof, crowned with deadly turns of horn. Now he is only a creature imitating itself, a shadow of a better self unremembered by even the oldest among the remainder. But it doesn't matter, not to C-432. Like many of his most successful predecessors, he is rarely introspective, barely curious. He does not wonder, only survives.

And now even that must come to an end.

C steers the bubblecraft at maximum speed, zooming back to the stable shelf where the behemoth crawler has always been crashed, its gray steel hull inset with outcroppings of pipes and sensor arrays, its flat roof covered with solar panels he has to constantly sweep clear of snow and other debris. Outfitted with eight sets of triangular tread-wheels, the crawler is nonetheless stuck, its hull listing several degrees atop two sets of treads broken against an obstruction some long-ago pilot missed from the squat polygonal command cockpit extending from the crawler's uppermost floor, a room C-432 has always avoided. This C has always been uninterested in the warrens of dilapidated machinery and well-scavenged halls, where surely everything valuable was long ago cast into the recycler. For the two years of his cycle, it's been the Ice that has demanded his attention, the Ice and the wreck of the Below, the buried past from which he's spent this entire life trying to extract his next.

Back inside, he makes the staggering passage from the bubblecraft to the hangar exit, then through the labyrinth of barely lit hallways to the recycling chamber waiting before the Loom. There he kicks the tarp inside the recycler's cylindrical tube, dumping its contents before throwing the plastic back outside. Wheezing for breath, his vision pulsing, he stumbles against the recycler's far wall, crumpling awkwardly among the splintered black roots; he smells bark and dirt and soil, the rust of his blood mixing with old-world decay, ancient lignin thawed and awoken. Woozy with shock, he folds his legs, pulls his hooves inside the crowded recycler. As long as the blood falls inside the recycler it's not lost: the blood soaks the wood, the blood circles the drain, the blood is due to be his blood again soon enough.

So much is missing, so much is lost; C has so much doubt about how the Loom might react, but he gives the necessary voice command anyway, the one that sets the recycler humming to life. The glass door slides shut and latches. A moment later a corded steel tentacle snakes out of the module's ceiling to slide its interface needle into the port at the base of his neck: the needle turns and locks into the rung, implanted deep inside the port; the tentacle pulls, the rung sliding from his spine with a long smooth rip only C-432 hears.

The remainder lives in the rung; after its removal, the voices vanish.

Now, as his life ends, C-432 for the first time hears no voice but his own, a senseless howling he barely recognizes. The only living creature on the surface of the Ice, he has never before been alone; what comes next he suffers without company or comfort. Micropores open in the recycler's ceiling, a hiss fills the air as the pores shower him with a hot pink liquid: viscous, acidic, melting; the pain is excruciating, unbearable, *new*. He turns his face away, his nerves screaming: one horn melts, then the other; fur sloughs off his face, then the face follows the fur. He squeezes his eyes shut, but the protection is temporary: his eyelid dissolves, then the eye. The peculiar feeling of the skull opening not with a blow but by dissolution, then the first acid droplets hitting the brain, burning bright holes through his perception. The body dies slow, but without the brain conscious agony ceases. One leg judders the floor involuntarily, the blood flowing from the injured arm sizzles when it drips into the pooling pink liquid, steaming fluorescence streaked brown with the mud of his melting body.

Dying, he lies amid the melting black roots of a tree whose species he thinks he's never seen alive: while his nose lasts, he smells the sweet scent of scorched applewood, barely recognized by the only part of the mind predating the rung's installation.

No one observes C-432's final agonies. His life ends, and it's possible to believe that before this torture it already had, perhaps in the moment when the rung was snaked free of its port. To believe this is to believe that what C is, what he really is, is not this melting flesh but the amalgamation of selves backed up in the rung, rebooted when the next body comes online.

But surely there is something alive in the recycler tube, surely there is *someone:* a creature suffering; a living being dying alone, coming apart in a shower of hot pink acid rain.

CHAPMAN

Chapman and Nathaniel are given to industriousness, they work most days from dawn to dusk; but then come days of waiting out weather, days of needing ground to thaw or floodwaters to recede, days of hunting and gathering instead of plowing and planting. The morning after the year's first nursery is finished, silent Nathaniel stalks into the underbrush, rifle in hand, leaving Chapman behind, sitting idly atop a fresh-cut stump. When a robin flutters from its tree, he studies the curve of its beak, how perfectly built it is for all the robin has to do, digging grubs and worms and caterpillars, plucking berries from blooming bushes, building a nest to attract a mate. Its locomotion is a highly evolved efficiency, nothing lost or wasted because loss and waste is the road of deprivation, despair, death; there is risk in being a robin but not recklessness.

The robin digs another grub from the dirt, sucking its meal

back with a jerking gulp. After it's fed it becomes more curious, cocking its head at Chapman's strangeness. The faun offers his hand, palm up, fingers loose, his shoulder steady, his elbow level but relaxed; the robin leaps into the air at this invitation, its wings aflutter as it lands in his palm. It walks a circle around his hand, only momentarily intrigued by his mossy smell, then crouches upon its twiggy legs, ready to fly off—but before it can escape, Chapman closes his fingers, surprising himself with how easily he catches the robin in the cage of his fist. "When I'm done," he whispers, feeling the robin's breast thumping inside his grip, its heart bold behind its splinter of breastbone, "there'll still be trees for you to nest in, but all will be only the trees I permit." As soon as he says it, he gags, his mouth filling with the acrid taste of bile; the robin squawks with agitation and Chapman lets it go, the bird flying panicking into the trees.

Afterward, he burns with embarrassed shame: Why had he said what he did? Was it something he believed or something he'd been taught? His brother fancies himself a conqueror, a man subduing the blank horror of the wilderness, but Chapman wants to believe there are other options, at least for him. Agitated, he departs the nursery for the dewy morning woods, where he restlessly searches out signs of other birds, a sparrow, a blue jay, a wild turkey, each seeking its particular seed or berry, claiming its share of the bugs chittering beneath wet rocks or fallen logs. It's difficult to distinguish the individual from the type, and the lower the creature, the more challenging the want for true encounter: not everything hooved is Chapman's cousin, but in the eyes of a deer he's spied a canny intelligence absent in the eyes of the jackrabbit or the grouse, the furtive stare of a lizard. Is it a matter of sentience or a matter of scale? Who is to say what the lizard sees, what a bullfrog contemplates?

Beneath the canopy of pine and oak and maple there is moss everywhere, softly striving mats of it climbing the scarred trunks of the oldest trees, colonizing boulders smoothed and discarded by glaciers impossible to imagine among all this greenery, the moss on the move generation after generation, a mindless and relentless life-form. This overripe abundance all around, the forest gagging itself upon a bright profusion of right living: flowers blooming, chicks crying out, infant rabbits in the brambles, and ducklings on every pond; bones everywhere, eggshells and carapaces, last year's antlers bleached white amid fallen leaves, loosed entrails covered in the white castings of maggots. The older the forest, the more the soil smells of death and rot, rankest fertility: in one narrow bramble-choked ravine Chapman can't take a step without crushing a beetle beneath his hooves, but the beetle quickly becomes food for something else, life sprouting out of life. Nearby a fallen oak exposes a ball of roots taller than any man, the roots clutching broken rocks in their woody grip. A tree takes what it needs and sequesters it into wood; death alone will not make it release its catch, only rot and dissolution; but even before a tree dies it cedes some part of its life to the termites scrawling trails beneath its bark, to the birds nesting in its heights. How quickly a nest tumbled to the ground is savaged by weasels, leaving behind some hen squawking after her loss: predation but without malice, opportunity the forest's only guiding morality. Do these birds remember their broken eggs? Certainly they're not distraught forever. Surely there is no loss so final a creature will not try again to gain.

Is nothing sacred or is everything? Nathaniel says he hates to feel the deep purposelessness he sees in nonhuman life, the utter lack of any higher calling, but alone in these woods Chapman imagines himself just as uncharged and nameless as any

beast, freed from the human here where there's no other creature who cares what he calls himself, where there is no creature
who calls itself anything: a muskrat scurrying home is something a man could name, but to the muskrat, the faun watching it go is simply a shape moving in the shadows, a darkness
stretching across a dappling. For a time the faun takes pleasure
in this shared anonymity, allowing himself to join the unexceptional state of being all around him, breathing in the scatter
and the spoor, tracking the ceaselessness of scale in the fungal,
the vegetal, the animal sprawl. Once this entire world was bare
rock and deep water and underground fire spouting choking
gouts of unbreathable gas; now it's a creeping, crawling body
made of many bodies, each unexceptional amid the endless
motion of the world, life all around, life unbroken from the forest floor to the tops of the trees, life leaving bare not one square
inch of earth. Nothing the faun sees or hears or smells is for
him, but he can take from it whatever he needs: here nothing is
denied, everything is permitted except waste.

Far from camp, but not as far as he'd thought, the sound
of a musket blast pulls him back to himself, renames him
Chapman. The gunshot is too close, reverberating through the
nearby trees; Chapman hides, afraid. A moment later a moose
appears, crashing through the brush, staggered by a skillful
shot, a clean kill in the making, and then Nathaniel appears
too, running after his bullet, lifting his knees high to clear the
brush between him and his target. The bullet has broken the
moose's ribs, its lead expanding to tear through one lung and
then the other; Chapman watches the stumbling moose's face
contort, its lips made flags of flesh, dripping ropy saliva; falling
heavily, its last lowing sounds are unmistakably distressed.

Chapman remains crouched in the shadows throughout

the grisly exhibition that follows. He looks on in horror as Nathaniel dresses the kill with his knife, the moose's fading heat radiating upward, its blood spilling wherever Nathaniel slices the skin to expose the solid ribs, the heavy guts: the four bulging stomachs, a hundred feet of intestines, kidneys the size of a man's head. Already the moose's wildness is gone, already what pale spirit it possessed in life has escaped; from his hiding place Chapman sickens at the metallic tang, the moose's body expelling so much hot blood, its many iron-rich organs soon left steaming in the open air.

For Chapman to reveal himself now would only embarrass Nathaniel, who has always done his best to shield his brother from this task, but now that he's seen it he will never forget how Nathaniel looked cutting this hooved creature into its component parts, piling viscera away from the butchered meat, separating what he desires from what he'll share with the Territory's scavengers, refuse that includes the monstrous antlered head, its eyes open and stupidly staring, its black tongue hanging from its dumb lips; most of all he will remember how, as Nathaniel worked on, he absently began to whistle, happy and proud of his kill so expertly butchered and disassembled, at the taken life of this moose piled into parts atop a blood-soaked tarpaulin, the moose made meat until it's a moose no more.

JOHN

How many others roaming the emptied lands west of the Mississippi must've felt the same persistent nag John thinks now, driving east: *Where have all the people gone?* But there are fewer people everywhere now, years after the Secession and the Sacrifice, after the unquenchable malaria outbreaks and the rising sea levels made much of the Eastern Seaboard uninhabitable—and no matter what the emergency was, always Eury Mirov appeared on every screen, offering slogan after slogan, each one a promise John had heard too many times before. Once Earthtrust had promised John a life he'd thought he'd wanted too, years ago, back when the company was an unremarkable midwestern start-up, just Eury and John and a handful of others paid entirely in then worthless stock options.

The work and Eury, for so long he'd thought he'd wanted them both.

John's grandfather had owned a small farm in Ohio, plowing his acres with a simple tractor, raising pigs and goats and chickens alongside a rotation of corn and wheat. This was land their family had improved for over two hundred years, right beside the farm where Eury had grown up, their two families close, the two kids childhood friends. John's father had expanded his holdings until he owned a swath of prime Ohio farmland covered in monoculture corn and soybeans, genetically modified crops stretching the soil's limits until every year a more resilient engineered seed was needed, plus more expensive fertilizers, ever more complex machinery.

The year John joined Earthtrust, the family farm was failing, its profitability declining as the weather warmed, as the rains stopped or else never ended, every spring a flood and every summer a drought, as tornado season started lasting all year. The first time John told Eury he was quitting was after all his family's land had been sold except for the original homestead, adjacent to the one her great-great-ancestor had bought in the 1850s; when John returned it was to live there alone, his parents dead of cancer and heart disease, of bankruptcy and heartbreak.

At Earthtrust, he'd wanted to make the world a better place, to help undo the damage other corporations had done. Earthtrust would be different, Eury had promised. Earthtrust's plants and animals—its "plant and animal products," as the brochures had read—weren't much like the crops and livestock John's grandfather had raised, and John was as responsible as anyone else for what they'd become. He'd helped design vast superorchards of genetically modified apple trees, then developed a series of synthetic nanobees to pollinate them; others invented strains of brown-leafed corn hardy enough to survive six-month droughts, their stalks growing imperceptibly slowly, producing kernels edible only to the cows Earthtrust bred to eat them. When John went home to his family farm, he'd planted only heirloom seeds taken from the company's archives, all acquired from the seed banks of hopeful organizations who'd helped Earthtrust in its early days, before it was obvious what the company would become.

For two years, the farm had grown, if not exactly flourished, John managing to get a beekeeping operation running in the apple orchard, a boon even at the height of the final colony collapse; during the second year, there'd been a promising explosion of earthworms and maggots, the soil turning and churning one more time—but then came a yearlong drought, exacerbated by the highest temperatures ever recorded in the Midwest. By the end he'd had to watch his soil blow away, all the earth his family had tilled gone, the farmland in Ohio and the other midwestern states turning to gray dust, cracked clay, bared rock. John had stood on the porch of his father's farmhouse, staring into a rust-orange sunset sky made newly beautiful by light refracted through rolling dust and windblown pollution, watching the dry topsoil lifting into the air in ragged strips, carrying with it the brittle bodies of dead earthworms, squirming maggots who'd never learn to fly.

The Rice Wars, the Corn Wars, the Soy Wars: How many lives were lost worldwide in the years of crop failures that followed that summer? Before they ended, Earthtrust owned John's family's land, then the entire county, then most of the state, Eury paying prices pretending the land was still farmable, that it wasn't besieged by dust storms and churning clodtwisters.

No one could afford to stay. No one could afford to say no to Eury Mirov.

Afterward she alone owned what had been, for more than two centuries, his family's and hers, and John had gone back to Earthtrust, desperate again for Eury's promises.

Driving faster now, John remembers: *A job for every man and woman who wants a job,* Eury had said, *an Earthtrust machine for every job you don't want.*

But also someone else's voice, a rebuttal from a book: *A man with a machine and inadequate culture is a pestilence.* Who wrote that? It's been years since John's read a book, years since he's done much of anything but drive and look, stop and fight. Two doctoral degrees, a career at Earthtrust, all of it in the past. He'd once thought of himself as intelligent, learned, sophisticated enough. Now what was he? A man reduced, a man made small. All the technology that had been put in the place of human dignity, replacing the natural with the artificial: Whose ideas lay beneath them? What was the culture from which his own inventions had sprung?

A vanished world. The things he'd cared about before, ideas about art and literature, ideas about justice and civilization, they'd been more fragile than he'd imagined. He doesn't know what can be saved. Surely there is something. But already he's forgotten so much.

THE SPEEDING CRUISER APPEARS IN HIS REARVIEW MIRROR TWENTY kilometers west of Cheyenne, its cycling blue and red lights dully cutting the midafternoon dust. This is what he's been waiting for. There's no such thing as a routine stop inside the Sacrifice Zone, but John wants the officers edgy, ready to pounce, too angry to ask questions. He accelerates, the truck groaning when the electric motor gives way to the combustion engine, then drifts left to ride the highway's center line as the cruiser charges, its siren wailing. He adjusts his rearview mirror to center the cruiser, watching how the aerodynamic curve of its black windshield hides the officers inside, how the driver's hands likely haven't taken the wheel yet, the officer letting the computer drive.

Dust swirls up and over the freeway, both vehicles tunneling through the blowing dirt, the cruiser giving him every chance to pull over. If John's truck were any newer, it'd have a kill switch built in, a way for the officers to shut off his engine from the safety of their cruiser. Another reason John's kept this old model. Its engines groan, the tires squeal when he fishtails to keep the cruiser from squeezing up alongside him.

Despite the demanding speed, John finds himself picturing Cal's face: the jut of her chin, the one crooked tooth visible in her smile, the heavy intensity of her attention, the violence of her grip. *What I love about you*, she said once, caging his body with hers, pinning him to a tent floor pitched atop a dead prairie, *is your wildness*. He'd never thought of himself that way. But she'd showed him how to find the something wild that dwelled inside him: not a recklessness—nothing wild was truly reckless—but a joyful abandon, a deadly serious sense of play.

John watches the cruiser slide right across the pavement, switching sides and speeding up. He yanks his wheel left, whipping the truck perpendicular to the freeway, leaving the pavement on two wheels. As the left wheels slam down with a bouncing jolt, he aims the truck across the horizon-spanning crust of clay, an expanse broken only by weather-beaten buildings in the far distance, by roaming dust devils closer up. He doesn't have much attention to spare—the ground is uneven, rutted, and cracked, every dip threatens to trap a wheel—but in the rearview he catches the slight hitch in the vehicle's previously smooth operation when the driver takes manual control of the speeding cruiser.

John presses the pedal down farther, sends the truck bouncing faster over the pitiless landscape, the ground crumbling beneath the wheels. One old myth of the West was that much of it was empty, barren, lifeless; a useful story, because one way to convince yourself to spread suburbs to the horizon was to tell yourself there was nothing there.

It wasn't true then, but it almost is now.

He takes a deep breath, tries to take in as much of the nothingness as he can. Nothingness is not emptiness. True nothingness, which existed nowhere on earth before humans made it so, is palpable, the earth's distress made physical, the silent sign of something gone terribly wrong.

John jerks the wheel and brakes hard, spinning the truck to a halt atop the cracked mudflat. Before the cruiser skids to its own stop, the first helmeted officer is out of his seat, advancing in a shooter's stance, pistol raised, his voice barking rushed commands. John waits blank-faced until the officer tears open the truck's door and hauls him out by his shirt, pressing his pistol to John's neck. John doesn't react, doesn't speak; he makes no apology or any sound of pain as the officer brings the pistol butt down on his forehead.

Then: fist and baton and boot, the officers beat him until they're huffing behind their face shields. John doesn't go under, doesn't fall unconscious. "It's okay," he says, giving in, giving permission. "It's okay." His voice sputters wetly. He wants to say, can't say: I'm afraid too. I'm afraid too, but there's always room for more fear.

Afterward they haul him upright, drag him to the cruiser,

cuff him, and shove him roughly into the back seat. There's blood in his mouth, a pounding ache in his temples, bright-flowering bruises blooming atop his cheekbones. He wants the bruises, invites their rising; hopefully the damage will hide his features from Earthtrust's facial scanners. He sticks out his tongue and licks away the blood dripping across his lip, down toward his chin. The blood tastes, improbably, like applesauce. But probably that's just a concussion.

John dozes fitfully. When he wakes, the cruiser is devour-ing the kilometers, passing the sporadic autonomous long-haulers with smooth ease, the day lost, sunset falling gloriously through the dusty particulate in the Wyoming air. One of John's eyes is bruised shut, his jaw so swollen it might as well be wired. He leans forward, puts his forehead against the bul-letproof partition, does his best to take in the two officers, their helmets removed, faces visible. Wherever they're from, it isn't Wyoming: Earthtrust security shifts its people from region to region, breaking local allegiances, local concerns. An old tactic. A man who grew up on a plot of land might not be able to stand its destruction, but a non-native with a paycheck might gladly brutally extract its resources, especially if he wouldn't have to live on the ruined land when it was over.

The younger officer turns around, clacks a gloved fist against the glass. "Lean back," he says. "You don't need to be so close." Less imposing with his helmet removed, old acne scars pock-ing clean-shaven cheeks, the cop could be anyone John grew up with in Ohio, back when rural life persisted, back when it was almost possible to have *a normal American childhood*—and wasn't John's the last generation to imagine such a life? Surely no one born today could expect a life like the one he'd been born into, a birthright of land and labor.

THEY REACH THE DETENTION CENTER IN THE DARK, THE CRUISER
pulling smoothly to a stop on a dimly lit charging pad installed
in the front row of the parking lot. John had expected the detention center to look like a prison, some imposing architecture surrounded by fencing and towering guard posts, but the
Cheyenne post is simply a repurposed big-box store, emptied
only a few years ago. In the Western Sacrifice Zone, every existing building might be put to new use: With so many structures
abandoned or evacuated, why build anything new?

Now we will be barbarians, John thinks, *living in our parents'
ruins.*

The younger cop opens the cruiser door and drags John out.
John walks forward in an injured hunch, past a series of temporary concrete barriers set in front of the building, meant to
prevent a speeding vehicle from slamming into the glass store-
front. The inside glows fluorescent, inviting even as it repels,
repulses: it's always been difficult for John to return from the
wilderness, to resume life in the world of connected technology, autonomous systems, endless electric lights. Days ago, he
was sleeping alone under the stars. Tonight he'll bunk in an
abandoned department store, a prisoner of the company he
helped found.

Once through the automatic glass doors, John's expectations are subverted again: inside the detention center he sees
no cells, no one else in cuffs. There are more officers here, but
none wear helmets or body armor, just slacks and short-sleeved
wicking t-shirts with the Earthtrust logo at their breasts, the
officers looking tired but not unfriendly as they process the incoming detainees.

The younger officer leads the way, supporting John's limping walk with a gloved grip. Without letting go of John's elbow, he leans in and speaks in a low voice. "You'll be charged with trespassing in the Sacrifice Zone, illegal driving, resisting arrest. You could go to the prison camps and serve your time, but why? When they ask you to Volunteer, do it. If all you have left is that truck, sign it over. You look smart, healthy. Go east. Work the Farm, earn a new life."

John seethes. How many times has this officer given this speech? How many times has he convinced frightened detainees to give up what little they have left? John holds in his anger, says thank you. A moment later, he's at the front of the line, the cop wishing him good luck as his identification passes the loose scrutiny of the intake officer, a stocky sunburned woman who offers the promised choice: imprisonment in a work camp in Cheyenne or a new life across the Mississippi, in the Ohio Volunteer Agricultural Community.

John signs the forms the woman shows him, the standard ninety-nine-year Earthtrust contract: he Volunteers, signing over his citizenship, his right to vote, his right to own property—all his guaranteed protections under the Bill of Rights—in exchange for a pardon and a leased home in the Ohio VAC, where he'll receive guaranteed work at a fixed wage, plus access to safe food and clean water, a selection of affordable consumer goods. He will not be free to travel outside the VAC; if he quits or flees or otherwise violates his contract, he'll find himself an illegal immigrant inside his own country.

The cuffs come off, because he's no longer a prisoner. Now he's a Volunteer, and as a Volunteer he has different privileges: he's taken to a medical station where his injuries are examined and treated by a kind pair of male nurses in pale blue scrubs; he's led to a private shower stall in a coed locker room, where he disrobes, discarding his filthy clothes into an overflowing bin. He exits his second shower in as many days to find a folded set of printed clothing waiting for him, blue jeans and a pale gray t-shirt, underwear and socks and sneakers. Everything functional, in his size or close enough. Another handler meets him outside the locker room, takes him to the next station where he's given a backpack containing a change of clothing, a box of nutrient bars, a tablet the handler says will start working as soon as he's inside the VAC.

"You are entitled," the handler says, in lightly accented English, "to whatever clothing, food, and services you need. Don't hesitate to ask. Not everything is possible, but we want you to be comfortable."

She passes her wand over his pebble and he flinches: it's invasive to scan a citizen without asking, but of course he isn't a citizen anymore.

"There," she says. "Earthtrust has advanced you your first month's pay, in case you need anything from the company store before your first pay period ends. This way you won't want in the meantime."

John knows this is all part of Earthtrust's stripping as many Americans as possible of their citizenship and their constitutional rights, but it's being done with such friendliness he can't help genuinely thanking everyone he interacts with, his tired and battered body and mind grateful for every kindness. By the time his processing is finished, it's three in the morning. He's been up for over twenty-four hours, hasn't had anything to eat since leaving Cal's bunker. The night's final handler leads John through the fluorescence to a darkened room containing rows of cots, good for a few hours of rest before he boards the morning bus to the eastbound train.

John sits on the offered cot to remove his shoes, then digs a nutrient bar from his pack. Chewing quietly, he scans the dim room, his eyes slowly adjusting. There are thirty or forty other people here, men and women and children, refugees from the fallen West, new Volunteers all. Anyone who turned down Earthtrust's offer is somewhere else, cuffed and unfed, out of sight in a cage of chain-link and razor wire. Most of the Volunteers John sees are asleep, but a few speak softly in the near dark. Their voices are gentle and sweet, fathers and mothers comforting their children, a surprising excitement in every sentence. They've sacrificed citizenship and home and belongings, rights and privileges it would have been inconceivable to relinquish before the troubles really began. But life in the Sacrifice Zone has been brutal for years now; the fact of these people's late arrival here in the detention center means they'd held out as long as they could. What awaits them in the Volunteer Agricultural Communities isn't the American dream they'd once been promised, a promise some of them have already wasted a lifetime futilely trying to earn, but perhaps it will still be better than what they've recently endured, the slow but undeniable loss of American possibility.

C-433

An assumption built into the Loom: any creature remade of many different materials remains itself. At the device's heart waits a domed stage, a hump of closed steel ringed by a series of extruder arms, each extruder outfitted with a rotating plate of printer heads capable of spinning out organic bioinks, inorganic plastinates, coils of various metals. Soon after the recycler finishes processing C-432, the dome opens, its interlocking lids sliding apart to expose a shallow pool of blue-white liquid heated to body temperature, temperature of the body about to be made. With the recombinant C confined to the unsocketed rung, flickering senselessly in virtual space as it waits for its next body, there's no one to watch the Loom work except the disembodied voice C calls O, the crawler's only other occupant. Housed in the crawler's data banks, O sings a harsh wordless sound, atonal, a rushing thud, a buzzing repetitive keening droning from speakers arranged throughout the chamber, clicking on in sequence as the Loom finishes booting.

Now the Loom's limbs move in concert with O's freed sound, the extruders slipping along their circular track in time with the sound, their hydraulics whirring as they lay down different colors and textures of bioinks alongside melted steel and fast-drying polymers, assembling C's next body layer by layer inside the viscous pool of milk-thick fluid, stacking organs and bones, lacing muscles to tendons, encasing the spinal cord in the bony sheath of the vertebrae, the brain within the shell of the skull; it prints the heart and the lungs, then all the other organs arranged inside the rib cage and the abdomen, each an algorithmically determined composite of bioink and plastinate. Immense numbers of nerve cells and blood vessels must be threaded throughout the accumulating body, a task of exquisite intricacy with only the tiniest tolerance for error: one hundred billion neurons in the brain, ten times more glial cells, one hundred thousand kilometers of arteries and veins.

Every time C is reprinted, his skull shows the evidence of a long-ago natural birth in its sealed fontanelle; always the creature bears healed breaks in both its femurs, an unremembered injury not one printed C has ever noticed. Then come the horns, rising in heavy layers from the forehead; then hooves capping the cloven toes, the left hoof keratin, the right polymer and metal.

Before the skin can be laid down, the Loom's ceiling opens, loosing two prehensile metal tentacles: one squirms between the jaws of the muscle-fleshed face, sliding between half-plastic teeth and over the muscular tongue to push into the trachea, starting the flow of oxygen into the lungs; the other stabs through the abdomen beside the navel, seeking out a temporary nest in the stomach to start a slow, sludgy nutrient drip, the creature's first sustenance.

The skin and fur go on entire: momentarily there's no mouth, no eyes, no nostrils or urethra or anus, the creature blind and deaf beneath the sheath of its face until the Loom sends a scalpel arm to carve the eyelids, the ears, the nose, and the lips. Then the blue fur is tattooed into the rubbery skin, one strand held in each pinprick, laid down a thousand pinpricks a second.

O's sound changes, the new noise as discordant and screeching as before, becoming a beseeching, an asking, a bringing forth. A summoning song. Powerful electrical charges jolt through the water in steady waves, continuing until the creature's muscle cells twitch, until the heart begins to *thump thump thump*. The body complete, a third articulating tentacle snakes from the ceiling, heading for a port installed at the base of the creature's neck. While it drops, the creature is only itself, instinctively fighting the machine making it, desperate to leap from the bloody bluish milk, wanting to tear the tubes from its stomach and throat, to lift the metal paddles holding it down.

In this moment, the creature has the same birthright of any animal, the right to be only itself, to make its way in the world for its own reasons. Self-sufficient, self-aware, self-willed.

Then the memory module locks into its port, the tentacle cranking its pin into place.

The module has had many names. Mostly every C has thought of it as the *rung*, the handhold by which he pulls himself up into himself. After it's installed, the creature becomes C, C-433 and also every other C besides, all alive again inside this one body.

C-433 drags his gasping body free of the Loom's pool, the lid sliding shut behind him as soon as his hooves come free of the fluid. He crawls down the Loom's slope and across the cold metal floor, shaking loose a milky trail from his fur. Lying heaving at the Loom's base, he aches everywhere, his body throbs inside and out with the hurt of having been made all at once. The worst pains are in his neck, where the rung was installed; in his throat, scratched as the breathing tube roughly extracted itself; in his navel, where the departing feeding tube left behind a raw pucker of seeping flesh.

Despite the pain, he can soon stand, wobbling on his hooves; not long after, he takes a few halting steps toward the chamber's exit, fleeing O's screeching voice. Everything he experiences outside the chamber's hatch is both novel and familiar: as C-433, he feels nervous and skittish and newborn; as C, he's taken every possible route inside the crawler thousands of times before. His fabricated hoof clangs across the crawler's steel floors, as the remainder guides his movements gently at first and then more insistently, steering him toward the life every C has pursued since finding the crawler, an event no remainder remembers but that the whole assumes.

The remainder is sometimes a single commanding speaker loud in C-433's mind; more often it's a murmuration of many voices. C-433 walks hallway to hallway, spinning open longshut hatch seals, steadying his shaky body on doorframes and exposed struts. Only a few chambers are fully intact: the Loom and the adjacent recyclers, the hangar housing the translucent photovoltaic bubble, a galley with seats for fifty where C eats alone, every meal taken from the stored biomass in the recycler tanks, every overindulgence risking some future self.

C was born nearly empty stomached, but the remainder implores him to keep himself lean, hungry, wanting, so they might live longer, so they might go on.

To live is enough, the remainder claims, its voices an un-subtle swarm inside his head.

If C has any other purpose, then 432 times he has failed to find it.

"This time will be different," he says aloud, hearing his particular voice for the first time, while in between his horns many similar voices repeat the same useless claim. He continues his tour, studying how the remainder dismantled the crawler's lab equipment and computer displays, how it fed tools and test tubes into the inorganic recycler; he remembers hooves almost like his kicking through the side of clear plastic crates whose raw materials might have helped the Loom make do after the biomass ran low. There are intercom speakers and various controls mounted on many of the rusting walls, but no matter what button he touches the only response is O's voice screeching through the speakers, a sound from which the gathered remainder recoils, the visceral blast of repetitive droning tightening C's stomach, setting his plasticine teeth to grinding.

Usually, the voice can be stopped with a single button press.

Other times, no matter what C does, the song blares on and on.

"What is this place for?" he asks, room after room, the crawler too complex to be the best way to traverse the Ice, much less suited to the task than his bubblecraft. C-433 hasn't been outside yet, but the remainder knows what he'd find if he walked the perimeter of the crawler: the treads on each side of the facility, the hydraulics attached to each axle designed to lift the crawler over obstructions; the way the various sections of the crawler are segmented, allowing the whole to stretch and distort and turn over the changeable landscape. C understands that the crawler is an extraordinary piece of technology, a last invention of the world that was, but under his command its promise has been nearly completely depleted, until the facility is almost as ruined as the wreckage beneath the Ice, the crushed trash of Below. Without the Loom, there might be no reason for him to stay here. But as long as the Loom functions—as long as each new C spends his life gathering enough biomass to buy more life from its recyclers—then the crawler will be his home.

Home, and also salvation, and also leash, cage, prison cell.

CHAPMAN

By May's end, Nathaniel and Chapman have planted three new nurseries, each twenty miles apart, one alongside what Nathaniel thinks is called Splitlip Creek, another beside a nearby river tributary, then a third hidden deeper in the bowels of the great black swamp, where Nathaniel says the nursery will be safe to flourish free from human intrusion until all the easier bottomlands to the east are settled. By the end of these weeks spent struggling in the swamp's wet gloom, the brothers speak less and less, their experiences so twinned there's nothing new to report or discuss, no stimulation except the endless daybreak to nightfall labor of their efforts.

Nothing new to discuss, and also nothing old: Chapman still hasn't told Nathaniel about his witnessing of the moose's butchering, despite the distance it puts between them, despite vegetarian Chapman's rising disgust as his brother ate his month of moose.

The frustration soon grows mutual. The morning the last nursery is finished, Nathaniel snaps at Chapman over a broken gimlet both can see cracked not from mishandling but overuse. Nathaniel's anger is misplaced but genuine: there's no way to replace the tool here in the swamplands, and a month's passed since they last met any human presence other than each other. Without outside contact, there's no news, no chance for barter, no change to their foraged diet of gathered berries and dug tubers and hunted game, supplemented less and less by the dwindling supply of flour and other sundries brought west from Pennsylvania. Items lasting years in settled lands disintegrate in weeks in the sodden, shelterless Territory, the constant exposure enough to undo even the best-made items the brothers could afford: Chapman wears only trousers, but his one pair is filthy, torn, and unseamed, unmendable; the sole of Nathaniel's left boot flops free of its glue, his hat brim breaks, the felt across its crown fallen to tatters.

The first morning of June, Nathaniel stares balefully across the cookfire, his reddened eyes signaling the return of a rage he bears constantly but rarely shows. An anger that this difficult life is Chapman's fault, that if Chapman had been born a mere boy, if his monstrous birth hadn't killed his mother, then Nathaniel wouldn't have to sleep outside, exposed and starving so one day they might make a dollar. Chapman waits for his brother to speak some such accusation, but Nathaniel says nothing until breakfast is finished, the fire smoldering out while he scours their dishes with dry dirt scraped from the maple trunks, above the foul waterline.

"We're out of supplies," Nathaniel tries, dissembling, casting his glance away from Chapman's too-wide face. "Cornmeal, tobacco, whiskey. We need a new gimlet, thanks to you; plus another blade for the saw. I'll be gone a week, if the weather holds. More if it doesn't."

Chapman knows he isn't invited. Even if he was, he couldn't walk the streets of whatever clapboard town Nathaniel intends to visit. Brotherly kindness means saying none of this. Brotherly togetherness means pretending they're mutually agreeing to part ways. Chapman says, "While you're gone, I can visit last year's nurseries, secure them against wind and weather, predation and theft. I'll be able to move faster without you." Because it's not only Chapman who holds Nathaniel back, but also Nathaniel who constrains what Chapman might otherwise be: without him, he can speed his return to older nurseries possibly at last ready to fruit, among which he might find his Tree. And if he finds it, without Nathaniel? Then the next time Nathaniel sees him, he will have become a surprise, a man instead of a faun, a brother come anew in a body to which Nathaniel's affections might more easily attach.

By noon the brothers have climbed free of the buggy swampland, both bitten often about the face and hands, both slicked with muck below their belts. They expect no sign of other people so soon, but at the waist-deep water's northern edge they discover a newly built levee holding back brackish water, further flooding the swampland on one side.

"This wasn't here when we came this way a week ago," Nathaniel says, frowning.

A hundred yards away, Chapman spies a dozen men digging beside the unsteady levee's loose hill of mud, dredging the swamp slop with shovels and mattocks, piling it high onto the next strand of levee.

The brothers hesitate, hidden halfway up the levee's steep slope. "They might have something to trade," Nathaniel says, taking another slim step upward, away from Chapman. "Otherwise I wouldn't leave you."

Chapman turns from his brother's renewed want for better conversation, for the sight of anyone else; if these other men will have him, then Nathaniel won't have to walk to town to meet the new company he craves. The logic is sound, but still, there's a hesitance in Nathaniel's voice, an unspoken ask for permission or absolution. Nathaniel has made his faunish brother into as much of a man as he can—he has dressed him in men's clothes, he has taught him to do a man's work—but sometimes it isn't enough.

What is it Chapman desires, in this moment and every other like it? He wants his brother to choose him. Fair or unfair, that's all. There are two worlds he knows he can't fully join, the human and the nonhuman, but every time Nathaniel chooses to dwell in the wilds of the Territory with him instead of returning to more civilized lands, Chapman's apartness doesn't have to become aloneness too. Chapman wants Nathaniel to choose him, but like his brother, he wants not to ask for what he wants.

"Go then," he says, waving a clawed hand at the cold stink of black mud around them. "I'll be fine in the swamps, alone."

There's no pleasure in anticipating more wet fur, no joy in mud ceaselessly clumped between cloven toes, but the only easy way to let Nathaniel leave without another fight is to leave him first.

Chapman descends the levee's bank to wade back the way they came, through doomed stands of ash and elm looming out of the rising floodwater. From beyond the tree line he follows his brother at a distance, walking parallel to Nathaniel but staying hidden. The ditchdiggers startle when Nathaniel calls out, then relax when they see his hands raised, far from the tomahawk slung through the strap of his bag, the hunting rifle secured across his back.

The ditchdiggers' foreman leans on his shovel, appraises Nathaniel, who appears beggared and destitute besides these better-provisioned men. "You're alone?" the foreman asks, scanning the swampland for compatriots, bands of thieves, whatever danger he imagines.

Chapman holds his breath. What is it he hopes Nathaniel will say? The impossible thing? That he has a brother waiting nearby, whose odd shape need be no reason for alarm or violence?

Nathaniel says, "Yes, I'm alone," with no quaver in his voice to suggest a lie. Chapman suppresses an angry snort, his face burning with hurt. Other than the last few of the brothers' dollars, there's nothing in Nathaniel's bag these men could possibly want, not with their own wagon full of supplies and a proper camp surely nearby. Chapman's too far away to hear every detail of the ensuing conversation, but it's not difficult to understand its progress, how Nathaniel details his purpose in the Territory, how the men explain their own: the levees they construct and the ditches they dig will drain away the swamp, making it possible to build better roads, plow broader fields, allowing more and more families to come to settle.

"You'll be able to plant anywhere you want next year," the foreman boasts. "No more tripping through the mud for you."

Ohio Company men, Chapman presumes. He spits into the water, expectorating his disgust for the Company bosses back east, wealthy men who want to own a landscape they have never seen. Men happy to know the Territory only in their ledgers.

Despite all Nathaniel's talk about making his own fortune, he takes a shovel from the ditchdiggers' wagon, knowing all the while that the men will reciprocate with nothing richer than a hot meal, a space around their cheery fire.

Chapman fumes, but what can he do? Let Nathaniel dig in the mud, let Chapman seek other pleasures instead.

WITHOUT ANY MAP TO GUIDE HIM, CHAPMAN FOLLOWS A TRAIL OF memory, searching anxiously for his trees. Some of what he sees next no other man will again, the levee due to reshape these acres of swamp, home to unique combinations of plants and trees, to the specific animals thriving in this one particular place. He spies a snub-beaked bird flitting in the dry branches above his head, then a white-furred weasel swimming bank to bank through black water. Harelipped suckers flit and skitter in the shallows, the fish hunting fingernail-sized clams and dun-colored scuttling crabs. So much might've already changed in the past year: at any moment a nursery can be lost to spring flooding, to autumn fires, to early frost; seedlings might be devoured by jackrabbits, shoots and seeds dug up in winter by starving squirrels. The wilderness moves both slow and sudden, and anywhere civilization touches lurches toward new and terrifying speeds: one year there'd been no need to guard their trees with even the simplest of brush fences and the next their nurseries were all overrun with half-wild hogs, the pigs loosed to feed wherever they could by newly arrived farmers. Chapman returned another spring to find a once flourishing nursery washed away, the river bar he'd planted turned to sandy silt as the water changed direction, some new dam upstream eroding the good soil he remembered.

Every tree gone is a lost chance to discover the apple Chapman seeks, but he tries to tamp down his nervous urgency: all he's truly lost is time; poor as he is, there's always more time. Time and apple seeds, Chapman's most honest currencies, all the wealth he's ever had.

By noon of his first full day alone, Chapman emerges from the unculled woods to the surprise of a stand of one hundred adult apple trees, arranged in the neat rows where he and Nathaniel once bent to plant their seeds. It's too early in the season for this nursery's apples to have ripened fully, but Chapman can't help plucking a dull fruit from the nearest tree, the apple gray green, mottled with pink flecks. His teeth, sharp as they are, struggle to pierce its waxy skin, the dense flesh within. It's impossible to guess what this apple's ripest taste will be: the early mouthful he spits out is wood and starch and stone, senseless disappointment.

Chapman tries another apple, but after each bite he remains wholly himself, unmoved and unchanged. Still, there are one hundred trees here, one hundred varieties of apple, one hundred chances. Moving faster, he tugs a purplish apple free from its stubborn stem, bites and tastes and swears before throwing the ungiving fruit into the bushes. He tries a green apple. A yellow apple. An apple striped and an apple stippled. The taste of sand, the taste of wood pulp, the taste of rind from skin to core. Apples too young even to be bug eaten, fly egged, worm riddled. Chapman's teeth soon set to aching. The air is flush with humidity, loud with the calls of frightened birds bearing witness to his anger. He stamps a foot and crushes an ant nest; he rakes his hoof back and forth, thrashes loose a warren of worms.

"I will turn this whole continent over to you," Chapman whispers to the uncaring trees, "if you give me what I want. I will plant a thousand thousand apple trees, a hundred thousand thousand. If it will earn me my right apple, I don't care if anything other grows here ever again." He's waited ten years for these apples to grow, he knows he only has to wait another month, two at the most, to learn if there's anything here for him.

He cannot force himself to be patient. Everything he does next is folly and waste, but he cares not. He cries out, then lowers his head and rushes a tree chosen at random, its shape no more offensive than any other. He slams his stubborn skull against the tree's adolescent trunk, he rakes his horns against the bark, then sets his claws to tearing loose chunks of pulp. He grabs hold of the tree's lower branches, shaking them furiously until their stems break to shower him with unripe apples, hateful orbs bouncing off his barked flesh. How useless such fruit is, how despised the tree that drops it! When he tires of battering the tree's surface, of snapping its branches—when his horns hum with the reverberations of repeated blows—he wraps his arms around the tree's trunk, he plants his hooves and lifts. His muscles ripple and bulge, his strength is greater than any mere man's. The tree's trunk protests audibly, its bark quivers and cracks. The air is so humid Chapman can't distinguish between the hot damp breeze and the sweat bursting from his fur. The ground gives way as he scrapes and pulls and twists, the soil collapses, his hooves slide into a trench widening at the tree's base. He grunts louder, leveraging the trunk until its bark splinters in a jagged tear, the tree crying out as its juvenile roots tear free of the earth.

Afterward Chapman lies beside the broken trunk, his anger gone, the blankness that follows a mismatch for the spectacle surrounding him. The tree destroyed, he stands and shakily considers the scene: the root ball exposed, the suckers covered in clinging dirt, the trunk slashed and scored and splintered. All the apples knocked free, doomed to rot instead of ripen.

What if this was the Tree. What if this tree's apples would have become the apples he sought, if only he'd allowed the tree to grow.

If Nathaniel had been here, this wouldn't have happened. But Nathaniel isn't.

Now Chapman chooses his own mistakes, makes regrets only he owns.

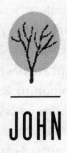

JOHN

The maglev train streaks across the Sacrifice Zone, floating centimeters above its enclosed rails as the landscape blurs by. Eury Mirov's likeness is omnipresent onboard, her voice speaking from telescreens mounted in the headrest of every seat and from larger screens decorating the walls, all looping the same mix of Earthtrust advertisements and promotional videos. Restless by noon, John gives up his bench seat to a pregnant woman and her wife, the second woman's forearm encased in a cast, likely broken during their capture. Limping through the train's many cars, John watches what was Wyoming imperceptibly give way to what was Nebraska, the old signs marking the state lines since removed. The burned brown landscape rushing by outside is a stark contrast to the farmlands in the looping videos where Eury plays leader, muse, mother, an object of adoration and generosity, promising safety, security, favor to any who follow her.

In every video John watches, Eury wears the same black suit and white blouse, her hair trimmed short, stylishly militaristic. In one, she tours a cavernous barn with a cluster of hale Volunteers, smiling men and women in Earthtrust-printed clothing working spacious stalls crammed with black-and-white cows, the shoulders of each bioengineered animal taller than Eury's. "These are not your grandparents' cattle," she says, reaching up to pat one of the passing cows. "There's nothing quite like the real thing, even better than you remember." Cue a clip of a beautiful child in a white sundress, using both hands to lift a glass of fresh milk to her smiling lips. When was the last time the train's newest Volunteers had milk that didn't come from a can or a powder? When was the last time they saw a pastured cow, safe and happy, dumbly chewing its cud?

In the next video, Eury's voice languidly champions her Volunteer Agricultural Community: horizon-busting fields of crops, fruiting superorchards, rows of white concrete houses with printed yards, children playing inside identical plots, a life hard to imagine while staring out at the Nebraska deadlands rushing by the train's windows. "This is your future," Eury says, walking now through a superorchard of supertrees laden with bright red fruit, "if only you will believe, if only you will strive, if only you will sacrifice for the greater good." Each apple above her a perfect globe, the grass between the trees impossibly level, improbably green. Eury holds out a hand and a bee lands on her palm, the camera smoothly zooming closer: it's not a real honeybee—America's honeybees have been extinct for years— but a miniature robot, part of the nanoswarms Earthtrust created to pollinate the VACs.

Some of the other passengers ooh and aah each time the robot alights on Eury's hand, but not John. The bees, after all, were his idea; the superorchards doubly so. In their earliest meetings with investors, Eury had begged him to talk about the apple trees he wanted to grow, the first part of the Farm they'd envisioned. Everything else she'd built since had, in one way or another, started with his trees and his bees, with the first time he showed her an awkward prototype crawling across the back of his hand, its carbon-fiber legs drunkenly summitting the hairy spines of his knuckles.

The train scrolls on, its tube tunnel suspended over cracked surface roads full of abandoned vehicles. The conductor makes no announcements, but eventually John recognizes the Iowa he once knew in the red barns and white farmhouses planted alongside wasted fields, wind-tilted cornstalks evidence of last harvests so poor they weren't even worth plowing under, combines left beached along the roadside, dust scoured and rusted. This American emergency—the coasts quaked and drowned, the center burned up and blown away—John knows this wasn't the world anyone wanted. A sullen midwestern dystopia, with only Earthtrust coming to save us.

He walks stiffly toward the train's sparsely populated last car, where he can sit alone and watch the curve of the train's tube snaking back across the countryside. Eury's voice speaks on, listing Earthtrust's many future achievements as if they've been accomplished, their promised world already manifested. The city-sized macrofarms of corn and wheat and soybean on which all can live; the skyscrapers of vertical chicken coops cleaned daily by drone handlers, their eggs gathered by Volunteers working alongside the robots; the many square kilometers of meat and dairy barns where Volunteers will spend their lives caring for genetically perfect pigs and cattle, reconnecting each Volunteer with an agrarian past thought lost, now rescued. A promise of the imagined past, packaged in an imagined future.

"This is how we save our country," says Eury. "This is how we save our world." Images flash by of other VACs worldwide, established throughout the unsteady European Union, in warring Russia and Ukraine, even in sub-Saharan Africa, where the desert has been reirrigated and revitalized, made greener than it has been in millennia; in China and India, where whole tracts of wasted ground have been rejuvenated into endless wetlands of rice; in Japan, where rising sea-level and a series of tsunamis and earthquakes caused an economic collapse Earthtrust was quick to exploit.

"It's not only this planet we were meant to inhabit, to settle, to improve," John hears Eury say. "There are worlds other than this one, and Earthtrust wants to take you there: the next frontier, destined to be settled by the bravest of Volunteers." As Eury's CGI future appears on-screen, the same vision comes into view outside: dust rises from a massive construction yard outside what was once Des Moines, one of the biggest projects John has ever seen, Earthtrust's bridge to an extraplanetary future, rising from Iowa's failed corn.

The spaceport isn't complete. It might be decades before any ship leaves it, if ever. But John has heard Eury's vision for this spaceport and for the colony ship she says will enable humanity to settle deep space. *Mars,* she told him once, *is too limited a vision. We go to the stars.*

Since childhood, Eury had dreamed aloud, and while some of her dreams had indeed become real, many more were gossamer things, chatter destined to excite boardrooms and investor rounds but never meant to materialize—like Pinatubo, another dream John had once thought impossible, now apparently closer than ever.

Pinatubo, named for a volcano that erupted decades ago in the Philippines, whose violent explosion launched twenty million tons of sulfate aerosols into the stratosphere. For the next two years, those aerosols had blanketed the globe, temporarily dropping temperatures worldwide by half a degree Celsius. "It didn't last," Eury had explained during a late-night conversation in the first apartment she and John had shared, "because a volcanic eruption eventually ends. But with the right technology, we could maintain the same cooling effect indefinitely."

The concept wasn't new, but that hadn't stopped Eury from branding it, making it hers. John squeezes his right hand into a fist, waits for the rainbow of lights to scroll above his pebble. All his friends alive, all hopefully on their way to the Farm, Earthtrust's original prototype for the VAC, where now Cal believes Eury plans to geoengineer the stratosphere. Years ago, even before the Sacrifice and the Secession, she'd pitched Pinatubo to the floundering American government, then to the European Union, to Beijing and Moscow, to anyone who'd grant her an audience. She'd wanted, in those more idealistic days, for the world to choose this together.

But after the global economic collapse, the wars everywhere abroad and the Secession and the Sacrifice at home, the worsening climate disaster, and the collapse of the worldwide food supply? Maybe now Eury didn't need anyone's permission, for anything. She did business in every country, and her security forces administered failing and failed states worldwide; she controlled more than enough land to build whatever she wanted wherever she needed. Now the world's governments couldn't risk standing up to Eury Mirov, to Earthtrust.

The journey almost over, John returns to the front, pushes through the other Volunteers crowding forward. The view outside is all fast-moving streaks of a landscape baking in the sun, at least until the old Ohio border—a border marked not with a welcome sign but with drone-surveilled chain-link and unmanned solar farms—whereupon the train enters the greenest lands left on the continent, the first realization of Earthtrust's earliest promises.

This is the Farm, with its bustling Volunteer neighborhoods, its rich fields and orchards, its stockyards and vertical coops. At its center rises the Tower, a gleaming structure John once watched Eury sketch on her personal tablet, sitting at their kitchen table: the Tower's use had changed in the years since—Eury hadn't known then what Earthtrust would become—but the structure looks strikingly similar to that first image, her dream lasting as the waking world around it disintegrated.

The Tower's black skin gleams in the ceaseless noon sun, its entire surface coated with photovoltaic paint. Four twenty-story-tall legs float the main structure off the ground, creating an atrium underneath where much of Earthtrust's first superorchard grove continues to grow, fed by a cunning system of mirrors moving sunlight into the shaded trees in a mimicry of the sun's transit. The main structure rises fifty sloping stories, then narrows to a needle-shaped spire spiking higher toward the sky. At the top waits Eury Mirov's penthouse, the office where even now she might be surveying her domain, including the land where John and Eury grew up, the farms where generations of their families lived.

Since the beginning, John had wanted to go back to the Garden, to remake the world as it might've been before the doom of everything natural, everything pristine, everything wild and free. But that wasn't exactly what Pinatubo promised.

Eury wanted to save the world too, but she'd never wanted to return to the Garden. Eury wanted to save the world only if she could also choose the future that came after, if she could be the one to decide what the human future should be.

C-433

Being born is no easy task, no matter the method, and the Loom is an especially cruel mother, fleshless and cold, brutally efficient. The first days of C-433's life are hounded by lingering hurts, and not only in the thick black scab crusted where the rung's port was screwed into his spine or in the unscratchable itching rawness where the exiting breathing tube tore his throat; his printed bones burn in their stiff sockets, his extruded muscles are sore despite having never been exerted. Despite his many pains, the pitiless, pragmatic remainder pressures him to put aside his aches for another excursion out onto the Ice: if all he does is stay inside the crawler and eat, there won't be enough biomass to regenerate his body; plus there's the winch to retrieve, from where it was abandoned by injured C-432. If the unsteady crevasse ledge collapses, taking the winch with it, then so goes C's best method for descending into the Below.

Not yet, C thinks—and then he says it aloud too: "Not yet." It's only when he hears his own voice that he feels in conversation, his thoughts needing to be made voluble to separate them out from the remainder's, that second person made of many persons.

You are not the first to think this, the remainder complains, as C returns to the galley for another globby meal of nutrient paste, the paste tasting like paste, provoking memories of only more paste. His is a world stripped of simile, everything itself, only a little less so than before. Whenever he wakes in the chamber full of rotting blankets, he moves his clawed hands over himself, cataloging the body that is not exactly the same one C-432 or any other was gifted by the Loom: only three of his front teeth are enamel, two less than in C-432's mouth; his horns are spiraled slightly tighter to his head, hiding how much shorter they are; his blue fur is ever thinner, so that C-433 will shiver more than C-432, who shivered more than C-431.

Despite these latest diminishments, the remainder expects C-433 to be as industrious as C-432, as incurious about the crawler. It wants him outside, on the Ice. The remainder tells him he should be healed and rested, but still his tight muscles tire easily, still his rung port scab leaks yellow pus, gummily trickling down the back of his neck. The remainder demands he retrieve the winch, but C doesn't see how he can—even dragging himself along on the irregular handholds breaking up the hallway walls, he can't walk from one end of the crawler to the other without wheezing. The morning of his seventh day, he vomits the previous evening's nutrient paste, the lumpy gruel gray and tasteless both ways. At the remainder's command, he cleans the mess from the floor and carries it in his paws through the crawler's hallways to the recycler chamber, where it whirls down the drain in gray-pink streaks.

The same drain C-432 melted down, not so long ago.

C stumble-walks the crawler's halls, the remainder's angry cacophony of voices a maddening companion, debating itself inside his skull. Perhaps there's something wrong with C-433. Perhaps they'd be better off recycling him and starting over. But the winch, left outside and possibly doomed by the shifting surface of the Ice; but the dwindling biomass, a supply too strained to print a better body.

Recycling is a lossy process, the remainder complains, this sick creature won't make a wholer one. They need C-433 to become the scavenger they were, to spend his life as they spent theirs, extracting the world Below, bringing back enough past to buy more future, but only C-433 has agency over their shared body. On his tenth day, he realizes the remainder can be made to retreat simply by entering any room where O's voice spills from the speakers. He moves chamber to chamber, pressing intercom buttons to free the trapped song, filling the crawler with its noise, the same wrenching drones repeating until C's blue hackles raise, until his jawbone warns it might vibrate into splinters beneath the rhythmic gnashing of his teeth. Being born is no easy task, childhood no easier, and despite being born into an adult body, C-433 is in many ways a child, forced to rely on the remainder's dribbled instructions, offering an unearned familiarity with the crawler's machines. But once his mind is set free by O's gut-clenching dirge, he discovers the remainder hasn't told him everything.

At the front end of the crawler, just before the gutted and recycled cockpit, C finds a heavy hatch he can't force himself to remember: whatever the remainder knows, it isn't sharing. The hatch is sealed with a handwheel, stuck with rust and disuse. C strains at its mechanism, his hooves scrabbling on the cold steel floor until the wheel turns over. With a heave, he forces the door open and steps across the threshold. His breath catches in his sore throat as he enters a room unlike any other he's found: the room's dusty but intact, not ransacked or scavenged. At its center is a conference table of white plastic, yellowed with age; the walls are covered with maps depicting the landscape before it was covered with ice. A half-dozen chairs are pushed in neatly around the table, except for the one at the head, tipped over on its side.

C circles the table, a new feeling bubbling his upset stomach: anticipation, replacing the dread of being sent out on the Ice, of being bullied into recycling himself. He rights the fallen chair, pushes it back into its place, then circles the room before trying to make sense of the binders on the table. He reads and reads until his new eyes tire; without context, he struggles to connect the passages he scans at random, each next binder stuffed with more maps and charts, hyperdetailed instructions and nested protocols.

C replaces a book, reconsiders the room. O's voice hasn't followed him inside, the song's droning stuck in the hallway. The remainder is similarly quiet, reduced to a simmering murmur. There's something else different about this space, beyond its intactness: the map room, as C-433 comes to call it, is entirely analog. There's no speaker embedded near the door, no screens on any of the walls, no machinery at all. There are only the charts and the maps and the books, all printed on slippery sheaves of plastic, their pages tear-proof, stain resistant, meant to last.

No books, no maps, the remainder says, its anger rising. *The bubble. The Ice. The winch.*

"No," C says stubbornly, picking up the next binder, its black cover blank except for its title: ORPHEUS PROTOCOL. And beneath that, in smaller text: BIOSPHERE RESTORATION PROCEDURE: DO NOT ATTEMPT WITHOUT MEASURED VIABILITY PROBABILITY ABOVE NINETY PERCENT.

Inside the binder, he discovers blueprints of the crawler's interior: rooms labeled as genetic testing laboratories, stocked with lists of equipment and supplies; bunk rooms, galleys, and storerooms filled with synthetic clothing for a variety of possible climates. Here the cavernous hangar is filled with other vehicles, plus a pair of the hovering bubblecrafts, even though now there's only the one, and in the lower levels of the crawler—areas inaccessible from the level C has occupied since emerging from the Loom—he sees a series of steel storage tanks, reservoirs holding the Loom's stockpile of biomass, a stockpile he knows he's nearly depleted.

In another binder, C finds a PERSONNEL BUILD ORDER, by which the crawler's crew was meant to be printed by the Loom: the project's commander would be printed first, to employ the crawler's sensor array to determine the viability probability of the outside world. If the viability readings checked out, then the commander would summon the rest of the crawler's crew: pilots, scientists, engineers—a team brought to life in order of importance to the Orpheus Protocol.

"You might be reading this a hundred years after the project began," the binder states.

> You might be reading it a thousand years later.
> You might have read this page many times by now, in many
>   different years.
> You may be disoriented, frightened, overwhelmed.
> You must become brave, determined, devoted to doing what
>   is right, even if it's hard.

By your efforts and the efforts of others like you, the earth
    will be reseeded and rebuilt.

C looks up, his heart racing. It's been many cycles since anyone has entered this room. Mostly the recombinant C never did.
For most of his four hundred and thirty-two cycles, he's chosen
survival over this mystery. But surely whatever happened here
wasn't what these binders suggest should have. Surely some
error's been made, surely mistake after mistake must have been
made for events to have gone as badly as C's lonely existence
suggests they have.

You are not the first to think this, the remainder has told C-433
repeatedly, filling his head with its dismissals. But when C
speaks next, when he says, "What could I do to fix this place?"—
then the remainder remains silent, all four hundred and thirty-
two cycles of it.

"What could I do to fix this place?" he says once more,
louder, more urgently, more earnestly, for the first time won-
dering something honestly unexpected, something no recent
remainder has dared.

In the silence that follows, he looks at the binder again, traces
the words with the tip of a claw: *what is right, even if it's hard.*

CHAPMAN

Roaming alone through uncut forests, frustrated Chapman kneels in the deep shade to dig the loam with his clawed hands, working the moist life of the humus between his fingers, every handful of dirt riven with beetles, maggots, worms, bits of decomposing plant matter, seeds, and shells slipping between his fingers. He scrapes at the raw earth with his hooves, the earth only seemingly solid, seemingly permanent, its every inch telling a story of passing sunlight and rain, of birth and growth and death, of ice and snow and heat and drought, the earth itself never static, always being shaped by weather and erosion, by the tectonic shifting of the earth's plates, by the tremblings of earthquakes in distant parts of the continent, by the slowly sloshing movement of cold water captured in cavernous aquifers, buried deep between drowned pillars of ancient stone.

How much slow focus it takes to read such a story! Still bereft of his brother's constant conversation, lonely Chapman has nothing but time and attention. Pausing at a meadow's edge, he turns a hand, watches a flea crawl harmlessly through the fur along the back of his wrist. Surrounding him and the flea is the uncut forest, an organism made of many kinds of life, many kinds of nonlife too, some visible only once his attention lingers, once he learns the names other men have gifted these pieces of the world. Oak and maple and pine. Deer and elk and moose. The gray wolf, the common coyote. Blue jays, cardinals, robins, ravens, and crows. All their barks and yips and birdsong, carried along on airs scented by bloom and branch.

The faun puts his hands to a granite boulder taller than any man. Leaning his weight into its solidity, he tests its immovable resistance, the heft of its weight anchoring it in time; as a glitter-scaled lizard skitters over the boulder's hulking bulk, he marvels at how the rock's knobby surface appears softened by clumps of lichen and moss, by streaks of guano and bird shit. His breathing slows; he focuses on each breath filling his lungs, each breath emptying out his mouth and nose. Horseflies land in his fur and he doesn't shoo them away, he lets them bite him if they choose; a dragonfly buzzes by his head, diving through a gathering of gnats off his left ear. Bright birds flit from branch to branch of their own accord, a red fox wanders by without a glance, padding lightly on nimble feet; a black bear cub appears, snuffling through the underbrush, hunting for nuts or berries.

Chapman lets his attention fall lightly on the cub, not risking disturbing it; time passes, the sun moves, the trees' shadows shift, but the cub stays, rolling around in the fallen leaves, then resting gently on its side. It's harder to see if the old-growth trees accept Chapman's willed impartiality, but he hopes they're as happy to be left alone as any creature might be. He imagines the slow life of a tree, of many trees living together, of anything rooted in one place, taking on whatever weather might come; fur and bark, feather and leaf, whatever else the forest is, it doesn't require Chapman, it doesn't crave his thoughts or desires or impositions.

If this forest is self-willed, living only for itself, then what of Chapman's nurseries, what of Nathaniel's saplings, the trees he means to sell to the west-bent settlers whose grateful dollars Nathaniel claims will make the brothers rich?

Chapman considers the stumps that might be removed, the rocks that must be carried away, the earth needing to be tilled before the planting can begin; the building of brush fences, the pruning of suckers, the weeding of other plants trying to claim the cleared space. The brothers' apple trees flourish wherever they are planted, they are in many ways indistinguishable from wild trees, but their lives exist first and foremost only to fulfill human desire.

Nathaniel speaks in the eager language of the settler, proud of *stewarding* the land, of *improving* the country: for him the Territory is earth not put to its right uses until its swamps are drained and its forests made passable to man and horse and ox and wagon, until roads climb every hill and bridges cross every river, until the mountains are mined for their deep treasure troves of ore, riches owed to any hardy man strong enough to drag their glitter into the light.

The given world wasn't perfect, Chapman remembers Nathaniel saying, but it could be made so by the efforts of good men. God had made the world, God had given the world to men, and men would show God their thanks by perfecting His creation. After all, if it was by good works that a man showed his worth, could the world not be improved by the same, by being made into the shape in which it might best be used?

Heaven on earth is our goal, Nathaniel had said. *Nothing less than heaven on earth, with two kingdoms carved out of it, one for you and one for me.*

At dusk, Chapman descends a narrow ridgeline into a salt lick marred by poorly grown birch trees, the lick populated by a dozen elk does standing ankle-deep in scummy water: their brown bodies shine in the late light, weak sunbeams falling through the canopy, softening the edges of their fur. He comes upon the elk gently, passing between their number without any intent, wanting to be nothing more than a hooved beast among hooved beasts.

At his approach, the largest doe lifts her swollen head, shaking her waddle of fur in unmistakable warning. The doe snorts and Chapman snorts back and the doe returns her attention to the ground, noisily licking loose minerals trapped in clay. The sun shines but the shadows are chilly, and Chapman shivers when he sees poking from the ground a series of preserved white ribs, stony bones not belonging to any elk, and beside them the curve of a single tusk, piercing the earth from below. How uninterested the elk are in these half-buried fossils, in whatever unseen mammal bore the ribs and tusk: gone, gone, gone, like so much else.

Five years after this century turns, the last buffalo in Ohio dies. And then sometime after goes the last timber wolf.

The last black panther. The last lynx. Every wild turkey soon dead and served for dinner. Every duck and goose and prairie chicken. The Ohio black bear, gone. The Ohio white-tailed deer, gone. The Ohio elk at this Ohio salt lick, every other one like them soon Ohio dead. By the time Nathaniel dies, other men like him will already be restocking new woods, placing tame deer beneath planted trees. But not every animal will be replaced, not every plant: only the ones men desire, and only if they do as men wish. Deer in the woods but not in the fields. Trees in the yard, their roots hacked back from the foundation. The given earth reduced to what belongs to man, populated by what man allows.

This salt lick will vanish sooner, washed away by rushing water moving along new paths, spring floods able to track everywhere the forest was cut, the drained swamps no longer there to absorb the surge of floods. What comes next? Only Nathaniel's dream: flat farmlands divided into neat squares of rowed crops, fenced-in acres for cattle, goats, sheep, and, for some of those homesteads, an orchard of trees planted by Chapman and Nathaniel.

For ten years, Chapman has labored without complaint to make Nathaniel's world appear, to make Nathaniel's imaginings solid, touchable, ownable. His brother has told him this dream world is the world that's meant to be, the one God tasked man with making, but Chapman knows what kind of world that will be. No place for elk, and no place for fauns either; a place made only for men, men and what men desire.

Today the elk move freely about Chapman, no longer paying him any mind. Their wants are local and immediate. The elk have their pasts and futures, but Chapman doesn't think they live much in either. Their past is gone, their future undiscovered. For them it is only the now that's present, it's only the present where they can act.

Separated from Nathaniel and far from his nurseries, Chapman envies the elk, doomed as they are: at least they are not beset by unsolvable doubt, by unreasonable want. Chapman is only half a man but that half doesn't know how to want less than the other settlers, how to say, *This world is already enough*, that it's enough to be a mere part of it, taking nothing more than the one real moment constantly renewed, the present in which it might be possible to stay rooted simply by ceasing your craving for *more*.

He says he doesn't know how to want less, but what he means is that he's choosing not to learn how, choosing not to give up his desires, the treasures he wants only for himself.

After all, it's not only Nathaniel's wants driving the brothers ever deeper into the Territory, year after struggling year, but Chapman's too: for him, there has been the Tree, above all else. Now his faith wavers. Can't he admit that the Tree is only a story he tells himself, a twisting of a half-remembered tale torn from a holy book Chapman has never even seen?

Maybe so—but stories have power too. Chapman believes this, has watched it in action: Isn't the story Nathaniel is telling, that all the other settler men like him tell too, the most powerful tool come to shape this Territory?

Story becomes belief, belief makes action, action creates reality. If Nathaniel can do this, so can Chapman—and if so, Chapman might never have to abandon his self-appointed quest for the Tree, despite the failure his search has so far engendered. Better this than the alternative, because Chapman can no longer avoid the truth of what giving up the story of the Tree would mean: if he decides to plant no more apple seeds, then perhaps he abandons Nathaniel too. And that faithful Chapman still tells himself he won't choose, can't choose, not even while hating how easy it was for Nathaniel to leave him first.

JOHN

The newest superorchard trees are the healthiest specimens John has ever seen, with those in the outermost plots of the Farm growing three times taller than any heritage tree, their too-symmetrical crowns precisely pruned and girdled to the specifications of the algorithm sorting the hydration and nutrient data captured by soil sensors and the air quality reports of the nanobees buzzing through the branches. Most of the new Volunteers smile at these wonders, their faces cautiously curious, happy enough as they parade down a packed dirt lane. John mimics their surprise at seeing for the first time the enormity of the trees' black branches and shockingly green leaves and perfectly glossy apples, all the while looking past the trees to study the swarms of nanobees floating between the rows. He waits for the right moment, then steps out of line to let the thrumming yellow hum of the closest swarm break scattershot over his body, the drones buzzing angrily, spinning to protect the bright boluses of pollen sucked tight against their rotors.

The first bees pellet against his skin, their shapes sharp as the stingers of the insects they've replaced, but the rest quickly modify their trajectories, the swarm rerouting around John like a school of fish avoiding a shark. These bots are an iteration of his earlier designs, now faster and smaller than he'd ever managed to make them. Subsequent generations would've been designed by artificial intelligence working with little to no human intervention, taking advantage of corresponding advances in printer technology, in sensor resolution and flight-ready materials; whatever else has changed, he can only hope no one's discovered the security backdoor he installed years ago, in the first-gen nanoswarms.

John's out of line for only a few seconds, just long enough to squeeze his right fist to set his pebble vibrating. A moment later his pebble buzzes again: the bees messaging back, confirming his command override. Good enough. He hurries to rejoin the other Volunteers, keeping his bruised face painfully smiling as their tour continues. The Earthtrust guide explains: The Farm is laid out in a spiral grid of discrete plots, with the Tower and the oldest supergroves occupying the spiral's center, surrounded by orchards containing newer generations of trees, plus other plots designated for growing resilient strains of corn and potatoes, soybeans and rice, new breeds of cattle and hogs and goats. In between are the neighborhoods of printed homes—stacked walls of quick-drying cement strands, solar roofs placed overhead by a rolling lifter—where these Volunteers will live, each family given their own house, plus a pale square of green-enough drought-resistant grass or bright turf printed directly into the hardpacked ground.

John knows it'd be more efficient to build multifamily residential complexes painted with the same photovoltaic paint as the Tower, buildings that could be sustainably operated in ways individual family homes can never be. But the Farm is both fantasy and promise, a re-creation of a dried up and blown away dream: a house for every family, health care and education, real food grown in real fields, all paid for by meaningful manual labor.

Real people, Eury said once, *have a right to real work. If nothing else, we can give our Volunteers back their dignity.* No more standing under fluorescent lights wearing a name tag beside a stack of clearance t-shirts screen-printed with brand names. No more clearing filthy plates off a table where you'd never be invited to sit. No more crushing your spine in an office chair, hunched in a cubicle, your blank expressionless face reflecting a monitor's glow.

The first morning in his newly printed house, John wakes to a work assignment doled out by the Farm's central planning algorithm. An hour later, in the nearest superorchard plot, he picks bright red apples alongside several hundred other Volunteers, men and women of many ages, various ethnicities and backgrounds, come to the VAC from different doomed parts of the country. Children are exempted from work, assigned instead to education centers or day care facilities, so the children playing in the manicured grass today are other new arrivals, allowed to stay with their families until they acclimate. John smiles at their play, laughs at the jokes of the people working nearby, each Volunteer wearing a printed-weave bucket strapped around their chest, slowly filling it with apples designed to maximize size, color, resiliency. Backs ache and knees burn, but John doesn't hear any complaints; there's a golden quality to the light today, they're outside in newly green lands, every tree they harvest is so bountiful it's possible to forget the dust bowl they've all fled, to ignore the way some Volunteers are too thin for the smallest clothes the Farm had to offer.

Malnourishment has weakened teeth and softened bones, diminished muscle mass, jaundiced skin: the Volunteers arrive hurt and tired, but the Farm will make them healthy, get them happy, give them hope. Every hour, loudspeakers crackle with Eury Mirov's voice, repeating promises made when the VAC was established, when the federal government invoked eminent domain to grant Earthtrust the land it wanted. "Every Volunteer is important, necessary, productive," Eury's voice says. "Individually, we struggle, but together, we feed the world." And every day this promise comes closer, the Farm and the other domestic VACs now producing enough food to feed the country, if only because there's less America left than ever before.

The Volunteers aren't sharecroppers renting the land from Earthtrust, they're not employees working for room and board—they are, Eury Mirov says, "heroes saving the world, after which it will be their world." The work will not be easy, Eury admits; it took centuries to destroy this land, it might take decades to put it right, a task to be finished by this generation, the next generation, some generation to come, all so their children or grandchildren can live in the America they were promised.

Eury's voice says, "When the land is made right, Earthtrust will give you back the land."

The fulfillment of that promise is many years away, but today, the only day John can do anything about, is a good day.

He jokes with his fellow apple pickers, he shakes hands and introduces himself, taking special care as he repeats his fake life story; he uses his body to work hard, he feels his strength and his capacity for the task he's been assigned. By sunset, he's freshly sunburned, a musk of sweat emanating from his printed clothes; he is, despite why he's come back to this place, genuinely happy. He isn't alone. The Farm wouldn't succeed if it were a place of misery, a dystopian slave state. The Farm is, for most of the Volunteers, a good way of life come to replace one fully failed.

If John and his compatriots succeed, they might take away this new world and its promise. He doesn't yet know what that will cost, what stopping Pinatubo might cause to happen next, but in the meantime he worries: Isn't it a crime to take a world from someone, no matter how wrong that world is, if you can't guarantee a better world to come?

LIFE AT THE FARM HAS A ROUTINE, MUCH OF IT FAMILIAR ENOUGH. Before sunrise, John's assignment is waiting on his telescreen, preceding the arrival of the electric trams shuttling Volunteers to their work. Three days after his arrival, John wakes to new orders, the day's task taking him farther from his row of printed concrete homes and bright green turf lawns than he's ever gone. He rides the tram to a cattle farm, where a thousand head wait hidden behind slat steel fencing. The cattle are bred and modified from Holstein and Chianina stock, the resulting animals frequently exceeding two tons and growing heavier every season, two-point-five meters tall at the shoulder, long horned, frightening to behold but also modified for extreme docility.

John watches a rancher leading a parade of cattle toward the processing barn with nothing more than a hand gesture and a well-practiced whistle, stepping easily between the animals. His own assignment will require nothing so skilled. He and the other Volunteers file into the processing barn's locker room to be fitted with yellow hazardous waste suits, baggy helmets at first unbearably stifling, then, once they've been shown their task, thankfully so. For ten despairing hours, John works the processing barn's stalls, shoveling up truckloads of muddy manure. What both the apple picking and the shit shoveling have in common is that both jobs are cheaper to have humans do than to automate, an easy decision for the Farm, which has nothing in more abundance than surplus human labor.

One of the Farm's goals—according to Eury Mirov's omnipresent voice—is *zero waste*.

As John works, he detects slight pings from his pebble, vibrations indicating a hacked nanobee flying nearby, part of the swarm zipping around the clumped cattle to read the pebbles inserted behind each cow's right ear. Dump trucks come and go; flies and nanobees use the same entrance to move between the cattle and their waste. The flies stick to John's suit and mask, his gloves and his shovel; the nanobees never land on any human but pass overhead with their cargos of air-sniffed data and gathered microsamples, collecting statistics on the efficiency and productivity of every Volunteer.

Late in the day, one of these nanobees drops nearly invisibly out of formation to buzz John's head, wirelessly passing a bit of information to his pebble; with his gloves on he can barely feel the telltale vibration marking the data packet's arrival. He looks around the barn at the other yellow-suited, shit-spattered Volunteers, tries to empty his expression of curiosity or alarm. The bee buzzes his head a second time, the pebble vibrates again, and this time the sensation doesn't abate. John clenches his fist, grunts behind his mask as blood vessels above his wrist break, the skin purpling beneath the sleeve.

It's several hours before he can return to the locker room to shed his protective gear, but even after he's showered and clean, dressed in a printed gray t-shirt and blue jeans, he presses his arm to his side, keeping to himself on the crowded tram ride back to his neighborhood. Back at his house, he studies the widening bruise on his inner forearm. One of his hacked bees must've found Cal, pinged her pebble; she sent a message the only way she could, via a bit of code of Noor's design capable of bursting an inkblot of broken blood vessels across John's arm. At a glance, the bruise seems accidental, but Cal is a technician, precise in the ways she hurts him: the swelling mark soon resembles the face of a goat, a goat of blood swimming beneath the skin.

Old Goat, Cal had dubbed him, soon after they first met. *Stubborn and sad, chewing over something no one else wants.*

Cal's made it into the Farm, is close by. The inkblot bruise thuds as John's heartrate accelerates, thinking of her, thinking of the others, thinking of what's next. In the parklands, he'd tried to convince himself he didn't need the human world anymore; now, returned to Earthtrust, he's ready to fight for it one more time, to struggle for the better world he still believes he could be a part of, a world for which he knows he'd trade his life.

C-433

C hurts less every passing day. By the end of his second week, he begins to regularly keep food down, then to sleep through the night. Waking from his scratchy nest of blankets, he uses O to restrain the remainder, its many voices recoiling from the broadcast song's earsplitting volume. All the while he refuses the remainder's screamed entreaties to travel the Ice to retrieve the winch, to delve into the Below; inside the map room's relative quiet, he continues reading, studying the many binders and charts. Previously incomprehensible texts begin to connect once he discovers an explanation of the mobile facility's purpose, the greater scheme it was meant to serve: his crawler is one of a dozen dispersed across the continent, each uniquely loaded with the schematics for printing a certain distribution of flora and fauna, the plants and animals who might thrive after the Ice melted.

The map room binders explain that the crawler's commander would have been reprinted on a regular schedule, to check the outside conditions, to adjust the AI's orders as necessary. If the viability probability was too low the commander was to make the same choice C did at the end of each cycle: he would feed himself into the recycler, letting the pink acid melt him down, restoring most of what was taken to make him to the storage tanks.

What the crawler demanded: the choice to suffer now so you might live again later. You and only you alive for centuries—and then one day the whole world, living anew. But something had gone wrong: instead of a world, only more C, forever.

On the wall-mounted map, most of the crawlers are represented by a red triangle, each one surrounded by a red circle indicating the radius of its territory. One in the upper-right quadrant is painted blue instead, a difference C decides denotes his crawler, assigned approximately one-twelfth of the map's depicted landmass. Far left of center is another symbol, not a single triangle but a group of three larger ones the binders name Black Mountain, the place where the crawlers were meant to return only after they'd completed their task.

C searches the messy table, digging through the toppled stack of binders until he finds the text he seeks. "Only at Black Mountain," it reads,

> will a continuous human presence be maintained. It's likely there'll be no way to contact the staff there—the terrestrial communication grid is already collapsed; given the timescale of the Protocol the satellites currently in orbit will fail and fall. But Black Mountain must prevail. And if Black Mountain prevails—if each of you prevails too—then the world can one day be put back to right.

C is healing, but he accumulates new stiffnesses from sleeping on the shifting blankets, from spending his days in chairs not meant for his shape. The world he inhabits is ill fit for him and he begins to wonder why. In the room where he found the heavy hooded cloak he wears are piles of boots sized for feet other than his, synthetic wool hats that won't fit over even his stunted horns, much less the taller spirals the remainder claims he once had. His stomach cramps constantly; he's hungry but he eats as little paste as possible. The more he eats, the greater the risk should he die: the more food he feeds his body now, the less body might later exist.

He tires fast from making sense of the world the binders describe. In one, C discovers a list of other creatures, creatures whose aspects he can't imagine: What would they have looked like? Would they have been horned and hooved and clawed, like him, or would they have had wholly different bodies, as different from his as those of the others who were meant to inhabit the crawler, those who would have worn the boots and helmets he's found? The binder of names is labeled GREATER OHIO REGIONAL RESPECIATION BUILD INVENTORY; each name it contains is followed by a serial number, used to instruct the Loom to reprint this menagerie of beasts, if only the blueprints hadn't been deleted for some reason, perhaps to make room for C, the only creature the Loom still seems capable of printing. In the empty stale cold of the map room, he reads the names aloud, one after another, memorizing all the entrancing titles of the unimaginable beasts who once inhabited this Ohio, the lost world buried beneath the Ice.

He reads:

AMERICAN BADGER AMERICAN MINK BLACK BEAR BOBCAT
COYOTE ERMINE GRAY FOX LEAST WEASEL LONG-TAILED WEASEL

RACCOON RED FOX RIVER OTTER STRIPED SKUNK WHITE-TAILED
DEER EASTERN COYOTE GRAY WOLF PIPING PLOVER KIRTLAND'S
WARBLER GREAT HORNED OWL BLACK RATTLER MOUNTAIN LION
VIRGINIA OPOSSUM ALLEGHENY WOODRAT AMERICAN BEAVER
BROWN RAT COMMON MUSKRAT EASTERN CHIPMUNK EASTERN
FOX SQUIRREL EASTERN GRAY SQUIRREL EASTERN HARVEST
MOUSE HOUSE MOUSE MEADOW JUMPING MOUSE MEADOW
VOLE NORTH AMERICAN DEERMOUSE PRAIRIE VOLE RED
SQUIRREL SOUTHERN BOG LEMMING SOUTHERN FLYING
SQUIRREL THIRTEEN-LINED GROUND SQUIRREL WHITE-FOOTED
DEERMOUSE WOODCHUCK WOODLAND JUMPING MOUSE
EASTERN COTTONTAIL RABBIT SNOWSHOE HARE AMERICAN
PYGMY SQUIRREL EASTERN MOLE HAIRY-TAILED MOLE NORTH
AMERICAN LEAST SHREW NORTHERN SHORT-TAILED SHREW
SMOKY SHREW STAR-NOSED MOLE BIG BROWN BAT EASTERN RED
BAT EASTERN SMALL-FOOTED BAT EVENING BAT HOARY BAT
INDIANA BAT LITTLE BROWN BAT NORTHERN LONG-EARED BAT
SILVER-HAIRED BAT TRICOLORED BAT MOURNING DOVE
AMERICAN CROW BALTIMORE ORIOLE BLUE JAY BOBOLINK
BROWN-HEADED COWBIRD COMMON GRACKLE EASTERN
MEADOWLARK ORCHARD ORIOLE RED-WINGED BLACKBIRD RUSTY
BLACKBIRD YELLOW-HEADED BLACKBIRD DOWNY WOODPECKER
HAIRY WOODPECKER NORTHERN FLICKER PILEATED
WOODPECKER RED-BELLIED WOODPECKER RED-HEADED
WOODPECKER YELLOW-BELLIED SAPSUCKER THRUSHES, MIMICS,
AND CUCKOOS AMERICAN PIPIT AMERICAN ROBIN BLACK-BILLED
CUCKOO BROWN THRASHER EASTERN BLUEBIRD GRAY CATBIRD
HERMIT THRUSH YELLOW-BILLED CUCKOO WOOD THRUSH VEERY
BLUE GROSBEAK CEDAR WAXWING DICKCISSEL HORNED LARK
INDIGO BUNTING NORTHERN CARDINAL ROSE-BREASTED
GROSBEAK SCARLET TANAGER SUMMER TANAGER TUFTED

TITMOUSE AMERICAN GOLDFINCH AMERICAN TREE SPARROW
CHIPPING SPARROW DARK-EYED JUNCO FIELD SPARROW
EASTERN TOWHEE GRASSHOPPER SPARROW HENSLOW'S
SPARROW HOUSE FINCH HOUSE SPARROW LARK SPARROW
LECONTE'S SPARROW LINCOLN'S SPARROW NELSON'S SHARP-
TAILED SPARROW PURPLE FINCH SAVANNAH SPARROW SONG
SPARROW SWAMP SPARROW VESPER SPARROW WHITE-CROWNED
SPARROW BLACK-CAPPED CHICKADEE BLUE-HEADED VIREO
CAROLINA CHICKADEE CAROLINA WREN HOUSE WREN MARSH
WREN RED-EYED VIREO SEDGE WREN WARBLING VIREO WHITE-
EYED VIREO YELLOW-THROATED VIREO WHITE-BREASTED
NUTHATCH ACADIAN FLYCATCHER ALDER FLYCATCHER BANK
SWALLOW BARN SWALLOW BELTED KINGFISHER BLUE-GRAY
GNATCATCHER CHIMNEY SWIFT CLIFF SWALLOW COMMON
NIGHTHAWK EASTERN KINGBIRD EASTERN PHOEBE EASTERN
WOOD PEWEE GREAT CRESTED FLYCATCHER NORTHERN ROUGH-
WINGED SWALLOW PURPLE MARTIN TREE SWALLOW WHIP-POOR-
WILL WILLOW FLYCATCHER AMERICAN REDSTART
BLACK-THROATED GREEN WARBLER BLUE-WINGED WARBLER
BLACK-AND-WHITE WARBLER CERULEAN WARBLER CHESTNUT-
SIDED WARBLER COMMON YELLOWTHROAT GOLDEN-WINGED
WARBLER HOODED WARBLER KENTUCKY WARBLER NORTHERN
PARULA NORTHERN WATERTHRUSH OVENBIRD PALM WARBLER
PINE WARBLER PRAIRIE WARBLER PROTHONOTARY WARBLER
WORM-EATING WARBLER YELLOW-BREASTED CHAT YELLOW-
THROATED WARBLER YELLOW WARBLER RUBY-THROATED
HUMMINGBIRD BRANT CACKLING GOOSE CANADA GOOSE
GREATER WHITE-FRONTED GOOSE MUTE SWAN SNOW GOOSE
TRUMPETER SWAN TUNDRA SWAN AMERICAN BLACK DUCK
AMERICAN WIGEON BLUE-WINGED TEAL CANVASBACK CINNAMON

TEAL COMMON GOLDENEYE COMMON MERGANSER BARROW'S
GOLDENEYE BLACK SCOTER BUFFLEHEAD GADWALL GREATER
SCAUP GREEN-WINGED TEAL HARLEQUIN DUCK HOODED
MERGANSER LESSER SCAUP LONG-TAILED DUCK MALLARD
NORTHERN PINTAIL NORTHERN SHOVELER REDHEAD RED-
BREASTED MERGANSER RING-NECKED DUCK RUDDY DUCK SURF
SCOTER WHITE-WINGED SCOTER WOOD DUCK COMMON LOON
EARED GREBE HORNED GREBE PIED-BILLED GREBE AMERICAN
AVOCET AMERICAN COOT AMERICAN GOLDEN PLOVER BLACK-
BELLIED PLOVER BLACK RAIL BAIRD'S SANDPIPER BUFF-
BREASTED SANDPIPER COMMON MOORHEN COMMON SNIPE
DUNLIN GREATER YELLOWLEGS HUDSONIAN GODWIT KILLDEER
KING RAIL LEAST SANDPIPER LESSER YELLOWLEGS LONG-BILLED
DOWITCHER MARBLED GODWIT PECTORAL SANDPIPER PURPLE
SANDPIPER RED KNOT RED-NECKED PHALAROPE RED PHALAROPE
RUDDY TURNSTONE SANDERLING SEMIPALMATED PLOVER
SEMIPALMATED SANDPIPER SHORT-BILLED DOWITCHER SOLITARY
SANDPIPER SORA RAIL SPOTTED SANDPIPER STILT SANDPIPER
UPLAND SANDPIPER VIRGINIA RAIL WESTERN SANDPIPER WHITE-
RUMPED SANDPIPER WILLET WILSON'S PHALAROPE WILSON'S
SNIPE YELLOW RAIL BLACK-LEGGED KITTIWAKE BLACK TERN
BONAPARTE'S GULL CASPIAN TERN COMMON TERN FORSTER'S
TERN FRANKLIN'S GULL GLAUCOUS GULL GREAT BLACK-BACKED
GULL HERRING GULL ICELAND GULL LAUGHING GULL LITTLE GULL
POMARINE JAEGER RING-BILLED GULL AMERICAN BITTERN BLACK-
CROWNED NIGHT HERON CATTLE EGRET GREAT BLUE HERON
GREAT EGRET GREEN HERON LEAST BITTERN LITTLE BLUE HERON
SNOWY EGRET SANDHILL CRANE YELLOW-CROWNED NIGHT
HERON AMERICAN WHITE PELICAN DOUBLE-CRESTED
CORMORANT AMERICAN KESTREL BALD EAGLE BROAD-WINGED

HAWK COOPER'S HAWK GOLDEN EAGLE NORTHERN GOSHAWK
NORTHERN HARRIER OSPREY PEREGRINE FALCON RED-TAILED
HAWK RED-SHOULDERED HAWK ROUGH-LEGGED HAWK SHARP-
SHINNED HAWK TURKEY VULTURE BARN OWL BARRED OWL
EASTERN SCREECH OWL GREAT HORNED OWL SHORT-EARED OWL
AMERICAN WOODCOCK CHUKAR GRAY PARTRIDGE NORTHERN
BOBWHITE QUAIL RING-NECKED PHEASANT RUFFED GROUSE
WILD TURKEY BLACK CRAPPIE BLUEGILL SUNFISH GREEN SUNFISH
LONGEAR SUNFISH ORANGESPOTTED SUNFISH PUMPKINSEED
REDEAR SUNFISH WARMOUTH WHITE CRAPPIE HYBRID STRIPED
BASS LARGEMOUTH BASS ROCK BASS SMALLMOUTH BASS
SPOTTED BASS STRIPED BASS WHITE BASS WHITE PERCH
FRESHWATER DRUM SAUGER SAUGEYE WALLEYE YELLOW PERCH
BLACK BULLHEAD CATFISH BLUE CATFISH BROWN BULLHEAD
CATFISH CHANNEL CATFISH FLATHEAD CATFISH WHITE CATFISH
YELLOW BULLHEAD CATFISH CHAIN PICKEREL GRASS PICKEREL
MUSKELLUNGE NORTHERN PIKE COMMON CARP GOLDFISH GRASS
CARP BROOK TROUT BROWN TROUT CHINOOK SALMON CISCO
COHO SALMON LAKE TROUT LAKE WHITEFISH PINK SALMON
RAINBOW TROUT LAKE STURGEON PADDLEFISH SHOVELNOSE
STURGEON AMERICAN BROOK LAMPREY AMERICAN EEL BOWFIN
BURBOT LEAST BROOK LAMPREY MOUNTAIN BROOK LAMPREY
NORTHERN BROOK LAMPREY OHIO LAMPREY SEA LAMPREY
SILVER LAMPREY LONGNOSE GAR SHORTNOSE GAR SPOTTED GAR
BIGMOUTH BUFFALO BLACK BUFFALO BLACK REDHORSE BLUE
SUCKER COMMON WHITE SUCKER CREEK CHUBSUCKER GOLDEN
REDHORSE GREATER REDHORSE HIGHFIN CARPSUCKER LAKE
CHUBSUCKER LONGNOSE SUCKER NORTHERN HOGSUCKER
QUILLBACK CARPSUCKER RIVER CARPSUCKER RIVER
REDHORSE SHORTHEAD REDHORSE SILVER REDHORSE

SMALLMOUTH BUFFALO SMALLMOUTH REDHORSE SPOTTED
SUCKER BANDED DARTER BLACKSIDE DARTER BLUEBREAST
DARTER CHANNEL DARTER DIAMOND DARTER DUSKY DARTER
EASTERN SAND DARTER FANTAIL DARTER GILT DARTER
GREENSIDE DARTER IOWA DARTER JOHNNY DARTER LEAST
DARTER LOGPERCH DARTER LONGHEAD DARTER ORANGETHROAT
DARTER RAINBOW DARTER RIVER DARTER SLENDERHEAD DARTER
SPOTTED DARTER TIPPECANOE DARTER VARIEGATE DARTER
BRINDLED MADTOM MOUNTAIN MADTOM NORTHERN MADTOM
STONECAT MADTOM TADPOLE MADTOM BIGEYE CHUB CREEK
CHUB GRAVEL CHUB HORNYHEAD CHUB RIVER CHUB SHOAL
CHUB SILVER CHUB STREAMLINE CHUB BLANDING'S TURTLE
EASTERN BOX TURTLE EASTERN MUSK TURTLE EASTERN SPINY
SOFTSHELL MIDLAND PAINTED TURTLE MIDLAND SMOOTH
SOFTSHELL NORTHERN MAP TURTLE OUACHITA MAP TURTLE
RED-EARED SLIDER SNAPPING TURTLE SPOTTED TURTLE WOOD
TURTLE BROAD-HEADED SKINK COMMON FIVE-LINED SKINK
COMMON WALL LIZARD EASTERN FENCE LIZARD LITTLE BROWN
SKINK BLUE RACER BUTLER'S GARTER SNAKE COMMON RIBBON
SNAKE COMMON WATER SNAKE COPPER-BELLIED WATER
SNAKE EASTERN BLACK KING SNAKE EASTERN FOX SNAKE
EASTERN GARTER SNAKE EASTERN HOG-NOSED SNAKE EASTERN
MILK SNAKE EASTERN SMOOTH EARTH SNAKE EASTERN
WORM SNAKE GRAY (BLACK) RAT SNAKE KIRTLAND'S
SNAKE LAKE ERIE WATER SNAKE MIDLAND BROWN SNAKE
MIDWESTERN WORM SNAKE NORTHERN BLACK RACER
NORTHERN BROWN SNAKE AMERICAN BULLFROG COPE'S GRAY
TREE FROG EASTERN CRICKET FROG GRAY TREE FROG
MOUNTAIN CHORUS FROG NORTHERN GREEN FROG NORTHERN
LEOPARD FROG PICKEREL FROG SPRING PEEPER WESTERN

CHORUS FROG WOOD FROG AMERICAN TOAD EASTERN
SPADEFOOT FOWLER'S TOAD COMMON MUDPUPPY EASTERN
HELLBENDER RED-SPOTTED NEWT ALLEGHENY MOUNTAIN DUSKY
SALAMANDER BLUE-SPOTTED SALAMANDER CAVE SALAMANDER
EASTERN REDBACK SALAMANDER EASTERN TIGER SALAMANDER
FOUR-TOED SALAMANDER GREEN SALAMANDER JEFFERSON
SALAMANDER LONG-TAILED SALAMANDER MARBLED SALAMANDER
MIDLAND MUD SALAMANDER NORTHERN DUSKY SALAMANDER
NORTHERN RAVINE SALAMANDER NORTHERN RED SALAMANDER
NORTHERN SLIMY SALAMANDER NORTHERN TWO-LINED
SALAMANDER SMALL-MOUTHED SALAMANDER SPOTTED
SALAMANDER SPRING SALAMANDER STREAMSIDE SALAMANDER
WEHRLE'S SALAMANDER BURYING BEETLE SEVEN-SPOTTED LADY
BEETLE FIELD CRICKET KATYDID BLACK-LEGGED DEER TICK
BLACK-AND-YELLOW GARDEN SPIDER BLACK WIDOW BOLD
JUMPING SPIDER BROWN RECLUSE COMMON HOUSE SPIDER
WOLF SPIDER DADDY LONGLEGS HONEYBEE DAMSELFLY
DRAGONFLY CRAYFISH SEVENTEEN-YEAR CICADA . . .

By the time his litany trails off, C's voice is raw and scratched, fresh pain layered over the aging hurt of the breathing tube. His heart pounds, rattling its bony home; his lungs crash against his ribs. Sometime during C's recitation, O's voice singing from the speaker outside the map room door abandoned its accustomed drone: now it sings a new melody.

In all his short life—and maybe in the many lives preceding it—C has never heard anything so beautiful. Head cocked to better listen, he absently reaches up a claw to scratch an ache at the joint of his neck and his left shoulder, where he's startled to find not a new sore but a dime-sized spot of mottled bark pushing through the skin, the rough-textured wood fresh from his flesh, distinctly not *him*, distinctly *other*.

After all these cycles, none of the remainder believed there would ever be another surprise, and yet here C-433 is, surprised: something new sprouted from the only ground available, the fragile flesh of C's neck.

Without knowing why he does it, he puts the claw of his index finger against the barkspot, then pushes the tip all the way down. The pain is immediate, worse than any other hurt, so powerful his legs buckle, C nearly collapsing as he grabs at the table, desperate to steady his legs—but despite the hurt, he doesn't fall. Instead he *flickers*, his mind flashing upon the blinking blackness somewhere or somewhen inside the rung where he's sometimes not only C-433 but many selves, many beings, a self that's simultaneously all that the remainder contains.

It doesn't last. Afterward, with his claws scratching grooves into the table as he flails against it, with his slumping weight threatening to tip it over and dump the binders onto the cold floor, who is he then? Again only C-433, this creature printed, last of his kind or else the first.

Whatever the line of C has been, now C-433 becomes whatever species of creature it is upon which a tree might be seeded. Fresh possibility, returning to the world after an unmeasured but immense absence; and also grave responsibility, a charge the remainder is already objecting to, a charge C will nonetheless have to answer, his body having committed before his mind could weigh the cost.

A tree, a tree, a tree, planted here at the end of all else, planted in the only ground there is, C's fleshy blue-furred shoulder; the remainder had dragged centuries of broken, frozen branches and roots from Below but had never imagined seeing a tree grow, not even after every next life was born of nothing more than the fragmented forests brought above the Ice and added to the only other biomass that remained, the ever more meager bodies of the creature C.

CHAPMAN

By late July, Chapman retreats deeper into the Territory than ever before, past anywhere he and his brother have planted, past anything he knows from any of Nathaniel's tales. *For a time let there be no more stories,* he thinks, *let me indulge only in the phenomenal present of the world*—but in the uninhabited and inhospitable great black swamp, the beauty he's worshipped elsewhere in the Territory gives way only to more difficulty. The swamp's stands of beech and birch are treacherously thick, the way forward sometimes nearly impenetrable. In places the water stands to his knees, and even the land above the waterline is never solid, instead perpetually sodden, slick with rotted wood and leaves and softening remains making springy humus. Hour after hour, he drags his furred legs through the sucking muck, the mud so persistent that he eventually stops bothering to stomp his hooves free in the rare moments he emerges onto more solid ground.

The way is difficult but for a time there is pleasure too. Freed of Nathaniel's constant cant, Chapman's ears truly have begun to hear more; with no one to talk to, mostly his tongue lies dumb in his mouth. He listens for the smallest forest voices, the clicking language of squirrels and rabbits, the chatter of mice in the underbrush; he hears hawk chicks exploring their nests, woodpecker eggs hatching far above his head, hidden in holes pecked into towering trees. A breeze wafts by, a local wind suffused with local smell—something floral, something overripe, something rotting—moving through these woods and only these woods, present one day and gone another. If these trees were cut down, he thinks, this particular breeze would be cut down too; if different birds chirped and tittered here, then the breeze would carry new sound; if there were no bears or skunks wandering the swamp, then the breeze would lack their musk, its most potent texture.

The breeze is a small god, something entirely local, bound to this place and time and circumstance. Chapman snorts, huffs out his breath; the breeze retreats and returns.

Maybe you couldn't empty the world entirely of such small gods, but you could damage the ones who appear, could reduce their splendor, their variety of specific natures repeating nowhere else. Clear the trees for fields, divert the stream for irrigation, take smooth stones and cut boards for fences and walls, and still a wind would appear here, just not the one wrinkling his nose today. This was what Chapman had done for the Tree, what he'd done for Nathaniel. For his wants, for his brother's. But now he eats only when he needs to eat, he sleeps whenever he needs to sleep, he drinks calmly from cold streams without gulping, his belly never stuffed and stretched, never wholly slack. He tells himself he is satisfied, but he is not fooled—it is only the animal side of him that has enough here, never the man.

Chapman trudges onward, pretending he has no destination and no need to find one, until finally one afternoon a cold rain sweeps across the swamp, its pitter-pattering drizzle turning quickly to a drenching downpour. This rain is hardly different from any other, but today the faun cannot suffer its arrival. The damp must of his wet fur, filthy with matted mud, plus the proposition of more weather and worse: whatever stoic spell had recently ensorcelled Chapman breaks. Now he looks with despair at these limitless swamplands where Nathaniel left him, now he turns on all the small gods who inhabit it, all utterly defenseless against the enormity of his ego, against the harm a human-enough ego can do.

The rain falls fast enough to flood the swamp, drowning the barely visible humps of spongy marshland; defeated, Chapman turns back the way he's lately come, deciding too late to return to their newest nurseries, where Nathaniel might be waiting for him. With the first step to the east, Chapman's most lasting desires return, coming one after another: his wants for his brother's company and comforts, and his want for the Tree, his story he'd pretended he could've abandoned, if only he'd found another to take its place. If Nathaniel is ready to apologize, then Chapman will forgive him; if Nathaniel is angry, then Chapman will beg forgiveness. It doesn't matter, not anymore, as long as they are reunited, as long as they can resume their life together.

He tells himself these tales but they do not satisfy, because as greed resumes so does his anger at his failures, at this Territory that has so far denied his desires: "I want what I want,"

Chapman screams, howling hoarsely into the pouring rain, his declaration swallowed by the storm, unanswered by the world. "I want what I want!" No voice responds, and no beast or bird flees from his sound; already the animal world is sheltering, as he should be. He stomps east, sulking, as the cold rain and blackening sky further dampen his spirits, even more so once already heavy rain transforms into a deluge accompanied by a spectacle of lightning and thunder.

Horns lowered, Chapman slogs through the drowned black forest, its already perilous navigation made more difficult without light, with sound reduced to the cacophonous noise of heavy water cascading through the high canopy. Late in the day, soaked and shaking, he comes on the ruins of a failed inhabitation, a squat cabin collapsing against a high curve of riverbank, the holding bounded on three sides by fallen fences and on the fourth by a stand of corn gone wild, other untended crops making a chaotic go. Normally he cannot stand to step inside any man-built structure, but this house is almost broken, likely already inhabited by enough animals to be part forest. Whoever fled this place will not return. No one will object to Chapman's trespass, if he waits out the storm here, drying his fur inside these creaking logs. He reaches the cabin stoop in a bound, then pushes the unsettled door from its hinges. Stepping through the thick cobwebs hanging from the exposed rafters, he considers what's left, all that couldn't be carried back east by some family fleeing the unfriendly frontier: A rough-hewn table, bench seats on either side. A bed frame but no bedding. A cradle, kicked over by a man or else upturned by some curious creature. The droppings of rats, dried kernels of corn. Surely the settlers here had wanted too, had believed they deserved everything Nathaniel plans to earn; but in the end all had been taken away, this life they'd led not lost but abandoned, as this unlucky family fell to ruin.

Thunder rolls, and after the booming peals have passed, Chapman hears through the open doorway something equally as unexpected as this distant homestead, a sound coming fast through the trees: a song, sung by a single voice, the song no hymn or folk ditty but a dirge droning on in no language Chapman knows, maybe no language at all.

Was he wrong that this homestead had been abandoned? Are its owners returning through the rain? He turns back, considers the fallen door, the abandonment within, then, heart pounding, he steps back out into the storm, shielding his eyes against bright amber flashes of forked lightning, as thunder for a moment obliterates all other sound.

Despite the fur-flattening downpour, Chapman's hackles rise. He grinds his teeth, sets a cavitied molar to complaining; he shakes his head, grabs his horns in distress, moans against the fast-approaching song, louder even than the rain ceaselessly drumming against the cabin's tin roof. Visibility becomes broken, difficult, staccato, strobing; lightning flashes and the song is closer; it flashes again and the song arrives. But it's no settler family that brings it.

A lightning bolt strikes the ground nearby, its shock backlighting the scene: here is the abandoned homestead, its weather-flattened corn, its crooked fenceposts; at the barely discernible line between the farm and the forest, three bulbous figures step forward, their bare feet toeing the broken barrier of the half-there fence, their naked white skin brightly ablaze against the dense black swampland.

At the sight of Chapman, each of the figures howls in an inhuman voice, shaking loose a tangled veil of thick dark hair, the wet mess falling over her face and shoulders, her naked torso. As wild a creature as the faun is, he's not half as wild as these three. All three women are fleshily voluptuous, ripples of seductive fat flowing over powerful muscles, mountains of engorged breasts, and a sunken valley of belly, skin slick as damp rot, looking the spongy consistency of poisonous mushrooms. Their tangled manes cascade to their hips, they wear no clothes except the mud of the swamp and whatever bleak things they might feed upon: wet smears of rabbit ichor and robin yolk, the blood of fox pups dragged loose from buried dens.

Witches, Chapman nearly screams, a word he knows only from stories Nathaniel's told him, the rumors other men have repeated across the Territory. The three are horrible, but they're not what scares Chapman most, they're not what pulls a frightened whinny from his throat. He squints through the slashing rain to see the song isn't coming from their mouths but from a shape the rightmost figure holds in the crook of her naked arm: a disembodied head, decapitated but still singing, its deathly pale face half obscured by stringy blond hair, some of it gathered into a messy topknot. Bloodshot eyes roll in their sockets, the nose snots and bubbles, broken veins fracture sunken cheeks, but the mouth is open and singing, impossible as this is, for a head attached to no lungs.

The witch takes the head by its topknot, aims it at Chapman. As the singer's gaze focuses on the faun, the voice shifts its aim in his direction: its voice is a beautiful nightmare, a rising, keening dirge, a droning repetition of unbearable loss. Chapman staggers as the drone rolls over his body, his bowels loosen; he fears he's seconds away from vomiting or shitting or both. "Who are you?" he moans, then flinches as the witches answer, their sound unlike anything he's heard: the witch on the left speaks like moss covering a stone, like claws pushing through fur, a voice that's also her name; the center witch names herself the crackle of a great spotted egg hatching; the rightmost is called the unheard sound water makes rushing through underground aquifers, the secret sloshing between the pillars of the earth. Their voices primordial, pre-language, born of dirt and rock, earthquake and storm and struggle.

Now the beheaded singer's mouth shifts, slackening, stretching into a round shape, making the only name he has to offer, a letter that is not all of an answer. The singer sings on, the song not a name but a dream given voice until its substance fills Chapman's skull, until his teeth grind and his bones burn and his skin shakes on its stitchings, until the dream-song becomes story, a flickering accusation spanning horn to spiraling horn.

THE FIRST FAUN

THE MYTHIC EARTH

Long before mortal Chapman, the first faun was born into the simultaneity of myth, a woodland being unlike any other, made to shepherd the flocks, to watch over the bees and the vineyards and the orchards, and to entertain the gods, to dance and to lust, to revel and to feast. But in the days of the myth into which the faun was born—in the eternal day that is the truest nature of myth—the faun was never only reveling or only feasting, so that at every moment he reveled, he also feasted; at every feast, he was also cavorting with the wild women of the woods; and wherever he was he was also an invited guest at his nephew's wedding, watching his nephew vow himself to his niece, watching his niece vow herself to him; and when he was at his labors, taming his bees and pruning his vines and teaching men how to produce beer and mead, even then he was already in the wedding tent among all the other thirsty guests, lifting a wine barrel overhead to glean its last purple drops; and he was also outside the tent beneath the fullest moon he had ever seen, a moon waxed full, a moon already waning—and what is a moon waxing and waning but a reminder of *mythic time*, how time in a story such as this paradoxically passes even as it repeats?—and he was stumbling on unsteady hooves toward the bride, his niece, his nephew's wife, his cousin too, a nymph and a man and half a man, all related because in those days so close to creation weren't we all each other's nephews, all each other's nieces, all birthed moments ago by the same meddling inconstant gods; and the faun was also stalking closer, lolling his long tongue through the bristle of his wine-stained beard; and he was also holding his tail in his hands, the telltale appendage twitching in his grip; and he was also standing right behind her, his niece now a new wife, a nymph of the woods made to appear gorgeously human in her wedding dress, rustic lace and dowry bead; and the faun was also pausing, weaving hoof to hoof, wanting to be anywhere else but there, wanting to be a character in any story but his own; because while he was at her wedding he was also attending her birth, where she was gifted the remarkable childhood he'd been denied; and he was also walking through her dale, the meadow she'd been charged to tend while a child, a meadow around which an apple orchard sprouted and grew and fruited; and he was also playing with her in her sun-dappled dale, where as a small girl she loved to dance with her feet atop his hooves, laughing with joy in her heart and fear in her eyes, fear of the future they shared, because she too was in every moment of the myth at once; and always he was smelling her bloom in that same place, as it would be sometime later (and at the same

time), when she had grown into the first years of her woman-
hood, a teenager picking dale flowers, their blossoms scented
like her skin, the faun caressing the flesh of petals carrying the
scent of her hair, everything in her domain sticky with her
bright pollen; and as the faun fled the dale he took with him a
stolen handful of her soil, thick black loam smelling of his
niece, earth he coveted because he did not want to covet her;
and all those times the faun was in the dale he was also already
standing in the bright pavilion, he was there with all the other
guests watching his niece speak her wedding vows, her voice
lovely but not as lovely as her husband's, because whose voice
was better than his, this man whom the gods had given their
best music, who the gods said spoke for them and for all men;
and at the same time the faun was reaching out to her at the far
edge of the wedding tent's penumbra of lamplight, at the very
border between this civilized space and the wilder myth beyond; and the faun was overcome as he'd been the day he'd
held her soil to his nose, the day he'd put it in his mouth, the
day he'd swallowed the dirt down into his gut; and that day
was this day, even though it was long ago and this was now;
and his niece was then and always turning toward him, her
eyes wet already with grief for what she knew would happen
next, what was already happening, had already happened—
and no matter how many times the faun was there, which is to
say *always*, always he never knew why she was crying, what had
been said to her inside the wedding pavilion to make her flee,
he knew only that it was not he who'd caused her exit—and she
said, *Uncle*; and she said, *Uncle*; and she said, *Uncle, no*; she said
all three things at once, she was always saying all three—and
he said, *I only want to comfort you*, a lie written for him by
another—and always he was stepping closer, his throat cot-

toned with wine and his nose full of her scent, the blossom and the loam, and in those days what a faun wanted was what the gods wanted him to want; and wasn't what happened the fault of the gods; and wasn't it their fault even though they always said it was his; and in this moment, almost his last in the myth even though it had happened many times before, he was always saying the words he could not bear to remember but could not forget (and he was apologizing already), and she was always stepping away from him (and he was saying *no* too), and he was always grabbing her by the soft flesh of her arm, his fingers hard as branches, his claws sharp as thorns, and he was always saying, *I am not myself tonight*, and she was always pulling away, slipping free from his grip; and he was always tearing at her gown as he tried to stop her escape; and he was always speaking and his niece was always screaming; and always from behind them he heard his nephew's voice, the call of his niece's past and present and future husband, himself the best hope of man, a hero of the civilized world, always charging across the damp grass, always drawing his sword, always crying out in his voice like no other, a prophet's voice, a voice the gods said would *make the future*; and always the whole host of the wedding was always following the groom, taking up their own arms against the faun; and always the faun knew he was caught; and always he was already regretting what he had done, *what he had been made to do*; and always the faun said he was drunk and always he said he loved her and always he said *forgive me* and always he stepped away and always she ran, even as he withdrew, and always with her next step she tripped, always she tripped, over his retreating hoof, the hoof upon which she had once stood to dance (upon which she was even in that moment dancing); and always she fell down the hill on which her

wedding pavilion was perched (always she was falling), the
brocade of her dress ripping on branch and thorn, and always
his gaze was drawn to her face, then to her upturned feet fling-
ing loose her wedding shoes, then back to her face, her face, her
lovely face, her expression stunned the exact same shade of surprise he'd seen on the day of her birth (which was in every way
this day); and always at the bottom of the hill there waits a pit
of vipers, and only the gods know why, only they know what
necessary sense the snakes make in their story, the pit placed
exactly in the right place at the very creation of their mythic
world, meant by the gods for this instance and this instance
alone; and always the waiting vipers attack not in anger but in
fear of the falling body, the snakes instinctively rising to sink
their many fangs into her flesh; and always the faun and his
nephew and all the gathering wedding host cry out as the bride
is bitten, as the many doses of venom enter the most beautiful
of the nymphs, whose name in one telling means "wide justice"
and in another "the world," and again as she is pulled from the
pit by her groom, whose sweet voice becomes forever sweeter in
its sadness and also terrible beyond belief, for what a monster
is any man divorced from justice and the world; and all the
while the faun laments, all the while he falls to his knees, all
the while he is ashamed; and always when he looks up he sees
a host of men gathering around him with their swords, always
he assumes he's once again about to die.

In this story the faun was born into, that he was even then
living in its entirety all at once, in his myth he dies, then and
there, by the righteous fall of many swords, all the host cutting
and stabbing and rending his body, until all that's left is to cut
the horned head from the neck, a blow saved for the faun's beloved nephew, the new widower made fearsome by his gigantic

grief, this greatest of all singers already beginning to voice his eternal elegy as he lifts his blade.

This death happens over and over, it is always happening, the faun is always dying, but then one time there's instead a glitch in the myth, a mistake in the weave, a skipped stitch or a dropped note: this time, as the faun reaches the climax of his myth, as his niece falls into the pit of vipers and his nephew starts his dirge, this time instead of repeating, the story *ends*— and in its ending the faun is only broken and screaming and painfully alive, bereft of every horror and help born of simultaneity, ripped from the endless now's complicated joy.

Now the wedding host *flickers*, now the faun's niece and nephew *flicker* too, and through the strobing first note of the nephew's song come three other guests the faun would've sworn had never been there before, not any of the innumerable times he's ruined this wedding: the three witching women who are sometimes the fates and sometimes the furies.

Wordlessly the three witches measure the faun's punishment against his crime. Without explanation they cut from him his misdeed, then him from the story. Against his screaming pleas they stitch up what is left, leaving the faun's shape broken, leaving his simultaneous self set adrift into linear time.

The faun will live, the witches say, but not as he had.

Afterward the faun made his way a year at a time, into the vast uncertainty of limited life. Now time took the faun only forward, now he had only his memories to tell him who he'd once been. But as he aged—as his fur turned gray, as his teeth loosened and his horns hollowed, indignities he had never imagined suffering—even his memories grew less reliable, more inflected by doubt and despair. Could it have been true that even in her youth, the nymph he called niece was already afraid of him? That she loved him as an uncle and feared him as her attacker in equal measures?

When as a child she danced with him in her dale, he was already killing her. Could that be correct? She'd known and he'd known too: what would happen, what had happened, what was always happening to a faun and a nymph and a man, all wedded to one another by circumstance, by myth. How was it fair that he be held responsible? How could anyone be expected to pay for crimes committed only because he couldn't help being born into his inescapable story, without the agency to escape into some better tale?

At the end of his myth, the witches had hurt the faun, but when they cut him from the story of his birth, they'd also given him choice, free will, control, all too late to do him any good.

As the faun died, old and alone, barely able to still believe in the looping life he'd lived inside the myth, still he wondered: Why hadn't the witches interceded hours earlier, at the beginning of the wedding instead of at its end? Why hadn't they come when his new free will could've saved his niece, his nephew, even himself, when his injury at the witches' hands might've saved their world such death and grief? Why give him his choice only after it was too late for him to change the ending?

CHAPMAN

Time wrinkles, folds, stretches. Chapman stands in the pouring rain, lightning streaking from the sky, thunder shaking the earth. The three witches wait at the clearing's edge, each much changed from how she appeared inside the song, their once civilized shapes regressed to fit this wild American frontier. Clutching the screaming head of the singer, one witch howls like an injured beast, another releases a huffing breath muffled as fog, all three pace the tree line, passing the screaming head back and forth as they stalk the rent edge of the homestead, seemingly unable to advance.

Chapman remembers how as a child he couldn't cross the farthest row of a field of tilled corn without bodily struggle or pained screaming. Are the witches what Chapman might've been if he'd had no brother to civilize his ways? Pure wilderness, creatures whose power persists wherever man hasn't yet come to dominate?

How much stronger might their allergy to settled lands be than half-domesticated Chapman's? For a moment, the faun wonders if he's safe on the cabin's stoop, but then the singer's song changes, then the homestead's clearing begins to shift and fade and *flicker*.

As the song washes over him, Chapman sees the plot of land as it was when the family who built it inhabited it: hot summer sunshine, golden autumn hope, then a winter of despair and death and abandonment. He sees pasture grass growing tall, the corn in need of weeding, the fence falling in. Snow drifts in the past, thunder booms in Chapman's present, a sunlit future appears, the house gone, its foundations long ago removed, the forest vanished and replaced with vast structures he can't recognize, buildings made of materials unlike any he's ever seen. The homestead plot flickers back to some-when closer to his own year and he sees the witches ready to pounce, the one in the middle holding aloft the singer's head, seeking to find the verse containing a time not far off, the year when the cabin collapses, when the fence rots away, when the corn is dispersed and devoured, when the swamp reclaims this plot into itself.

When the land is again wilderness, in the slim gap before it's settled again.

The scene *flickers;* the right moment appears alongside fresh lightning, a bright finger of electricity bolting from the sky to strike the abandoned cabin, the air around Chapman exploding with static and heat as the house bursts into flames.

Chapman covers his head as the rotted wood blows apart,

throwing burning boards across the plot. The three witches advance through the rain and the fire, the scene warping around them, past and present and future sliding across one another: he sees a vision of a young girl laughing as she chases a rust-colored rooster across the yard; a moment later a mass of metal screeches across a flat black road laid where the girl had been, the machine coming louder than anything Chapman's ever heard; before the screech fades he sees the forest once again completely intact, as it was in the years before the homesteaders arrived here, or else how it'll regrow many years from now, after their absence. Then the forest vanishes, the girl and the screaming metal and the black road vanish too, every world momentarily lost within a howl of blowing snow, a blast of frozen air.

The witches advance through every time Chapman sees at once, placing their steps in whatever moment suits them best, holding the crying head aloft, his song unsettling the way.

Chapman flees, fast as his legs will carry him. Stubborn branches slap his face, thorns tear his fur; his hooves slide on slick rocks, he slips and stumbles, tumbles into knee-deep muck, climbs out with soaked trousers, his satchel heavied with mud. Rain falls, lightning spikes the sky ahead of pealing thunder. Chapman tries to distance himself from the inhuman hollers of the witching women, plus the echoing song they carry, its dense drone pounding, reverberating off boulders and tree trunks, disorienting and confusing the landscape, the ground slippery mud or fresh-poured road or cracked dry clay or glassed ice.

No matter how fast Chapman runs, his pursuers do not flag, not even when the landscape ahead flickers. He leaps a fallen log whose trunk is several feet high and one of his hooves snags a broken branch; he somersaults into a spray of icy powder, he regains his feet to crash through a field of golden corn, snow melting from his beard in the autumn heat. His leathern bag bangs against his bruising body, his skin is cut and ripped and scraped from innumerable falls; in every landscape he crosses he sees how the song eventually becomes a blight, its sound withering plants, turning soil to dust, shattering icy surfaces, setting his muscles aching deeper than even a full night's running should. Mostly but not always he remains a faun, running on a faun's hooves, but at least once he looks down and thinks he sees himself changing too, his body a sudden nightmare of upset flesh and fur; mostly but not always he thinks the rushing witches chase him on the same naked feet he'd seen in the clearing, still human enough.

Mostly but not always. Once Chapman sees a black panther, larger than any he's ever imagined, loping through the trees, its mouth spilling a pink tongue from between daggered yellow teeth; another time he leaps past what he's sure is a grizzly bear huffing free from the trap of a dank, mossy cave, its hiding place nearly buried beneath rising swamp water; throughout the night's pursuit, he sometimes hears a gigantic vulture soaring overhead, its gargantuan wingspan swooping over the high treetops, its grotesque bald head cawing to chill Chapman's blood.

Whatever these witch-beasts are, they come hauntingly close but never catch him. A faun was made to run, and so Chapman runs: as the miles accumulate, the witches' charges become less frequent, and after each such attempt their crashing, loping, soaring noises fade farther into the distance; as they fall back, the song fades too, its drone rising and falling then retreating altogether, after which the ground at last ceases its shifting beneath Chapman's hooves.

Chapman is fast and strong, but by dawn's twilight he's exhausted. Eager to escape the swampy muck of the forest floor, he climbs a grassy hillock, gasping at the cleaner air above the canopy, placing hands on knees to propel his tired legs. As the rain trickles off, the thunder and lightning retreat, withdrawing their enervating energies as Chapman crouches to hide his profile. The still-risen moon emerges, a yellow lamp parting black clouds; the distant horizon glows with the first sign of the coming sun. Chapman doesn't know if the coming day will save him, but he begins to hope he might escape. He searches for signs of fire back the way he came, hunting for where the lightning struck near the abandoned homestead, but he can't see even the thinnest tendril of lingering smoke.

How far east has he come? He doesn't know. In every direction, all he spies is a profound profusion of trees, miles and miles of barely inhabited landscape offering no sign or suggestion of giving way to the coming civilization Nathaniel promised will conquer this land.

Because Chapman is a faun, and because it's in a faun's nature to fall in and out of trouble, he thinks tonight he will not be caught. Whatever his pursuers claim he did in some past life, before he was Chapman, tonight he will not be punished. He turns toward the more inhabited lands of the east, the rising sunlight world of men where he might be safe, where he might reunite with Nathaniel. He can't see himself from below, but if he could he'd see his unique shape silhouetted against the revealed moon, its yellow gaze turning him to strangest shadow: a creature slowly rising, his hands leaving the earth as his body unfolds, rearing out of his bestial crouch to throw back his horns. His mouth opens to let out a defiant cry, loosing a whinnying whoop of triumph—but then he hears the singer's voice rise in response, the voice hoarse now but still making way for the commotion of the witches' passage through the trees, shoving aside branches and thorns and briars by making visible a future in which no swamp exists.

The witches rush from the west, the singer's voice preceding them; Chapman rises on his hooves to face the pursuing song, the flicker advancing before its sound like a wave, a wave of future possibility overcoming the hillock at the same moment a single rifle shot is fired from below, from the east, the direction where he'd hoped to find his brother. Chapman turns toward the unexpected sound, the grieving drone washing over him from behind in the same instant a musket ball reaches his chest, its impact spinning the faun off his hooves.

Falling toward the ground but never hitting it, taking the would-be fatal bullet with him as he drops through the song's strobing sound, Chapman cries out his beloved brother's name, his voice rising even as his body strobes and fades into the passing flicker: *Nathaniel, Nathaniel, NATHANIEL!*

And Nathaniel *is* close by. Nathaniel, who used to promise not to hunt when Chapman was nearby so as not to mistake his brother for his quarry, who has for the past week been desperately seeking his brother, sorry to the bone for what he said, for how he acted the day they met the ditchdiggers, climbs fast through the horror of what he's suddenly sure he's done. Terrified by the injured voice he knows he heard calling his name, he searches the hillock in confusion, his smoking musket clenched in his trembling hands. From far off in the forest to the west, he swears he hears simultaneously the roar of a monstrous bear, the screech of a great cat, the sharp cry of a giant buzzard—but then those distant voices are drowned out by his own rasping breath, by the speeding grieving sobs already choking his throat.

PART TWO

JOHN

John labors three days in a superorchard, two in the stock-yard processing room, one pitchforking ripped or soiled clothing and broken furniture into a truck-sized shredder, prepping the refuse for recycling; on his first assigned day of rest he forces his stiff, sore body out of bed before dawn, setting out on foot as soon as the sun rises. The northern road out of his neighborhood is bounded on one side by rows of super-trees, on the other by a field of brown-leafed drought-resistant corn, the plants pushing their stalks high over the heads of the Volunteers. Between the clatter of the passing trams, he enjoys the warm sunlight, the rare dew about to vanish from the grass and corn; nanoswarms buzz nearby, and if he closes his eyes, he can pretend they're real bees. He listens for birdsong carried on the morning air, but all the Farm's birds are city birds, squawking or silent: pigeons, seagulls, starlings, the occasional hawk, a lone barn owl he's heard hooting in the late evenings. There's wildlife here, but no one would mistake the Farm for a nature preserve.

Walking the narrow tramways, John continues studying the disguised industrial agricultural architecture, all the while wishing in vain for the return of the farms and rural landscapes he'd once known, plus the wilder smell of something no longer possible to find: the deep rot of fallen trees left undisturbed, the strangely patient life of moss and lichen and fungus, the way every thriving forest floor is a bed of decomposition and regeneration, death and life lying down together. But now there's no pristine wilderness left even in the preserves once set aside—and John knows this Ohio River valley, settled and farmed since even before colonization, was never really set aside.

John doesn't forgive those who came before, but he tells himself he also doesn't flee his own complicity: there's no crime in being born into a harmful story, but surely there's sin in not trying to escape. The story of how we got here, the story we refused to abandon; if that was all the human world could be, then he wants a different world. A world of mud and rot, a world of green life blooming everywhere without human intervention; a world of migrating megafauna, of birds of prey hunting bountiful meadows and bright-sparkling river streams; a renewed story of hooves and horns, of broad wings and bright scales, with a smaller, gentler humanity living as part of the whole, not better or more important. Humanity as equal to, not greater than.

Earthtrust offers another possible future, built on a culture where the endangered many Volunteer to preserve the better lives of a privileged few, the last citizens. What Cal wants instead—what she's convinced John to want—is a world where the powerful might be forced to save everyone else. *No take-backs*, Cal said before they parted ways. *Either we all survive, or no one does.* John believes this. He tells himself he does. But he believes it best when he's near Cal telling him what to believe.

At noon, John enters the next neighborhood's brightly lit cafeteria, an ornamental red barn full of Volunteers standing in line or seated at long plastic tables, many making cheerful conversation. He tries not to make an impression while he waits in line, every so often squeezing his right hand to send out pulsing pings from his pebble, impatiently hoping for some response. By the time he reaches the front, he's surprisingly hungry, his long walk in the sun having awoken his appetite. John piles his plate high with food the Volunteers surrounding him have grown and raised and cooked: a slab of fried Farm ham, a side of roasted Farm potatoes, a generous slice of apple pie, its fruit picked fresh from the Farm's superorchards.

It's all so earnest that it's possible to pretend everything John sees isn't a heavily managed experience, that Earthtrust hasn't predetermined every choice he's allowed to make. *A transition*, Eury would say. *One day we won't need to manage this land or these people. One day the Volunteers will be ready to manage themselves again.*

One day, but not any time soon, according to Eury.

Despite these nagging thoughts, the pork and potatoes are truly delicious, undoubtedly the best meal John's eaten in months, a far cry from his dehydrated dinners and nutrient bars, the simple meal he shared with Cal in the barn above the bunker. But then, after eating most of the ham and potatoes, he takes a first bite of the apple pie.

He blanches as he chews, has to force himself to swallow.

The perfect-looking apples he picked during his orchard

shifts, heavy and round, with unblemished red skins: Why hadn't he tasted one as some of the other workers had? Maybe he already knew what he'd feel between his teeth: a new fruit made to survive new seasons, a product pushed until it's no longer what an apple is meant to be. This wasn't what he'd intended, when he'd made the first-gen supertrees.

He's never had an apple that wasn't domesticated, that wasn't a human product. But the apples in this pie are something else, something worse, a mockery of what an apple had become over its thousands of years of human interaction. A generation or two from now, no one might be left who remembers the taste of what John thinks of as a *real* apple.

He sets down his fork, the pleasurable spell of good food broken. His hand buzzes as he does so—he glances down to see the purple and blue lights blinking beneath his skin. Looking up, he finds Julie and Noor standing across the table, then stepping over its bench to sit down. Julie, the sides of her head freshly shaved, the remaining hair gathered into a black braid falling between her shoulder blades; another ex-Earthtrust soldier like Cal, another scarred veteran of the Secession, plus abbreviated campaigns in Europe and South America, in the oil wars fought across the already-devastated Alberta tar sands. Forty years old, she's fought half her life, is fighting still. Noor's the youngest member of their cell: bright and quiet, dressed in long sleeves as always, her slim hands resting calmly before her on the table, hands John has seen move quickly across a keyboard. She's a far better programmer than he'll ever be, her hacker's mind possessed of an intelligence John can only envy, her skill a tool on which they all rely.

Julie picks up John's fork, spears his last bit of pork. "The pigs are the only animals here I'm willing to eat. You've seen those freakish cows your ex is growing? I wouldn't try one of those monsters if I was starving."

John almost points out that some Volunteers likely had been starving not long ago. Instead he pushes his tray at Julie. "They'll give you your own lunch, you know," he says.

"Not hungry," says Julie, talking around her mouthful. "Anyway, it's time for a tour of one of those superorchards you're always going on about."

Back outside, Noor and Julie walk hand in hand, following John into a superorchard plot freed from the seasons by Earthtrust modifications, populated today only by the buzzing nanoswarms visiting branches full of blooms, flowers nature designed to attract now-extinct pollinators. Beneath the trees, John squeezes his fist: pebble vibrating, he reroutes a friendly bee, commands it to lead the nearby nanoswarms away. The buzzing recedes, leaving behind only the wind, only branches scraping against branch, leaves rustling leaves, a few birds chirping nearby.

"When did you get here?" John asks. "I've been looking for you."

Noor says, "We came in three nights ago. Surrendered ourselves to the detention center in St. Louis, driving an old gas-guzzler I hotwired in Kansas City." She cocks a thumb at Julie. "You should've seen how she was living when I found her. Camped out on the top floor of a half-scorched Holiday Inn, living on minibar vodkas and condensed milk, cold cans of expired beans."

"A good place to watch the freeway," says Julie, smirking, "so I'd be ready when Noor came." Noor returning from Montana, her Jeep packed with pilfered solid state drives, server storage modules full of proprietary data left behind by shuttered mining companies, decommissioned power plants, supposed departments of natural resources and environmental quality. She couldn't process all the data, but there were others who could, hacker cooperatives safe in the new Northwest, in Freed Scandinavia, and who knew where else. Atop the Holiday Inn, Noor spent a week decrypting internal memos and corporate research reports, looking for further proof of government collusion, purposeful failures to prevent what might've been preventable. What she found wasn't news but it was more evidence. She'd searched the offices then set her bombs, turning inside out whatever Earthtrust salvage crews might come to save.

John tries to picture their last free days. The damaged Holiday Inn swaying unsteadily in the gales rolling across the plains. Noor working long hours, boiling water on a backpacker stove for instant coffee, her laptop powered by a portable solar panel flagging from an open window; Julie pacing the floor, her rifle in one hand and a lukewarm drink in the other, watching the empty freeway for Earthtrust convoys, Bundyist raiders. When Noor was finished, the two women hauled a satellite uplink to the roof, set a timer to start the upload as soon as they'd gone.

"I don't know if anything we sent will be useful," Noor says. "But we did what we could."

"Tell him the rest," Julie says. "Tell him what else you uploaded."

"A lot of video," Noor says. "A dozen hours of footage from Montana, from a week spent following the Earthtrust crews around."

"Cal told me. The dronedozers, scraping the soil off the earth."

Julie says, "Earthtrust is carting away the surface of the West, all the dead grass and dead trees, the dead animals. What can't be gathered by hand can be dredged with machines, hauled to sorting facilities where the organic materials can be separated out. We've been calling the West a sacrifice zone for years, but what's it a sacrifice for? Sacrifice zones used to mean making the present easy and cheap at someone else's expense, but the West isn't some fracking town with polluted wells, where we're fine with someone else's water being ruined as long as we get cheap natural gas. This is half a country we're talking about. And who, right now, is gaining from it?"

"No one," says Noor. "Not in the present."

"But for what?" asks John. "What's the goal?"

"We don't know," Noor says, giving Julie a conspiratorial glance. They're trading lines, combining their pitch. "But sooner or later, your face is going to heal. Eventually the scanners will tell your old girlfriend you're here, if they haven't already."

John touches his fading bruises, the yellowed flesh tender. "You want her to find me."

"Mai's already inside Earthtrust, but she has only so much access," Julie says. "Noor might be able to hack a way into the Tower. Cal and I can shoot us a path, if we have to. But you might be able to enter at Eury Mirov's side, ride her personal elevator right to the top, ask some questions from the throne room. Questions it would take us a year to answer might be revealed to you in a brag. You tell us what else Eury is planning, then we'll work to stop it. We came for Pinatubo, and it's surely the beginning. But there's no way it's the only goal."

"What we want to know," Noor says, "what Cal told us to tell you she needs you to find out, is what does Eury Mirov want with all that biomass?"

For once, John doesn't have a clue. Whatever Eury is planning, it's nothing she ever shared with him. Some new ambition, arrived only after he left. "And if she won't tell me?"

"There's more than one way to find out," Julie says. "But you're the best chance we have to do it without violence."

Without violence. Julie the soldier, pitching John the pacifist. The sun tips toward the trees, the shadows shift and lengthen and swell. For a moment, they don't speak, only rest together in the sweet-smelling air moving beneath the trees. Two weeks ago, they were deep in the Western Sacrifice Zone; now they're reunited in this thriving place, seeing how life might flourish again on heavily managed earth, how data and technology might create a community, even if that goodness isn't without cost, when everyone here has to give up their free will, the agency to make their days their own.

"We're almost out of time," John says. They need to be back in their assigned neighborhoods soon, need to be sure their pebbles don't register outside their homes after curfew. "And I've got a long walk ahead of me."

"Better you be where Earthtrust can find you," Julie agrees, pushing him gently in the direction of the road. "Because sooner or later, Eury Mirov is coming to collect."

"Before we go," John says, flexing his hand, watching the colored lights scroll beneath the skin. "Have you seen Cal? Is she back?"

Julie says, "She's here, John. But it's better if she stays away. We want you to get caught. We don't want Cal to get caught with you."

John starts to object, but what else is there to say? There are no guarantees, only risks they should minimize if they can. The sunlight slants through the trees, red-winged blackbirds flit through the branches, the breeze carries the distant joys of happy Volunteers. Whatever they do next, John wants to do it without endangering the laughing people he hears, the people

for whom this Farm has become a refuge. No matter how compromised it is, no matter how suspect Earthtrust's motives are,
it could be home enough for many. But if Eury can't be convinced to abandon Pinatubo, then stopping its launch might
mean dismantling Earthtrust, which might mean the end of
the Farm—and if the Farm fell, where else could its people go?

It was something they'd only rarely discussed, in all their
years of planning. It'd been easier to imagine a victimless success from the abandoned Sacrifice Zone, already evacuated and
uninhabited. There, he'd been able to free the land without
hurting anyone else; at the Farm, nothing would be so morally
simple, so bloodlessly clean.

Walking the tramways alone after leaving Noor and Julie,
John admits to himself why he hasn't tried to learn the names
of any other Volunteers this past week, despite long days working alongside them, despite sharing meals and watching their
children play. He knew he couldn't risk knowing them, couldn't
risk his small circle of affection getting any larger, not so close
to the end.

Risking Cal and Julie and Noor and Mai—risking Eury
too—was already as high a price as he could bear.

C-433

The translucent photovoltaic bubble whirrs pleasantly over the frozen surface of the glacier, its gyroscopic floor leveling C as the craft pops and bobs over half-remembered ice ledges and ridges of snow-crusted rock. The memories are the remainder's, but the remainder is C too, its multitudes continuing to collapse into him as he ages into his third week, offering knowledge he needs: he studies how to operate the bubble's controls, either with the rung-summoned haptic console or through the rung itself, his every thought translatable into motion; he learns the double tap of the right temple below the right horn that overlays the AR display, then how to mute O's captured voice when the keening becomes unbearable.

C navigates the glacial shelf with a combination of thought and automation, swerving the bubble around questionable stretches of thinner ice, avoiding obvious crevasses leading Below, into the dark world he no longer believes he'll see. Passing the place where C-432 was fatally wounded, C-433 refuses to retrieve the abandoned winch. What would be the point? Even if he descended Below and retrieved something usable, he would have to return to the crawler to recycle it, and that he'd made sure he'd never be able to do again.

A choice made not for his sake but for the sake of the barkspot.

As the bubble veers west, C worries the new growth, his fingers polishing it into a smooth keloid of worn wood, one undeniably growing, spreading, multiplying. As he'd prepped a store of nutrient paste and the other supplies he'd need to leave the crawler, another barkspot had appeared lower on his neck, twice as wide as the first; while he readied and loaded the translucent photovoltaic bubble, another had grown on his left cheek, begun from a sore he felt forming inside his mouth, where he'd explored its sharp weight with his tongue. By the time he discovered how to download O into the bubble's computer, leaving the crawler entirely uninhabited, there was bark beneath his temple, bark atop his left biceps, along the ridge of his left hip. Another, another, and another, all together making a constellation of wood creeping down his left side, while the original barkspot on his left shoulder tripled in size overnight before producing a single bumpy bud, a gnarled pea bulged atop the skin.

A *bud*, a word C barely managed to remember until, as he left the crawler forever, the bud burst open, C yelping with surprise as from his shoulder there spilled forth a tiny thorned branch bearing a single green leaf, the world's longest winter granting this smallest of springs.

C-433 ISN'T THE BEST CREATURE IN HIS LINEAGE, NOT THE brightest nor the most whole. His skin itches everywhere, he frequently shakes with muscle tremors and disturbances of the bowels, his vision is poor and his hearing muffled; his bones are partly recycled plastics and metals, his loose joints rattle and scrape in their sockets without relief. But despite all this creature's weaknesses, there is boldness too. Before he left the crawler forever, he'd entered the Loom chamber, accompanied by O's careening song playing as loud as the room's speakers would permit. With the remainder's complaints drowned out, he did what no other creature like him had dared, in however many unimaginable years they'd each inhabited the crawler:

C-433 lifted a rusted red fire axe in his clawed blue hands, the barely audible remainder screaming for him to stop as he set out to destroy the Loom.

At first the damage the axe did didn't seem like much, hardly enough. After all, the Loom had been built to last, and C-433 was such a dismal creature. But then he remembered the organic recycling tube, its glass walls, without which the pink acid that had melted his hundreds of bodies would leak uselessly across the floor. With a single blow, he shattered the glass, the housing crashing apart into thousands of shards. Gingerly lifting his sensitive hoof over the sharp debris scattered everywhere, relying on his metal other to take the most dangerous steps, C-433 left without looking back.

Four hundred and thirty-three creatures named C had emerged from the Loom's extruders, a lineage of approximate sameness producing a being who was both ancestor and descendant, a creature who hadn't otherwise propagated, hadn't made any mark except deprivation, who hadn't evolved, hadn't thrived, who'd done nothing but continue recursively, looping back, spiraling in, making himself and the world smaller and lesser with every turn. Now, with the Loom destroyed, C-433 commits himself fully: no matter what, he can never retreat. Unless he reaches Black Mountain, unless he protects the barkspot and delivers it to this one facility the map room suggested might still be populated, unless he finds there a way to save whatever tree the spreading bark might become, unless he accomplishes all this, he knows he'll be the last of his line. He and his tree are saved together or doomed together. He leaves no other way.

FROM C'S PERCH AT THE CENTER OF THE BUBBLE, HE SURVEYS A landscape that in every direction is only gradations of bright white, dull gray, shiny blue. Before leaving, he'd cut down the map room's wall-sized chart depicting the twelve crawler sites across the continent, plus Black Mountain far to the west. Unrolling its scroll, he tries to match the map generated by his rung with this plastic copy, but the two worlds lack enough correspondence for him to plot a route directly, and despite its autonomous systems the bubble cannot navigate itself—its sensors read SATELLITE FAILURE and UNKNOWN LOCATION when C tries to feed the haptic console the map's coordinates. But the bubble can follow compass directions, so: west then. The local terrain the map suggests remains buried beneath the Ice, its topography surely reconfigured by the glacier; what lies beyond is impossible to guess. C steers the bubble west then southwest then west again, routing around icefalls and crevasses and rocky outcroppings looming skyward; he travels every day beneath a sky-spanning solar halo floating above the glacier's surface, the pale orb of the sun ringed white against white as it moves across the sky; at night, he rests inside the motionless bubble, seeing through its curves dark sky-obscuring cloud cover only rarely broken by the dim pinpricks of stars, their distant light too dull to fully penetrate the atmosphere.

Without the advancement of the bark, how would C clock the passing of time? A new day passes, almost the same day that passed yesterday. So little distinguishes one kilometer of flat glacier from any other that novelty approaches zero. There are obstacles to avoid but all of a type, the bubble deviating from its heading to skirt unsteady surfaces, to swerve around icefalls and fields of broken stone; the bubble corrects course as soon as it can, turning west a dozen kilometers south of where it left its route. Floating a half-meter above the surface, the bubble leaves no trace of its passage, the ice remains unmarked in every direction C looks. His stomach rumbles but he rarely eats; every mouthful of nutrient paste strains his limited stores, while his stomach revolts at its nothing taste, the nausea that followed him out of the Loom seemingly permanent. Eating does nothing to forestall the cramps, leaving him doubled over atop his hooves, racked with croaking cries until his stomach unclenches. The barkspots advance day by day, C checks their progress after every rest: he touches the bark obsessively, careful to avoid handling the leafy stem too often, instead running his fingers over the rutted wrinkles of bark climbing the left side of his throat, his jaw, his stiffening cheeks. At the bark's many edges, his skin furrows then hardens alarmingly, but for now any dismay he feels is tempered by the surprise of new-ness, of seeing a living thing striving to thrive.

The Ice is without ecosystem or community; C expects to find neither life nor civilization until he reaches Black Mountain. He has only the map room's binders' description of the world beyond the Ice to guide him, having memorized but barely understood their protocols for tilling the thawed earth, for how to use the Loom to replant the soil or repopulate a biome, all purest fantasies to this creature who's never seen soil except in the caves and tunnels Below, who's never seen any other living thing except these barkspots, his woody parasites.

The bubble has an array of sensors, but mostly they tell C what he already knows: the flatness of the glacier, its only occasional changes in elevation, the predicted time of sunrise and sunset, the cycle of the moon. C navigates a narrow valley of blued ice, the bubble's glass scraping as he squeezes around tight corners; he zooms quickly across a snowless expanse lacking either obstacle or landmark. He accomplishes other crossings, makes other passages through and across and over features he can't name. Much of what he sees meets in him a profound ignorance, a lack of language for the conditions he traverses: wherever the first C originated, he must not have needed to name the many kinds of snow, hadn't had to learn to read the dangers lurking in slight variations in glacial conditions.

C travels hundreds of kilometers without the landscape appreciably changing; wherever he goes, his ignorance travels along. The Ice offers no quarter, only its expanse. The bubble's computer and the rung in C's neck conspire to keep the bubble on a generally westward trajectory, toward where the map scroll suggests he'll find Black Mountain. The days pass slowly, offering few prompts or triggers for C's memories; he becomes restless, walking circles around the constrained space of the gyroscopic floor. As time seems to stall, he combats his melancholy by focusing on the barest signs of progress: the digital odometer on the command console, its number slowly climbing; the inexorable march of the barkspots, the once discrete keloids growing together into inflexible stretches, wood slowly overtaking the surface of his skin.

With no one to talk to, C's facial expression rarely changes; he doesn't realize it's become difficult to speak until the bark's weight begins dragging down the left side of his face. He struggles to choke down his next mouthful of nutrient paste, his feeding tube clenched in one panicky fist. Paste dribbles from his lips and he starts again, forcing himself to swallow carefully, working around some obstruction, his throat restricted by the hardening barkflesh running now from temple to shoulder, cheek to jowl.

The next day he wakes to discover he can no longer fully open his left eye, his expression forced into a squint by the bark covering his cheekbone, the wood dully warm to the touch. Before noon, the eye disappears completely behind another patch of fast-growing black bark, and now C panics, what joy and surprise he once felt having fled in an instant. He summons his toolbox from the cargo container beneath the bubble's floor, his left hand shaking as he retrieves an orange-handled knife, its edge pitted with rust. Clenching it tightly, C musters what courage he has, then places the blade against a low ledge of bark, at the edge of where it's slowly advanced across his right forearm. With a trembling grip, he slides the blade along the base of the bark's farthest growth, seeking a protruding lip under which he can slip the knife, something like the edge of a scab lifting away from the skin.

He expects pain, but the first stretch of bark comes off easily, falling to the floor in woody chunks. Where the bark was, the skin beneath is reddened, raw, but undeniably skin, a reassuring sight—but then when C moves the blade farther in that differentiation disappears. Where the bark's too stubborn to flake away from the flesh, he tries to cut into it from above, setting the unserrated blade to sawing at a stretch of bark farther up the forearm, near his stiffened elbow.

This time the hurt comes immediately, as soon as the blade bites the barkspot.

As C moans, O's voice cries its own painful song, O's old complaint merging with C's new one. He presses down again, angrily sawing until he can't take any more pain; when he yanks the knife free a red sap pulses from the wound, oozing down his arm.

Blood and not blood. Creature and tree, leaking together.

C drops the knife to apply pressure to the cut, but the wound is not flesh, the skin not skin. The sap globs through his fingers, not clotting as blood would, only hardening as sap does.

Afterward, C's good hand is sticky and filthy, his cut arm is covered with the reddish amber of his blood-sap, hardening into the crevices of the cut bark. Still, the operation is at least partially a success. He might never be able to reverse the tree's growth, but at least he's learned to prune it. Day after day, he'll have to trim the bark back from his arm and face and neck, flaking away new growths to slow the bark's advance.

If this tree has made C's body into its earth, then when he is finished, he tells it, it can have all of him it wants. It's a

ridiculous statement but he doesn't know why. He's too new a
creature, the coming of the barkspots too novel an event. He
doesn't understand that nothing truly wild was ever controlled
without pain, that no living world was ever conquered without
consequence.

CHAPMAN

Nathaniel fires his musket in 1799, aiming uphill at what he thinks is a wild goat, his mistake unknown until halfway through the pull of the trigger. Afterward he spends ten confused, brotherless years grieving and planting alone, tending nurseries alone, traveling alone between the wild Territory and the settled east, then across the State the Territory becomes into lands beyond, lands Territory still. Ten years seeking new undrained swamps, new uncut stretches of virgin forest, new rivers undammed and undiverted and maybe still unnamed and unmapped; ten years of planting seed after seed as every spring the advancing civilization chases him farther west, as first the Territory and then the State fill with human towns, human cities, the human sign spreading until the wilder places are cut off, until they shrink and separate and disappear.

Nathaniel spends these ten years always searching what wilderness remains, in case his brother lives, because it was only in the wild where Chapman was ever comfortable. Ten years of aging, ten years of drinking, ten years of thickening flesh, of graying hair, of exile and grief and returning every year to climb the Ohio hillock where, in the breaking light of dawn ten years ago, he swore he saw a wild goat—but in the second he took his shot didn't he see his prey was no animal, rising as it did to stand on two hooves?

Ten years of waking shaking and sweaty in his bedroll, dreaming of a terrible accident he'd caused but couldn't understand.

Ten years now past.

Now Nathaniel is there on that hillock, now Chapman's there too, returned as Nathaniel's bullet finishes its transit, ten years after it first met Chapman's skin, the until-now-paused lead ball burning through the skin to mushroom against the rib cage in an Ohio so changed it might as well be another world from the one in which Nathaniel's bullet was fired.

And where was Chapman in the years between? Where was he with Nathaniel's bullet?

Escaped into the flicker, riding the singer's song between the stations of the seconds before and after the bullet's impact, safe in an interstitial reprieve unable to keep the bullet and his blood apart forever, every hurt sooner or later returning to the earth from which it sprang.

GRIEVING NATHANIEL, OLDER NOW, REUNITED WITH HIS LOST brother, still young; skeptical Nathaniel, dropping disbelieving to his knees at the injured faun's side; faithful Nathaniel, arriving as the final strobes of the flicker recede, as his bullet at last starts killing Chapman: steady Nathaniel wastes no more time. He hooks his arms under his horned brother's armpits, then drags him from the exposed hill. Below the tree line, he shucks his possessions—his satchel, his bedroll, the same rifle he used ten years ago—then takes his knife from his belt. Kneeling beside Chapman, Nathaniel places his free palm on his brother's bare chest, trying to soothe his rocking movements, his inhuman moaning.

"Hush, brother," Nathaniel says, peering into the bullet wound, its seeping entry a decade and a moment old.

"Nathaniel," Chapman says, wheezing past sharp teeth. "We have to go."

Nathaniel shakes his head. "Not until I get the bullet out of you."

"There's no time," Chapman says. He tries to sit, fails, wraps a furred hand around Nathaniel's spotted forearm. "Can't you hear them coming?"

Chapman's last word garbles into a cough, punctuated by a bubble of blood. Nathaniel tries to hear whatever it is Chapman hears, but there's only a slight wind blowing, a few squawking birds scattering away from the commotion.

"Lie quiet, brother," he says. Knee on Chapman's hipbone, knife in his hand, Nathaniel surveys his brother's bloody wound: the bark of his brother's skin is harder than hickory, Nathaniel's knife only a farmer's tool, not a doctor's scalpel. With a whispered apology, he digs the knife's tip into the entry wound, searching for the mushroomed musket ball. If he's lucky, the lead might be near the surface, crashed against bone without breaking through. If not, the bullet might've shattered the rib cage or slipped between its slats to lodge in the lungs or the heart.

But probably then Chapman would already be dead.

The wound isn't deep, but Nathaniel can't find the bullet. He can't even move the knife below the skin, because whatever a faun is, its flesh is made of sterner stuff.

"If you were a man," says Nathaniel, "I wouldn't have shot you."

Chapman only moans, pain robbing him of language as Nathaniel tries again to move the blade inside the bullet wound, as he's again stymied by his brother's stubborn flesh.

"If you were a man, I'd save you," he says. "A man wouldn't need to die."

Nathaniel is half right, but today half right is enough. When he tries for a third time to explore the entry wound, Chapman howls, the beastly sound shivering Nathaniel, setting his hands to shaking. He pauses, lets his brother's bucking slow, then tries again—and this time as the knife reaches the wound, Chapman changes skins. Nathaniel sees the faun he has known his whole life, then the man he's asked his brother to be instead, a man whose chest contains the same bullet hole as the faun's. The vision is unstable, the body shifting moment to moment: Chapman's a faun then a man, then a faun and a man; he has feet then hooves, then one foot and one hoof; his skin blooms fresh fur, the fur ripples away in shed sheets to reveal hairless flesh. The horns spiral up out of the man's head, as the face widens and sharpens, grows faunish; they spiral back in as the face flattens out, leaving only two circles of shiny skin blazing the forehead.

Nathaniel's mind is quick, his spirit steady. He puts the blade against the bullet wound in the faun, then when the faun becomes a man, he moves the blade.

The flesh of the man gives, the flesh of the faun resists; Chapman's body bucks, his moans elongate pitifully, his voice sounds one way from the mouth of the faun and another from the man's, both voices hurting, hurting.

Now Nathaniel hears the slightest clink as the steel blade taps lead, the smashed mass turning the knife tip aside. He holds his breath, steadies his grip: if he pulls the knife loose before removing the bullet, he'll have to start over. He studies the man turning faunish, studies the faun becoming a man; he adjusts the blade, moving from the top of the bullet to its side, then below. Now his knife cuts into Chapman the man, now Nathaniel worries his brother the faun will kick his hooves or lash out with his claw: if Chapman decides to buck him free, there's nothing Nathaniel will be able to do, not with the arthritis in his joints, the chronic aching in his muscles. But as new blood wells around the blade's entry into the wound, Chapman's changing body stills, his shape flickering more slowly, sometimes pausing somewhere in between: not the perfectly proportioned half-man, half-beast the faun was, but something monstrous, something never meant to be, truly half a faun, half a man.

As smoothly as possible, Nathaniel works the knife like a lever, slowly lifting the musket ball through the flickering layers of skin and muscle. He moves when he can move, he pauses when he has to pause, he waits for his chance.

His whole life, Chapman has been the wild one, given to flights of fancy and boundless curiosity, while Nathaniel has been steady, unplayful, a stodgy plodder. This was the man Nathaniel believed he had to be, but who could love the role, choosing stoic readiness over excitable joy, quiet perseverance over quick-blooded passion? As the bullet rises, his pulse does not elevate, his breathing remains unhurried. At last the bullet comes free from this brother he shot ten years ago, whose life he'd already saved twice before, once when Nathaniel's bullet sent Chapman into deepest flicker, a no-when where the musket ball could wait arrested while the witches who might've torn him limb from limb lost his scent, and once even earlier, forty years ago in a story never fully told, of the day teenage Nathaniel lifted the newborn faun in his arms, rescuing a child unloved and unnamed in still-wild woods, abandoned to death by exposure by Nathaniel's grieving stepfather, who would not love the horned babe that was his own firstborn son, whose mother-killing shape the man couldn't ever again stand to see.

BY THE TIME NATHANIEL FINISHES CONSTRUCTING A LEAN-TO IN A nearby copse of cedars, Chapman's bandaged shape is once again only a faun's, injured but no longer dying. Despite his long absence, Chapman looks exactly as Nathaniel remembers, unchanged and unaged. Unlike Nathaniel, who after the surgery feels every one of the last ten years.

He moves Chapman's unconscious form inside the lean-to's crooked structure as gently as possible. This isn't an ideal camp—it's too far from water, too exposed—but Nathaniel is thankful for the time each next task takes. He gathers up Chapman's few possessions, the poverty of his well-worn leathern bag holding only a dusty last handful of dead seeds, plus the broken gimlet they'd fought over a decade earlier. He digs a depression for a firepit, gathers wood kept dry beneath the biggest trees. After walking a half mile to the last creek he crossed, he fills his newer waterskins and his brother's aged pair, Chapman's bladders seeping at their seams. Back in camp, Nathaniel builds a fire, sets a pot to boiling while he peels gathered roots and carrots, guiltily gnawing a knuckle of dried venison as he works. A man makes a mistake but still he needs to eat. The vegetables go in the pot, he lets them cook until they soften to a watery mash. He fills a cup, takes it to his brother in the lean-to. His brother needs rest, food to restore his strength, fluids to replace lost blood.

Last night's rain is ended, the grass is wet, but above the boughs the clouds part to let the sun pass. Chapman shivers and stirs, but is he awake? Kneeling beside the bedroll, Nathaniel tips the cup to his brother's mouth, but the mash only dribbles into the scratch of his beard.

Nathaniel drinks what Chapman refuses. He's sitting closer to his brother than he has since they were children alone in the Appalachian woods, their first home after fleeing their father's house. In those first years, Chapman's body grew faster than a human child's, but inside he was a toddler desperate for whatever poor parenting Nathaniel could provide. Chapman's birth cost Nathaniel his family, his inheritance, whatever life he might've had back east in Massachusetts; his birth gave Nathaniel the many years they worked the wilds of the Territory, work Nathaniel has finally come to love for its own sake.

The leftover mash goes cold. Nathaniel busies himself with darning a pair of socks, with sewing a button back onto his last decent shirt, then wrapping a cracked adze handle with leather stropping. He builds the fire past the point of comfort, not sure how much warmth Chapman might need, the faun shivering under the lean-to despite being wrapped in both their blankets. Nathaniel sweats as the afternoon gives way to evening, as the evening gives way to night. He gnaws a second strip of jerky and paces the camp to cool himself, then returns to his vigil.

Sitting beside his resting brother in the dark, Nathaniel doesn't think he'll sleep—he'd have to lie blanketless on the ground, something his arthritic joints would likely protest—but then his eyes flutter closed and suddenly it's hours later, Nathaniel startling himself back awake, still sitting in the dark of the lean-to, his aging legs jumping involuntarily.

Looking down, Nathaniel finds he's holding Chapman's hand, something he hasn't done since his brother was a child-faun, fresh on his hooves. But here they are, one brown-furred and clawed hand held in another, liver spotted and pale.

Nathaniel and Chapman, man and faun, brothers forever, despite everything.

AT DAWN, CHAPMAN WAKES TO DISCOVER NATHANIEL BESIDE HIM, his brother barely awake, his body listing but his hand still holding Chapman's. He tries to sit too quickly, winces and clutches his bandaged chest, then tries again, more slowly. "Brother," he says, rising to his elbows. "You're here, but—" He shuts his golden eyes against his confusion, then opens them to take in Nathaniel's face again. "But you're so old now."

Nathaniel drops Chapman's hand, embarrassed. He strokes his gray beard, runs his fingers through his thinning hair. "It's been ten years, Chapman."

The faun holds up one arm, studying the fur there, all of

it as deep russet as ever, without the slightest sign of the gray shooting through his brother's hair. "What happened?"

"Ten years ago I shot you atop this hill, mistaking you for a wild goat. By the time I saw it was you, it was too late to stop my trigger, and after I climbed the slope . . ." Nathaniel shakes his head, curses. "A little blood, a clot of fur, and no brother to be found." He tells Chapman the rest: how he's worked their apple planter's life alone, how for ten years he's returned to this place, the pilgrimage here often his last task before looping back through their older nurseries on his way east. He explains that this year's *east* is a destination farther west than before, as it's possible now to comfortably winter near the new towns of eastern Ohio, in this State the Territory's become, instead of crossing the mountains back into Pennsylvania.

"You saved my life," Chapman says. He opens the bedroll, then rises slowly, swaying unsteadily. He tentatively smiles his toothy grin, then stamps his hooves to move his blood. He taps an index finger at the makeshift bandage covering his bark-brown torso, then pushes in a claw. He winces, but no new blood spots the linen, the faun healing fast now that the bullet's been removed. "You saved my life not once, brother, but twice," he says, then pauses: How to explain the night of the rainstorm, the fleshy witches, the beheaded singer, the chase through the changing wilderness? "I was being chased," he says at last, "by some who planned to punish me for a crime I didn't commit."

Nathaniel imagines a mob, armed and dangerous, a throng of violent, suspicious men like the crude and uncouth ditch-diggers he'd left Chapman for, all those years ago. "For what crime? What did you do?"

"I think it was an accident," Chapman says, then falls si-lent. The forest floor here is springy with spongy soil, humus, and moss; the trees are old, scarred, ancient kings, their broad branches full of birdsong; everywhere there is the sign of deer and bear, wolf and fox, rabbit and squirrel, all Chapman's old comforts, his oldest joys. But in the witches' shapeshifting, in the beheaded singer's song, in the flickering vision they gave him and the shifting landscape through which they gave chase, there was something else too, something new, something he both fears and craves: true magic and deepest mystery, the re-vealed existence of forces perhaps as inhuman as he is, pos-sessed of some power by which much that seemed impossible was made to happen.

Chapman had nearly been ready to forsake his self-imposed quest by the night the witches and the singer appeared; now his hopes are renewed, because any world in which creatures such as these existed might be made a world in which his Tree did too. He has seen the singer's song move the landscape through time, changing it, shaping the ground to make it possible for the witches to more easily advance—what if the song could do the same for him, he tells Nathaniel, what if it could show him the future in which his Tree exists?

"I don't understand," says Nathaniel, his normally placid face contorted by confusion. His brother has babbled for five incoherent minutes, the fantasies he relates surely divorced from reality and sense.

"Neither do I," says Chapman. The faun absently rubs his horns, the whole then the broken, then makes a decision: even if the witches could help him, his fear remains greater than his hope. He scans the way east, the direction Nathaniel would've been planning to travel anyway. It was in the wild places the witches had found Chapman; he fears it's in the wilds they'll hunt him again. "We have to go, brother. Back east, back anywhere it's better settled. No time for stopping this year either. Our nurseries will have to wait."

Nathaniel nods, giving his assent even as his furrowed, sunburned face twists in confusion. "There's something else I need to know," he says. "When I found you last night, you weren't only yourself. You were—"

Chapman considers his steady, stoic brother, who once possessed no lick of superstition or belief in anything more supernatural than his Christian god, this brother whose lack of imagination had persisted despite his many years in the company of a creature whose true name they'd had to learn from a book of stories. He asks, "What, Nathaniel? How have I wronged you?"

Nathaniel grows visibly frustrated, his reddening face betraying the return of the intractable anger that broke their fellowship. "Have you always been able to do it?"

"Have I always been able to do what?"

"Have you always been able to make yourself a man? Could we have been two men this whole time, proper men together?"

Chapman laughs. "Brother, no! This is me. I could no more change my shape than you can change yours." But suddenly he isn't so sure. He considers again the shapeshifting witches and the mutable landscape, driven before them by the singer's song; he raises a hand, recalling how strange he'd felt after Nathaniel's bullet struck, held softly aloft in the flicker, a sensation he can still feel tugging his seams.

He tries, best as he can, to put just one part of himself back.

What happens next is no meditation or prayer, no parlor trick or spell, but it's hard to pretend it's not magic: Chapman's hand become a man's, the hand of the man from whom Nathaniel dug a bullet.

The brothers startle. The hand changes back in an instant, furred and clawed again, then with effort Chapman makes it pale and hairless once more. Surprised anew, his concentration quickly breaks, his hand this time rippling over slowly, until the skin is sheathed with its accustomed fur, fur this faun has somehow learned to wear on the *inside*.

JOHN

It takes her another week to come for him. Returned to the cool dark square of his assigned house, its fresh-printed concrete still stinking and curing, John turns on the solar light to reveal Eury Mirov sitting at the kitchen table, dressed in the same black suit she's worn for countless promotional videos and press briefings, the same white blouse donned for board meetings and Senate depositions, her tight black slacks cropped above low wedge boots. The outfit's too fashionably cut for the spartan space of the concrete house, but Eury's also not her television self, not so made-up and well lit: this is the real Eury, taller than John even without her heeled boots, her fingernails chipped, her face tanned and windburned. "I knew you'd come back," she says, uncrossing her legs, then using a bootheel to push back the table's other chair, gesturing for him to sit. As if he has a choice.

"I hoped you wouldn't notice," John says, taking his seat, already exhausted. He wants to be sharp, careful, attentive; knows he's not, his body worn from hours of digging irrigation ditches for an AI-planned soybean field. "How did you find me? Cameras? Bioscanners? Facial recognition?"

Eury laughs, leans back in her chair. "So dramatic, so paranoid, always. Yes, there are cameras and drones, here at the Farm and in the Sacrifice. Yes, we use facial recognition, sniffer sensors, biometrics of all kinds. But it doesn't mean we're constantly watching. The data merely ensures health and safety, efficiency, maximized capacity. It's not about controlling the people who live here. It's about enabling this land to be its most productive self. Still, we do sometimes find something interesting."

She retrieves a palm-sized projector from her pocket, places it on the table. The projector hums to life, splashing a series of images across the white concrete wall: John, crossing the fence line of a stilled power station outside Phoenix; John, using his truck as a battering ram to dislodge a row of gas pumps in a deserted desert town; an explosion dismantling a dam over a snaking canal, while a tiny figure in forest-green flannel runs; a fracking well winched from the ground and dragged, John plainly visible behind the wheel of his now lost truck. More images follow, a montage of his minor crimes, all the controlled demolitions and half-hearted destruction shot at such a distance that even the explosions look futile, amateurish.

Eury pauses on a photograph depicting John staring up into the sky, his profile stark against a field of waist-high brown grass, a half-dead river sparkling behind him; she advances the projector one more time, displaying a last image of the same place, this time taken from a lower vantage: a close-up of John's face, bearded and sunburned, furious and frightened.

Yellowstone, the Lamar Valley. The first view from the drones taking away the bison; the second from a wolf that wasn't a wolf, or that was a wolf but was also something else.

"We weren't tracking you on purpose," Eury says, "but you kept showing up in routine machine scans, from our drones, from left-behind camera systems still active in the Sacrifice. Every so often the system flagged your passing by, even when your pebble was turned off. A neat trick, that. Our engineers assured me they couldn't be deactivated without removing them from the body first. I'd love to hear how you accomplished it."

John offers her nothing, for now reserving even his questions. First and foremost among his unasked queries: What had Eury done to make a wolf into a camera? Maybe it wouldn't take much: the Earthtrust-made pebble implanted in his thumb controlled a retinal display he could summon at will, plus a satellite tracker and other tech; the nanobees carried visual sensors that were much smaller than anything you'd need to mod an animal the size of a wolf. But just because it was easy didn't mean it didn't also offend. It was bad enough what they'd had to do to the apple trees, all the genetic manipulations, the cross-splicing of genes from dozens of species until what an apple tree was became meaningless. It was worse how they'd reshaped the livestock. But still the wolf upset him most of all. Heir to the inheritance of every ancestor too proud to become a dog, it should have either stayed free or died away. Even extinction was better than becoming another toy for this woman who had everything, who every day owned more of the world.

"I shouldn't have come back," John says, his cheeks flushing. He thought he'd feel anger when finally confronted with Eury again. But all he feels is the shame of his wasted years, of having accomplished so little while telling himself he was doing something important, while every minute Earthtrust grew and Eury got stronger. "I should've stayed away."

"But I'm glad you didn't," says Eury, pocketing the projector. She stands, smooths out her blouse, adjusts her jacket. "Will you come with me?"

"Do I have a choice?" He knows he needs to go: Julie told him this is what Cal wants, but he can't resist indulging his petulance. "Do we Volunteers even have the option of refusing you?"

"If this square of concrete is where you want to live, I won't stop you, but you and I both know Volunteering is a waste of your talents." Eury waves dismissively at the walls still curing, the utter lack of decoration, every blankness evidence of how John has barely inhabited this house. "We're way past where we were when you quit. We're making real progress now with our redundancies and resiliencies, preparing the Farm for what's coming next. That field of soybeans in the next spiral over? The plants are really designed for the *next* decade's heat, when we predict they'll be twice as productive. They're not just drought resistant but hungry for droughts. When that future arrives, we'll be ready. No one has to starve, no one has to suffer."

"I didn't come here to help, Eury. You have to know that." John says this carefully: it's true, but it's not the whole truth. He's always been a bad liar, and more so where Eury is concerned.

Eury stands, gestures toward the door. She's tired too, he sees, as her mask momentarily slips, before her calm enthusiasm reasserts itself. "At least let me show you the view from the Tower. It really is spectacular. After we're done, maybe you can tell me why you're sneaking back into my Farm, instead of just coming home to me. By now you must know I wouldn't care about a couple bombs out west, not if the blasts let you burn off some of that crippling guilt, still as boring as ever."

EURY'S PENTHOUSE IS SET AT THE PEAK OF THE NEEDLE NARROWING skyward from the Tower's main structure, an ostentatious addition to the already overwrought office building. After riding a private elevator up from the fiftieth-floor Earthtrust executive offices—offices where John might've worked, if he'd stayed— Eury leads John through a small antechamber to the penthouse's double doors, ornately inlaid with a forest scene: dense trees and dozens of woodland creatures, a mountain hovering over the horizon. Unlocking the automatic doors with a wave of her hand, Eury steps aside to let John enter first, revealing a well-appointed office flush with sunset, red-orange light setting every surface to glowing, especially the heavy mahogany slab of Eury's desk, its empty surface polished to a high sheen. There are no visible metals, plastics, polymers, only warm woods, handcrafted textiles laid over gleaming marble, burnished leather chairs, and the smell of wood polish and pipe tobacco.

All that—and also a wolf.

Lying before Eury's desk, its nose tucked beneath its paws, is a sleepy double of the lone animal John saw out west, the one he now realized led the lifter drones to the herd of dead and dying bison, then sent an image of his face to Earthtrust: the same gray fur, the same clever green eyes, the same preternatural calm when confronted with a man.

"I call this one Ghost," Eury says, gesturing as she walks behind her desk, turning her back until she's silhouetted before the window by the sunset expanse of the Farm.

"Ghost," John echoes, arms crossed. "You call this one Ghost, or all of them?"

"Just this one," Eury replies, refusing the provocation. "You're quick to judge, but you weren't here these past years.

You don't know how steady a hand it took to make this possible. The world outside the Farm ended. It was up to us to make the future, and you left." She clicks her tongue loudly; Ghost rises and yawns, its pink tongue lolling free as it pads around the desk to sit beside Eury. "Come here, John," she says, absently scratching behind the wolf's ears. "Come look at the world we made."

We? Not we. Her. The Farm is her invention, her vision come true. John refuses his share of the responsibility, despite his bees, despite all the work he did to make the first super-orchard trees survive this new Ohio. He hadn't wanted to re-make the world, hadn't wanted to own the future. All he'd wanted was for there to be apple trees here, on the land where he grew up.

All he'd wanted was for there to keep being *bees*.

John joins Eury at the glass wall, Ghost resting between them. The view is vertiginous, the land below healthy but also deeply unnatural, its spiraling plots arranged in an agricultural model far removed from any traditional practice.

"You've transformed our home into another factory," he says. "The technology is new but the end result is the same as any other industrial farming operation. There's no *here* here, not anymore, no Ohio, nothing natural or wild. It's all Earthtrust, in every direction."

"When we built the first VAC here, there wasn't anything left to save," Eury says, her gaze distant, seeing not just the Farm but the ruins it was built upon. "Just grids of dead or dying farms, shuttered factories and empty downtowns, suburbs full of abandoned malls and sprawling parking lots. A totally failed state. We had to tear up all the roads, tear down all the fences, till a quarter of the state into new soil. Isn't that the work you were doing out west? How is this different?" She waves a hand dismissively before he can object, before he can differentiate between rewilding the land and reusing it. "Parts of the Farm are too polluted to grow anything edible, so we're planting special rotations of crops to leech out the poisons. When they tried the same technique in Detroit back at the turn of the century, the process took decades, but at Earthtrust we've invented some promising corn products designed to suck up every contaminant in a single planting. The Farm's not wilderness, I'll grant you that, but everything you see is becoming healthy, productive land again, and we've got the technology to keep iterating as conditions change. And they are going to change, John. We're not going back to some pristine wilderness without a single human in sight. That world's gone. All we can do is prepare for what's next."

"As if those are the only choices." His voice is flat now, his anger level. "As if all we can choose is wilderness or a factory farm."

Eury turns, her expression intense, beseeching. As always, it's not enough if he only agrees with her: she wants him to believe. In her. In the world she wants to make. In the world she wants to make together. "We never did make us last," she says. "But we don't have to try again. Just come back to me, John. The world is over but a new world is coming. Maybe there we'll be friends again." She gestures at the Farm. "When we were children, our parents' generation said the planet might be uninhabitable if the temperature rose a mere two degrees Celsius. It's risen that and more, and they were right: the planet has become hostile to human life. Soon we'll be the only mammals left. We've abandoned half the United States and still our government is too slow, too beholden to old interests, old powers.

But the world they're protecting is finally truly over. It's time to make a new one."

"Pinatubo," John says, staring out the window, watching the sun fall over the sprawling fields, the spiraling orchards and stockyards. "You're talking about the Pinatubo Project."

"You remember," Eury says, smiling slightly. "Worldwide stratospheric aerosol scattering to return the planet's temperature to where it was at the beginning of the century, maybe even all the way back to preindustrial levels, if it works as well as I think it will."

"But cooling the air isn't enough. What about ocean acidification, what about mass extinctions, what about wildfires everywhere, all the compound extremes to come? Climate change isn't one problem but a million interconnected crises. There'll be unforeseen consequences. People will suffer. Who benefits from this, Eury? Who wins?"

"We all win," Eury says, her voice tight now, her eyes flashing. "This is about protecting everyone on earth. Pinatubo will pause the clock, give us time to invent more lasting solutions, to put those solutions into action." She frowns, glares. It's not anger, only disappointment. "Tell me if you're with me, John. Tell me if you're back. This is what being back means."

"I'm here," he says, hating the frustrated defeat he hears in the words. He straightens his posture, evens out his voice. This is exactly where Cal needs him to be. All he has to do is go along a little further. "I'm here, aren't I?"

"I should've come to you sooner," Eury says, as Ghost whimpers, rises, and pads away. "But I've been busy, shuttling between here and Syracuse, to the United Nations and the European Union, Moscow and Beijing and New Delhi. There's so much timidity, so much hand-wringing, but we can't cling to old powers forever. It's time to do something. Something bold."

"You say it like it's that easy. Like no one will get hurt. Like we can flip a switch and change the world." And wasn't that exactly what Eury was proposing? A technological fix, surprisingly simple, surprisingly cheap, all things considered, launched by a great woman brave enough to do what no one else will.

"I'm a realist but I'm not afraid to act," Eury says, barely pausing at John's objections. "The Farm is proof. It's bold and complex, but it works. The Chinese have their own attempt, but they don't think it's viable long term, which is why they let us build a VAC there too." Eury smiles her enigmatic smile that rarely exactly signals *joy*. "But then our Farm isn't viable forever either. Not without Pinatubo."

John senses his resistance withering, paling in the face of Eury's confidence, all his questions small-minded, feebly nay-saying do-nothings. "What happened to your talk about new kinds of drought resiliency, the next decade's heat-tolerant crops? Just more PR spin?"

"No, no, all that is true. One of the best parts about being good at your job is you don't have to lie to the press. The Farm is as future-proof as I've promised, at least for a couple decades, if we do nothing. But I do not plan on doing nothing."

"Why you, Eury? Why should you be the one to get to make this decision? How can you possibly decide?" This is the one real objection, the root of Cal's anger, of his own: Why *her*? Why Eury Mirov, claiming the right to choose for everyone, after first hastening the dismantling of the nation's democratic institutions, always fragile, always endangered, now almost vanished. "Why you?" he asks again, his voice rising.

"You want to save the world, John. What do you think saving the world is, except deciding for everyone? The world is
worse for most people now than it was when we were young,
but the old world was pretty bad too. Now it's ending, one way
or another. All I want is to give us more time to prepare for
what's next."

Whether they act or don't act, some will suffer, there will
be winners and losers, but is John willing to gamble on the
hope that more will be saved than lost if he lets Eury Mirov decide what's worth saving? He considers the twilight landscape,
the glowing orchards and fields. He thinks of the Volunteers
below, doing their best to live the good life Eury's promised.
He objects to this place, but his objection doesn't rob it of its
majesty.

"John," Eury says. "John, please look at me."

This is his childhood friend. This is the woman he loved.
Once he thought he'd do anything Eury asked him, no matter
the cost.

"I'm listening," he says. "But first, tell me what your drones
were doing in Yellowstone."

Now Eury offers John her real smile, not the practiced, in-
scrutable expression she saves for the telescreen cameras, but an
animal's grin showing too many of her too perfect white teeth.

This is Eury Mirov, a wolf in a white blouse, ready to remake
the world.

"I don't know if you're ready for all that," she says. "But
maybe I better show you."

C-433

A tree grows sneakily, it is rare to see one move; C goes to sleep with quiet reverence for the beauty of his barkspots, despite their danger, then wakes the next morning grotesquely heavy with new growths, his breathing further strained and his flesh flushed with fever, his skin throbbing everywhere it remains skin. He coughs until his eyes water, he wipes snot and drool from his broad lips with the back of his hand, leaves yellow mucus hardening blue fur; the wan sun still lies low in the sky as he pulls his legs up into his chest, wrapping his arms around the bony knobs of his knees, a creature who was never a fetus finding the fetal position. As his temperature spikes, he hears voices he can't believe are the remainder's; to beat back these auditory hallucinations, he recites the litany memorized from the map room binders, the names of animals he'll never see, then all the trees the binder says once inhabited the buried world, a world so rich it was home to more than one tree.

Only after his fever recedes do the voices fully abate. How much daylight has C wasted listening to them, sick and suffering while the bubble shakes in the wind? He rises unsteadily to study a gale unfurling across the flatness of the Ice, seeming to blow from beyond the western horizon; as he sets the craft in motion again, its curve pushes back against the turbulent gusts, bobbing and dipping across the Ice's rippling perturbations, slowly jostling up powdery white dunes or skirting dangerous drop-offs. He makes progress in the light that remains, then rests as best he can in the dark. The next morning, he begins again by pruning the nighttime progress of the barkspots, before hurtling over the frozen landscape fast as he dares. If it snows, the lessened sunlight fails to fill the craft's batteries and he loses progress; if the gale reappears from the west, the bubble trembles against it, the battery again draining faster.

With the craft floating above the ground, C often misses minor changes in grade, but now whenever he summons the control console its gauges reveal that the craft has been slowly, subtly descending. Over the next fifty kilometers, he navigates still-rare signs of the buried human landscape, occasional architecture brought to the surface by glacial movement, its deepest layers inexorably lifting their caught material. Kilometers above what the map scroll suggests should be a river valley, the ice becomes studded with half-submerged steel structures, toppled over, blades bent. The relentless wind blows twisters of clodded snow across the wreckage; the sound of metal cracking against metal fills the air as one blade creakingly spins.

Other remnants of the Below begin to appear more frequently, in seams of debris thrust upward, all the previous world pulverized to gravel by pressure and weight and the slow friction of ice age time. Gravel of aluminum siding and steel girders and blacktop, gravel of roofing tiles and mailboxes and security gates. Gravel of countless vehicles, gravel of innumerable computers, gravel of televisions and radios and medical devices. Gravel of petroleum-based carpeting, gravel of throwaway flat-pack furniture. Gravel of marble countertops, of ceramic dishes, of stainless steel appliances. Gravel of fences and roadways, gravel of streetlights and traffic signals. Gravel of plastic chairs and plastic dishes and plastic children's toys. Gravel of libraries of printed books, gravel of record collections, gravel of oil paintings and framed photographs. Gravel of bones, gravel of last humans, of last human children, last children's pets. Gravel of bones too fine to be worth scavenging, too bright white to pick out against the sparkling glitter of the Ice.

Two weeks out from the crawler, this garbage-strewn but still slowly sloping shelf gives way again to more uneven ice, the flatness cut by breakages and crevasses, steep icefalls cascading for hundreds of meters. The sun shines daily, but even when every cloud recedes its energy is often palely diffuse, offering too little radiation to make travel worthwhile. There's no option but to wait for the unseen blockage to disperse, C begging for a trickle of sunlight to recharge the craft. Even when the sun shines, he starts and stops, moving fitfully as the days of travel accumulate. It takes more sunlight to charge the batteries in motion than it does when stopped, and always the waning remainder warns against running the craft's engines when the batteries are dimmest.

If C ruins the batteries, he'll have to abandon the craft. If he abandons the craft, there's no chance of reaching Black Mountain with these barkspots intact, their thorned branchlets surely more susceptible to frost and cold and darkness than furred C is; and then there is O to consider, the only companion he's ever had, because if the craft dies then whatever O is dies too, wedded as he is now to the craft, unable to be separated by any knowledge C possesses. As C mulls his responsibilities, O's song unmutes itself again, the drone setting the barkspot to new burning, C's now ambient fever flaring as a new bud sprouts beneath the one leaf growing from his shoulder, as others break through in other places, the skin surrounding each bud swelling as new leaves break free of the bark.

C watches these leaves flutter in the recirculated air, each reaching toward the wan sunlight, its glare too weak today to thaw the slightest trickle of water from atop frozen ice. He sees how every leaf seems to dance to O's song, and how when he mutes the song the leaves go limp again, crumpling in on themselves—and so what choice does C have but to let the song resume, no matter how much O's drone hurts him to hear?

The bubble spins westward, O sings his song, the barkspots sprout more branchlets and buds as the glacier continues to drop, the Ice sloping toward some plain C cannot quite picture. With his imagination stunted by his vocabulary, he'd initially pictured his entire journey taking place across a landscape as frozen and featureless as the region nearest the crawler, one high flat plane reaching thousands of kilometers to Black Mountain, but surely there are other possibilities hinted at by words the remainder still knows, good words setting C's heart skipping with anticipation: *earth*, he says, he says: *dirt, ground, soil*. There was dust in the crawler, but dust is not dirt. The remainder offers flickering memories of descents Below where some previous C found better evidence of the earth that was— dried clots of dead soil caught in the bark of mummified tree trunks, better than the root ball C-432 died for—but no C ever found any living earth.

To calm himself, C resumes his litany, all that lovely Latinate, all that lovely Greek, languages C cannot name, plus names for this frozen earth itself: should there be no humanity left in Black Mountain, whoever comes next will not call it *earth*, from the Old English *eorthe*, the Dutch *aarde*, the German *erde*. There will be no more English, no more Dutch, no more German. Never again. If one day some next intelligence emerges to name this planet—which will not by that intelligence be called a *planet*—the intelligence will name this ball of scraped rock and frozen water and magma something other than *home*.

Now come days of bad weather, pale mornings of slow battery-draining progress, afternoons of heavy clouds lying low, icy rain streaking the bubble's surface. Visibility dropping, the bubble's clarity obscured, C relies on the craft's sensor arrays to pilot blind. When the bubble runs low on power, he pauses, passes time restlessly stomping his stiffening left leg and its bark around the constrained space of craft. He repeats his litanies, the flora and fauna of Greater Ohio, while every day the tree colonizes more skin, the creeping bark relentlessly increasing its territory despite his trimming its progress. When the barkspot first appeared, it was possible to believe he might still choose to cut it free with a minor surgery. Now that belief is rendered moot: the barkspot has become true wood, making a trunk of his left side, its innumerable thorned branchlets grown into scrawny branches bearing buds and leaves.

The bubble makes its slow way westward, navigating undulating dunes of packed snow, the craft rising and falling over hour-long slopes, dodging crystalline twisters come to shatter against its sides. C trims the wood as much as he can, he plays O's voice at deafening levels, the drone arresting the bark with one song, setting its branchlets and buds to frenzied growth with another. And then one cloud-obscured afternoon the bubble climbs what C believes is only another snow dune, but as the bubble crests the dune an alarm cuts through O's howling drone.

The command console pops into view, its gauges lit up with flashing red warnings. C looks out the glass, then back at the gauges, then out the glass again, his experience insufficient for his imagination to comprehend the improbable sight before him, an unexpected danger that does not disappear no matter how hard he stares: below the bubble's perch atop this drifting dune, there waits a five kilometer sheer plummet into a layer of clouds, a drop C sees no way to safely descend, at least not anywhere near where his path touches the Ice's edge, the end of the only world he thinks he's ever known.

CHAPMAN

The brothers begin their journey east several days out from Licking Valley, several more from Zanesville. An hour after breaking camp, they stop to reapportion their loads, discarding whatever might slow their passage, then better distributing Chapman's weathered possessions and Nathaniel's newer gear between the two of them. Despite his wound, Chapman is as strong as ever, while Nathaniel's heavied, aged body soon wheezes against their haste. In the next days, they'll cross plenty of land not yet carved with roads or separated into plots by split rail fences and rock walls, but everywhere between are pockets of inhabitation newly established since Chapman last saw this country: a dirt-pathed village, stove smoke swirling out of every brick chimney; homesteads bounded by piles of rubble dug from lands soon to be planted fields.

"We have to hurry," he says, reliving again the long night's chase, as recent for him as the wound burning in his chest. "We have to go east by the most direct route, fast as we can."

"Brother," Nathaniel says, squatting to rest beneath tall ferns shading the narrow track, his back stooped beneath his load. "Tell me again what happened. Make me understand this time." Chapman had tried to explain in the lean-to beneath the hillock, but Nathaniel had taken his tale as injured confusion, the aftershocks of the trauma of his makeshift surgery. But if there is some truth to Chapman's tale, then Nathaniel is willing to try again to hear it.

"The sin my pursuers showed me, brother, the crime wasn't mine. Surely not. Surely I'm only myself, not responsible for every past faun." Chapman shakes his head, then nervously whinnies, remembering the flicker-myth he saw in the beheaded singer's accusing song. "I'll tell you everything," he says, "but first we must leave all this behind."

Nathaniel lets it go. "There's a farm a few weeks' travel from here where I planned to work through the winter," he says, then holds up a hand against Chapman's incoming protest. "It's not weeks of *forest*, brother. We'll be out of these woods in another day, two at most, then we can walk the rest of the way on better roads. But you'll be exposed the whole way."

Chapman's never slept beneath any roof, he's never been able to bear to walk a field even during the fallow months of winter, and he suspects his pursuers follow the same rules that govern him: until the singer's song transformed the abandoned homestead, the witches hadn't been able to step forward. He thinks now that if the brothers can reach planted lands, then he might be safe enough there, as long as he's also a man. The discovery is shocking, attractive, tempting, infuriating; as the brothers walk, he experiments, tries to force one body and then the other: claws appear and disappear, his facial features shift and rearrange themselves, the width of his faunish face grows narrower, sharper, more like his brother's. Never have they looked as much alike as they do now, although at first Chapman's skin remains darker than Nathaniel's. He picks up a hoof and puts down a foot, his leg is covered in goosefleshed bare skin one step and thick brown hair the next.

By the time the brothers reach the road to Zanesville, Chapman's glamour must be ready. The next day, he practices holding the shape, a minor act of will keeping his fur hidden inside his skin, his hooves inside his feet; he shivers through the cool evening and the colder night, the bark of his faun skin gone the way of his claws, his horns. In the morning, Nathaniel borrows his brother's cleanest shirt, whose fabric scratches and itches Chapman's torso; without hooves or boots, his feet soon begin to ache, then to bleed, his pace slowing. He complains as Nathaniel passes him on the trail, as the wound on his chest seeps blood, pinkening the makeshift bandages. Despite the pain, he knows this time as a man is almost the boon he'd hoped the Tree would grant him, only not nearly good enough: instead of his body truly becoming human, he feels merely turned inside out, his horns and hooves and claws not gone but only hidden away, his faunness a broken beast whose many wild parts can't help but scratch and claw at him, eager to escape this imprisoning skin of a man.

"Turn back already," Nathaniel says, watching Chapman bleed. It unnerves him to see his brother's human face, his human shape; having gotten used to brothering a monster, he can't yet square his affections with the man the faun contains. Chapman transforms himself again, but instead of a smooth progression of enveloping fur and emerging horns, his true shape returns this time in stuttering bursts, minor flickers: he's a man and then both a man and a faun and then only a faun, a faun relieved by the returned solidity of his barkskin and the surefootedness of his hooves, by the wildness he was born into, the animal he'd for so long fervently wished to shed and forget.

THE STATE THAT WAS THE TERRITORY IS NO LONGER THE LAND Chapman remembers. As Nathaniel promised, they reach the dirt road to Licking Valley in two days' time, after which Chapman forces himself into his human shape—every time the change comes faster, easier—and then waits shivering as Nathaniel flags down wagon riders willing to barter. A passing tinker sells Nathaniel a pair of shoes fitting Chapman well enough, plus two gray shirts, a pair of trousers, a slim supply of dried fruit and hardtack.

"That's all the money I have, brother," apologizes Nathaniel, "but when we get to Zanesville, I'll collect on our nurseries there."

The road into town is wider than any Chapman has previously seen, its ruts deep enough to trap wagon wheels in their tracks, forcing others to detour into the mud. The brothers pass whole acres of clear-cut forest turned into arable farmland, the homesteads closer to the Pennsylvania border devoid of any stumps indicating their fields were ever anything but flat black soil, land perfect for the rich harvests this good year promises.

Nathaniel's expression sours fast, his frustration at the proximity of others obvious. "Once," he says, "we were nearly the only men here. Now look."

Chapman follows the sweep of his brother's hand, sees

only the world his brother told him would come. For the first time in his life, there's a human voice always within earshot, every hour, dawn to dusk. Forests made farmlands, trees made houses and churches and general stores. Rocks dug from the earth and stacked into walls, branches cut into rails separating homesteads into discernible plots and parcels. Cattle and pigs and goats roam open pastures once dense swamplands, every river and stream and creek diverted to irrigate the many new farms. A windmill turns one millstone, another is powered by a waterwheel beside a creek bed; everywhere human ingenuity puts the land to work, everywhere human will makes the land productive. Corn in perfectly painterly rows, roaming sheep attended by herding dogs, an apple or pear orchard beside many of the new homesteads, thirty trees all any farmer needs to make his claim. How many of these apple trees did Nathaniel and Chapman plant? Not all but many. Nathaniel will try to collect as they pass by, but the economics of the squatter planter have not and will not make him rich.

In the evening the brothers make their bare camp along the wagon road, laying out their bedrolls, cooking their meal in a hastily dug firepit. With fences abutting both sides of the road, there's less common space than ever before, with what once belonged to everyone now claimed by only a few. A creek runs nearby, but the easiest access to its trickling water lies within a settler's fence so that Nathaniel must climb the house's stoop to stand with his hat in his hand, begging permission to fill his waterskins. Chapman worries at his brother's barely contained rage, at how what was once his or anyone's is now only this one settler's, at how this man came west already possessing the resources Nathaniel lacked, enough money to buy the right to try his hand at settling any acreage he desired.

"The land belongs to the Ohio Company," Nathaniel reminds Chapman, once returned from the creek, "but the trees?
The trees are ours."

Once a squatter, always a squatter, Chapman thinks. Nathaniel's been planting apple trees in Ohio for decades, but
he's no closer to his own homestead, the kingdom he promised
Chapman he'd own.

Not yet even to Zanesville, already the brothers are tired of
other people, weary of their bland planted lands. Despite summer's end, more and more settlers clog the road, driving more
wagons than Chapman can count, their progress slowed only
by the road's inability to fit so many wheels and hooves and
boots. Every road turns to deep rutted mud, causing more stoppages, then more detours to be made around the stoppages, the
industrious would-be settlers hacking back saplings and young
brush before resuming their passage.

Nathaniel needs no such assistance, scowls at those who
do. "It's not necessary to destroy the world," Nathaniel says,
speaking to no one, loud enough so anyone might hear, "just to
make your way through it." He repeats himself until Chapman
absently agrees, all his attention trained on his glamour, every
distraction increasing the difficulty of his task.

Another day wanes. Chapman has no choice except to bed
down in his human shape, with his bedroll beside Nathaniel's,
their blankets laid out under the stars, their camp ringed by the
tents and wagons of other travelers, too many settlers gathered
around too many fires for the crowded stretches of free land.
Some make their beds in the middle of the road, planning to be
awake by dawn, hoping no one coming west decides to travel
by the light of the full moon. They could be killed in their sleep
by trampling hooves or rolling wheels, but probably they'll be

kept safe by the light of campfires up and down the road, fires
burning low in the wee hours, leaving smoke hanging over the
valley, tonight's wind insufficient to push it over the hills. Gas
lamps gutter, bored men walk the camp sharing whiskey until
they're fighting in the dirt, and amid all this nocturnal activity
there's Nathaniel, too furious to sleep, and there's Chapman,
not sleeping either, too afraid he might dream of hooves and
horns until he sprouts them both.

After Nathaniel's frustrations finally turn to angry dreams,
after all the other settlers have fallen beneath the spells of darkness and tale and cider and whiskey, restless Chapman leaves
camp to explore the nearby homesteads, his human chest aching where the bullet clattered against his ribs. Beside one cabin
he finds a homely arrangement of trees, inexpertly transplanted
but likely some of theirs, each tree unique, not grafted from
some already established stock. It's possible someone might
see him, but inside the orchard he relaxes his glamour, allows
his anxious attention its rest. He hoofs slowly among the trees,
scratching absently at his itching wound as he studies the character of every apple, the hope he wishes to suss out from its
shape.

His Tree of Forgetting, if he ever finds it—will it be more
beautiful than other trees, will it be taller or stouter, will its
crown loom above its brothers and sisters? Chapman knows
not everything good is beautiful, despite the dumbly persistent
superstitions of simple men. Perhaps the fruit he wants will be
horrid to see, or else unassuming, dull to the eyes and duller to
taste. Whatever its shape, however warped or rotted, he chooses
to continue to believe it will work the magic he desires, will
set him free. From the death of his mother. From taking from
Nathaniel the life he would have had. From the crime he saw

in the song, attached to his shape if not his person. More than anything, he wants to be freed from this shape itself, sometimes hated, sometimes beloved, always defining him and constraining him, these contradictions unchanged by the false, impermanent trick he brought back from the flicker, the sleight by which he hides himself inside himself.

He wanders the orchard, putting his rough hands to the trees' gnarled trunks, running his fingers down their varied barks, each tree its own being, half wild despite being planted only to satisfy human wants. He picks an apple, bites into its flesh with his sharp teeth. He lets its juices run from his broad lips, into the bramble of his beard. *Only an apple*, he curses unfairly, as if the apple need be anything else. He picks one from each tree, he takes one bite of each before tossing the rejects to the ground. The stories these apples tell Chapman are of simple things, the simplest things always the greatest: weeks of sunshine, much-needed rain, good soil tugged by good roots, the hasty visits of pollinators, the way the wind whistles through the boughs, rustling changing leaves and shaking ripe apples from softening stems.

More than enough for apple trees, but far from what Chapman wants.

Only later does he think he should have gathered some apples for Nathaniel, who might've enjoyed these literal fruits of their labors.

Perhaps, perhaps not.

Nathaniel, Chapman soon realizes, is unbelievably sick of apples.

CHAPMAN WALKS DAILY NOW AMONG MEN, A MAN HIMSELF. HE hears all around him their loud voices, conversations, jokes, frustrations, buying and selling, bartering and bragging. New neighbors talk across the bounds of new fences, while cows low, goats bleat, pigs grunt. Children chase each other along packed dirt lanes, laughing shrilly in the moments before they are caught: How are there already children here, in this place where last Chapman came there was nothing but filthy white-faced men? As he travels east all the noises he hears are of the same sort, their slim variations repeating daily, hourly. The apple trees transplanted behind neat raw-board homes, the wheat and the corn, the sows and the steers—all of them are only human desires brought to life, everywhere made plentiful. Among this living want he feels a fear never felt before, not even near the Pennsylvania villages where the brothers wintered for so many years. Here, where his apple trees dot every plot he sees, there's no denying his responsibility. He once promised that all the world might look like this before he was finished, all the world turned over and plowed under and tamed, made every inch safe and the same. He and others like him will want and want and want until there is nothing left; every man Chapman meets carries within his skin his own creature of endless appetite, forever widening its greedy gnashing mouth.

The brothers tarry only enough for Nathaniel to try in vain to extract some few pennies from each homestead graced with seed-grown apple trees, likely transplanted from one of Nathaniel's nurseries. But Nathaniel's claims are impossible to prove, and the supposedly good Christian men of the State rarely pay debts they cannot believe they owe. Again Nathaniel stands before a roughly set door making his ask, time and time again he is denied or sent away with a fraction of what his trees and labor are worth. "God has made us a gift of these trees," one well-scrubbed settler piously tells Nathaniel, and by the time the brothers leave the valley by the old roads along the river—not the fastest way east, but the quickest escape from this sudden civilization—Nathaniel's face is crimson with fury, he's cursing and muttering, kicking at blameless rocks and complaining loudly enough to flush every nearby bird from cover.

Chapman commiserates, comforts, cajoles. For now he wants Nathaniel to stay the course, to keep returning to the frontier as long as he's physically able, to plant as many trees as they can each season. But where the trees fruit—whether along a riverbank or in the yard of some settler's farm—Chapman doesn't care. Either way he'll test his teeth against the skin of their apples, either way he swears he'll eventually earn the Tree he's again determined to seek, a Tree whose fruit he decides now might ease Nathaniel's anger too.

Many miles east of the Zanesville bounds—once he can hear no voice but Nathaniel's—Chapman relaxes, reclaiming his first shape, but as soon as he's a faun again he fears he spies evidence of the witching women's presence. He lopes cautiously through stretches of forest transformed by fire and rain and human hands, he smells seeping water falling slowly through untouched trees, he discovers clearings previously unseen, and wherever some wild spot remains he finds hidden signs: in certain copses wait the scorched marks of bonfires, surrounded by the scuff marks of unshod feet ecstatic in their dancing; he spies twine-bound branches weaved into sigils hung high in the trees; wind chimes made of bones tinkle over the faint tracks of a forest cat, muddy signs leading to denser, uncut groves where Chapman thinks a black panther's rubbed itself raw against the sides of trees, ground sprayed with pungent yellow piss, the markings of a beast in heat, mad with an unseasonable lust.

Chapman makes himself a man again, then hurries back to Nathaniel's side, urging his tired brother onward, translating his fear into urgency. "How far is it," he asks, "how far to the place where we'll stay the winter?"

Nathaniel stops, considers. "Two days until we reach Splitlip Creek," he says, then claps his brother across his broad shoulder. "Don't worry, Chapman. A sweet family lives there, the Worths, who gave me shelter in return for work on their farm, in return for the trees we planted the year you went missing. In two days' time, we can rest against those trunks and talk again of better days."

As they walk, Nathaniel fondly describes every detail of the Worth homestead, its fine and humble house, its well-built barn, its ever-expanding fields and pens, until a new idea lights his face.

"Splitlip Creek isn't so civilized," he says hopefully. "There are plenty of woods nearby, if you'd prefer to sleep outdoors. But perhaps now you could sleep beside me, amid the heat and the light and the good company."

"Yes, brother," says Chapman, nodding his hornless head, still unaccustomed to its lighter weight. "For you, I'll try."

A rare grin cracks across Nathaniel's face; Chapman smiles back, his expression a queasier version of his brother's open joy. An entire winter indoors, dressed in the skin and clothes of a man? His feet encased in uncomfortable shoes? It's impossible to fathom.

But the wilderness has become dangerous to Chapman as never before; now like any other man he must hide in buildings of wood and brick and stone. Better to say nothing more of his fears, better to let Nathaniel think he remains a man out of brotherly affection. Let Nathaniel make-believe they could become a normal family, that they too might one day inhabit a house like the one toward which they're headed, where they might be farmers, landowners, bachelor kings.

Surely a lie can last a winter. Surely by spring Chapman will know what he needs to do.

JOHN

Eury leads John and Ghost down a staircase hidden behind her office's false wall, into a tall vaulted room, a private museum housing rows of ventilated cubes of blast-proof glass, each set on a marble plinth. Beneath columns of late light falling through the high angular windows, Eury narrates the living displays: a Galápagos tortoise born over a century ago, its shell broken decades ago then inexpertly glued, its movements slow and deliberate, as if it's trying to remain unnoticed by time. An eighty-year-old alligator, crawling through a mucky manufactured pond. A blue-and-yellow macaw, its feathers undimmed but its beak slowly softening; Eury says her handlers have to feed it by a dropper bottle. The bird, one hundred and seventeen years old, alive in a world where a wild macaw hasn't been born in decades. They pass a pair of peak-backed tuataras, the male a century old, the female in her eighties, the two uselessly mating, the once supple leather shells of their eggs coming out hardened, the insides still. Last, last, last, Eury explains, each of these is the last of its kind. Finally: an Andean condor far from its native mountains, one huge wing injured, the other clipped, its talons scarring its perch, its hooked mouth gasping from a head bald and terrible, ringed by a high collar of white feathers.

After all these aged creatures come exhibits containing the taxidermied remains of other lasts Eury's people couldn't keep alive, rows of specimens made a diorama of the end of the world, each animal arranged on its own plinth: the last American panther, its coat glowing in the soft light; the last coyote and fox and bobcat, each gifted the same shining glare. The last grizzly bear, dead in its forties; the oldest rhino, preserved at forty-five; a wild horse who improbably made it to sixty. John's heart pounds at the majesty of a posed elephant whose plaque declares it lived to be eighty-six years old, its last twenty years spent alone, Eury says, after its mate died, after its children died, after every last wild elephant in the world died. The terrible cruelty of an elephant, a creature so capable of grief, living past the rest of its kind.

Beside the elephant stands a taxidermied she-wolf, fangs bared, glass eyes glaring. John wonders: Is this Ghost's original, beneath whose preserved corpse the living Ghost rests, cleaning herself, tongue rasping over one forepaw and then the other? Maybe, maybe not. It's impossible for John to compare the vitality radiating off Ghost with the preserved, taxidermied other, its staring glass eyes and posed snarl.

His anger mounts: last, last, last. "Why are you showing me this?" he asks. "Why would you ever think I wanted to see this?" He stares at Eury, furious at her tall, slim frame, her black hair swept back, her green eyes dancing, her usual outfit, accented now by a black-and-white cloak she'd retrieved from her office, its sharp angles flaring at her hips, its reflective fabric blazing when Eury walks. *What kind of monster are you?* he doesn't say. *What kind of monster would acquire the last Galápagos tortoise, the last macaw, the last everything, and then keep them for herself?*

"You think I'm showing you the end of the world," Eury says. "But this is the beginning of the next one." She returns to the condor, gesturing at the bird's ancient face. "She was doomed in the world. Fifty years ago, she was doomed and no one did anything. But we're going to make a world where condors can live again. Maybe not today, maybe not tomorrow. Maybe I'll be there, maybe you. Either way, a condor exactly like this one will be, because we'll have sequenced its genome, blueprinted its body, copied its mind. The last shall be first, John. She'll live again, her species starting over from a specimen exactly like her. With the appropriate modifications, of course, to make sure she can survive in the environment where we release her." Eury unfolds her hand against the condor's glass cage. "John, in the new world, I will make you another condor."

"It won't be a real condor, Eury. It'll be just another thing you own."

Eury doesn't turn from the condor, but John can see her judging his reflection, his expression mirrored by the cage's surface. "You're disappointing me. I thought you wanted to save these creatures."

"Yes. Not create pale imitations, more bad fakes."

Now Eury pushes away from the cage, frustratedly tapping the glass to capture the condor's violent attention one last time. "What are your nanobees but useful fakeries? If we didn't have them to pollinate the supertrees, the trees wouldn't fruit. Your fakeries are keeping people alive." She gestures at the room, all the dead and dying lasts, her expression going placid as she turns. "You're not convinced. Let me show you what else we've done since you left. After all, Pinatubo is only phase one. Orpheus is phase two, and it's the key to everything."

"THE MYTH OF ORPHEUS AND EURYDICE," EURY EXPLAINS, LEADING John deeper into the maze of glass cages and taxidermied mammals. "The two young lovers marry, but on the night of their wedding, Eurydice is killed. A snakebite, according to most of the stories, from a venomous viper, accidentally stepped on while she danced, although in other tellings her foot finds the viper while she's fleeing a lecherous shepherd. In some of those versions this would-be rapist is a beekeeper. The inventor of beekeeping, in fact. Didn't you invent some bees, John?"

John starts to object—to which accusation, exactly?—but Eury stops him. "A joke, John. Stop looking guilty. Eurydice dies; it doesn't really matter how. Grief-stricken Orpheus wanders ancient Greece singing the most terrible dirge, begging the gods' favor until they consent to let him enter the underworld. He descends into hell, where the gods make him another deal: they'll allow Eurydice to follow Orpheus back into life, if only he can make it out of the underworld without looking back."

Keep your eyes on the future, Eury says: that's the story's moral. "You remember what happens next: Orpheus flinches, looks back from the threshold of his victory. Doomed Eurydice returns to the underworld, dead forever. Orpheus goes insane all over again, his grief song driving the gods mad, until finally they have no choice but to have him ripped limb from limb. In some versions, a pack of wild dogs kills Orpheus. In others, it's a mob of women, witches drunk on wild powers." She smirks. "I'll bet you can guess which version I like best."

"Eury, what does this have to do with anything?"

She kneels to scratch Ghost's ears, waiting until the wolf pulls away before continuing. "Maybe nothing. But there's more to Orpheus than this myth. What do you know about the transmigration of souls?"

John's never been interested in religion, doesn't believe in past lives or ghosts. He shrugs. "Reincarnation? Something like that?"

"Close enough. The ancient Orphic mystery cults believed the soul was a prisoner of the flesh, aspiring to freedom. But after death, the freed soul couldn't bear to be parted from the earth, so it inevitably began life again in a new body." Eury stands, clicks her tongue at Ghost to follow; she clicks her tongue, John supposes, at him too. She's already explained that below the needle is the Tower's research layer, a labyrinth of glass-walled labs, some filled with rows of planters for germinating seeds, each containing a slightly different genetic variant of corn, soybean, or wheat, apple tree or pear tree; labs where the Farm's livestock are being continually refined one gene at a time, banks of centrifuges spinning up blood and cultures for analysis. The work has advanced in the years he's been away, but it's all the same kind of research he left behind. What Eury's talking about now is something else.

Despite inventing the nanobees, he isn't an expert in other kinds of biomimicry, artificial intelligence, genetic modification, three-dimensional printing. The bees were cunning enough, sharing intelligence and communication across swarms, capable of lifting the microloads necessary to spread pollen, but their programs are relatively simple, the results nothing like the habits of real bees. The nanobees mimic only what's needed by humans: when the last colonies collapsed, John's nanoswarms saved the fields and orchards real bees had once pollinated, saved them well enough it was possible to forget the bees were gone.

How difficult it is to notice the presence of an absence, the sound of no bees buzzing.

How quickly you adjust to whatever diminishments the world allows.

Eury shows John to the far end of the atrium, where a table displaying a series of perfectly square patches of gray fur waits. He looks to Eury for permission, then runs a finger along the edge of one of the squares, seeking the line where the fur meets the skin, where the skin meets the air; the edge is too regular, too smooth, missing any sign of a blade where the animal was skinned, the fur squared. He lays two furs side by side, then runs his hands through the hair, across the skin. Each must be exactly identical to Ghost's fur, to the fur of the Yellowstone wolf that was Ghost but not Ghost, maybe the fur of the dead wolf taxidermied in Eury's zoo of lasts.

Eury doesn't object when he opens a specimen cabinet beneath the table to discover other parts reproduced in bulk: a deep drawer full of jars, two dozen pairs of green eyes floating in formaldehyde; another drawer of tongues, rough muscles drowned in yellow liquid; then one of forepaws, of rear paws, of tails, all never having been attached to any animal; and in the bottom-most drawer wait six glass jars with six floating brains, each exactly the same size and weight.

A pack of wolves, Eury jests, printed in parts, never assembled.

"Your nanobees," she says, "are incredibly impressive, but

they're not *bees*, are they? You've been obsessed with what is real, what is pristine, untouched. I don't feel the same way, only because I don't believe anything is pristine anymore, if pristine means unchanged by humans. Pinatubo will give us time to make a sustainable future, to ensure human resilience. But it won't be fast enough for the large mammals, for the raptors or the big reptiles or so many other creatures, mostly already gone. Nearly everything else might go too." She sighs. "I know that's hubris, that I'm seeing the world from a human perspective. Not *everything*, then—there'll always be something alive somewhere—but even if we save humanity, what remains won't be the world we remember."

John closes the drawers, then returns to the tabletop squares of fur, digs his fingers deep into the soft gray hair. "If the world is only humanity," he says, "is it even worth saving?"

"That's exactly the question, John."

He looks up from the fur square he's holding to find Eury's triumphant expression waiting for him.

"Exactly it. But it'll still have to be humanity who gets saved first. The iguanas aren't going to fix the planet. If the chimps and the gorillas weren't already gone—and if they'd had another billion years to evolve—maybe they could have. Maybe somewhere deep in the ocean there's a super-octopus capable of abstract thought. But the only way to sell the future to the human world is to sell a human future. Once that's secure, then we put everything else back. That's why we invented Orpheus."

"In your story," John says, his eyes lowered to the square of fur in his hands, "you're the Eurydice who stays up on the surface, alive in the light, while it's every other creature who descends into hell. Then, once you're ready, you'll lead them all back out again, by some miracle of science you've dreamed up."

"Yes, John, exactly," Eury says, excited now. "Most people are already living in the underworld, in the dry lands, from which there is no escape without our help. We can walk out together, but only through an act of bravery and will. If we look back too soon, if we flinch or linger on what's behind us, then we lose everything. John, whatever happens, I do not plan to look back. Not now, not ever. I will bring humanity out of the dark. Later, once I've made the world right for us, I'll save everything else too." She picks up a jar holding a pair of wolf's eyes, shakes it teasingly in front of his gaze. "You know how I saw you in Yellowstone," she says. "That wolf wasn't Ghost, but close enough. A slightly different personality, a slightly different purpose embedded in the same body. Ghost's sister, perhaps."

He still doesn't understand, not exactly, but he's also no longer sure he wants to. Already he tires of Eury's self-aggrandizing explanations, her righteous justifications that have always made him feel small, unambitious. Which isn't to say he's not also attracted to her unending confidence, her enormous will. Unable to stop himself, he asks, "Ghost is some kind of organic robot? A cyborg?"

Eury laughs. "No, John. She's a wolf. And the wolf is an incredible creature. The first wolves evolved four million years ago, and they've been exactly like the one we made Ghost from for three hundred thousand years. All their incredible history, all that survival—all we did to them was make sure some might survive, not now but later. In the meantime, yes, we did modify a few for our own uses. They're sterile, of course, with trackers and other tech embedded, so they don't escape to breed or otherwise contaminate the remaining biosphere. Wolves like Ghost are only for this world, the one that's ending. Later they will just be wolves again, as unmodified as we can make them, freed of our wants and our uses."

Again John's curiosity overwhelms his reluctance. "Where are you storing the samples?" he asks. "Are they all here in Ohio?" Somewhere in the Tower, there must be a genetic library, DNA sequences, biological blueprints: instructions for how to populate a world. Whatever Eury first desired, whatever the Tower was originally designed to be, it has become an ark. An ark capable of destroying the world. An ark capable of saving it. Pinatubo and Ararat both.

Eury says, "We've designated gene repositories at various Earthtrust sites, here and abroad. We're keeping DNA samples in cryofreeze, as well as digital copies of each scanned creature, in case the samples are lost. The costs in both space and processing power are immense, but Earthtrust brings in immense revenue." She gestures around at the atrium, the Tower, the Farm beyond. "We are, after all, running most of a country here, and we're absolutely integral to the success of many others. Earthtrust VACs prop up governments all over the world now, and at each of our VACs we've constructed a version of this facility, with the same capacity to house endangered specimens, sequence their genomes, and prepare them for reintroduction once conditions improve. Each is also part of Pinatubo, one of the many injection sites necessary to quickly achieve reliable stratospheric coverage."

"And all those other nations signed on to this?" If so, Eury's grown even more cunning than he's imagined. She'd tried before, in the earliest days of Earthtrust, without success.

"No, no one has agreed," Eury says. "Not even the United States. Truthfully, the time to act was fifty years ago. Now more radical measures are necessary. While Pinatubo cools the globe, we'll deacidify the oceans, replant the forests, renew the soil. And when the work is done, we'll put back the plants and animals. Although that part isn't public, likely won't be for years." She mockingly throws up her hands. "The public still panics when someone clones a lab rat. How do you think they'll react when they find out I'm ready to print an entire biosphere?"

"But you're not ready to do that." He's sure of it. He's sure he wants to be sure. "Because it's impossible."

"Because there are complications. That's what Pinatubo is for: to slow down the crisis while we work. If we have another fifty years, another hundred, it'll be enough." Eury Mirov has never lacked for ambition. Never once has she flinched away from the biggest ideas, the boldest claims.

"Plus," John says, "if your plan doesn't work, you and a few friends can always move to Mars."

Eury laughs. "The spaceport! Yes, possibly. Who knows? We're building it. The scale of space travel we envision is incredibly expensive, incredibly difficult, and it will only become more so without a stable situation here to support and supply the effort. So yes, we have been working on terraforming technology, but we don't have to go to Mars to give it a try."

Her confidence! John has never once felt so sure of anything. Maybe Eury's telling the truth, maybe everything she promises will soon be possible. He doesn't know anymore, can't think straight: even after years away, her charisma is as intoxicating as ever, her quicker intellect just as capable of overpowering his slow and careful reasoning.

She says, "John, after Pinatubo, we'll terraform the earth back to what it was. Or else we'll make it better."

Eury moves to John's side again, this time to take the fur

square from him, an object he didn't even realize he was still clenching. Eury lays it down on the table, flipping it over to flatten it with a palm before returning it to its place: the back is too smooth, eerily lacking the connective tissues of real skin, but Eury doesn't seem to notice, or if she notices she doesn't care.

"Come on," she says, walking back toward the penthouse stairs, Ghost already following at her heels. "Let me show you how Orpheus works."

C-433

Cspends one restless night atop the glacier's sheer western wall, dreaming fitfully of abandoning the bubble to descend the cliffside hand over hoof, hacking holds into the Ice. Thanks to the remainder, weeks-old C already knows how to skillfully wield the ice axe, how to avoid the breakable crust of snow bridges covering crevasses, how to guard against shattering a seemingly solid wall. But despite all that knowledge, nearly every previous C died because of some presumably preventable mistake. And none of them also had to protect the barkspot, its branchlets, all the leafy emergent tree C's sworn to deliver to whoever guards Black Mountain.

In C's last dream before waking, he leaves the bubble behind, dooming the barkspots to wither and freeze and die; when he wakes up, sprawled and sore on the bubble's floor, he stands to begin searching for routes the craft might be able to navigate, finding the tree's burden even heavier than the day before. Shortly after dawn, he steers toward one possible route, manipulating the haptic controls carefully to guide the craft down a narrow chute dropping precipitously toward a landing spied from the level above. Next comes a series of ridges he wouldn't trust to hold his weight but that he hopes provides enough surface for the craft's repulsors to grip, the bubble bouncing above the unsteady ground. It takes an hour to plot a path to a broader shelf, a creaking expanse where he parks to study the route forward, a narrow way broken across the cracking surface of the Ice, which here splits into other chutes and moraines, boulder-strewn ravines leading down into ice caves, passages plummeting into crevasses, other topographical features C can't summon the language to describe.

On a slim switchbacking slope at the glacier's edge, a sudden gust of wind slams the craft against the inside wall of ice, the bubble's gyroscopic floor responding quickly but not fast enough to keep C on his hooves. Instinctually, he grabs at the command console, a confusion of haptics and actual substance; he falls through it to hit the curved wall with the bark side of his body, sounding a loud cracking noise he hopes isn't the bubble's glass. Fallen leaves strew amid broken bits of branches; his good hand roams his stiffening tree side, uselessly pressing fallen patches of bark back into place. O's song rises in alarm as the wind batters the bubble, the angry drone filling the air until C barks the command for *mute* more times than is strictly necessary.

The bubble quiets until the only sounds are the gusts rocking the exposed craft and C's wheezing breath. Sap leaks from the bark half of his face, his left horn aches at its root. It's dangerous to proceed but there's no other choice: even if he wanted to reverse course, the slope he's descended is angled too steeply for the bubble to climb back up.

C dismisses the command console, its pretense of solidity and control. He plants his hooves at the center of the bubble, pulls a deep breath into his battered chest, the lung on the bark side filling painfully slowly. The connection between C's rung and the craft's computer is invisibly wireless, but he imagines it as a silver tether tendriled between himself and the bubble, this globe in which he's spent the majority of this short life. *Take hold*, he tells himself, and then he tries, reaching out with his mind, wrapping a thought tight around the tether, and as he does so he feels the connection suddenly strengthen, the bubble's controls becoming more responsive to his urgings than ever before.

C's flesh is bruised and his bark is breaking, but he and his tree aren't finished yet. The bubble shudders forward again. He adjusts his mind's grip as fresh gusts thrash the craft against the ice wall, each impact threatening to bounce the bubble off its ledge. The slope is broken up by flatter shelves but the shelves are broken too, even the widest full of unsteady icefalls, spiked fields of blue and gray ice. The edges of the icefalls force the bubble's repulsors to shake and the craft to wobble; the gyroscopic floor holds C as steady as it can but not steady enough. He stumbles, he rises, he despairs; visibility diminishes as the craft makes its way lower, the bubble dropping through a thick layer of cloud until C sees nothing, not with his open good eye, not with his bad one, stuck shut. He closes both eyes to rely on the bubble's sensors instead, letting them feed data directly to his rung. The craft has short-range ice-penetrating radar and other arrays, their inputs synthesizable into a geometric model he thinks he can move through.

Fast-forming ice crackles across the bubble's surface, the moisture of the cloud layer fogging the inside of its walls. C is terrified but knows he must not delay. He proceeds in fits and starts, trying to navigate the model the rung feeds him. The glacier creaks and whines, the craft hammers the wall with each new gust of wind. He listens to his heartbeat, he tracks the blood pulsing in his temples, he hears sap moving inside the bark overlaying his left ear.

C hears all this, but what he doesn't hear is O's voice.

He unmutes the song, flinching as it fills the bubble at an earsplitting, skin-crawling volume, O's drone painfully repeating until C feels like a hammer is being rubbed against the contours of his skull.

O, he says, speaking not aloud but from somewhere inside the rung. *I need your help.*

What C needs is to pilot the craft down the glacial wall, through the layer of clouds, to the *earth* below, to whatever *earth* turns out to be—and whatever O is tries, whatever O is sings a new song meant to help, a song of passage, a song of escape, a song of *flickering:* the bubble falls; C falls inside it; the barkspot that's long since become anything but a spot falls with him. As the bubble descends the glacier, C feels himself giving up control, giving in. The invisible tether between him and the bubble's computer is still there, still thrumming with activity, but it's no longer his conscious mind that guides the bubble's movements along the narrow ice ledges, through the clouds frosting and freezing the bubble's glass.

After a time, C realizes, it's not O who helps him steer the bubble but somehow *the tree,* the tree that is or isn't still him is rooted now to the craft's computer, rooted through C by the tether he imagined. In the next moment the bubble breaks

through the cloud layer, zooming frictionless and fast, leaving
the icefalls for a rocky slope of gravel and frozen boulders and
trickling water, the first truly flowing water C has ever seen, a
sight he barely has time to register. The tree and the craft seek
the safest way down in fits and starts; the bubble's shell spins
and spins, but this time the gyroscope keeps C on his feet. After
hundreds of cycles lived atop the near flatness of the Ice, he enters a world of sudden altitude, of horrendous sucking gravity.
The world below is an impossibility approaching at ever greater
speed, rushing up to meet him, until, heart thudding, he feels
the craft spin to a stop at the bottom of the glacial wall, the
worst of the descent completed without any input from him.

C moves to the front of the bubble, puts his claws against
the glass. With his breath steaming the curve, he stares at so
much he cannot name, much of it unexpected, unprecedented,
unbuttressed by anything in the remainder's experience. For a
moment the landscape shimmers, blurs, then he begins to see,
to make sense: this is another world obscured by snow, visibility impeded by new flakes falling nearly sideways in the high
winds, but unlike every other world C thinks he's known, this
one is not entirely frozen over.

For what he thinks is the first time in his life, in all the com-
bined lives that constitute the remainder he carries, C looks
upon the bare surface of the earth, exposed ground open to
the air. So much of it monochrome, so much of it rock reduced
to gravel along with everything else pulverized by the passing
of the glacier, made broken stone dotted with black ice, covered by drifts of dirty gray snow. By the last light of today's sun
he spies his next destination looming on the horizon, a vision
of something he believes he's previously seen only in the fragments of the Below, twisted and shattered and ground down

beneath the Ice. Like with the exposed earth, he cannot at first make sense of what he sees, but as he stares the word to name it rises up in him, naming the sight into solidity: what he sees is a *city*, shimmering in the far distance, no mirage or illusion but a city real enough, abandoned but not buried, a ruin reachable by following a cracked and shattered black expanse C will any moment now remember to name *road*.

CHAPMAN

The Worth homestead at Splitlip Creek is a simple clapboard cabin, a few plain rooms organized around a stone chimney, a house not unlike the one where Chapman and Nathaniel were born, a home only Nathaniel remembers. A narrow stream bounds the back of the Worths' claim, the land a combination of natural meadow and clear-cut forest, the latter dotted with unpulled stumps. Behind the house, on the other side of a pen with three goats and a crooked chicken coop, wait thirty mature trees, grown right where Chapman remembers planting them, their ungathered fruit now heavy on the stem. It's all Chapman can do not to rush to taste their apples. Instead he concentrates on his shape, tries to keep his faunness tucked within, his hooves vanished inside feet encased in too-stiff shoes, his injury hidden beneath a linen not well enough woven to stop him scratching at his skin.

Nathaniel, worrying at the strain on Chapman's face, touches his brother's hand softly. "No one will suspect," he says. "The Worths will gladly open their home to you, the brother I thought I'd lost forever. The second winter without you, I went east to look for our father, our sisters. But our father is dead, our sisters married and dispersed, the town transformed. So many people crowded along cobblestone avenues, row houses where our farm used to be." He pauses, his mustache trembling. "I despaired at how impoverished I was, how there was no one anywhere who knew me. But when I came back across Ohio I discovered the Worths working this land we'd planted."

This was how the family had paid Nathaniel for the trees he planted: not with dollars but with a warm room where he might wait out his winter days. "You did well, brother," Chapman says, putting an arm around Nathaniel's stooped shoulders, their physical affection easier now that their shapes are aligned.

Nathaniel beams, then waves Chapman onward toward the cozily lit house. "Come and meet my friends, dear brother, and let them be your friends too."

THE WORTHS ARE JASPER, HALE AND CLEAN-SHAVEN, TEN YEARS younger than Nathaniel, dressed in a felt-brimmed hat and wash-grayed shirt and trousers; his talented wife, Grace, her dark hair braided in tight plaits, her skin freckled everywhere it escapes her long-sleeved dress; their clever daughter, Eliza, two years old, black haired and pale, sick with a cough the day the brothers arrive, secure in Grace's arms when Jasper opens the door.

"Come in, Nathaniel, come in," Jasper Worth says, hurrying the brothers into the house's main room, a cozy square of wood made of boards and logs Jasper cut, furnished with furniture he made himself, warmed by a potbelly stove radiating heat from the kitchen. "Bring your friend with you," Jasper says—and for the first time in their lives, Nathaniel has to introduce Chapman to someone else.

"This is my brother," Nathaniel explains, his voice cracking, his smile loosening the dirt lining his wrinkles. "This is the lost brother I was telling you about."

"The prodigal returns," Jasper exclaims. "Come in, come in, brothers, and let us celebrate your safe arrival."

Jasper and Nathaniel take their accustomed seats at the table, while Grace proudly shows her new guest the household she and her husband have made, baby Eliza carried along on her hip. She narrates the making of their household, showing curious Chapman the artifacts of her clever industry, of her husband's tireless endeavors: a rough-edged table hewed while Jasper learned his woodcraft, covered by a linen tablecloth she sewed last winter, made of finer fiber and with better skill than the one it replaced; the matching chairs are likewise draped with quilts Grace knitted, there being no stitch of fabric here she didn't sew herself. Elsewhere there's a larder stocked with salted meat her husband butchered, sacks of flour milled from their slim stand of wheat, jars of preserved beets, a cask of cider fermented from their trees.

"Nathaniel planted the apples," Grace says, smiling. "We're so thankful for his having preceded us here, for having prepared for us this place."

"I was here too," Chapman stammers, unable to keep from claiming his share of the credit. "Ten years ago my brother and I planted this land together." He remembers the sparkling creek

bed, the hot spring sun, the first nursery planted his last season, before the ditchdiggers and the long night. This land was
a place of promise then; through Grace's eyes, he sees it still is.

"I'm sorry," Grace says, frowning. "I didn't know."

"How could you? Nathaniel and I have been apart for many
years," Chapman says, although he can't feel that gap, which for
him passed in an instant, an instant in which his last nursery of
hoped-upon seeds somehow sprouted this thriving household.

Grace's expression smooths as she bounces Eliza on her hip,
the child no longer crying, now just as curious about Chapman
as he is about her. "We're glad you've found each other again,"
Grace says. "Nathaniel spoke of you often, in the months he
spent with us each year."

And what did Nathaniel say? Chapman wonders. What
could he possibly have said? Grace tells him of the humid summer she and Jasper struggled to stack the stone to make their
chimney, her husband young and inexperienced and not as
strong as he is now, her body then slim as a sapling, almost
still a girl's, years before giving birth to Eliza. The house grew in
size every year, Grace says: at first they had only one room, built
around the chimney, in which they ate and worked and slept;
then the next year they raised another for their own bedroom,
so their work and their rest might be parted; and then they built
a room for the child they wanted. One season they dug the root
cellar, another they built a crib, a child-sized bed, a child-sized
chair; and always the land was in need of improvement, Jasper
with ditches to dig, plow-breaking stumps and rocks to remove,
the planting of new crops in new fields requiring new fences,
everything needing more time and attention, the way a farm
demands a family give its life to make the land prosper.

"It's taken us our entire marriage to make this land the home it is," Grace says, "and there's always more to do. We're lucky Nathaniel's been such a help to my husband."

Chapman considers his brother, conferring with Jasper at the kitchen table, the two men leaned in, laughing over tin cups of coffee, close as brothers—Chapman feels again the jealousy he felt on the day Nathaniel left him for the ditchdiggers. How he worries his brother will forever be searching for someone else, someone better, someone more *human*. Even now, when Chapman's hidden his faunness away, his brother craves the company of others.

Grace shuffles Eliza arm to arm, the sick toddler whining as she's jostled. "You've listened enough, Chapman. Go sit with the others."

Chapman flushes. "I'm sorry, Mrs. Worth," he says. "I didn't intend any rudeness."

"After the snow falls, we'll have whole months to fill with nothing but talk," she says, soothing Chapman's worries with an easy smile. "Go be with your brother and my husband. When you tire of their company, I'll still be here."

Grace gives Chapman a light push—and how this touch lingers, when no one but Nathaniel has ever touched him—turning him toward the kitchen table, the free seat pulled back in welcome, the third tin cup he hadn't noticed. She carries sickly Eliza toward the bedrooms, the girl watching Chapman from her mother's shoulder. Her expression is serious, seeking despite her sickness, or else because of it: in her fever gaze Chapman worries Eliza might see what others do not, guessing at the beast hidden within the skin. But then she's vanished into her bedroom and Chapman is neither outcast nor mon-

ster, only one more man sitting down at a table of friends, unremarkable in every way.

THE BROTHERS MOVE THEIR FEW POSSESSIONS INTO THE WORTH
household, the Worths grateful to have Nathaniel's help earlier than usual, to have Chapman there too throughout the
busy weeks of the harvest and of preparing for the winter to
come. Nathaniel and Chapman labor dawn to dusk beside Jasper, bringing in the crops, patching leaky joins between the
house's boards, pulling stubborn stumps from ground Jasper
wants to plow the next year. The work isn't harder than anything Nathaniel and Chapman did in the Territory, only more
determined by the rhythms of the household, by the morning
and evening meals, by Jasper's insistence on reading scriptures
aloud after the night's meal and after Eliza has been put to bed,
while the four adults sip last year's cider from Grace's delicate
ceramic cups.

Jasper reads, Jasper interprets, Jasper shows Chapman the
words of the man whose ideas rule Jasper's own. "According to
Swedenborg," he says, "the soul is the gift of life from God and
the human body its natural clothing. You are shaped as God
made you, there can be nothing wrong with the flesh you are
given."

He slides his book across the table at Chapman, who takes it
but doesn't open it. He can't read, has never learned. He considers Jasper's words, weighs them against the faunish body he's
hiding. As a child unlike any other, Chapman had wondered
what it was he was called, but when years later he learned the
word *faun* from a book of tales Nathaniel bought and read to

him, he found it answered few of his questions, for the place the book claimed fauns were from wasn't like the place Chapman had been born, the wild country in which he'd lived his life. Was that all books contained? Knowledge but not answers? Then perhaps Chapman didn't need books.

Watching Nathaniel refill his cup with cloudy cider— refilling his cup too often, Chapman thinks, watching his brother's slackening face, his drooping eyelids—he asks, "But can the soul come back? Can the body die and the soul go on?"

Jasper frowns, retrieves the unopened book from Chapman's hands. "The Church teaches us there is Heaven, where the sunlight of God's love shines upon you, and there is Hell, the absence of such light. In between the recently dead travel a realm of spirits, where a man grapples with the events of his life until he dares admit his true nature. Only after his every deed has been confessed and heard and judged does he pass into Heaven or else descend into Hell."

Chapman cares not for this talk of Heaven and Hell: What does it have to do with one such as he, so bound to the earth? He tells Jasper good night, then drains his cup; he takes sleepy Nathaniel's and drains that too. His tongue thick with cider, Chapman says, "Come, brother. Let us lay out our bedrolls, let us get you to your rest."

Nathaniel's voice slurs, his movements unsteady. Chapman cares for his brother now as his brother once cared for him, pulling a wool blanket over Nathaniel, his brother already snoring before he's fully settled on the cabin floor.

The next afternoon, Jasper and Nathaniel set out to slaughter a goat Chapman can't bear to watch die. Begging off, he picks apples while watching Eliza for Grace, who takes his place in the goat pen. Eliza toddles beneath the trees as Chapman works; she laughs brightly when she topples over after chasing a chipmunk, then cooingly greets the worms she meets in the grass. Chapman picks apple after apple, the trees flush, glad to be growing in this good place, tended by this sweet family. As he works, Chapman tastes one apple from each tree. In the first he tastes no story more complicated than how sunshine turns water to sugar, how time and light and care are transformed into flavor and desire, nutrients and calories. In one apple there's flesh soft as melted butter; in this one, flesh dense as unbroken oak. In no apple does Chapman find even a hint of the Tree of Forgetting, the long-sought answer to his unusual life, without which he knows his secret self will always hold him apart from this sweet family, from the gentle love Nathaniel has found among them.

JOHN

At one end of the otherwise empty forty-eighth floor—a cavernous space waiting to be occupied by more fabricated labs—Eury pauses in front of an unmarked doorway, lifting her palm to the pebble reader bonded invisibly with the concrete wall until a light blinks green below the wall's surface. A moment later, a concealed door splits and slides open: inside waits a stainless steel platform a dozen meters across, a radial trapdoor closed atop its mounded floor, the platform surrounded by a series of multijointed extruder arms, obvious prototypes tipped with revolving plates of printer heads and cutting blades, plus needlers and staplers, paddles for shaping and folding, all controlled by an ordinary laptop on a rolling cart, the cart's wheels tangled in a messy nest of yellow network cables. A piecemeal machine, a fancy piece of kitwork assembled out of repurposed tech. Old dumb technology, not connected wirelessly to the rest of the Tower.

Whatever you wanted to do with this machine, you had to do it here.

"I call it the Loom," Eury says. "The heart of the Orpheus project."

"Cloning," John replies, still standing in the doorway. "It's a fancy name for cloning."

"Not exactly." Eury boots up the laptop, then begins moving around the room, turning on the other machines. "Cloning mammals usually requires living mothers to grow the cloned embryos, to nurse and nurture the offspring. It's extraordinarily time-consuming, it bears a variety of risks, but the inputs aren't difficult to produce in a functioning ecosystem: food, water, shelter, space. But our ecosystems are so battered. Conditions are going to get worse, and there's only so much Pinatubo can do to protect us. Already we have to modify our livestock to make them thrive here on the Farm, and it's a highly controlled environment."

"I'm not sure I follow," says John. "What happens here? How is this different?"

He follows Eury around the room's perimeter, running his hand over the steel tanks ringing the walls. The insulated metal is cool to the touch, the contents clearly refrigerated. Nothing in the room is marked, all of it too provisional and new for warnings or explanatory labels.

Once Eury logs in to the laptop, the patchwork Loom begins to hum, its extruders waking up, a low chug of liquid volubly circulating in the tanks. "The Loom is the first part of Orpheus," she explains. "It's a 3-D printer, partly, but that's selling it a bit short, since no other additive manufacturing process can do what Orpheus can. It'll be easier to show you than to explain, but before that you should know that buried beneath this Tower is a series of reservoir tanks holding a highly refined and stable form of liquefied recycled biomass, the Loom's most crucial input."

She says it like its nothing: *liquefied recycled biomass.* John stares, at first unwilling to comprehend what she's telling him. "Where does the biomass come from?" he asks, but he knows part of the answer already: the flying drones in Yellowstone, the dozers scraping the ground in Montana, the work crews pulling timber out of the western suburbs.

"When we built the Farm," Eury says, her fingers flashing across the keyboard, "we had to clear the land. Instead of piling the dead livestock and rotted crops into landfills, we harvested them, shipping what we could to be sorted and recycled at a facility outside Vegas, a first-of-its-kind refinery capable of separating polluted dirt and broken concrete from decaying plant matter, stinking animal carcasses. Everything organic gets broken down into one material, from which others might be made."

At first the process had required heavy chemicals, immense amounts of power and heat, coughing smokestacks ringed by white holding tanks, all the ugly industry John knew they needed to leave behind. "One last extractive industry," Eury says, waving away his concerns. "Scraping the surface of the earth before it blows away, so later we can reseed the planet."

All necessary technologies move quickly. Already the refineries were obsolete, replaced by a novel acidic compound invented in Earthtrust's labs, capable of dissolving skin and bone, keratin, cellulose, lignin, rubber, cotton, anything biological in origin.

Once emulsified with an antibiotic preservative, the resulting sludge could be stored indefinitely, forced through pipelines into storage tanks, even frozen into longer-lasting bricks.

"None of this was enough for the scale of Orpheus," Eury says, continuing to prep the Loom, occasionally looking up from the laptop to be sure each next piece of machinery has successfully turned on. "And it's insanely labor intensive and time sensitive. Even scouting with drones, focusing on the most easily available sources—abandoned industrial-scale agriculture, for instance—it was never going to work long term. That's where the Farm came in."

"Wait. What does the Farm have to do with this?" He tries to connect the supertree orchards with their tasteless apples and the stinking stockyards of almost mutant cattle to the sterile hum of this room, but fails. "What are you really doing, Eury?"

"John, did you think people were going to live in cooperative agricultural communities run by megacorporations forever? I keep telling you: Earthtrust is a transitional company. To bridge the present we have and the future we want requires using the tools available. We live in a capitalist country; I built a capitalist tool. But I don't care about the money, only what it can do."

"You've made an awful lot of it, though." This unavoidable petulance, always a source of self-loathing, and never more so than now—how much does John hate how small his objections always feel before the grandeur of Eury's ambition?

Eury doesn't look up from the laptop, but John knows she's rolling her eyes, if not outright scowling. "And I've poured every cent back into Earthtrust. Give me a break. I'm administering half of the United States from a research facility in Ohio. Not to mention our efforts abroad. This is all a means to an end. Democracy wasn't up to the task of facing the future. Too slow, too dispersed, too many safeguards. Do you have any idea how difficult it would have been to do any of this through national elections or ballot referendums? Starting late last century, corporate greed weakened democracy's safeguards; now, in the places where the safeguards are weakest, we're free to act. Now we exploit the gaps left in our democracy to save our people."

This was the world as it had always been to people like Eury, the visionaries of the next human age, the next human race: the future the promised land, the present a necessary sacrifice, the past irrelevant, embarrassing, dispensable, taboo.

A necessary evil, Eury would say, if John pressed.

"The Volunteer Agricultural Communities feed the world," Eury continues, still typing, her back to John, blocking the laptop screen. "But the ultimate goal is for the world to feed itself, once we've halted the rising temperatures and the climbing sea levels, once we've rebuilt the soil, once we agree upon a model for sustainable human agriculture as part of a thriving global ecosystem. It might take fifty years or a hundred. They might be ugly years. To bridge the gap, the VACs will grow as much as we can as fast as we can, not only for food but to stash as much biomass as possible. John, I don't care what a superorchard apple tastes like. Flavor is easy to chemically correct. The only marker I'm chasing is density of available organic compounds. I care only how tall the trees can grow."

John listens, his face darkening. He studies the activating Loom, sees the hoses leading from the storage tanks to the extruders begin to stiffen, thick liquid biomass chugging through them, pumped nearly fifty stories up from the underground tanks. "What are you doing, Eury? Why are we here?"

"Just wait," she says, pressing one more button before stepping away from the laptop.

Now the extruders rise, now the stage's radial hatch opens to reveal an oblong pool of bluish liquid, a milky sludge sloshing as the first extruder tip dips below its surface. A repetitive keening fills the room as the other extruders lower themselves, moving in time with the oddly melodic but grating loop of noise. John's heart pounds. The sound reminds him of something, but he can't concentrate enough to make himself remember, not with the extruders sliding along a series of interlocking circular tracks, performing a dance of hydraulics ready to deliver bioinks and fast-setting polymers. As the song-sound grows unbearable, Ghost moans, its head buried beneath its paws; John wants to comfort the wolf but not as much as he wants to watch the Loom's movements.

It takes only a moment more to understand what Eury's ordered: a full-grown she-wolf, another Ghost, another tame sibling to Eury's spy in Yellowstone.

Layer by layer, working from the inside out, a wolf is made, birthed already fully grown: the slow manufacture of bright white bones, the delicate threading of nerves and blood vessels. A mass of intestines appears, a stomach, a gall bladder, the kidneys and liver, each part assembled in its right place, as determined by billions of years of evolution. Bio-staplers zip shut the internal organs, secure the blood and the bones beneath printed muscles, leave the muscles twitching against the enwrapping skin. The wolf is pink and hairless and without life, no breath yet as a scalpel-wielding arm cuts the mouth free of the skin stretched over the skull, the cut exposing teeth clenched in a stilled snarl, then shapes the ears, the nostrils, the eyelids, under which the wolf's eyes might or might not be modified as the Yellowstone wolf's must've been. The keening rises steadily, its screech screaming through John's skull, its bass pounding at his breastbone, intensifying as the extruder needles pound millions of hairs into pink skin, finally leaving behind a perfect copy, floating lifeless in the Loom's viscous milk.

No creature was meant to be made this way; until Earthtrust, no creature ever was.

Now the noise gets louder. More piercing. Wrenchingly terrible. A flood of electricity jolts the tub of milky fluid; when the song stops, it's replaced by the sound of two wolves barking, by Eury clapping as Ghost rises to meet the twin bounding wetly from the Loom's tub, a wolf exactly as alive as John, as Eury, as any creature ever born.

JOHN CROUCHES BESIDE EURY TO JOIN HER IN PETTING GHOST AND its sister: here are the perfect muscles beneath the skin; the happy panting breath moving into Ghost's lungs, out of its sister's. The squares of fur he saw earlier are nothing like the same fur here, he thinks: to dismantle the living into pieces is to unmake reality, but maybe to reunite the parts into a whole is to heal a break in the world, closing the gap left when the last wild wolf died. Surely a world with wolves is better than one without them, no matter how the wolves came to be.

"We've all lost so much, but we don't forget everything." Eury scratches both wolves behind their ears, each wolf exactly as happy as the other. She says, "We all have some vanished part of the world we miss more than any other. The wolves were mine. Maybe the bees were yours. You and I are not so old, not so young. But the worst environmental devastation happened in our lifetimes, not to mention the political breakdown. This is why we have to act now, while there's still a generation who remembers what the world should be."

"As diminished as our childhoods were, they were the last real ones," John says. "I feel that too. But every generation thinks theirs is going to be the last."

"Sooner or later, someone's going to be right."

John thinks about the wolf he met in Yellowstone, the one both spy and camera. He says, "Why modify the wolves at all? Why not make the exact wolf you scanned?"

Eury gives him a withering glance. "Because wild wolves are *dead*, John. They couldn't survive. We made ones who could. Different tolerances for temperature, more efficient metabolisms, lower mortality rates in breeding. Every variable is adjustable, even if the consequences are difficult to predict." She raises a hand to cut off his objections. "And yes, the complications of reassembling an entire biosphere—while also modifying its individual parts—are staggering. But we're running simulations, applying machine learning, thinking ahead. I'll say it again: Pinatubo is our grace period. In the time it gives us, we'll finish the transition from fossil fuels to a sustainable energy culture, humanely draw the population down to an appropriate size, then determine where and how people can most productively live. Some people might live in places like the VACs, most others in highly designed and centrally planned megalopolises. The rest of the country could be left uninhabited, like the Sacrifice Zone. Over time, we'll terraform unused landscapes into new green zones, places where humans can grow crops and graze livestock, where we can reintroduce a sustainable wild world to live alongside humanity."

Is this what John had dreamed of when he was blowing up dams, when he was destroying fences and gas stations? Still on his knees, he runs a hand across the gray tile, finds a patch of fur loosed from one wolf or the other. A talisman, a reminder that everything he sees might not be real, not if *real* means *not of human manufacture.* He says, "It's a hell of a boardroom pitch, Eury. I almost believe you can do it."

"We are doing it, John. We could do it together." Eury trains her gaze on John, pinning him in place, about to ask whatever it is she plans to ask.

"Why did you bring me here?" he asks, unable to wait for her to speak. "You must've known I didn't come back to help you."

"Didn't you?" Eury arches an eyebrow, taunting him. "That's news to me."

I came here to stop you. I came here to plant a bomb.

"You have everything figured out," he says. "So why do you need me?"

"Because maybe there is something only you can do," she says, standing. She reaches out a hand, pulls him to his feet. "Pinatubo, John. I want you to finish it."

OUTSIDE THE LOOM, BACK IN THE BLANK OPENNESS OF THE FORTY-eighth floor, John agrees. Eury issues a series of commands to the Tower's AI, summoning a mobile fabrication drone to build a lab and living quarters nearby, plus furniture and appliances and whatever else John needs, all arranged in a configuration Eury's chosen: a replica of the lab John once occupied in Earthtrust's first offices, in the Columbus industrial park where Eury started the company.

"This will take a couple hours," she says, "but then you should get to work. Stratospheric aerosol scattering isn't a complicated technology but it has its nuances. Determining the size and reflectivity of the particles, the ideal density of cover; predicting exactly what might happen at different levels of dispersion. How much you cool the earth, how fast. We've modeled those out pretty well and pretty confidently. The tricky part is the delivery vehicle: How do you get enough particles into the stratosphere, and how do you keep replenishing the supply? We've explored airplanes and zeppelins, rocket volleys, low-orbit space stations, what's left of commercial air travel. All too expensive, too easy to disrupt or abandon."

John watches the fabricator work, unnerved by the emerging outline of his old lab, a place he'd thought he'd escaped forever. "What's the solution, then?"

"It's you. It's always been you." Eury kneels to bury her face in Ghost's furry neck, then its twin's, the two wolves already inseparable packmates. "More specifically, your bees. We remade them into miniature injectors, individually capable of aerosol manufacture and release, as well as perpetual self-repair and self-propagation. Set and forget geoengineering."

"Set and forget? What if you get it wrong?"

"I would suggest we not? One problem with any delivery system requiring constant human input or a static base is that someone could bomb your airfields, invade your facilities, disrupt your supply chain. We both know we're headed for less geopolitical stability, not more. We need to fix the planet in a way that isn't reliant on, say, what's left of the United States sticking around, because it likely won't. So we'll inject a nanoswarm into the atmosphere from VACs around the globe. The swarm has to be capable of harvesting materials to produce the aerosol microparticles and placing them in the stratosphere at the correct altitudes, at appropriate densities. This means the swarm needs a decentralized AI hive mind, continuously re-formed from all available bots. The bots would also need to be able to self-replicate, fabricate new parts, and permutate their own designs as conditions change, as well as be totally secure, safe from interruption or interference."

"It's a tall order," John says. He objects but he's already smiling. "Almost impossible."

"Almost, but not quite."

"No. If you're right, and the basic design is already there, then if it works—"

"If it works, then we'll have time to refine Orpheus, on top of everything else. Restorative cloning via bioprinting, a worldwide terraforming effort, the reshaping of our cities around sustainable agriculture and energy. These efforts are already within our reach. All we need is more time." Eury blinks, flicking her eyes through a menu or reading a message sent to her pebble. She stands, clicking her tongue to bring the wolves to attention. "But now I have to go."

"You're leaving?" John says, surprised. "For how long?"

"Just a few days. Meetings in Syracuse, then Brussels, maybe Asia." Eury pauses as the fabricator drone assembling John's office noisily slides free an extruded slab of tabletop. "There's more than one way to save the world, John. I'd prefer the world want our help. But I don't need its permission. One way or another, I'll do what's right. And soon. As soon as you make it work."

Eury leans in, kisses John's bruised cheek. He reaches for her waist, but she stops his hand with hers, twists away. Then she's gone, the two wolves following her to the elevator, leaving John alone with the fabricator. Watching the printer work, he flexes his fist, activating his pebble, then blinks through the series of command prompts that flash across his retinal display.

Immediately his pebble begins to burn beneath his skin, its processor overworked by one of Noor's riskiest worms, a program designed to decipher and copy one specific security key, a theft Noor had assured John was possible only at extremely close range.

All it took was John's hand on Eury's hip, all it took was her hand pushing his away.

C-433

In the shadow of the glacial shelf, C wakes to a dusting of plant material on the bubble's floor. He reaches up to explore his widening branches, finding more novelty, more change, but at first he can't resolve the new softness he touches into anything he knows. Craning his neck, cramming his still left shoulder blade uncomfortably into view, he finds more buds have crowded around each leaf stem, each decorated with more leaves than the ones that came before; around each of the branchlets the bark thickens faster, tugging and scratching the surrounding flesh, the borders between bark and skin now lined with stiff purple blades. At the center of some of the leaf clusters, velvety pink blossoms unfurl to display whitish pistils, stamen tipped with dustings of yellow pollen.

Flowers, he remembers, awed. He considers the purple blades lining the bark until a dozen different remainder voices tell him what it is he sees: *grass*. Something C thinks he has no memory of, but must have known, long ago, in one of his earliest lives.

The translucent photovoltaic bubble continues its zipping over lifeless broken ground, crossing frozen concrete and clay shattered by the dredging force of the glacier's retreat, leaving behind new glacial kettles, solid lakes dotted with rocky ice; blankets of till scatter the bottom of moraines, everywhere there are fragments of stone and cement and steel, the edifices of a civilization reduced to pebbly incomprehensibility—and there's the distant city, backdropped by the mountains beyond, the range in which Black Mountain must surely wait. But C barely sees this landscape, enraptured as he is with his study of his tree. How can he look away? Why would he ever take his eyes from the fresh attraction of the blossoms bursting their buds, the flowers unfurling, the bright insistence of their pollen-dusted stamen? A vision of new life—for what is a flower but a fruit in waiting, for what is a fruit but a demand for *more*?

If a fruit were to grow from the barkspots' flowers, then its seeds could grow independently of C's body, outliving this cycle of his existence. Despite this promise, C worries. He's ignorant of so much, the relevant memories of the remainder often wordless, imageless, thoughts reduced to bare hunches, barely understood: the blossoms need pollinators, without whose help they might die on their buds without producing the fruit C now desperately craves.

By evening a new pain appears, a deeper itching, lodged not in his insensate barkskin but beneath it, in deeper layers of his skin, or else the muscles beneath. He digs his claws at the bark, avoiding anywhere leaf stems grow; when that fails, he takes the orange-handled knife and saws through to the mess below, cutting around the flowers, poking through the bloody sap to discover a bolus of cysts nestled within the bony wooden mess of his shoulder, near where the barkspot first appeared.

The cysts are different from the buds, but different how? C lacks any helpful experience. They rise up beneath the bark, create pockets of pressure and pain; frustrated, C stomps in unsteady circles around the claustrophobic bubble until the craft reaches the city limits. Ice and snow, frozen brown clay, black asphalt broken and buckled, high roads collapsed off toppled supports, gray concrete made irregular boulders—the ruins here are more intact than those of the Below, but their intactness makes passage difficult, the cityscape not glacier-crushed, only left in a state of confused abandonment.

At C's direction, the bubble flits around and between and over every obstacle, penetrating the city by its widest arteries, the cold-buckled but not vanished roads often tens of meters wide. It takes C some time to recognize the wrecked hulks tossed alongside the road as other conveyances: wheeled vehicles piled high, wrenched metal and cracked glass and faded rubber, drifts of steel pushed before passing ice or unimaginable winds, cracked against concrete spiked by twisted rusted metal he remembers to call *rebar*, surrounded by shattered *stucco*.

The bubble passes beneath a sign reading WELCOME TO FABULOUS LAS VEGAS, the language recognizable but the sentiment unintelligible. C-433 is less curious about the world than many of his predecessors, but still, he has to resist the urge to exit the bubble, to explore the fallen-down structures he passes. He detours wherever the road is blocked by the collapsing mismatched architecture: he wonders at a towering green-robed figure, its neck broken, one arm raised to a shattered elbow, whatever object the missing lifted hand once held fallen among other rubble; he mistakes other half-nude statues for frozen bodies, likewise missing heads and limbs, their robed waists terminating in no torsos, none of the bodies hooved like his, none of the bodies horned. Columns of stone separate broken panes of colored glass, sparkling shards harmless to the floating bubble, the craft gliding over bent green signs offering incomprehensible directions, routes north and south to other boulevards and avenues half blocked by fallen poles caught suspended on their wires, dangling dead cables.

Wherever C looks he sees faded painted words, words whose meanings he can only guess at, CAESARS and BELLAGIO, PARIS and NEW YORK. The bubble moves unsteadily, its repulsors lifting it automatically over low obstacles, C piloting it manually around more complex obstructions. On one sign he sees a beast walking on four legs, its head maned, its back bearing two feathered wings: a creature made of other creatures, not so different from him. He thinks he's never seen a fountain before but then there are fountains everywhere, filled in with snow, including one surrounded by statues of stilt-legged pink birds, some species likely unnamed in the Ohio litany he memorized; he passes below a mural depicting four robed figures, one floating haloed above the kneeling others, all four faces scratched out, bullet holes riddling their bodies. What do all these figures represent? Are they invitations or warnings?

Maybe it's better not to know. Whatever this city believed, it wasn't enough to save it.

C retreats several kilometers, searching side streets for a route around a toppled filthy-white spire that blocks the road, its long-ago impact having cracked a rift in the concrete too deep for the bubble to cross. Everywhere he goes he finds debris he can't always name: punched-through screens, discarded conveyances, half-decayed fabric in a hundred colors, the decay arrested by the cold that killed everything else, although he finds no bodies in the streets, no bones secured in tattered winter clothes.

It's impossible for C to guess how many people once lived here. Staring out the curved wall of the bubble, he tries to imagine how many other cities there must have once been, how many buildings holding innumerable bodies, each body capable of housing as many lives as his. All gone, all gone, everywhere except Black Mountain.

Despite everything he's seen, C still actually believes this: that at Black Mountain someone will be waiting to receive him.

Off the Ice, less of his attention is required to pilot the craft. It should be easier and easier to give his attention to the world around him, but C is easily overwhelmed. Everywhere he goes there is some inanimate object whose name he can't always divine: the words are in him but he can't always rescue the language from himself. Other times the world names itself back with force, the remainder pressing upon him words he couldn't have guessed he'd forgotten: a *casino* or a *restaurant*, a *taxi* or a *limousine*, a *winged lion*, a *flamingo*.

After hours of slow travel across the rubble-strewn city, C gives up trying to make sense of what he sees. He listens to O's song, he watches the blossoms waving on their stems, the stems shivering on the bark of his body, he worries about what will happen when the flowers start to die, how he'll feel after they're gone. These are the first true seasons of C-433's life: flowers and not flowers—and then flowers again? He doesn't know. His left arm grows immobile, his right leg is stiffer every day, his stance sags leftward under the weight of the tree. Now the bubble smells richly of pollen, there's yellow dust and blue fur everywhere, the pollen shaken loose from the blossoms, the fur pushed from his skin thread by thread by the advancing bark. It's harder than ever to breathe, harder to swallow gagging slugs of nutrient paste thinned nearly past taste, made watery enough he might choke its dwindling supply down his tightening gullet.

C coughs, spits wet phlegm into his hands, wipes his hands on the furred side of his stomach. The city's claustrophobia of ruin extends in every direction, as oppressive as the Ice ever was. He scratches at the places where beneath bark and skin he can feel the cysts growing, rising through his burning flesh; he closes his eyes against the incomprehensible world and lets the bubble make slow progress while he dreams a dream of blackness, blackness unending, blackness numbingly cold and utterly boundless, totally lifeless, totally inert, a world where nothing more would be asked, where he could be still, finished, complete.

Hours later, C awakes not to the sound of O's voice but to a steady rhythmic bleeping, an alarm previously unheard. Dark falls outside, but by the bubble's light beam he sees a path cleared through the rubbled cliffs of frozen trash and broken buildings by the treaded passage of some enormous vehicle. Confused, he calls up the command console, studying the new indicator on its display, an alert reading only: BEACON ACQUIRED.

C mutes the alert, then taps his right temple. When he left the crawler behind, he brought with him only its insufficient maps, old-world knowledge no longer matching the continent he'd crossed. Now, as the bubble automatically makes a wireless connection to this distant beacon, the augmented reality display before him shimmers and swims: topographical features realign, the map adjusting to the changes wrought by unknown years of glacial progress, of ceaseless snows and violent winds, all the other phenomena capable of remolding the landscape.

When the new map is complete, a bright line appears in C's vision, pointing two hundred fifty kilometers west: a line leading directly down the canyon of ruined city the bubble is already navigating, the tracks spanning the makeshift canyon now obviously exactly the width of a crawler like the one where he was born and born and born. Why hadn't he realized it before now? Because he'd never seen his own crawler in motion. The promise of another's beacon, the fresh snow falling gently over the ruined cityscape—together they activate a deep need, a want for companionship, for someone to share this sight: the falling snow is beautiful, beautiful even without anyone to tell C what *beauty* means. When he begins to cry, tears fall only from the side of his face untouched by bark. His body is so stiffened by the tree in him and on him that he can only stand and lean against himself, leaning on the tree, its trunk strong enough to hold him. He weeps against his tree, its weight supporting the fleshier side of his body—and as he weeps something moves inside him: the cysts push all at once against his trembling flesh, rising beneath the bark, then breaking through.

What C thought were buried cysts are not cysts at all, but teratomas born of buried genetic material—not cysts but *eggs*. He wrenches his barked forearm up before his tear-streaked face, his joints moving slowly, the arm more branch than limb. Bloody sap leaks through minute cracks, and from those cracks climb first one then another then half a dozen translucent creatures each the size of a fingernail, made of parts naming themselves to C: *carapace, mandible, antennae, wing.*

Beetles, he guesses, choosing from among the words the

remainder has to offer, unsure if that's the right name for what he sees, these unlikely insects hatched from his body.

C shuts down the bubble's light beam, conserving energy. Darkness descends over the trench as he leans against his tree half, shivering at the tickle of the beetles' tentative steps, crawling through the grooves of his black bark, crossing the purple-bladed grass to part the blue fur printed into his dark skin. As early as tomorrow he might arrive at Black Mountain, a place he knows only as an icon on a map, a symbol where C hopes to deliver this tree—the first new life he thinks this cold world has made—where he hopes this tree might be made to live separate from him, before it takes so much they both die.

CHAPMAN

By midwinter, Chapman chafes at the captivity of the Worth household, its tight environs too much restraint on the faun trapped inside the man, who despairs at his shivering diminished self: as a faun, he knows, he wouldn't quake against the cold, wouldn't whine for more blankets, for warmer clothes than the ones Nathaniel bought him months ago. He misses the woods, misses the feel of pine straw beneath his bare hooves, misses all the wild smells the wind once brought him, all these sensations ejected from every human household. One midnight, under a full moon veiled by bright wisps of cloud, he can take no more. He leaves his boots beside the door, drapes his shirt over his boots, rolls his pant legs above his knees. Barefoot and bare-chested, he steps into the frigid night, his feet clinging to the icy slats of the porch, his skin threatening to freeze and tear.

Chapman doesn't hesitate. He takes his first steps on human feet, running across the Worths' frozen yard, but before he reaches the edge of their fields he is already galloping on faunish hooves, cruising over crusted snow to jump atop their split rail fence, cracking the top rail as he leaps off it to enter the woods beyond, running over frozen logs and frigid boulders. Chilled air slides over the bark of his skin, and he laughs at the contact of hoof on solid earth, so much more satisfying than cramped shoe on sanded board. For a few hours, he thrills at his loping passage through the snowy woods, he dwells within the right feeling of his returned faun body, his inhuman footsteps never breaking the wild quiet of the cold night, the creaking of frozen trees in the stiff wind, the settling of ice, the whisper of no living thing speaking. Only once he's exhausted does Chapman pause in the wintery dark, a faun closing his eyes to consider again the flickering blackness where this winter he's had to hide so much of himself.

How long can this blessed stillness last? He slowly opens his eyes but doesn't yet move. He scans the dark woods, cocking his head one way and then the other. Nothing living moves, nothing living stirs, not at first; the wind strains the ice loudly wherever it's frozen to a leafless branch, the woods speak with the voice of winter itself. But that's not all. Chapman's heartbeat rises, quickening as the song he cannot ever forget further penetrates his reverie—is what he hears coming his way a distant memory or a present nightmare rushing closer?

Whatever Chapman hears is enough to set his skin ashiver, to set all his fur to standing. He panics. Turning back toward the Worth homestead, he immediately misjudges a leap over a frozen fallen log, the toe of one hoof catching on a broken branch, sending him tumbling painfully across rock-studded

ice. Stretched out and panting, he listens again, he wills himself to locate the terrible dirge, if it's there, the feared song that
is elegy and threat, anger and future-making flicker—

Maybe he hears the song. Maybe he doesn't. But somewhere,
somewhen, surely the head is still singing its complaint, caught
crooked in a witch's arm; somewhere, somewhen, or maybe
here, maybe now, because now doubt vanishes, now Chapman
is suddenly sure he hears the singer's voice.

He rises in a rush, his footing falters as haste overtakes care.
Reaching the edge of the Worth homestead, he again bounds
over the cracked rail, already changing mid-leap, giving up his
faunness, so when he stumbles to the ground inside the fence
line he falls this time on bare human feet, his unfurred skin
burning at the earth's frozen touch. He picks himself up fast as
he can, then pauses shivering in the yard, his bare soles sticking
to the icy ground.

He hears nothing now, is no longer sure he ever did. A trick
of the mind, he tells himself, an indulging of fearful imagination.

Surely he's safe with the Worths, as safe as Nathaniel hoped
they would be.

Surely this land is settled enough to keep wild things at bay.

Disguised as a man, indoors upon planted lands, Chapman
hopes he can live freely.

But every moment he wears the man, he fears the faun is
shrinking.

JUST AFTER DAWN, JASPER WORTH LEAVES THE HOUSE'S WARM INTE-
rior to feed his goats; minutes later, he's back, pale and trembling. Jasper sits shaking while Grace makes him a cup of tea;
he doesn't speak until he's swallowed its heat in one scorching

gulp. "There's some danger in the woods," he says, returning his cup to the table, "unlike anything I have seen before."

In the night, he says, something broke the fence at the end of the yard, letting one of the goats escape through the shattered rail. Jasper followed the missing goat's hoofprints to a hollow thrashed through the crusted snow, where the black-and-white goat sprawled—its belly split, its entrails spilled atop bloody snow.

"A mountain lion?" asks Nathaniel, pulling on his boots. "A bear?"

"Could be either," Jasper says, swirling his tea, his eyes lowered to watch a clot of cream swim circles across its surface. "I should have been more careful, should've checked the tracks before I scuffed the ground with my boots. But whatever killed the goat didn't eat it." He shakes his head. "No, this is something else."

"What do you mean?" asks Grace. "What else could it be?" She bounces Eliza in her arms, the raven-haired child entangling her fingers in her mother's braids.

Nathaniel looks at Chapman, who can barely keep his eyes open, the man's body tired from the faun's night spent running; Chapman, whose fault it is the fence was broken, who in a single night called his pursuers to the Worths' door: Which one of the three witch-beasts, Chapman wonders, was it that killed Jasper's goat?

"Jasper, I should've already been out there with you," Nathaniel says, "helping you with the work." He looks to his brother: Will Chapman reproach him for his drunkenness last night, the cider that kept him from waking as early as Jasper? But Chapman stays silent, relieved for his brother's distraction, and for the ask that follows. "Chapman, can you mend the fence? Better one of us stays behind and makes sure no more goats go missing."

"Yes, brother," says Chapman, watching Jasper and Nathaniel dress themselves in fur and hide, then donning his own stitched furs, slid over bare skin he still doesn't think of as his. While the others are gone, he cuts a new rail from a stack of lumber, fitting it into the existing slots in the fence posts, hammering it home. He feeds the remaining goats, then checks the laying hens in the cramped chicken coop, delivering the day's eggs to Grace in the kitchen, where the stove's radiant heat sets his cold skin to pleasant tingling.

Before this, he'd never known the monotony of chores, the not unpleasurable way *what next* is here answered only with *now again*.

"Rest a minute, Chapman," says Grace. "Your brother will be back soon."

He sits, accepting a second cup of tea, always grateful when Grace joins him. Eliza plays in the corner of the room, watching Chapman as she prances a wooden horse across the cold floorboards. He smiles cautiously at the girl's attention, then starts when she rises, dragging her toy behind her to stand beside his chair, her thumb in her mouth, her horse clutched to her side.

"You can pick her up," says Grace. "She likes you."

Chapman lifts Eliza, hefts her surprising weight into his lap. Eliza digs her feet into his thighs, laughs as he bounces her as he's seen Jasper do. He's known no children, had no playmates of his own besides Nathaniel, who was parent first and brother second. House and farm and family—this was what Nathaniel always said he wanted. In the years Chapman was missing, Nathaniel found some approximation of that dream here, after coming brotherless to this place where now Jasper calls him *brother*, where Grace calls him *friend*, where Eliza calls him *uncle*.

Chapman's presence threatens to bring that good life to ruin. Somehow, he must try this winter to accept being a man. For his brother's sake, for the sake of this sweet family. How much easier it would be if he found his Tree, he thinks, his old story shifting to accommodate his new life: changed by the flicker, he can pretend to be a human now, but after his excursion in the wintry night he admits pretend is all it is. His fur itches the inside of his skin; he feels his hooves wanting out of his shoes, wanting out of his feet. The flicker has let him live inside the Worth house, but it has not made him human.

For weeks, Jasper keeps his rifle loaded beside the cabin door, ready to take aim at whatever creature preyed on his goat. Now the winter world grows quiet, the sounds of the forest reduced to the cracking of ice, the howl of freezing wind, the cries of the surviving goats as they squeeze together for warmth. Despite the forbidding cold, the Worth household is well provisioned, stocked with salted meat, jarred vegetables, tins of flour and sugar bought before the weather made travel impossible. Always there is sharp, pungent cider fermented from the orchard, and more than one evening is spent with Jasper and the two brothers lifting mug after mug, cheering one another in good company. Chapman enjoys the sound of others reading aloud, and so many hours are passed sitting on the floor beside young Eliza, with Jasper reading from his few volumes, his Swedenborgian tracts or a prized book of tales. Often the stories in this latter book are purest nonsense—a girl attending a ball in a pumpkin, dressed in a gown knitted from rags—but occasionally one rings truer. Chapman trembles to hear of a wolf prowling a forested path of needles, wanting only to devour a girl draped in red. The wolf, Jasper says, ate the girl's grandmother first, then dressed itself in her clothes, her housecoat and bonnet—

"And her skin," says Chapman, the trance of the story making him forget himself.

"What? No, no, of course not," says Jasper, repulsed.

Chapman scoffs, sipping from his cup of cider. So this wasn't a true story after all. Because how else would an animal pass as human, except by wearing human skin?

For the rest of the winter, the brothers help Jasper inside the house and out, assisting in minor feats of carpentry, or else digging more frozen rocks out of next year's fields, their shovels bending against the cold earth. The work is difficult, the rewards and the dangers often distant, but in the moment there's true pleasure in shaping the land. When the brothers first planted their nurseries, the people who would one day benefit were abstractions, hoped-for buyers of apple trees; here on the Worth farm, Chapman finds the beneficiaries of those efforts manifested, Jasper and Grace and Eliza set to enjoy their apples for the years to come.

The work eases Chapman into the more settled life of a man, but then it's spring again, and when the world wakes, Chapman's wanderlust does too. "Brother," he says, having waited until he and Nathaniel are alone beside the fire, stuffing their pipes with the last of Jasper's tobacco. "Our apple trees await us."

Nathaniel taps his pipe against the hearth. "What if we didn't go this year?" he asks. "Jasper would keep us on, we could earn our place here."

Chapman waves a hand over the human shape he's worn

nonstop since the broken fence, the body irritating his spirit as surely as his shirt scratches his skin. He says, "I want to be myself again."

"Brother," Nathaniel begins, then trails off. He stares into the fire, his pipe's scent filling the room.

Chapman waits for his brother to speak, studies what isn't being said when he doesn't. Nathaniel doesn't want Chapman to be a faun again. He's older, slower, fuller of paunch, poor as ever. He's shown Chapman that the Worth household is a good place, maybe the best place he can hope to secure. A life among these Christian people who treat him kindly, who accept him as he is: rough handed and rough mannered, given increasingly to drink.

Chapman could leave his brother here to go on alone, into the Territory. It would be safer for Nathaniel, given what chases Chapman. Likely it would be better for his brother in every way. Certainly a year at the Worth homestead would be kinder than another six months in the woods, scrounging a never-arriving living from the inhospitable wilderness, sleeping nightly on bitterly hard ground.

All Chapman has to do is say, *Stay*.

Brother, you stay—he could say those words—he knows he won't.

If Nathaniel stays and Chapman goes, then Chapman will be alone forever—and whatever else he wants to be, he no longer wants to be alone.

"I can't stay," he pleads, rising to his human feet. "And wherever I go I want you with me, at my side."

It's the most selfish thing he's ever said, the worst burden ever placed on his brother.

Nathaniel sits and smokes and watches the flames, fists balled, legs shaking nervously. "I will not lose you again, brother," he says at last, his eyes on the fire. "Where you go, I go."

"West then," Chapman says, his smile a mismatch for his heart's thudding fright. "West to wilder lands, where this year at last we make our fortune." *Where this year we must at last plant my Tree*, he thinks. Now or never, for if the Tree will take ten years to bear fruit, then he cannot stand to delay another day.

Their path decided, the brothers part for the rest of the night. Any day now, they'll leave the Worth homestead together, Nathaniel promising as always to return as soon as his work is done. They'll again gather seeds to plant all across this beautiful, invincible land, this surely inexhaustible green world from which they and all their kind have asked so much.

JOHN

All plots move humanward. Before Eury leaves the Farm, a herd of thirty bison appear in the meadow beneath the Tower, happily grazing the circular plain: all juvenile males, printed from the blueprint of the last bison John saw dying in the Lamar Valley dust. That night, up late in his lab, John thinks about how happy he was to see them, then how infuriating he found this instinctual joy. Always the mind and heart are eager to be tricked by forgeries of the wild, falling in love with trees planted in pots, animals kept in cages. He'd created the nanobees because he loved real bees but real bees were gone; the supertrees he'd designed the nanobees to pollinate couldn't live anywhere but the VACs, existing only to serve human desire, each one a human wish planted in chemically enriched dirt, fulfilling Eury's want for all the biomass a tree might make.

And the bison, printed from the biomass Earthtrust had collected? What were they? Only the present recycled, then wasted: an animal brought back from extinction, a token conservation in the present whose cost was a waste of what they'd need to reach the future, if Pinatubo and Orpheus worked.

All plots move humanward, all human plots move toward the human. If Pinatubo launches, then what it means to live on Earth will change forever; but if the human world someday ends, it won't be the end of the world. Even if everything goes as wrong as it can, it likely won't even be the end of humanity, only one particular way of living. But however much the human world has been diminished, humanity's diminished the nonhuman more. In the West, John had tried to connect himself to what remained, to erase the gap between himself and all the othered others. He remembers the faraway red rock canyon, the painted giants, horned and antlered; the parklands and the dying bison and everything he did in the Sacrifice Zone to give the world back, all the bombs he set to remove the heavy damage of the human mark, all the nights he spent sleeping under the stars in the years after he left Earthtrust, many with Cal but just as many alone with what remained of the world. But it's impossible to fully summon these fleeting memories from the forty-eighth floor of the Tower, as humancentric a monument as any he's ever imagined.

All human plots move humanward, he thinks, but what about the plot of the world? To what ends does it move, toward what triumph, what tragedy, what redemption? What does the world want, what is the world still capable of becoming? Where is the will of the world made most visible? Is it an angry force, felt in its earthquakes and hurricanes, in the endless wildfires, in the hot gales kicking up dead dust? How else is the agency of the world made manifest? In the slow shaping strength of a glacier, a behemoth of ice pushing mountains before its weight? Or in the profusion of life, the splendor of bounty and beauty that so many peoples have been convinced must be proof of some god, some higher purpose to existence? Are evolution and its abundances the expression of the world's will, or only the artifacts of its indifference?

As always, these questions remain outside John's knowing, which is not to say they don't matter, that their answers do not matter terribly to him—but what can he do now except continue along the path he's committed himself to, a human-focused plot if ever there was one? He squeezes his fist, blinks through menus to unlock the rest of the hidden subroutines. Bringing his hacked nanobees inside the Tower had been a risk, but he needs only a few: two dozen line his gums, deactivated and undetectable beneath his tongue, tucked against the molars. A moment later, he opens his mouth to release the activated bees, their false buzzing nothing like that of real bees, whose extinction broke John more than the death of his parents, more than the loss of his family's home. He remembers when colony collapse came for his farm: cleaning the last dead hives, prying loose tiny body after tiny body, looking for any living queen, any viable larvae; abandoning the beekeeper's suit halfway through his search, the protection unnecessary against the nothing there.

By the end he would've given anything for a bee sting, would have gladly allowed himself to be stung to death if it meant real bees could go on in his place.

Nanobees assigned and his lab assembled, John continues solving the problem Eury assigned him before she left the Farm. Once he understands how the Pinatubo swarms differ from his bees, it's simple enough to adjust some parameters, to tune the self-preservation protocol, to program self-sufficiencies and redundancies the bees had never needed. The nanobees were already capable of swarm thought, their hive minds coordinating to make higher-level decisions, but the Pinatubo bots also need to self-replicate; still, the technology to design printers to print other printers is old now, the materials the nanoswarms will need reasonably abundant.

The launch control chamber waits at the top of the Tower's needle, on the other side of Eury's penthouse, protected by layers of biometric security: a handprint sensor, an optical scanner, and a DNA prick, in addition to the usual pebble-based locks. Whatever parameters are set there at launch will quickly spread to the rest of the swarms, then become permanent. Because the swarms must not be allowed to be tampered with, and because anything that can be hacked will be, the safest option is to ensure their instructions can't be adjusted after launch, no matter what happens. Instead John programs precise drawdown triggers, instructions the nanoswarms will continually revert to, no matter what other modifications are made: when atmospheric carbon dioxide falls beneath a certain level, the nanoswarms will slow the sulfate injections until the white sky blues again, returning the world to a more natural state.

As if there'll be anything natural at all by then.

He builds in new firewalls to further prevent the swarms from taking revised orders but balks at removing the backdoor he left in the nanobees, a backdoor the Pinatubo swarms have inherited, unseen by Eury's engineers. He should delete it, but the assurance of its existence is too great a temptation: if Cal and the others fail to halt the launch, then this might be one more way to stop Pinatubo. Still, it'll be only marginally useful.

Activating the backdoor requires close proximity, so once the hive mind is established in the stratosphere, it'll already be too late to stop its orders.

Eury left him with the best projections from her climate engineers, all their estimates of the level of aerosol scattering needed to create a sufficiently dense coverage of sulfates to cool the global temperature by the necessary amount, which to Eury means simply maintaining the current status quo, without letting temperatures climb any higher. Blocking enough solar radiation to dramatically undo the two-and-a-half-degree rise in global temperatures isn't necessary, according to Eury, because civilization has already restructured itself to life at current levels. But what she means is that two point five degrees Celsius has already delivered a sufficient shock to the global system to allow Earthtrust to take over the global food chain, to bend world politics to Eury's desires. If conditions improve too much, what might happen to the control she says is necessary to save everyone else? Best for Earthtrust if the world needs the company to run it a little longer.

The work is interesting, just challenging enough to stretch John's mind in new directions. In a single day and one long night, he's solved the problems Eury suggested had been plaguing her scientists for months. But he knows how talented the best Earthtrust researchers are, had worked alongside some of them for years before he quit: there wasn't anything he could do that they couldn't.

What if Eury hadn't needed his help, only his complicity? Now he is implicated in whatever happened next. Now he is as responsible as she is.

It's two or three hours past midnight when John finishes. Pouring himself another bitter cup of coffee he doesn't need, he allows himself a moment of unreasonable pride. At noon, he'll meet the others, the five of them gathering for the first time since returning to the Farm; he knows he should sleep, knows he won't. Instead, he recalls the nanobees he sent flying through air vents and wiring conduits, eager to start assembling their findings into a map of the Tower. One by one, the bees report in, their memory banks full, their micro-batteries nearly depleted: without outside sunlight, there's no way for their miniature solar cells to charge; without being assigned a swarm, they can't download their data anywhere but his palm.

The bots finish downloading, one after the other. Once John has their data, he crushes each false insect between two fingers, the quiet crunch of their metallic exoskeletons giving way not so different from what he remembered of the crackling of real insect carapaces, like the many hundreds he unavoidably crushed beneath his boots in the grieving last weeks of the bees.

C-433

Dozens of beetles climb the bubble's curved wall, dotting C's view of the landscape with their scuttling blurs; when they fall away, their overturned carapaces and scrabbling legs mix with the crumbling blossoms blanketing the gyro-leveled floor. Dozens are already dead, but more emerge from the cracked ridges of C's tree, the half of him made bark and branch and bole, while the rest of his flesh shivers and shakes and starves. His left eye roves beneath a mask of wood, seeing only darkness, his breath shallows as new bark crosses the meridian of his sternum, binding his torso, covering his navel; he can no longer turn his neck, his left cheek completely stilled by the same tendrils wrapping his spine, straightening his posture. Only one ear remains free, listening to O's drone and the clacking beetles and the beacon's steady beeping, while the other

ear, buried beneath the bark, reports on life underground, under
bark, the scrabbling of bugs tunneling into his woody flesh.

Now the free ear hears the beacon's beeping accelerate,
as the photovoltaic bubble zooms down the unseen crawler's
trench, climbing to the edge of the place C's sought almost
this entire life: a rocky valley containing the approach plane to
Black Mountain, an expanse of massive black thorns partially
covered in drifts of filthy snow, rising dozens of meters tall at
angry angles, their every surface spiked, the thorns connected
by tendrils of rough walls made of the same matte material, an
unreflective synthetic rock made of hollandite, zirconolite, and
perovskite, materials C doesn't know he's seen, named with
words he doesn't know he knows.

C's good eye gazes despairingly from his half a face, his chest
heaves with the sluggish pumping of his sap-blood, his shallow
breathing. Arcing the bubble along the first row of thorns prodding the clotted white sky, he discovers the crawler he's been
following crashed against the thorns' immovable warning. The
crawler's steel hull is shattered, its many portholes dark, its triangular starboard treads as twisted as his own distant crawler's,
all the damage the only evidence he needs to imagine a failed
attempt to ram through the unbroken barriers.

His chest aching with the bark's weight, C searches the ir-
real landscape ahead. The crashed crawler blocks the most viable way forward, but surely there must be a path the smaller
bubble craft might take, however slim, however difficult. The
longer C looks, the more the scene settles, until at last he sees a
narrow path he might be able to navigate through the thorns, if
he pushes the repulsors hard enough to lift the bubble over the
lowest parts of the snow-caked walls.

With a strangled cry of relief, C urges the craft forward,

crossing ice crusted in the shadow of the doomed crawler. O's drone fills the darkness; the bubble's sensors report mild changes in altitude as the craft climbs the first of the barriers, threading a narrow gap picked out by the light beam. The bubble advances slowly, the crawler's shadow elongated by the time of day. A third of the way along its length, C realizes he should've waited to proceed until the hidden sun was directly above: now a warning light fires on the haptic console, the light beam and the repulsors and the heat and air pumps all straining the stressed batteries in the bubble's belly.

To C's left lies the snow-blotted surface of the thorns, the walls' irregular shapes; to the right looms the riveted steel hull of the crawler, its many protuberances of piping and tubing and sensor arrays. Looking ahead, he follows the path of the beam, the light leading the way, the craft wavering and bumping over low walls not meant to stop progress, only to slow it. C understands this at a glance: he is inexperienced but not unintelligent. The more thoroughly Black Mountain was secured, the less safe its contents would have been: instead of a high fortress wall, there looms this warning of thorns, a sprawling black sculpture making passage difficult enough to dissuade the curious but not so impossible as to make them insist on trying.

It's been days since the remainder spoke directly, the voices of all those who came before having slowly integrated into C-433. But the passage beneath the broken crawler prods the remainder to more distinct speech, awakening its old warnings, its cowardly commandments.

The Mountain holds nothing for you. If you bring the Mountain the tree, it'll cut you free of the wood, steal your blossoms and beetles. What then?

It says, *The Mountain is death, but the crawler might save us.*

Every room exactly as in ours, everything where we left it. A new recycler, a new Loom.

C considers the surface of the crawler, its frost-ridden hull already halfway past, obviously damaged and almost certainly lifeless, with no evidence anything inside is functional.

But the beacon works. But the beacon has worked all these years.

C-433 has been alive for only a short while, and yet in the rung are lifetimes stacked on top of lifetimes, each remembering whatever could be lived between his emergence from the Loom and his return to the recycler, lives now indistinctly intertwined, each too much like another, their individual strands impossible to separate. He cannot help but bend before the remainder's aggregate pressure: he imagines stopping here, dressing in cloak and goggles and glove—only one glove needed, since his left fist is no longer a hand but a wooden gnarl—and heading out into the snow, the trunk leg dragging a furrow behind him. Limping along the crawler's underside, he would search for a hatch whose seal he might pry free from the rust and the ice. Digging his claws at the cracked rubber seams, finding purchase in slim crevices filled with powdery silt, pulling at the hatch with his one good arm until the door opens. Wandering the crawler's dark hallways, veins of cold scrawling the walls like roots of ice, C not knowing if the solar panels are intact, if their deployment mechanisms can be unstuck. The remainder remembering: how C's crawler was kept functional by never letting its power dwindle or shutting off the heat pumps, by clearing its solar panels of debris in all but the worst weather. The remainder had known how to use the failing fabricators in the crawler's bowels to make new panels or heat couplers, how to replace the miles of tubing and wiring the crawler required, easy enough for as long as enough feedstock remained.

But every time a broken part got recycled, a little more was lost. Another lossy process never meant to last so long.

The remainder doesn't care for C's objections. The remainder does not want to be a tree, a flowering freak made a home for beetles. It wants to be a blue-furred creature with two good-enough hooves; it wants to be a creature of sharp claws and spiraling horns, lone survivor of a world in which everything else has died.

But C-433 is not the prime version of himself, only the runtish last of his lineage, the smallest C ever printed. One of his horns is plastic; the other, brittle keratin, chipping now where the encroaching tree pushes against it. One hoof a fabricated slab, heavier than the organic other, the imbalance having given his gait an uneven limp even before his leg was stiffened by bark.

The crawler tempts but C resists. It promises a safety he no longer wants, that C-433 never accepted. Even if this crawler's Loom works, even if it could rebuild him, it would rebuild him not as himself but as someone less. It's only the tree—its bark and branches and buds, its grasses and its flowers and its beetles—that might make him more.

C-433 knows so little. But even he knows better than to want to be less ever again.

C drives the bubble out of the crawler's shadow and into the afternoon sunlight, navigating the forest of frozen thorns. "I am not afraid," he says aloud, but the urge to turn back isn't so easily dispelled. The shadows of the towering spikes fall across the bubble, black, angular, forbidding, dangerous; C pilots, O sings, the beetles crawl quickly around the bubble, dispersing the heady bouquet of pollen into the stuck air. In many places the thorns crowd the bubble and drive it sideways, but C continues his careful passage, looping in ever-elongated arcs, looking for the easiest places to cross the low walls and the drifts. Hours pass like this, his progress slow and methodical but always eventually forward. Finally the thorns begin to shrink, the walls between spreading out and then vanishing, until the path once more smooths into rolling snowdrifts, prompting a confident half-smile to cross C's face, creasing the half of his face capable of smiling.

Just before sunset, C enters a narrow valley between the mountain's first slopes, an icy reach inset with columnar structures made of the same polished black synroc as the thorns: dozens of monoliths arrayed in a regular grid of diagonal rows, easily navigable. O's voice ebbs and flows, coming at C's lonely prompting, going at his frustrated irritation; as the bubble approaches the first monoliths, its song gets louder, the keening banshee dirge climbing to a new and more terrible register.

Distracted, C summons the command console, fingers the haptic button marked MUTE—but nothing happens. The drone C hears sounds similar to O's, but it's not coming from inside the bubble. It's coming from outside, from many directions, from the monoliths, from all the monoliths at once. Whatever O's song is, this is the same droning amplified and condensed, weaponized as a sonic wall, a black bruise of noise buckling C's courage, testing his will. His teeth grind, his free eye waters and twitches, his exposed skin burns, and then the bark burns too, the tree's flowers folding their petals, the beetles crawling back into the cracks from which they emerged.

The sound bashes against C's refusal to retreat. By the time the bubble passes the first row of monoliths, his nose has begun to bleed from his one free nostril, the red slop dripping across his mouth and into the bark crossing the meridian of his chin, the accompanying pain blinding enough he almost misses the dense lines of glittering silver language that cover the monoliths, dozens of scripts orbiting the circular columns.

He wipes his face with the back of his blue-furred hand, then spins a tight circle around one of the monoliths. He reads logograms representing nothing he has ever seen, glyphs from regions unknown, words more like paintings than language, though he thinks he's never seen a painting; he finds scripts made of characters he recognizes but whose words remain senseless, words similar but not similar enough to the only language he speaks, the language of the rung, of the crawler's binders, of the bubble's displays. His vision pulses, his temples burn; the drone from the monolith is a thudding violence, but he holds his course, circles one more time around until he finds the one language he speaks, only to be disappointed that the message seems not worth the effort or the pain, the same message the monoliths and the noise-wall and the thorns have already wordlessly communicated:

THIS COLUMN IS A MESSAGE, PART OF A SYSTEM OF MES-SAGES. THE MESSAGES ARE ALL WARNINGS. NO ESTEEMED DEAD ARE BURIED HERE. NOTHING OF VALUE IS BURIED HERE. DO NOT PROCEED. RETURN TO WHERE YOU CAME. THE SOUND YOU HEAR IS A LAST WARNING. THE NEXT PART OF THE MESSAGE IS DEATH. TURN BACK. TURN BACK. TURN BACK.

Disappointed, C pilots the bubble away, seeking a place inside the grid where he'll be equidistant from a number of the monoliths. He wants to flee farther, but he's misjudged how much daylight remains. The sun drops fast, taking with it any hope for recharging the bubble's perilously depleted batteries;

with the sun gone, C can't safely retreat outside the field of monoliths. The bubble makes it only a couple hundred meters in the direction where C believes the entrance to Black Mountain waits—it must be close, if he can no longer see the mountain face through the snow swirling before the bubble's headlamps. The wind blows, but even in the highest gusts the bubble barely rocks, its repulsors powerful enough on flat ground to keep it steady in a storm; the wind blows more and more violently but not loud enough to block the monoliths' sound, their repetitive keening threatening to send C fully mad.

BUT THEN, A MINOR MERCY: THE SINGING MONOLITHS TURN OUT to be solar powered. They must've once had a continuous power source, some buried battery now degraded or else a generator long unfueled and unmaintained. In those years, the monoliths might've relied on the pale sun only for backup, but now, as the sun sets, so their harsh rendition of O's song slows, its effectiveness failing as its sound distends; after dusk, a snowstorm arrives, further dampening the broadcast as column after column is blanketed by snow, the chorus of voices becoming fewer until there's only a single voice, then none. A relieved moment of silence follows, before O's voice rises inside the bubble, this time with a new melody utterly unlike the harsh keening that had accompanied C across the continent. This is what music once was, how it sounded at its best, in a world C cannot remember: a comfort, a beauty, a pleasure. His heart thuds, but not with fear, not with terror. With all the face he has left, he crooks his stiffened lips into an expression he has rarely known, something like *joy*. This is song as unfiltered sunlight, this is song as gentle rain, this is song as dank soil, this is everything a tree needs that the frozen earth no longer provides, with its bright white sky dulling the sun.

C's body droops against the supportive trunk of his tree. He could be dreaming or hallucinating. With his woody neck making it difficult to turn his head more than a degree or two, he can barely lift his heavy left arm to see how its enlivened bark swells, flush with more moisture than could possibly be leeched from his parched flesh. It's night outside the bubble, but under its dim interior light all the blossoms flare their petals, stretching their flowers, opening themselves to a sun they cannot see but instead hear, exposing pistil and stamen, loosing clouds of bright yellow pollen into the bubble's cramped curves, its sweet smell carried aloft by recycled air. A moment later, dozens of C's cysts pop open at once, his bark spilling forth new black-and-yellow beetles, their no-longer-translucent bodies climbing to the surface, their carapaces freshly moist, their hungry mouthparts clicking audibly in the near dark.

When the new beetles take flight, C cries out first in alarm, then in delight. All this time, he'd thought a beetle was a thing that *crawled*.

The air fills with buzzing and clacking, bright music, the creaking of bark, a human voice expressing joyful surprise. The translucent photovoltaic bubble is tonight a globe full of life, life barely lit beneath a dim heat lamp but warm enough and temporarily safe within a sustenance of song, the bubble's globe a glass world around which heavy wet snow falls and falls and falls.

C's joy doesn't last. When he wakes the following morning in silent gray light, he finds his flowers wilted, their blossoms drooping. A few beetles buzz the air, but without last night's frenzied ardor; others litter the floor, their upturned bodies unmoving. Summoning the command console, he stares at the barely lit battery indicator, hopelessly willing its bar to fill. He can force the bubble forward, but if he empties the reserves, he'll face the same fate as the inhabitants of the dark crawler crashed against the field of thorns; if he proceeds, he risks not just forward movement but heat and light, air and water. If he stays, the snow might bury the bubble, preventing it from charging.

Everything is running down: the bubble's battery, C's overtaken body, the dying beetles. He reaches out his good hand, sends a ping from the rung to call the nutrient tube snaking up from its port in the flooring, then sucks greedily at the paste's thinnest gruel yet.

The weak sun remains masked behind dense clouds dumping more snow, the combination enough to keep the monoliths nearly silent, a grid of creaking, crackling speakers, the carved messages now obscured. C checks the craft's battery level, notes the quick-dropping number. As long as the sun breaks through, there'll be enough power to move forward safely. But at midmorning the clouds blacken, then spike with green lightning. The bubble steams as C wipes down its fogging glass in broad circles, trying to keep visibility clear, though all there is to see is more snow falling, drifts piling up around the bubble, forcing him to lift the craft higher into the air, expending more power to keep it from being buried.

It snows until dusk. And then it snows all night.

And in the morning, the second spent among the monoliths, it's snowing still.

A whole day wasted. C's furious with himself, but there's nothing to do to fix his mistaken delay but hurry on, beginning too late through the eerie silence of the snow-covered monoliths, toward whatever next obstacle lies beyond.

The monolith grid fills a valley several kilometers deep, but at its far edge its uniformity breaks down: here some columns are toppled and shattered, while others are riddled with holes or bolted with cracks. The bubble exits the cramped valley into a wider bowl, a flat oval covered in fresh powder. The bubble's radar sweeps the path ahead, offers C's rung a provisional map: visibility is nearly nil, but C believes that if the snow lifted he'd find the entrance to Black Mountain across this last plane, buried in the hidden rock face. The only other features he can see are two mounds a hundred meters off, humps of earth whose purpose he can't imagine.

C pilots the bubble slowly forward, O's voice rising as they accelerate toward the mounds, then barking out sharp exhalations as the bubble's repulsors begin to brown out, not all at once but in random sequence, the bubble's battery no longer able to power all the repulsors continuously. The bubble lists and jostles, its gyroscopic floor tilts unsteadily. C leans against his tree side for balance and hears a sharp crack as the bark near his left knee breaks painfully. Somewhere below the kneecap, he's bleeding sap; he grits his proper teeth against his plastic ones, rights his balance the best he can, and pushes on.

As the bubble approaches the twin earth mounds, he hears a new noise: a grinding, a clattering. He looks back and forth between the two mounds, O's upset and upsetting voice making thought difficult. C watches as the top of each mound slowly rises, revealing the lid's mechanism, and from within each mound a perforated barrel slowly comes into view, turning grindingly toward the bubble. *Machine gun*—the name comes quickly enough, its danger vivid even in C's dim mind. Now he reconsiders the cracked and pitted monoliths he passed: as the machine-gun nests continue their creaking turn toward him, he imagines the last crawler's inhabitants crossing the approach plane on foot, having navigated the field of thorns and braved the madness of the monoliths, only to be gunned down on this last stretch of open land, bullets riddling their bodies, clattering off the columns behind them.

C should flee, but the bubble's battery is depleted, his breathing is shallow, and his stomach empty. If he advances, the turning weapons might fire. If he retreats, he'll die against the monoliths, with O's voice torturing him until the bubble's power dies, then the columns eternally singing their dirges over his spherical grave, keening on whenever the sun shines.

He pushes forward, the command bouncing from his rung to the bubble's repulsors; when the craft lurches, he catches his balance with a second sick crunching in the trunk of his left leg, a spraying seep of blood-sap puddling the floor. Only a lucky failure of ancient machinery offers any jolt of hope: the leftmost machine gun slips its track, falls over uselessly. But the other continues to rise, tracking the bubble's progress, tracking C, the human-enough being peering through the bubble's translucent shell.

"There must be something we can do," C says to the remainder, what little is left, its many voices so assimilated into his own personality that when it responds, isn't it only C-433 answering himself, his frustrations accusing and angry, viscerally felt?

We never should have left. We could've lived forever, if only we hadn't been you.

"No," C says. "Or yes, but I don't care. Because I chose this life. Because I choose it still." The snowfall is unceasing, the way forward unsure, the destination close, the intervening danger present: with a thought transmitted through the rung, with a gesture of his right paw against the haptic console, C chooses again. He chooses whatever future might lie beyond this moment: Onward toward whatever happens next, toward the moment where his story ends, whether the machine gun fires, whether the machine gun does not. Through the dim light and the blowing snow, he watches the functional machine gun nest loom closer, its barrel spinning up, the ungreased sound of its revolutions audible across the last fifty meters, now the last forty. Any second now. The craft rocks forward unsteadily, its repulsors firing on one side and then the other—and then thirty meters from the machine-gun nests the repulsors fail completely, the translucent photovoltaic bubble dropping to the ground with a deafening crack.

O screams—O, whose existence is tied to the bubble and the battery and the data bank into which it's been downloaded; O, who's been so long disembodied, so long unable to speak in anything other than song—O screams a single unbroken note so brutally sustained C's eardrums pop and his nose bleeds and his beetles rise into the air to buzz fiercely against the bubble's curves. Outside the glass the machine gun spins its perforated barrel faster and faster, the belt feeding its chamber starting to vibrate with malice.

C's fur crawls with fear, his leaves quiver atop their thorny branches, amid wavering purple grass. He closes his eyes, waits for the end—but then the machine gun's barrel slows instead, emitting a rusty whine.

By the time C finally dares to look, the machine gun is still, its whine quieted. Now two figures appear from the far edge of visibility, both emitting a pale green light whose glows cuts through the snowstorm's blank white accumulation, both exactly unlike anything C thinks he's ever seen.

C's never seen another mammal, much less another living

person. He has, until this moment, thought that what it meant to be fully human was to be like him, with horns and claws, hooves and fur.

Before this, he never imagined he was the anomaly.

But then it's not like either of the figures approaching the bubble is exactly human, not what was last meant by the word, in the long gone world that was.

PART THREE

EURY

At dawn Eury Mirov appears on every telescreen in the Farm, shaking hands in Syracuse, Brussels, Beijing: the American president, the president of the European Commission, the Chinese general secretary. Three geographically distant and asynchronous events presented as if simultaneous, a seeming impossibility even though the Chinese newscast and the American one are each labeled LIVE in the corner of their feeds. One or both are surely erroneous, but so much news is misleading, if not outright faked, that it's impossible to know which one might be wrong. In all three cities, Eury Mirov delivers the same speech, each video playing side by side, each Eury announcing the Pinatubo Project's readiness with the same exacting precision, in the same well-practiced cadence. Her speech is grandiose, sweeping, promising everything but purposely vague, the most granular details unnecessary, she says.

"In three days," Eury explains, three times across three feeds, "Earthtrust will deliver a massive payload of sulfuric aerosols into the stratosphere, beginning the process of cooling our shared planet. We funded the research, we tested the results and designed the fail-safes, we have prepared ourselves to successfully lead the most audacious effort in human history. Our teams in each Earthtrust VAC—in Ohio, in Bavaria, in Overberg and Sichuan and the Punjab, in Chile and Brazil and so many other places—all have gathered the necessary materials, technology, and expertise."

She presents no facts, no figures; offers no diagrams or video mock-ups. The only evidence on offer is Eury Mirov herself. Three times, she says, "By itself, this effort will not save the world. And still there will be sacrifices to come, there will be unforeseen hardships. But together with our Volunteers we will push back the danger to our civilization another hundred years, maybe more. We will give ourselves time to save our children and grandchildren; we can make time for our children and grandchildren to save themselves."

What Eury doesn't say is how geoengineering is a trap disguised as a solution. If Pinatubo succeeds, then yes, its stratospheric aerosol scattering will give humanity time to draw down new carbon emissions and to sequester what's already in the atmosphere, after which the solar-blocking aerosols could safely be allowed to dissipate—but if carbon emissions continue to accumulate, as they have for three hundred years, then any disruption to Pinatubo might result in global temperatures quickly and irreversibly rising four or five or six degrees Celsius, causing every worst-case catastrophe to arrive everywhere at once.

What else Eury doesn't say: even if Pinatubo works, our

children will grow up beneath a white sky, the blue every human has known hidden above a cooling layer of glittering sulfates.

Two-thirds of the way through Eury's speech, the Beijing feed is interrupted by an unheard commotion off-screen. The Chinese camera slides sideways, then falls over, leaving Eury speaking in Syracuse and Brussels while the feed between them blue-screens.

In the two remaining feeds, Eury says, "Ten years ago, governments everywhere believed it would soon become impossible to feed their populations, but Earthtrust found a way. Our engineered orchards of supertrees, our drought-resistant crops, our incredibly productive cattle and pigs who can be raised to twice the size on half the water, these were our gifts to your peoples. We've taken your refugees onto our farms, we've given them safe shelter, clean food and water, education and health care, meaningful work. Our Volunteers come from every country and practice every religion, but their differences do not exclude them from our united purpose, laboring to feed the world. And are you not fed? Whoever you are, wherever you are, our Volunteers put food on your table. While the rest of the world burned, our Volunteers regreened the earth they were given, making the soil beneath their feet productive again."

All over the world people stop to watch Eury speak, Eury dressed in her monochromatic asymmetric cloak, futuristic clothing for a woman promising to make the future; Eury with her practiced gestures identical in the streams still broadcasting from Brussels and Syracuse; Eury locking eyes with the camera and smiling her famous Eury Mirov smile, saying, "One way or another, Earthtrust will always do what is necessary."

In Brussels, the parliament of the European Union votes

to denounce the plan, over the objections of certain members who have to be dragged from the chambers by EU soldiers, the representatives of the nations hardest hit by rising sea waters and other disasters screaming for Pinatubo's necessity. In Syracuse, at an emergency meeting of the United Nations Security Council, the Chinese and Russian ambassadors veto any chance for approval of the project, their vetoes loudly objected to by an unconvincing American president.

What's left of television journalism explodes, speculation and righteous anger leaving twelve pundits on-screen at a time, everyone speaking over one another, no one listening.

An hour later, Eury appears again, her image pushing the angry screaming faces to the periphery. On the steps of the repurposed capitol in Syracuse, Eury speaks while behind her stands the American president, his hands clasped, head down, cowed. "The United States government," she says, "in accordance with the terms of Earthtrust's territorial governance agreement over the Western Sacrifice Zone and the continental Voluntary Agricultural Communities, has pledged its support for the America-first deployment of the Pinatubo Project. The rest of the world has three days to accept our offer, or else Earthtrust will proceed alone."

Now Earthtrust proves it's become one of the world's superpowers, an empire dispersed, based everywhere and nowhere. The company's agreements overseas are substantially the same as in the United States: each VAC is in practice a sovereign land governed by its own laws and rights, not answerable to the host country from which it was carved. And because there's no nation left that can grow enough food to feed its people without Eury Mirov's help, any country that attacks the VAC inside its border dooms its food supply.

On every telescreen in the Farm—on every screen in all the VACs she controls, in all the territories she's conquered across the world—Eury Mirov beams while the American president cringes, red-faced, hair amiss, beaten.

Raising one black-gloved hand, Eury brandishes an unnecessary prop, a red button set in chromed steel, brought along to sell the moment's drama. "In three days," she says, "we save the world."

At the press of the button, a timer appears in the corner of each feed, the countdown quickly spreading to every other channel, pushed to every screen worldwide.

In three days, Eury promises, the world changes forever.

CHAPMAN

The first spring of Nathaniel's last decade, he and Chapman gather their seeds from a cider mill only miles from the Worth homestead. For the first time, they compete for supplies with other apple planters, winter-worn cash-poor homesteaders going directly to the source. In the mill's yard, Nathaniel shouts curses at a rival arrived early, a black-eyed man half his age and twice his size; for his trouble Nathaniel gets shoved down in the muddy lot. With his faunness hidden inside his human skin, Chapman's nervous, unsure in a fight. He's never hurt a man in his life, but at least as a faun he'd had the latent strength of his claws, the ready power of a hooved kick or a toss of the horns. As a man he is only calloused hands, wiry muscle, unremarkable in this state where every man's body might be reduced to calluses and scars, his spirit made a pragmatic meanness born of desperation, fed by greed.

Chapman pulls the attacker off his brother, but the man's already gathered the best of the mill's offerings. The brothers content themselves with what remains, less viable seeds shattered by the millstone, reluctantly dug from the stinking shoveled piles of already-rotted pomace.

"It's not enough," Nathaniel says, looking into the ruin of apple flesh inside his half-filled bag. "Barely enough seeds for a single planting."

"That lack gives us time to tend last year's nurseries," Chapman soothes, thinking of all the trees he's not yet tested, all their untasted apples going to waste. "And then on the way back, we'll collect what we know we're owed."

Nathaniel scowls, but at least it's a plan. A single nursery, planted as far west as they can manage, then a loop through the orchards Nathaniel sowed while Chapman was missing. And all the while, Chapman can search for his Tree, safely avoiding his pursuers, who cannot seem to find him in his human form. It's a good plan, he thinks, as they begin again their yearly pilgrimage, but now there's less forest waiting, now there are fewer isolated campfires in sheltered dales, now many trees they once knew almost by name have gone missing, cut down for log cabins and general stores, for millhouses and mine outbuildings, or else burned to make space for cornfields and barley, grazing grasses for cattle or sheep, pigs or goats.

"This," Nathaniel says, surveying the still-new State before them, "this, brother, is where we'll make our fortune"—but before he's finished speaking another settler burdened with his own heavily laden pack shoulders by, pushing Nathaniel roughly aside, transforming his accustomed speech into a furious stammer.

That first night, Chapman lies restless on his bedroll, trying to will himself to sleep, to dream of the Worths' sweet laughter, their kind words. Instead, one of the witching women appears, a nightmare crouched low over spindly legs, her gums smacking, yellow teeth clacking woodenly around missing others, her shape hunched and bulging. The witch's skin is wet with perspiration or precipitation, her mane of hair falling over a topography of flesh, mountains of engorged breasts and a sunken valley of belly, her shape less a body than a landscape; a blizzard begins, piling white and clean atop the witch's shoulders, blessing the scene Chapman dreams with a false holiness, as if such a creature as the witch could be beautiful, as if such a monster could be innocent as the driven snow.

Chapman wakes with a start, his fur threatening to ripple out from beneath his skin, revealing him; once his shape is back under his control, he counts the dream as one more reason never to pass a winter anywhere called *territory* or *frontier*. In the morning, the brothers strike camp eagerly, ready to be gone into the continued unscrolling of America. The spring is pleasantly warm and lushly green, but there are fewer opportunities for foraging and hunting along the roadside, new fencing leaving nowhere to pick berries or dig tubers, while the game animals are all hunted or routed or else unreachable without crossing some other man's claim. Still Chapman whistles as he walks the crowded road west, more at ease in the company of others after his sojourn at the Worths'. Atop one quiet wagon he spies a young man absently stringing a fiddle, and he begs the boy to play his instrument loud and lively, until all in his dour company are laughing and dancing their way down the rut-pitted road. When the music stops, the cheered family invites the brothers to travel with them as far as they'd like, but Chapman weighs Nathaniel's glower, thinks better of accepting the offer.

He shakes his head and whistles on, humming a snatch of tune learned from little Eliza Worth, *The Lord's been good to me, and so I thank the Lord*, an earworm carving out the rotting apple of his brain.

Chapman sings, Nathaniel scowls, the roads finally become less crowded the farther west they travel. What used to be mere days of travel becomes two weeks, then a month, the distance to be covered farther than ever before. Before they've planted a single tree, they've consumed half the provisions meant to last the summer, food eaten early because the lands they passed through were not free for Nathaniel to hunt on or for Chapman to gather other foodstuffs.

Nathaniel grows angrier with every mile, the pomace in their bags drying fast, the bad seeds getting worse. It's May already when the brothers pass the last homestead at the edge of an undrained stand of swampland, what might be the new edge of what frontier is left in Ohio. Seeking a suitable nursery site, they discover instead more human signs: a trapline strung through the dark woods, steel-jawed traps baited with gutted rabbits split at their seams, with squirrel corpses dusted with powdered poison. Traps meant for wolves the homesteaders blame for lost cattle, missing goats; traps for wolves even before there are many cattle or goats to lose.

At first the brothers see only the loaded traps, but soon they find the wolves, trapped: wolves struggling in steel; wolves dead of bloody injuries and poison. Wolves with broken forepaws, shattered skulls; wolves with black tongues, bulged eyeballs. At the next unsprung trap, Chapman takes his walking stick and depresses the trigger plate, slamming the jaws on a poisoned rabbit left for bait. The rabbit is harder to disarm, because even with the trap sprung, anything eating of this rabbit will die.

"Brother," Nathaniel says, "this isn't your problem."

"Brother," Chapman says, uselessly tugging at the stuck rabbit, "if we don't help, who will?"

Nathaniel huffs with impatience but doesn't stop Chapman. All he might say has been said a million times before. That time wasted is paid in trees not planted. That without planted trees, they cannot make their fortune.

But by now Nathaniel must know a delay barely matters, if unplanted trees are its only cost.

Chapman kicks off his boots, rolls his trousers to his knees. He crouches, rocks back and forth to dig his leathery heels into the soil. His toes grip the dirt, he closes his eyes, he tugs the earth toward himself as he slips out of one skin into another. Once he's a faun again, he reaches for the poison-dosed rabbit, digging the claws of his first two fingers into its stiff fur to tear it from the trap. It takes only a few minutes to dig the rabbit a shallow grave, his claws more than capable of loosening the forest floor. When the work is done, he slides the rabbit into its hole, smooths the dirt with the flat of his hand, rues the impossibility of keeping the harm humans do confined to any one place. No matter what he does, the poison in the rabbit will eventually find its way into some other living thing: if not the scavenging birds and mammals, then worms, maggots, the burrowing insects alive beneath the earth.

"Are we going to bury every rabbit we find, brother?" asks Nathaniel—but when Chapman turns, Nathaniel knows the answer. The trapline is laid along the same path the brothers planned to take; they discover more snares, some already sprung, some waiting, the traps coated with beeswax or animal blood, anything to cover the human scent.

Chapman quickly buries the dead. The poison will spread

if it isn't contained; the forest is a system of interlocking cause and effect, nothing can be made so discrete: a dead wolf eating a poisoned rabbit becomes poisoned itself, could poison the crow or raven who feeds on its corpse. Even with Nathaniel adding his trowel to the effort, the work is extraordinarily slow, the devastation widening. When the traps disappear, more brutal methods arise to replace them: now the brothers find sleek coyotes and slender foxes, poisoned. Then a black bear, eyes bloodshot, belly distended, breathing its last in a watery ditch; dead owls, their wings broken when they fell from the sky, their flat faces rictuses; a bald eagle, its neck twisted, a string of raw meat flagging from its beak. Along their path are innumerable deer shot through their ribs, bright red lung blood matted into fur powdered with strychnine, their bodies surrounded by dead and dying wolves, mouths foamed, steps staggered or stilled. Everywhere they go they find more carrion birds, they watch the bare heads of doomed vultures digging into so much poisonous flesh, the big black birds impossible to scare away, even to save their lives.

Defeated, Chapman and Nathaniel walk on silently, grieving in death's wake. Chapman broods, his vision swimming with rage. Nathaniel's gorge rises visibly. The smell of hot blood, wet rot. The fury both men feel. Right now Chapman doesn't know if he could retake his human shape, doesn't believe its lesser form could contain this much anger, this burning a grief.

Late in the afternoon, after the sweltering heat has turned the many corpses to stinking, festering ruin, Nathaniel raises a hand to Chapman, motions for him to stop. "Look, brother. Through the trees." Chapman follows Nathaniel's pointing finger: a hundred yards away, a giant of a man sits astride a coal-black horse, the man dressed in dark furs despite the heat, the horse straining to drag its overladen sledge. The horse advances slowly, whinnying its disgust or fear at the slaughter all around, the giant leaves everything behind but the wolf skins, all the proof needed to collect his bounties.

An ingenious entrepreneur, this man. Another American innovator, accepting all the collateral damage of his method, as long as he earns what he's owed.

The giant turns in the direction of Nathaniel's voice, leaning over his pommel to peer into the pines. By the time Nathaniel says, "Hide, brother," Chapman is already vanished into the brush, his face burning. He's not a violent creature, or he wasn't before, when he lived only as a faun. But some of man's volatility must've followed him back into his other shape, because now he knows he intends to hurt this trapper.

"Who's there?" the giant says, his voice booming. He swings a leg over his horse, drops down to draw a rifle from his saddle's scabbard. There's a rifle in Nathaniel's hands too but Chapman doubts it's loaded: it's only used for hunting, and never again in Chapman's presence.

"Why are you doing this?" Nathaniel says, his voice choked. He steps past Chapman's hiding place, his jaw set, a vein pulsing at his sun-freckled temple as he closes to within twenty feet of the trapper. "Why would anyone do this?"

"A dollar a pelt," the giant replies, his voice matter of fact as he dismissively gestures at the nearest dead wolf. He spits, exposing a mouthful of missing teeth, the phlegmy wad of tobacco barely escaping his beard. "I'm going to be rich once I get all these back."

Chapman slips tree to tree, moving closer through the shadows, shuddering whenever the wind rustles the canopy, close enough to smell the giant, his rotten slaughterhouse stench. Deciding Nathaniel's no threat, the man sets his rifle on the ground, then pulls a dully gleaming knife from beneath his fur cloak. Nathaniel stares, Chapman seethes, the giant hacks the fur from a wolf's skull, unzips the skin from the bloated torso, then begins undressing the hind legs with a series of jerks, pulling crudely until Nathaniel says, "Stop. Stop, goddamn it. This isn't right. Look at everything you killed to skin a wolf."

It's not only the animal in the trap, half stripped. An overturned hawk lies bloated a dozen yards away, its wings raised in rigor mortis; a pair of coyotes lie unseen in the brush Chapman slinks through, foam leaking from muzzles pressed nose to nose as they expired.

The man sneers, a fresh dribble of tobacco crying out the side of his mouth. He says, "You'd rather someone's sheep get taken? Someone's calf, someone's pig?" He stands, not picking up his rifle but brandishing the knife, the pitted blade slick with wolf's blood. "Maybe someone's kid, a girl in pigtails playing in the trees?"

Nathaniel raises his musket. "Stay back," he says, his voice quavering.

How old he's become, already fifteen when Chapman was born, then aging ahead of him while Chapman was gone in the flicker. From his hiding spot, Chapman watches quivering Nathaniel, never tall nor brawny, now reduced to sunspotted leather stretched over scrawny bones, but still brave enough to face the giant alone, with only his unloaded musket to protect him.

Not that Chapman has to let him. He lets the trapper advance another step before he violates the one rule Nathaniel gave him as a child, a rule he has until this moment hewed to without question: now the faun reveals himself with a roar, baring his sharp teeth, shaking his horns in warning. He flexes his clawed fists, he stamps a hoof; a barking grunt escapes his snarl. As the giant turns, the man's face twists in slow, dumb horror, barely reacting in time when his terrified horse rears at the faun's unnatural voice, yanking its tether from the ground with a jerk of its thick neck.

At the last second, the giant ducks the flying spike at the end of the whipping tether, then dodges past the horse's panicking hooves to snatch its whipping reins. In the moment it takes him to mount his bucking horse, Nathaniel cries for Chapman to hide himself again, but it's too late, there's nothing Nathaniel can do to stop him, the hooved faun already trying to run down the hooved horse. The horse is fast and powerful but still tied to its sledge of wolfskins, the sledge now slamming over rocks and logs, banging against the trunks of trees.

Chapman runs steadily after, leaping over the same obstructions with ease, his body nimble, quick, happy to flow into motion; he's never given chase before, but he's well built for the task, his shape eager to be moving at faunish speed after months spent in a man's skin.

Then it happens again, just as he should've known it would.

He's a dozen strides back when he hears the song. He hears the beheaded singer's terrible noise, and then he sees the first of the witches: not the woman but the panther, its yellow eyes flashing as it leaps through the air, dragging the giant from his saddle; and then the grizzly appears too, surging from a bramble to grip the horse's throat in her jaws, knocking the animal off its hooves. The giant is the one dying but it's Chapman who screams the loudest, stumbling to a stop as the slaughter begins. The witches have become furies, righteous protectors of these lands, come for the trapper for reasons different from why they come for Chapman, or so he at first thinks. But what if it's not only the crimes of the past the witches seek to punish? What if the violations of this life count against him too, crimes committed against the wild world he helped undo, that he and the other settlers so carelessly uproot?

"What do you want from me?" he cries, his voice rising above the unfolding carnage. "Anything but this," he says. "Anything to make this stop. Tell me what you want and I will do it."

The grizzly and the panther show no sign of having heard, instead continuing their attack, the earth beneath their paws thrashed and rent and churned to bloody mud until the forest clearing is made an abattoir. The grizzly drags the horse by its throat, pinning its head to the ground while its body bucks and jerks, its hooves kicking in the air; the panther buries its dark head to the ears in the giant trapper's opened torso, its jaws making a wet squelching sound almost loud enough to drown out his screams.

"Tell me what you want," Chapman repeats, his voice halting now, sickened by what he sees, what he's caused. He'd planned to hurt the giant too, had believed the trapper didn't deserve mercy after what he'd done, but could anyone deserve this?

The dead wolves, the dead bears and deer and elk, the dead rabbits and squirrels and owls, the doomed vultures circling them all. All that death was the trapper's fault, all that death would be paid for by his own death, coming any second now. But it was Chapman's change that called the witches. It was the call of Chapman's faunness that brought them here, in this moment.

He admits this even before he hears the third witch speak: the violence he sees before him is his fault too.

With the bear and the panther occupied, it's only the woman who is also a vulture who can answer Chapman's cries. With the singer under her arm, she turns toward the faun, her bird-self hidden inside human-enough skin, the witch-beast no less a shapeshifter than he is. When she opens her mouth to speak, it's in a voice like underground water, the deep secret of a hidden river rushing with ancient rain-seep, its currents coldly crashing through limestone conduits. There is sense and syntax in the sounds she makes, Chapman's sure, but the meaning of her speech remains foreign. He grows frustrated at her refusal to speak as a human would; she's likewise visibly agitated at his incomprehension.

At last the witch's voice falls silent as she extends her arm to brandish the singer's head: if Chapman cannot listen, then he must see instead. For a moment there is only more ripping flesh and crunching bones, the vengeance of the witches and the world they serve; then a sudden vision takes shape, its reality born into being upon the singer's song, a manifested glimpse of a frozen world devoid of life, a white world where all lies silent and utterly cold, where no one screams except a horse and a giant, the latter at last silenced only after he's torn limb from limb by the bear and the panther.

Chapman can't look anymore, can't make himself watch whatever might happen next. Even if this is the only part of his answer he can understand, he wants it not. He turns on his hooves, fleeing this vision of bloody revenge and frozen future for the Territory he knows, for the pale body he has to wear

there now, this shell of a shoeless, frightened man, who soon
finds his brother where he left him, still shaking in the falling
dark: here is Nathaniel, far from the melee, weeping uselessly,
furiously trying to load his musket, too late, too late, too late,
his terrified paralysis breaking only after Chapman yells for him
to *run*.

JOHN

Volunteers crowd the viewing platform at the base of the Tower, their lunching families squeezed against the railings to look down on the re-created herd of bison grazing among the original supertree groves, a habitat edged by buried electric fences, cornered by the Tower's legs. The park is a gift to the Volunteers from Eury, at first glance as relaxing and cheering a place as any in the Farm ever was—but John knows that the park's potential for continually attracting visitors means that the gathering Volunteers will create a continuous shield of innocents around Eury Mirov's sure-to-be-targeted headquarters, hopefully promising enough collateral damage to pause a planned military strike.

If all goes well, that hesitation is all Eury is going to need.

John twists through the rear of the gathering, leaving the better angles to the other Volunteers. It's barely been two days

since John entered the Tower, but already the outside feels unfamiliar, strangely alien. The Volunteers' collective oohing over
the bison mixes with scattered nervous chatter about Eury's
pronouncement, but neither the cloning nor the promise of
eminent geoengineering seems to provoke true anxiety or anger. These Volunteers have been rescued, their sacrifices made
noble by Eury's rhetoric, their children guaranteed a future
thought lost. John's father was born before the twenty-first century began, when it was possible to choose to believe in growth
forever, in market forces solving every social ill. Those promises proved false, but here was another come to replace them,
a story by which the world might be saved, or at least made
understandable again.

John finds the others leaning against a stretch of rail two-
thirds of the way around the viewing platform. Julie and Noor
are dressed in the muted colors of the Volunteer wardrobe, gray
or blue pants, equally plain t-shirts and button-downs, and
work boots; only Mai wears clothes purchased off-site, her
yellow dress a conspicuous burst of color against the monochrome others. Julie and Noor look out over the bison herd,
their hips gently knocking; Mai leans beside them, tossing her
shiny black ponytail, laughing at a joke John isn't close enough
to hear.

It's Cal, standing on the far side of the group, dressed in
gray jeans and a pale blue shirt, her sleeves rolled to her powerful shoulders, who sees John first, the others turning toward his
approach only after she speaks. "You're late, old goat," she says,
then steps forward to pull him close, mashing her lips against
his. John flushes with embarrassment; the others laugh, as always. He steps away from Cal to greets his friends, the reunion
happy enough but their small talk fizzling fast. Soon they're

leaned against the rail, standing close enough for their pebbles to link up via near-field communication, their retinal displays activating at Cal's command.

"Twenty-four hours to launch," she says, her usual teasing good humor banished from her voice. "We don't have much time left. Everyone seeing what I'm seeing?" She taps her temple, centering the synchronized image mirrored in their retinal displays, overlaid across the pasturing bison. "Good. This is the Tower as mapped by John's bees, incomplete but likely good enough. Mai's been inside for the last year—are we missing anything important?"

Mai leans forward, her eyes blinking rapidly as she manipulates the blueprint, clicking downward through the cross-sectioned floors. The shared display shifts with every squeeze of her hand, its focus plummeting down the needle to the executive suites at its base, then past the research layer below, then more administrative offices, the medical wing, other more mundane parts of the complex. "Not that I can see. But I've never been to the research floors or into the needle, so only John can answer for those parts of the Tower. When you get inside tomorrow, the first place you need to reach is the security nexus, sticking out right there from the south side of the Tower, on the first main floor above the Tower's legs. If we can take the nexus, we can control access to the elevators, reprogram the Tower's pebble readers, shut off security cameras."

"That'll be your job then: we'll get Noor to the nexus, then you'll help her hold it. You're going to have to be ready to fight." Cal pauses, drums her fingers along the railing. "Which brings us to our next problem. The neighborhoods have programmable printers, but anything usable as a weapon or an explosive will be flagged as contraband, triggering a security check."

In the Sacrifice Zone, Earthtrust security forces were fully militarized, but on the Farm, security seems to be mostly plainclothes officers, maintaining an illusion of peacefulness; despite this, the bees had found several armories, hidden in unmarked rooms in the Tower, in unmarked compounds dispersed throughout the neighborhoods. Julie flexes a hand, calling up an overhead view of the spiraling superorchard plots and cornfields closest to the Tower, then the neighborhoods tucked between, their viewpoint zooming toward a structure blinking blue with Julie's attention. "This is the closest armory to the Tower. John's bees didn't see any guards outside, and if it's only a pebble lock on the doors—"

"Then it's hackable," Noor says. "Anything but biometrics is easy enough. Honestly, security everywhere in the Farm is laxer than it should be. Earthtrust isn't scared enough of its Volunteers. Eury must not have expected them to ever resist her, not when the alternatives to living here are all so much worse than this." She shrugs. "The short answer is that I can get you into the armory, and then you'll have to get me into the Tower."

"But crossing the Farm armed is going to draw attention," says Cal.

Mai says, "I can fab what you need in the medical wing, if you can give me the schematics. The alarms will go off, but if you're already inside, it might not matter."

Julie says, "Let's meet halfway. We need rifles and body armor, but fabbing them is too complicated when we're in a hurry. We'd have to print the weapons in pieces, then assemble them. Better to source those directly, despite the risks. Then while we take the security nexus, Mai can print the rest of what we need."

"Which is?" asks John.

"Plastic explosives and detonators. If Noor can help me re-move the restrictions from the medical wing fabricators—"

"No problem," says Noor, blinking to transfer the neces-sary schematics to everyone's pebbles, burying the knowledge in the same hands that will plant the bombs.

"Then Mai will print the explosives at the last moment, on her way to the nexus," says Cal. "She'll stay with Noor, while Julie and I bring the explosives up to John in the penthouse."

"You'll have to take two elevators," John says. "One to the fiftieth floor, where the executive suites are, then another up the needle to Eury's office. There are two ways in: the second elevator opens into an antechamber outside the penthouse, where the door can be easily bypassed now that we've cloned Eury's pebble. The other entrance is in the atrium below Eury's office, accessible through a staircase inside the office and from another running up the side of the needle, starting at the fif-tieth floor. That's another two dozen flights of stairs, at least."

"But if the fiftieth-floor elevator is disabled—"

John nods. "Then you'll have to take those stairs."

"Okay." Cal blinks the overlay away, zooms elsewhere. "John and Mai will be inside the Tower. Julie, Noor, and I will enter at one of the legs, then make our way to the security nexus, where we'll connect with Mai. Once the nexus is ours, Julie and I will ascend the needle, where John will already be waiting in Eury's penthouse to access the Pinatubo launch chamber."

"That's the next problem," says John. "The launch chamber access controls are locked with biometrics: a handprint reader, a retinal scanner, a DNA check, a voice-activated lock. And I think we all know whose biometrics are the key."

"You're saying we need to take Eury Mirov prisoner?" asks Julie.

"I wouldn't mind," says Cal. "But that's the hardest road to go down."

John says, "Is there another way to stop Pinatubo? Do we have to be in the actual launch chamber to set the bombs?"

At John's mention of the bombs, Julie and Cal share a look he can't read. He almost asks what's wrong, but the moment passes too fast, Cal already answering his questions. "The launch is global," she says, "but our plan has to be to stop it here. This is Earthtrust headquarters. The fail-safe controls will be here and nowhere else. Once we've shut down the launch, we'll bomb the Tower, or at least the penthouse. It might not be enough to permanently derail the project, but now that Mirov's shown her true intentions, maybe the world will do something to stop her before she can try again."

They pause, each considering all that might go wrong with their plan, this heist in reverse, not taking something out of the Tower but smuggling themselves in. "We do have one more trick," Noor says, breaking the silence. "The data I uploaded our last night in Kansas City, through the satellite link we left behind? Enough made it out to the collectives I contacted from out west. They're waiting for our word to broadcast as much of what they've assembled as they can, for as long as they can, while simultaneously leaking the raw data in a single dump. I don't know what's all there, or what might happen when it comes out. But if it takes Earthtrust's gaze off us for even a moment, it's worth it."

"Tomorrow then," Cal says. "If they broadcast at dawn, local time, it might create enough confusion to get us inside." She plants her hands against the rail, then blinks to blank their displays, leaving only the world as it is, with its crowds of Volunteers, the bison herd below and the Tower above, gleaming black against what might be the last blue sky they'll ever see. Still clenching the rail, Cal says, "Julie and I fought in the Secession and then fought on for Earthtrust afterward. I won't ask to be forgiven for what I did then. But when we went west, we all told each other we could fight back without hurting anyone innocent. I don't know if we'll be able to make the same promises tomorrow. If you won't accept the possibility of other people getting hurt, I won't fault you for walking away. But I promise you those same people will be hurt anyway. Because what Eury Mirov plans is nothing more than replacing our world with a future of her choosing, a white sky hanging over an earth to be restored only when she says, containing only what she desires. That's not the world I want. I'll gladly give my life to stop it from happening. I know I'm asking you to risk yours, but I won't take it from you."

No one flinches, no one balks. These five prodigal Ohioans, come home to the last days of Ohio: once committed to seeing their task through, what else is there to say?

When it becomes clear Cal and John are going to linger, the other three say goodbye first, Mai heading back to the Tower, Noor and Julie walking away hand in hand, easy amid the other Volunteers gathered on the viewing platform, populating the picnic grounds below.

Once they're alone, Cal asks, "Are you ready, John?" No nicknames, no teasing now. Before he can answer, she says, "I wish we could stay together tonight," uncharacteristically direct.

"Me too," he replies, pushing against her, summoning her arm around his waist. He tries to think of something better to say, but that's not their division of labor: Cal gives the speeches, he believes in the cause. They've sacrificed before. They will sacrifice this too. "We're doing the right thing," he says, trying not to look to Cal for assurance.

"But the work isn't done," Cal says, her mind moving away from John but her grip not yet loosening. "Somehow, before tomorrow, we have to solve the launch control biometrics."

"Actually," John says, pulling away to access his pebble, "I have an idea about that too."

With a squeeze of his fist, he spins the Tower blueprints back across their displays, scrolling up to an overhead view of the forty-eighth floor. He zooms in, highlights a room that remains stubbornly blacked out, its secure contents impossible for the bees to scan.

"This," he says, "is what Eury calls the Loom."

CHAPMAN

Chapman, a man again, chastened and jailed by his body's contradictions: his faun shape balks at the settled lands, but in the wilderness it never fails to attract the attention of the witches. After the death of the trapper at the hands of the witches, he admits it's unsafe to ever be the faun again, because everywhere he goes he sees more of their signs, more evidence of the witches' growing fury at the destruction of the wilds, their vengeance most visible anywhere civilization is only half established, wherever the forest and the swamp might reclaim a broken human inhabitation. Near the undetectable border where the Territory resumes, the brothers find an old tomahawk claim abandoned, its corn wilted on the stalk, a dead and bloated hog slashed open not in the yard but inside the shattered cabin itself. As if swine should hide inside a house. At another homestead: a well laced with arsenic, a sick family packing to return east. Nearby, a rock dam collapses, sending torrents of water rushing along old pathways to flood already-planted fields, ruining crops needed for the settlers to last the winter. Even some apple trees go sterile, their blackened blooms falling to dried ground, their dead leaves crackling with the crumbled husks of honeybees.

This was the work of witches, Chapman worries, unless, as Nathaniel argues, it's only everywhere the effects of men competing for what men want: land to own, on which to live and to build, to husband and harvest. But how to know which signs mean what, which atrocities are the fault of the witches and which are only some more mundane ruin? One week, the brothers come upon a strand of burned and blackened log cabins, the destruction rumored to be the sign of returning natives or of advancing government cavalry, impossible to know for sure. Wherever Nathaniel's sure it was the cavalry who'd caused some violence, they're soon to find a half dozen uniformed men ambushed and riddled with gunshots, or else torn by claw and fang and beak. Other times Chapman is sure it's the witches who caused the damage he sees, only to discover again the everyday negligence of common men: a stand of trees burned to hastily expand a pasture at the cost of every acre's every bird's nest, squirrel hollow, and fox den, so much ashy soil eroded into runoff. Elsewhere he finds a river dammed, its trout and bass and perch trapped in reshaped waterways ill-suited to their needs, unable to reach feeding spots and spawning pools they once returned to instinctively; then another stretch of swampland drained, leaving behind acres of stinking catfish, their slimy bodies flopping in the drying mud, barbels twitching, gills heaving against mud made from water they used to breathe.

All around Chapman the natural world flees west. Every improvement men make to the land is an incursion against the wild, the Territory a shifting borderland temporarily neither settled nor pristine, where for a time both men and witches might act, where a faun could move with ease, if only he'd risk it. Meanwhile more and more men follow Nathaniel and Chapman's progress, building homes and establishing industries and ensuring there'll soon be no space for anything else. White-tailed deer fall before human hunger, wolves and other supposed threats are exterminated in turn, no one trapper's gory death enough to save anyone or anything.

On the edge of all this strife and struggle, Nathaniel's aging body leaves the brothers ever more separated. Spring turns into summer and the days grow longer, the hours Nathaniel can work lessen weekly; Chapman had always been the one to crouch in the dirt to plant the rows, but now he offers his brother this easier job, even though Nathaniel's strained back and creaking knees balk after seeding only a few rows. Gently Chapman helps Nathaniel to his rest, setting him against the broad trunk of an uncut oak before bringing him a strip of salted pork, a bladder of bartered cider. He returns to the work alone, the hot sun beating down on his newly burnable skin as he hums Eliza's tune—*The Lord's been good to me*—he plants a row of seeds, another and another and another—*and so I thank the Lord*—he wipes his filthy brow, wrings out his sweat-soaked hair. At day's end he surveys the half-finished nursery, the already-hoed rows needing to be planted before the soil dries out, the brush fences that must be erected, the many other hours of work remaining.

For what, he thinks, for what? Once he'd known the answer to this question without hesitation. Now he can no longer pretend any part of what he does is for Nathaniel's sake, this brother snoring beneath his tree, the empty cider skin beside him, his heavy beard tugging his head to his chest. After all, how many years does Nathaniel have left to make his fortune? He is fifty-five hard years old, years gifted to Chapman, a brother who couldn't be left in anyone else's care; years wasted on the Territory's settlement, work for which no one but the Worths has given fair recompense. And now? If nothing changes, his last years will all be spent fleeing the civilization he'd once hoped to make manifest. An entire lifetime wasted on the fraying hem of a world whose warp and weave Nathaniel no longer fit.

CHAPMAN PLANTS A SEED, HE PLANTS A HUNDRED SEEDS AS HE'S planted thousands before.

Chapman saws the trees, Chapman hauls the logs, Chapman clears the brush and pushes the plow and swings the hoe, Chapman plants and plants and plants nearly every seed himself. Some days Nathaniel manages once more to work dawn to dusk, but the next he's tired, irritable, too sore to stand, stuck on his hands and knees, his back bent as a saddle-broke horse's, tears streaking down first Nathaniel's face, then Chapman's. More and more Nathaniel's again useless by the noon meal, unable to return afterward to the sawing of trees, the plowing of cleared earth; still, by August the brothers have managed to plant two nurseries, a slim success even if their paltry seed haul means there's no good reason to start a third. Instead they pack up whatever's worth saving, abandoning broken tools and worn clothing to a tidy rubbish pile, then begin their long walk to the Worth homestead, visiting their past nurseries and orchards along the way.

Wherever he can, Chapman sneaks among their fully grown trees, testing an apple here, an apple there, praying that the magic he's spent his life trying to find lives in one tree or the other, a miracle at last grown within the mundane. But everywhere they go is busier now, the State's towns populated by growing families, their many children playing in the streets, all of the brothers' trees now captured behind fences and walls, made private property. This is the world Nathaniel had promised, but its arrival makes him no happier. "Soon Cincinnati will be New York," he complains, but in truth most of the State still reeks of cow shit, the deep stink of too many pigs in one place, too many hooves tearing the earth to mud.

Men had transformed the world but the world didn't stay as they put it. The brothers see topsoil running off poorly graded farmland, they see streams choked with silt, flooding one farm and starving another. Old-growth trees are cut for log cabins, then for fuel to heat the cabins; when the forests are gone the settlers dig coal instead, every lump of coal made of what used to be a tree. Malaria sweeps through village after village, smallpox and cholera kill dozens of people in one town while everyone everywhere is always dying of dysentery. Then comes milk sickness, the slows, the trembles—the settlers call the disease different names but can't identify the source. *The witches,* Chapman thinks, watching another homesteader bend to puke beside his split rail fence, a worry Chapman harbors until a Shawnee woman married to one of the white farmers teaches the rest about white snakeroot, a plant unknown in Europe, here tainting the milk and meat of cattle whenever the cows are driven into the woods to forage.

Now the brothers see cows slaughtered but not butchered, their carcasses stacked in heaps and burned before they attract the few wolves left, if there are wolves at all, because who'd seen one recently in this county, this newly organized county named by men living in Boston or Philadelphia or Washington. Around campfires or in village taverns, the brothers listen to squatters who've spent decades settling Ohio discuss the cavalry sent to drive them off, the military captains charged to eject anyone living anywhere better men might claim to own.

"We told the captain, 'Yes, we'll leave,'" says one squatter, grinning, "'as soon as we harvest our crops. But should we not save our cattle? We'll need to feed the poor beasts from our grain stores through the winter, then graze them through the melting season. But the cattle fertilize the land with all their shit and piss—and if we were to leave, then we couldn't carry that shit and piss, not with a hundred buckets, and without our fertilizer, how would we plant elsewhere, on some other unprepared land? Who would compensate us for our loss of shit and piss? In what ledger could such a loss be tallied? It's better if we plant our seeds here in the spring, on land properly readied. Come back after planting, good captain,' I said, 'and by then we may be ready to leave, as you so kindly request, right soon as we bring in the harvest and feed our cattle and fertilize our land and plant our gathered seed.'"

If the cavalry couldn't negotiate with the squatters, they meant to burn them out instead. But everywhere last season the brothers found a cabin burned, this year two more are built nearby. Every dam torn down is already replaced, every irrigation ditch unblocked, every windmill repaired, every single yard of broken fence rebuilt and reinforced. When the cavalry came, the squatters hid in the woods, emerging afterward to repair whatever damage was done. The squatters—who do not think themselves *squatters* but *settlers*, landowners by right of inhabitation and improvement—refuse to be dislodged. Never mind that the land they inhabit was stolen from another; they swear they will not let it be stolen from them next. Now the destruction done by the cavalry binds them together, makes their isolated holdings into a community.

Is there any such community for itinerant Nathaniel and Chapman, any place where they might be celebrated for their contributions? They've so rarely been paid for their apple trees or the decades of labor those trees represent; now Nathaniel's bartering for a fair share reduces him to prideful begging, the farmers who owe him often refusing to pay in anything but cider. In Hebron and Granville and Millersport, Nathaniel comes away with nothing but his skins refilled, day and night drinking his spoils to ease his aches, until the sweet smell of fermentation leaks from his pores and his teeth darken with rot. "If this is all anyone will give me," he tells Chapman, hiccuping as he drains another fireside cup, "then I will take all I can get."

"This is new, brother," Chapman says. Never has he seen his brother so drunk, day after day delaying their travel until he sobers enough to walk.

"What do you know?" Nathaniel slurs. "What do you know about what is new?"

Chapman knows this isn't the body into which he was born. He knows every day he spends as a man diminishes him. He knows the future they spent their lives trying to make arrived and then overtook them. They are living in the past, but the past is gone. Every moment a world ends, every moment a new world begins.

"Brother," Chapman says. "Brother, it's time to go home." A word they'd never used before the Worth homestead, which nonetheless could be home enough for Nathaniel. It had been once already, in the decade Chapman spent lost in the everywhere everywhen of the flicker.

"Home," Nathaniel sneers. "Home is *nowhere*. Because you—" He stops, slurs, stupefied or else pretending to lose his place. Loving the faun-child Chapman once was cost Nathaniel everything, left him reduced: all he is now is half a brother for half a man. But what Chapman has never said, what he has never pursued, is what Nathaniel cost *him*. The story of Nathaniel and Chapman is that Nathaniel saved Chapman's life, gave up his own future for the vulnerable faun. But what if Chapman didn't need Nathaniel, even then? He could've lived in the forests, would've forever fled the progress of man. He might not now be opposed by the witches, the wild women who want to punish what man has done, what Chapman, a once wild faun, did in man's name. If only he had learned to speak their language instead of Nathaniel's, he could have been their ally against the progress of a civilization of which he might then be no part.

Without Nathaniel, Chapman would never even have needed the tale of the Tree, a story he thinks of less every day he spends as a man. Instead of that story's promise, Chapman has only his brother's love, as Nathaniel has his, instead of the riches he sought—but look what brotherly love has cost them both.

IT'S OCTOBER THE FIRST TIME CHAPMAN AND NATHANIEL RETURN
together to the Worth homestead. When they arrive, Eliza
Worth is three years old, but she doesn't stay three for long.
Years pass; the brothers arrive, they winter, they depart; and
whenever they return Jasper and Nathaniel work the land while
Grace lets gentle Chapman help inside the house, fixing furniture, mending clothes, churning butter, and jarring preserves.
Every year Nathaniel comes back weaker and angrier, his body
reduced to loud popping bones and jaundiced skin and a flabby
potbelly hanging over scrawny legs; he drinks more than his
share of the Worths' homemade cider and store-bought whiskey, the blood vessels of his face bursting with drink until each
night Jasper begs Nathaniel to stop, until every spring he begs
Chapman to take his brother away.

Yearly the brothers return from longer journeys to more
distant frontiers in what is becoming Indiana, and when they
return Eliza is six, then eight, then ten, then twelve. Eliza grows
tall and straight, lean and strong, the only person Chapman's
ever observed growing up, so that at each winter's joyful reunion he's eager to see her new inches, the new evidence of
her intelligence and quick wit. A town rises around the Worth
homestead, but Eliza is no city girl. She memorizes Bible tracts
and her father's Swedenborgian apocrypha, she holds forth on
Heaven and Hell, but despite her theologies it's the living world
of her father's farm she loves best.

Chapman watches her at eight, moving through rows of
cornstalks taller than she is, her hands brushing the stiff leaves,
the stalks bending toward her touch.

He watches her at ten, nursing a sick sow back to health,

its piglets anxiously squealing whenever Eliza is not there to comfort their mother.

He watches her at twelve, a farmgirl striding to the edge of her disapproving town with her father's rifle in hand, her black hair braided down her back, off to hunt the last few deer living in the slim forest from which her town was carved.

Chapman watches Eliza but they rarely speak. Chapman knows he loves her as he loves Nathaniel, with as much affection as he feels for Jasper and Grace. But Eliza knows only the human half of him, not him entire. How would Eliza—the kindest soul Chapman knows, lover of animals, the best steward of the land she and her father and mother have shaped—how would she react to him, a monster stuck in the skin of man?

"Our mother's name was Elizabeth," Nathaniel tells twelve-year-old Eliza one night, his voice tired, his eyes fluttering shut. "Just like yours."

He wants to say more but instead coughs into his fist, hacking until his voice sputters out. Sitting nearby, staring into the fire, Chapman starts. Nathaniel has never told Chapman this, has never in all their years spoken so directly of their mother, the woman Nathaniel loved, who died giving birth to Chapman's kicking hooves, his clawing fingers, his head already studded with budding horns.

Later, Chapman spreads a blanket over his brother's dozing body. Eliza wipes sweet cidery drool from Nathaniel's lips with her handkerchief, then takes Chapman's hand in hers as together they watch his brother shake and buck against his dreams. *Elizabeth.* It's enough. A name to attach to all the longed-for memories Chapman will never possess. A container into which might be poured their imagined relationship, once desperately craved, a want never faded.

THE YEAR BEFORE NATHANIEL DIES, THE YEAR BEFORE ELIZA WORTH turns thirteen, Chapman is suddenly famous—but where do the tales begin, who is their first teller? The frontier has moved on, this Territory settled, and now the new people of Ohio and Indiana make their own myths, raising up the pioneers who came before, erasing crude violence and genocide in favor of edifying local legends and entertaining folk tales. There are ten thousand apple trees in the State that was once the Territory, trees planted by *someone*, and why not *John Chapman*, why not *Johnny Appleseed*, this wild-eyed man who never needs shoes no matter where he goes and no matter the weather, who always has his tune floating from his lips—*The Lord's been good to me*, he sings, *and so I thank the Lord*, over and over—Chapman begging door-to-door while Nathaniel coughs behind him, Chapman saying, *Let me tell you where some good apple trees are*, saying, *Let me sell you ten good apple trees for that sack of cloth*, a sack grudgingly given, then gifted to Nathaniel, who refuses to replace his thread-worn shirt with this object that is not clothing, and all Chapman wants is whatever is best for his aged and embittered brother, even as Chapman effortlessly attracts the legends born of their shared life, these tall tales told among people only recently arrived in the State or the Territory beyond, about the Johnny Appleseed who once charmed and tamed a wolf with cider, made the animal his constant companion, *a dog that followed him everywhere*, and then drunken Nathaniel says, *Am I the drunken dog they see?* but no, it's only a story, Chapman says,

dragging his brother through the muddy streets of some stinking hovel, away from some village green where they tell a tale
of how Johnny Appleseed once hid from a band of marauders
by lying at the bottom of a creek, sucking air through a straw of
reed, and Nathaniel says, *What creek was this then?* and Chapman names a dozen creeks it could've been but wasn't, because
the story isn't any more true than the fable of his tin-pot hat,
and every time Chapman says, *They're talking about anyone other
than me, you've been with me every minute of this curious life, and if
anyone was to be a hero to men it is you, Nathaniel, the best of our
settling kind, who invented every scheme we ever hatched.*

Cider-drunk Nathaniel seethes. All the labors of his spent
life and he remains poor and unknown, and now it's his brother
who is famous while unknown Nathaniel remains as penniless
as the day he began. Childbirth to gravedeath, this poverty is
to be his life, Chapman's fault every inch. If only the faun had
been suffocated by his caul, the membrane wrapped around
his head at his birth, just like a goat's; if only their father hadn't
been such a coward when the time came to crush his foul wind-
pipe. If only the witches they'd spent years fleeing had caught
him, witches Nathaniel still claims he's never seen, a rumor he
now accuses Chapman of using to keep them from ever staying
in one place enough to truly live.

If only Nathaniel hadn't saved his brother's life, ten years
after he almost murdered him.

If only, if only, if only.

What Chapman doesn't know, what he'll never know: the
slug of lead Nathaniel dug from his brother's chest waits in
Nathaniel's pocket, a charm he fingers whenever he worries
he'll say the words to break their long fellowship, their often

tenuous brotherhood. Despite everything, Nathaniel loves his brother, his Chapman, the one thing in the world unlike any other, the one thing that was his alone to know. Or so it was before the faun became a man, a man almost like every other Nathaniel has known, a man who Nathaniel sees in the year of Chapman's fame is better loved everywhere they go than he will ever be.

JOHN

John waits calmly for the concealed entrance to slide shut behind him, the air pressure changing as the Loom chamber's hermetic seal closes. There are only a few locations in the Farm without surveillance, without connectivity, but he believes this room is one such place: he squeezes his fist and sees the colored lights on the back of his hand blink red as they fail to find a signal. All is silent except for the hum of electronics on standby: the extruder arms surrounding the platform with its hidden bath of milky fluid, the stainless steel tanks with their refrigerant, the laptop on its rolling cart, and the other jury-rigged electronics waiting for his touch. In the dark, everything is still possible, but once John turns on the lights, he'll know for sure: either the Loom will be able to do what he promised Cal it would, or else he'll have to come up with another plan, somehow, hours before Pinatubo is supposed to launch.

There's no point in further delay. John squeezes his fist again, switches profiles: with Eury's spoofed authorizations loaded, the lights come on, the machinery whirrs to life. The Loom's interface is provisional, unfriendly, meant only for Eury, who likely wrote the code—but if John doesn't know exactly how the console works, he at least knows how Eury thinks. Her program has a search function, but before he tries it he manually scrolls through the currently loaded database, checking Earthtrust's progress:

AMERICAN BADGER AMERICAN MINK BLACK BEAR BOBCAT COYOTE ERMINE GRAY FOX LEAST WEASEL LONG-TAILED WEASEL RACCOON RED FOX RIVER OTTER STRIPED SKUNK WHITE-TAILED DEER EASTERN COYOTE GRAY WOLF PIPING PLOVER KIRTLAND'S WARBLER GREAT HORNED OWL EASTERN CHIPMUNK BLACK RATTLER MOUNTAIN LION VIRGINIA OPOSSUM ALLEGHENY WOODRAT AMERICAN BEAVER BROWN RAT COMMON MUSKRAT EASTERN CHIPMUNK EASTERN FOX SQUIRREL EASTERN GRAY SQUIRREL EASTERN HARVEST MOUSE HOUSE MOUSE MEADOW JUMPING MOUSE MEADOW VOLE . . .

The list goes on, but already John understands that this section of the Loom's database is intensely local: this is all the fauna of Ohio, all the vanished species of the last century, endangered when he and Eury were children, lost in their lifetimes. Her plan to restock the world is, by necessity and by choice, also a plan to rebuild the world of their childhood. The Loom's database is an expression of hope, fueled by ambition; the fact of its existence, like her zoo of lasts, is despair embodied.

John grips the laptop's glass bezels, breathes deep, then begins to type: first he tries Eury's name, then HUMAN FEMALE.

No. Too much hubris, even for Eury.

He searches everything he remembers about Eury, every story she's told about herself. It won't be randomized or scrambled. The entry will be a single word or a phrase, possibly a joke. It might, if he keeps scrolling, eventually jump out at him. But there are thousands of other entries in the database, so many animals and plants already missing, waiting to be restored.

All her life, Eury has loved her name, loved the myth it referenced. He thinks of the story she told him the day they visited the Loom for the first time. Eurydice, the girl trapped in the underworld, doomed by the weakness of men. *Me and not me*, she'd said once, correcting the story even as she told it. *I'm not her, I'm who she would have been, in a better story. The one who escapes, the one who saves herself, the one who is enough to save everyone else.*

Eury always tells the part of the story she likes best, but that's not the whole myth. Before Eurydice went down to the underworld, before she was married off to mortal man, she was a creature of the forest, a spirit of natural places, an integral part of the wonder and the splendor and the abundance.

John types NYMPH into the console, hits a few other keys.

A moment later, the Loom awakens.

AT FIRST, THE PRINTING OF A WOMAN ISN'T SO DIFFERENT FROM the printing of a wolf.

It begins with the opening of the radial trapdoor, the blue-white base liquid filling the hollow, sloshing like a bathtub of buttermilk; the extruders beginning to move, their whirring confident, precise. John watches in mixed horror and fascination, an unimagined voyeurism: this is Eury Mirov, his childhood friend, his once-upon-a-time love. This is the making of her organs—her heart, her lungs—all their bloody mess slowly caged in by a rack of bones; this is the bones threaded with blood vessels and marrow. Her brain, printed in layers; her teeth, built up exactly opposite of how John imagines they might be ground down; her tongue, a slab of muscle slid into the mouth and fastened into place. This is the breathing tube snaking into her throat, ready to inflate her lungs. This is her stomach tucked into its right place, her intestines coiled to fill her abdomen. This is the manufacture of the scar tissue around her missing uterus, evidence of the partial hysterectomy she had a decade ago, her recovery the only time John can remember Eury even slightly out of control, pain medication making her tell him stories he'd never heard, dreams of a surreal imagined world, an emotional landscape he hadn't known she'd tended. Eury floating through green forests, Eury living alone in a glade—

No, not a glade. What was it she had called it? A similar but different word.

A *dale*. In Eury's dreams, she had lived in a dale.

"You were there too," she'd said, her pupils wide, irises obliterated by painkillers.

"You were there, but you weren't you," she'd said, and then she'd held her hands to the sides of her head, splayed her fingers, wiggled them. Hands made horns, maybe antlers.

"Spooky," she'd said, then laughed. A laugh he hadn't liked, that she hadn't liked either.

This is Eury's body, exactly as John remembers it. This is that body being zippered shut, skin stitched to skin. This is the chest heaving shallowly, mechanical breath being forced into the lungs. This is the moment when padded grips descend to hold the body in place, to immobilize the chest and the legs and the head.

This is electroshock, jolts applied to start the heart. This is the same drone-song that played when the wolf came to life: John's skin crawling, his teeth aching at the digitized scream screeched out, looped, repeated at various speeds. This is the final touch: one more extruder reaches down, its arm swiveling on articulated joints, holding a circular port in its steel grip.

The printed Eury thrashes her head, causing the paddles astride her skull to tighten as the arm aligns the port with the base of the neck, then punches it in. The clone tries to scream, the sound swallowed by her breathing tube; her wet flailing kicks pound the hollow tub, their clangs reverberating about the soundproof room; she slackens as the tentacle-arm retracts, momentarily silent as the paddles release her, as the milky liquid drains from the Loom's chamber.

John watches the clone breathing, this new Eury alive in the same lived-in body John has known: an old scar blazes behind her right shoulder, reprinted exactly as it was, and there's a raised bit of burn tissue on her forearm, where she injured herself on a college lab Bunsen burner; he recognizes a once familiar constellation of tiny moles reprinted on Eury's neck, descending the left side of her chest. The skin around the implanted port in her neck is puckered and raised, future scar tissue forming around the steel. It's an ugly wound, holding some kind of networkable module, perhaps with a faster processor and higher capacity than a pebble, but cruder, crueler.

John clenches his fist, directs his pebble to send out a series of exploratory pings.

The module responds quickly, at first sending back only an

identifier: E-5. Whatever else the module is capable of remains a mystery, but he won't figure it out by standing here staring. He covers the clone with a printed blanket, slides it under her body, lifts her to his chest. Her hair's wet, her skin soft; she smells, he realizes, exactly the way new babies smell.

A moment later, she blinks open her eyes, her vision momentarily blurred; when John's face comes into focus, she starts with surprise; then, in a voice John has known nearly his entire life, this new Eury begins to speak.

E-5

I know you.

I remember. I remember you and I remember me. I remember us.

I remember us as children, chasing each other through the apple orchard between our parents' farms, the trees in both our backyards, a friendly border: not mine and not yours. Ours.

This is one of my first memories. It is and isn't mine.

In it, you are you, but am I me?

Not exactly. Eury Mirov is me. But I'm not her, not right now. But if you call me by her name, I'll answer.

You say there must be others like me, but how do I know? You tell me today's date, the year, but for me it's two years ago, it is another season entirely. I went to sleep in the winter and I woke up in summer. Or so you tell me, since inside this facility it could be any day, any year, any season.

In the first memory I have of us, it's autumn, the air crisp and cool, the apples heavy on the trees. They were never delicious, those apples: pocked with worm holes, squishy or gritty. But you and I ate them anyway, because the orchard was our space, the apples ours, the one place on both our family farms where no one cared what we did. The golden light, the sound of your laughter, the cries of birds in the trees, the crackling of leaves, the far-off voices of adults finally calling us back home, taking us away from each other.

We grew up, we went to college, we founded this company. We started this together, and then you quit, left me to do what needed to be done. I fought while you fled, into exile and retreat; you never sent word but I saw you in security footage and drone captures, I watched everything you destroyed burn while I stayed here alone, building a better future.

Most of my memories, all of which are only *hers*, have nothing to do with you. It's only from your vantage point that you've seen my life revolving around yours, how my choices serve the story you're telling. The most human error, you once judged this, even as you couldn't escape it: to see other life only as it relates to you. The man putting himself at the center of the living world as he once believed Earth the center of the universe, when in truth the universe cares nothing for this one blue bauble of a world, when in truth the life blanketing the earth most often barely notices the human man, except to flee his endless appetites, his unceasing destruction.

A Eury thought, that one, not quite a *me* thought, this me that right now isn't Eury.

If you asked, I could tell you some of the other memories I hold. Of years of worry and struggle, of building this company, of fighting its fights. Of years of preparing for the shocks

I saw coming, shocks many saw coming but few took seriously enough to act as boldly as would be required. I could tell you how when the time came Earthtrust was ready because I was ready. How when the Secession began, Earthtrust fought to control the peace that followed. When we forcibly emptied the Sacrifice Zone, it wasn't only to save human lives, but to be able to save enough *life* to supply the future we were making.

Right now, I feel nothing about any of this. I am—detached? These memories are here so I can perform her, but they're not really me. Two years have gone by, you say, two years you know and I don't. But even so, I remember what comes after the Sacrifice: Pinatubo. Orpheus.

If this is my Tower, the Tower I dreamed up years ago, as you say it is—then it's time.

I'm strong enough to walk, but I think you'll have to tell me where to walk. I'll tell you anything you want, but you have to ask. Whatever I did to myself to make me this way, it's made me slow to act, slow to speak.

But if you tell me what to do, I'll do it.

I know I've been made to trust a handful of people. The captain of my bodyguard. A handful of senior advisors. Drivers, pilots, household staff. Other people I haven't met yet, handlers nevertheless imprinted upon me.

And you. Of course you.

John Worth. I know you. I trust you. I always have.

Why are you here, John? And what do we do now?

JOHN

The broadcast begins at dawn, local Ohio time. Every telescreen in the Farm is on a linked circuit, every telescreen in every VAC worldwide is synced to the same, so Eury Mirov can broadcast to her Volunteers any time she wants: now all those screens all over the world turn on at once, their single remote access code a simple enough thing to hack. It's possible, in the broadcast's earliest moments, to believe this is more corporate propaganda, with the same fields of corn, the same orchards, the same grazing cattle, familiar from so many Earthtrust videos. But this is old footage, of the world long before Earthtrust, before the unceasing droughts, before the endless fires, before the new antibiotic-resistant infections, before the rise of acidified seas and the spinning mobs of tornados and hurricanes. Before the soil died and dried up, before every city street required a mask, before the rolling mass extinctions became the total annihilation of the natural world.

This is the world that was stolen.

What follows is one story of how it was lost, about who cost us what, about what they intend to do with what remains. It is a story told in excerpts of Earthtrust documents, in passages from secret government memos now read to narrate bulldozers piling up an acre of dead trees or knocking down century-old family homes, in footage of soldiers pulling families from houses in Arizona and New Mexico, Colorado and Utah, so many men and women and children forced at gunpoint into trucks, onto trains. Soundless video of armored soldiers advancing through burning streets follows, the gunfire and destruction accompanied only by the narrator's voice, vaguely feminine, utterly calm, as she reads Earthtrust orders to evacuate the cities and to level the towns. The narrator's voice reads Eury Mirov's words: public speeches given, transcripts of secret presentations to the federal government, the negotiations to sell the West to Earthtrust to form the Sacrifice Zone. Militarized corporate-speak. A clip plays of a Phoenix suburb, concrete and stucco, pinkly beige homes with clay tile roofs, with black-clad soldiers in filter masks pulling heat-burst bodies out of house after house, piling them into quadcopter cargo lifters; a series of jump cuts offers flashes of automated trucks filled with people killed by exposure, starvation, abandonment, their bodies Earthtrust property, carted away to the refineries now appearing on-screen, the biomass recycling plants built in secret in the newly barren West.

It's shaky handheld footage, acquired at great risk. The inside of one of the plants, at first indistinguishable from any other refinery, then a concrete room where hazmat-suited workers shovel body parts into a roiling pink sludge, the skin and hair and bones melting fast, seeping toward a drain in the middle of the room. A series of still photos of similar scenes, other remains: human, animal, vegetal. Eury's words, read in the narrator's drawl: "recycling," she says, "reclamation," she utters over a close-up of a drain, swirling with steaming pink liquid.

"The world to come," she says, "can only be built from the world that was. The past irretrievable. The future the good world, the promised world. This is a story we can tell.

"But first," the narrator says, slowing down, enunciating Eury's words as the screen goes black, "but first we have to be willing to sacrifice the present."

On-screen, the countdown to Pinatubo reappears. Four hours until the world we made together ends, before a world of Eury Mirov's design begins.

As the broadcast concludes, Volunteers spill out of their homes, confused and angry in the morning light, refusing their work assignments, overwhelming the neighborhood avenues, blocking the passage of the trams and other Earthtrust vehicles. Voices rise to yell incoherent slogans as throughout the Farm crowds gather, masses whose anger hasn't yet been given direction. Other Volunteers are only afraid, wanting to be left alone, to not have the life they'd found disrupted, the gathering demonstrators a frightening reminder of the Secession and the Sacrifice.

In one neighborhood close to the Tower, a ponytailed woman climbs atop a trapped tram car. Cupping her hands, she calls the other Volunteers to listen, while in other neighborhoods, many women, many men, many individuals are doing the same. Saying, *Listen.* Saying, *Let me tell you what's next.* Saying, *These fuckers do not get to decide the future for us.* Pushing their way through the crowd, Cal and Julie and Noor watch these leaders emerge. How cheered they are to see them, to learn they're not the only ones resisting, that what they do in the last hours before Pinatubo launches will not be done alone.

Exiting the commotion outside, the three women rush into the opened armory among a troop of frantic plainclothes security officers still dressed in standard neighborhood garb, their infiltration simpler than it should be thanks to the surveillance state's reliance on technology instead of people. Noor's hacked pebbles spoof the credentials they need as they shoulder past the others, Cal and Julie not waiting for confirmation as they file inside. Once admitted, they move with unfeigned confidence, following the officers to racks of flak vests and smart-visored helmets, loaded assault rifles snapped into wall mounts. The three women suit up fast, hurrying to be anonymous behind the face shields of the helmets, Julie rushing to help Noor with her confusion of straps and buckles and snaps.

Cal and Julie grin despite the danger, knocking each other on the shoulder pads with gauntleted fists. It's been years since they went into battle together, longer since they felt righteous about the war they were about to fight.

Cal shoulders the reassuring weight of her rifle, checking the tactical scope, the light mounted under the barrel. The women leave the armory in lockstep, blending in alongside the soldiers already dropping every pretense of civil service, their military-grade riot gear and heavy weapons readied to suppress the Volunteers they'd previously promised to protect. But Cal knows every police force protects power first, that property is always prioritized over people, that the plans of the powerful are always paid for by the violence they're willing to inflict upon their citizens.

And these Volunteers are no one's citizens. Eury Mirov has seen to that.

FAR ABOVE THE TROUBLE BELOW, JOHN AND E-5 TAKE THE SHORT elevator ride to the fiftieth floor, not speaking, E-5 dressed in the same monochromatic outfit in which John last saw Eury, including the pair of gloves she'd worn to press her prop button, plus a printed replica of the hip-length garment from when she'd shown him the museum of lasts, its high white collar now hiding the black metal port at the base of E-5's neck. Dressed for the part, she is and isn't Eury. She has Eury's face, Eury's body, Eury's voice, but not Eury's ambitions, not Eury's sense of control: E-5 is more accommodating than Eury ever was, even in her lightest moods.

Was? Is? John struggles with verbs, tense, personhood. What is she to him, this clone he's printed: a person or an object, a weapon or a tool? Maybe a better question is: What would she have been to Eury? In the night, E-5 followed John from room to room, from the apartment to the lab and back again, rarely speaking unless prompted, eagerly waiting for commands. He asked her to move aside and she did, immediately. He asked if she needed anything and she told him exactly what she wanted: a quantity of food, a certain amount of water, to use the bathroom. Eury had clearly programmed E to be trusting, pliant, capable of taking directions, with a minimum of agency. For what purpose? Why would Eury want a lesser clone of herself? John doesn't know, isn't sure it matters, as long as her biometrics are the same.

The real Eury has compromised John his entire life, has made him a danger to everyone else. He has fled her, fought her, returned to her. Now all John needs of E-5 are her finger-prints. All he needs are her eyes opened to the retinal scanner. All he needs is a drop of blood, her genetic combination, the final key to reaching the Pinatubo launch chamber at the nee-dle's pinnacle, accessible only through Eury's penthouse.

Before they left, John printed himself new clothes too: black pants, black shirt, black boots, a jacket with too many pockets, the uniform of someone wanting to be no one. A pacifist still, or so he tells himself, he takes no weapons. Out west, bombing dams and bridges and destroying fence lines and fuel depots, the goal was the removal of infrastructure or industry, never injuring people. In the Sacrifice Zone, it was possible to be as careful as you wanted, ensuring structures were uninhabited and bridges unoccupied, to know that blowing dams over dry rivers wouldn't flood anyone's home.

What they're doing now will not be so clean. Whatever they choose—whatever they do or don't do, whatever they cause or allow others to do—inevitably people will be hurt.

The elevator lifts John and E-5 ever closer to the levers of power, to the imagined red switch that sets off an apocalypse or else stops it. There, there'll no longer be any way to stay neu-tral. Whatever he does or doesn't do, John has made himself complicit in the *what next*.

So be it. He has one more printed tool, stored in one of his jacket's cargo pockets: a jet injector with a single pebble in its chamber, another perfect spoof of Eury's own. Seconds before the elevator doors open, he smiles at E, takes her hand with his. With the other, he places the injector against the space be-tween her thumb and forefinger. She balks, tries to pull her hand away, but he offers a reassuring lie.

"Don't move," he says, "and this won't hurt."

He pulls the trigger, fires the pebble into her flesh. Born without enough agency to protect herself from harm, E-5 nonetheless cries out, surprised by the first pain of her brand-new life.

EURY MIROV PROMISED TO KEEP THE VOLUNTEERS SAFE, BUT HERE are her soldiers, marching against them with riot shields raised, with assault rifles and tear gas at the ready. At the direction of the ponytailed woman, the gathered Volunteers link arms, chaining their bodies across the tramway as Earthtrust security exits the barracks, armored and armed. The Volunteers are from Ohio, from Indiana and Illinois and Michigan, from Missouri and Wyoming and Louisiana, from California and Texas and anywhere else the collapse reached; they are former Americans, stripped of their citizenship, made a community of refugees inside their own borders, today ready to resist as one people, united in deciding that they will not let these soldiers pass.

"Stand together!" the ponytailed woman yells, leaning recklessly into her words, her straining body supported by the Volunteers beside her. "Whatever happens, we all stand together."

The armored soldiers stop ten meters away from the human chain, not advancing but not backing down. Hundreds of Volunteers, breathing hard in the hot streets; fifty soldiers, standing across from their swelling ranks, a standoff that can't last. More Volunteers arrive, thickening the human barrier, but there are no more soldiers coming, not here, not right now. And then there are three fewer, as Cal and Julie and Noor peel away from the rear of their ranks to make for the Tower instead. They're less than halfway there when the fighting begins with the telltale hiss of tear gas canisters, then hundreds of rising voices screaming in agony and anger and the muted crash of bodies throwing themselves against riot shields, before the first bursts of gunfire ring out. There are more Volunteers than there are soldiers, but the only weapons the Volunteers have are their bodies, their numbers, their resistance. The battle might yet turn in their favor, but however it ends it begins with their blood.

"Just keeping walking," Cal says, her voice hard, her pace quickening. She can help the Volunteers or she can complete her mission, but she can't do both. After years of waiting and weighing every option, now every second there is another unexpected choice. A moment later she reaches the Tower doors, then steps into the southwest lobby's blast of cool air-conditioned air, the waiting quiet it promises. The lobby is locked down, but the door's scanners glow green as the women's spoofed pebbles pass inspection; a dozen armored soldiers are stationed inside, the usual reception area staff dispersed. As soon as the three women clear the pebble scanner, a soldier in a captain's stripes holds up a gauntleted hand, stepping forward to block the route to the elevator.

"No one else is going up the Tower, soldier," he says, his square jaw and twice-broken nose all that's visible from under his helmet's visor. The world outside is tense, but this soldier is calm, ready. "Director's orders," he adds, pointing his index finger toward the ceiling, toward Eury Mirov's office far above them. "Where are you supposed to be stationed?"

"The security nexus," Cal says, trying to suppress her awe at the lobby's spotlit timber columns, massive supports carved from supertrees John invented, trees cut down when their technology was deemed obsolete by the scientists who took his place. "We're part of the third shift rotation. As soon as we saw the trouble start, we suited up and came to help."

The captain shakes his head. "That's not protocol and you know it. You should have stayed in your neighborhood, helped secure the situation there. Who's your commanding officer? I'll let him know you're on your way."

Julie hefts her rifle, taking a few steps to place herself in a row with Cal, close but not so close they can be taken together. She says, "We're already here, though. Might as well lend a hand."

How fast could she turn the rifle from target to target? Faster than a dozen shooters? Maybe, maybe not. Noor bumps nervously against Julie, her body too close; Julie reaches back to gently nudge her away, only to find Noor's fist clenching and unclenching, rapidly activating her pebble.

Noor has given John plenty of gifts, hacks and shortcuts; now here comes one he made just for her.

"You're not getting in the elevator," the captain says, "without direct orders from above."

"Five more seconds," Noor says, her voice calm, her gaze fixed.

"Five seconds until what?" The captain jerks his rifle to a firing position, the move bringing the other soldiers to attention. They take aim, some of them stepping sideways in a flanking maneuver, surrounding the women. "Maybe you three should stand down."

"I don't think so," says Cal—and then the lobby's outer wall explodes into a shower of flying glass, the Earthtrust soldiers ducking instinctively as a swarm of thousands of John's hacked bees zooms inside, their bodies striking the soldiers in a confusion of tinny rotors, minuscule shells shattering against armor plating, embedding into exposed skin.

The bees are more distraction than weapon, but a distraction is all Cal needs. She aims her rifle, fires. Her ears ring as Julie fires beside her, as Noor squeezes three-shot bursts into the screaming surprised soldiers, their bodies falling to the granite or slumping against the timber columns. Shards of supertree take wing amid the kamikaze nanobees, the cordite-choked air filling with broken bots, the deadly detritus of John's best invention.

ONCE THE FIGHTING BEGINS, IT'S IMPOSSIBLE TO CONTAIN, BUT not every angry Volunteer clashes with Earthtrust security. Others attack the Farm's infrastructure, charging into the fields and orchards they've been made to work, tearing down the pebble readers and security cameras that watched them; there are few military weapons available to the Volunteers but there are the tools, the shovel and the axe and the hoe, all the other instruments of this reinvented agrarian pastoral. Already the superorchards west of the Tower burn. The fire takes slowly, the trees designed to be wildfire resistant, but *resistant* does not mean *impervious*. The fire spreads tree to tree, the wood roasting, apples baking, the smell frustratingly entrancing. The grass burns fast too, the chemically treated ground beneath blackening and blowing away, exposing the Farm's buried infrastructure: subterranean sprinkler systems, irrigation pipes, electric cabling, heat and moisture sensors, microprocessors, listening devices, all the apparatus of an agricultural surveillance state. Somewhere a server fills with the sound of crackling flames, of supertrees crumpling in the heat as the fire spreads to a service road, where for a while it stalls against the gravel. But the winds are high today—the winds are always high—and soon a flaming trunk lifts off its shallow roots, the freed root ball burning, the blazing crown floating into the next square of unburned orchard. And then another tree flies upward. And then another, another, another.

THE ELEVATOR DOORS OPEN ON THE TOWER'S FIFTIETH FLOOR, THE administrative level reserved for Earthtrust executives and the commanders of Earthtrust's security, decorated with the same opulence as Eury's penthouse: the gleaming stone floors, the hardwood arc of the reception desk.

"Director Mirov," says the receptionist, rising as John and E-5 approach. "We thought you were—" She looks again at E-5, then turns to John. "Dr. Worth," she says. "I'd been told you were back, but I didn't realize you were escorting the rung today. My apologies, it's been a confusing hour. The leadership team is in the west conference room, speaking to the director from Beijing. You'll join them?"

What do you mean by the rung? John wants to ask, but there's no time. Here on the fiftieth floor, everyone has always spoken so knowingly, because at the top of every organization secrets become power, knowing becomes rank; everyone here, even this receptionist, might be complicit enough in what Earthtrust has done. John looks past her: if the bluff of E-5's presence fails, he's made no alternative plan for crossing to the next elevator at the center of this floor.

"There must be a mistake," he says. "As you can see, the director's right here."

"Yes, of course, but—" The receptionist half rises out of her seat, turning to check the frosted-glass walls of the occupied conference room behind her.

While her back's turned, E-5's eyes flick to the receptionist's nameplate: John had coached her on what to say here, assuming she'd know everyone on the floor, but this receptionist must be new enough that this version of Eury doesn't know her name. Someone hired in the past two years then. "Ms. Khan," E-5 says, snapping her fingers to get the woman's attention, delivering the lines John had given her. "The Farm is on fire, and we're two hours from launch. Should we stand here discussing the particulars with you, or can I go up to my office and get to work?"

Faced with Eury's voice, warned by the snarl threatening at the corners of E-5's lips, the receptionist flinches. "Yes, Director," she says, chastened. "I'm sorry. I'll notify the rest of the team that you're here, if you'd like them to join you?"

"No need," says John, already leading E-5 past reception, cringing at the way her force of personality collapsed the moment she'd finished playing her part. "Anything the director needs, they can provide from here."

He hurries E-5 past offices housing executives he'd once worked alongside; she dogs his heels, something the real Eury would never do. It's only a short walk from the desk to the next elevator, its doors guarded by two security officers already stepping aside for John and E-5, whose pebbles transmit all the right access codes, whose performative confidence is convincing only as long as they move quickly enough to not get stopped.

They hurry, but when John looks back he sees the receptionist's confusion resolve into action, the woman reaching below her desk for the alarm installed underneath, her voice rising in a shout as the elevator doors close. Inside are only two buttons: the fiftieth floor, the seventy-fifth. At John's touch, the elevator takes off smoothly, its ascent fast but not fast enough: a moment later it slams to a jerking stop, throwing John and E-5 against the mirrored walls. The elevator lights turn red, a siren blares. E waits, docile and unconcerned, while John paces the square box of the stalled car. If they'd never entered the elevator, they could have tried the stairs, but with the alarm raised, returning to the fiftieth floor is no longer an option.

"What now?" E says, her voice placid, patient.

John points at the ceiling, where a square trapdoor leads up and out. He shakes his head. Twenty floors to go. "Now we climb."

THE FARM'S AUTOMATED TRAMS ARE QUICKLY LOCKED DOWN, BUT other equipment is easier to commandeer. A Volunteer drives a solar-powered bulldozer down the length of every fence line she meets, mowing posts and rails out of the ground. She does more than is necessary to release the animals, the over-fattened calves, the sows so swollen they can barely walk; she frees the land, unboxing it, unparceling it. *The land must not be contained.* It's the last thought she has before an Earthtrust sniper fires the bullet that flings her instantly limp body across the bulldozer's cockpit.

At the Tower's base, the original superorchard burns until it ignites the parkland around it, the heat crumpling the recently erected viewing platform; beneath it, the printed bison run terrified along the edge of their flaming prairie, unable to cross the buried sensor barrier sending electric shocks to their implanted pebbles, a fence sparing humans its unsightliness but just as ruinous to the animals it pens in. Now the American bison is made extinct for the second time, this time on a stretch of burning grass Eury Mirov might've been able to see from her penthouse's floor-to-ceiling windows, if only she was at the Farm.

CAL AND JULIE AND NOOR REACH THE TWENTIETH FLOOR WITH the adrenaline from the lobby gunfight palpable in their stink of sweat and blood, the three firing now at every moving shape:

a mail drone gets riddled with one burst, a uniformed officer spins to the tile beneath another. Julie and Cal lead, moving from cover to cover, clearing the way for Noor to follow. The nexus is easy to find, housed in a glass trapezoid protruding from the otherwise flat structure of the Tower's southern wall; a short hallway leads from the warren of glass-walled offices to its sealed doors, a red light swirling its warning over the doorframe.

"Just down there," Julie says, emptying a side hallway with gunfire, barely waiting for the hit bodies to reach the floor before turning away. "How do we open the doors?"

A sound from behind: someone running too fast and slipping, skidding across the smooth tiles. The three spin, their rifles ready—but here comes Mai, her marathoner's physique sleek in formfitting athletic gear, each hand hauling a backpack containing the printed explosives and detonators she'd promised, her black ponytail whipping side to side with every quick step. The other three women whoop to see her. "The furies," Julie says, pumping a fist. "We ride again."

Mai laughs, opens a backpack. She reaches in and takes out a clump of claylike plastic explosive, its lumpy surface still warm from the fabricator. "Let's get this door open already."

After the smoke clears and the gunfire stops, Noor charges into the nexus, moving console to console, looking for an undamaged workstation left carelessly unlocked. She can hack a password but it takes time. She can reboot a computer with root access but that takes time too. Ditto for pebble spoofing, especially if she can't simply copy the information she needs from another. She steps around the unarmed officers slumped in their chairs, blood pooling beneath their consoles. Noor isn't a soldier but she's willing to do what needs doing. She's never forgotten the civil wars and regional conflicts of the first twenty years of her life, followed by her violent exodus out of Iran to un-receptive Europe, then a second escape from the predatory governments in the Balkans to the States, her family arriving mere months before the borders were closed forever. She's fought for what she wanted, has been hurt and has suffered, has hurt others. The world they have isn't the world anyone wants, because the world they have is a human world. For years, all she's wanted is to take as much of the world from human hands as possible.

Noor considers her options. With the security officers dead, their pebbles are unpowered and inert. She could copy them, but only with even more time, plus equipment she doesn't have with her. Meanwhile the elevators are frozen, halted as soon as the Tower went into lockdown. She can at least start undoing some of the security measures, making it easier for others on the ground to follow them into the Tower: most of the chaos remains in the neighborhoods and the wider Farm, but sooner or later it will come here. As firewalls and passwords fall before her, Noor unlocks the sliding elevator doors on every floor, then opens every other door she can, beginning at the top of the needle and working her way back down to the nexus.

Far above Noor, the elevator door to the antechamber of Eury Mirov's empty penthouse slides open over a yawning shaft, its drop plummeting vertiginously to a stuck car far below, above which two figures climb slowly up the narrow emergency ladder, a long way from the top but already far ahead of anyone else making the ascent.

CAL AND JULIE WORK LANDING TO LANDING, CLIMBING THE Tower's southwest stairwell, rifles shouldered, tactical lights lit and leading the way. They move with ease, all their old habits returning, the ways they fought beside each other in Sarajevo and Rio, then in Seattle and Portland during the Secession. The worst was clearing building after building in post-Sacrifice Phoenix and Albuquerque, dragging families out of tinderbox suburban homes left without power or water, their rooftop solar panels obscured by blowing dust. Wherever Cal and Julie were, whomever they were working for, they stayed together, watched each other's backs, kept each other alive. Together they left the military, resigning their commissions after their last European campaign; then together they joined Earthtrust, hoping to rebuild the country; and together they'd quit, after it became obvious Earthtrust wasn't interested in their kind of rebuilding, at least not west of the Mississippi.

They didn't always agree, but always their disagreements stayed within a tolerable range. The only topic they'd ever truly fought about was John Worth. Cal had loved John but never fully trusted him. Julie hadn't liked John but she loved Cal. When Cal said John could be useful—he was angry the same way they were angry, he was disillusioned with Earthtrust, even though he'd helped found the company, even though he was a childhood friend of Eury Mirov's and her former partner—then Julie had trusted Cal, had trusted Cal to not trust John the right amount, no matter what her romantic feelings became. And so when Cal told Julie about the job within the job, Julie knew Cal had done the right thing.

John could do it, Cal had said. He could get access to Eury Mirov. He wouldn't even have to really try. In fact he'd probably waste time trying not to go to Eury, becoming all the more convincing because he'd think he was doing the right thing by resisting. When he finally gave in, he'd be doing exactly what Cal wanted him to do. But he wouldn't know there was one more choice to make until the last possible moment, and even then only if someone showed it to him.

One more reason Cal and Julie need to make it to Eury's office before John does anything stupid.

Gunfire rattles down the stairwell, fired from a floor above—Earthtrust security pushing back at their advance. The women flatten themselves against the wall, return fire blindly. Through the reinforced concrete walls, they hear an explosion outside the Tower, close enough the metal stairs vibrate beneath their boots. The gunfire from above pauses at the sound; Julie waits two beats, then steps out of cover, finds her target, and aims. Two quick bursts, bullets clanging into metal, striking concrete, digging into armor and flesh, then a soldier in matte black armor topples over a railing to fall through the stairwell's open center, a bullet having spiked through his bare neck.

Cal yells to Julie—"Clear!"—her voice echoing, the echo interrupted by the sound of a door opening somewhere above, fresh boots on the stairs, another spray of bullets aimed at her voice, its mistaken declaration. She throws herself to one side, her shoulder striking the wall, jostling her weapon out of position. She swivels behind a railing, but she can't see well, can't move without exposing herself. Pinned down, she waits for Julie to dislodge the Earthtrust soldiers blocking their ascent, holding on to the perpetual high ground.

There's no way to know how many more Earthtrust soldiers are above.

It's impossible to prevent others from following from below.

And as long as the elevators stay deactivated, every path leads to these stairs.

All Cal and Julie can do is climb, climb and kill, climb and hope.

IT'S NOT ONLY IN THE OHIO VAC THAT THE PEOPLE RISE UP. IN St. Louis, two hundred would-be Volunteers attack the Earth-trust train depot, all of them refusing to be sent east, refusing to let anyone else be sent east against their will ever again. The processing center burns, but the security guards are invited to surrender, the other employees are allowed to exit peacefully. Only the maglev conductor refuses the Volunteers' mercy, making a lonely escape in his train, fleeing across the Mississippi to find the track already bombed on the other side, a problem that doesn't come to the conductor's attention until it's too late to prevent a violent derailment, his empty passenger train flipping off its tracks to shatter its tube, sending buckling wreckage to churn up rolling clouds of dead Illinois dirt.

JOHN EXITS THE ELEVATOR SHAFT FIRST, CLIMBING INTO THE ANTE-room outside Eury's penthouse. He reaches back: then it's her hand in his, Eury's hand gripping his; Eury's hand but not. E-5 climbs free as the penthouse doors open, just as Noor promised they would—but then the previously hidden blast doors inset before them start to slide shut, the heavy steel moving haltingly, a never-before-used mechanism jerking on its rails.

"Hurry," John says, dragging E-5 as fast as he can, disoriented E yelping as Eury never would, stumbling through the blast doors seconds before they close. Eury's ornate office is as sunlit as before, the polished desk waiting, the curving wood chairs inviting, everything expensive, bathed in bright light. Through the glass walls, John watches black smoke plume into these heights where Eury lives and works and rules.

"This way," John says, pointing E-5 toward the security

console embedded in the far wall, the entrance to the Pinatubo control room. He squeezes his fist, checks the row of lights: orange, purple, green, blue; Cal, Julie, Mai, Noor.

All still alive. He sighs with relief—and then the green and blue lights blink out.

AT THE HALF-BUILT EARTHTRUST SPACEPORT OUTSIDE DES MOINES, two saboteurs in bomb vests are gunned down before they can trigger their explosives. Their rigged bodies fall, slumped at the base of rails meant to guide the not-yet-built starship into launch position. Over the next hour, two more sets of saboteurs attack, each pair repelled by gunfire, riddled with bullets before they can explode their suicide vests. Soon armed drones patrol the airspace above the construction yards, blockades are permanently erected across every remaining freeway. And still the saboteurs keep coming, not just today but in the years to come, crying, *No escape,* crying, *No escape for anyone unless there's an escape for everyone.*

FOR A TIME, MAI HOLDS THE ENTRANCE TO THE NEXUS ALONE, BUT her luck can't last forever. The next bullet burst strikes Mai in the shoulder, spins her to the ground behind the metal weapon crates stacked across the doorway to the nexus, an improvised barricade hastily erected after Cal and the others blew their way inside. She moans at the pain but doesn't scream, doesn't want to give away that she's been hit. Before infiltrating Earthtrust, she'd served as a field doctor during the Secession, first on the American side, then for the disorganized western resistance. She's removed bullets from thrashing bodies, she's amputated limbs, performed emergency surgeries whose complexity boggles her, when and if she makes herself remember.

All that, but before this, she's never been shot.

Her breathing slows; she meditates on the pain's pulse, counting surges of blood like breaths. She tries to lift her body atop her knees, then into her shooter's stance. Without her suppressing fire to stop them, the Earthtrust soldiers will charge in seconds. But she's rising too slowly, her injured arm unable to lift her weapon. "Noor," she cries. "Noor, they're coming."

Noor turns from her console, her eyes taking in Mai only partially, her focus emerging out of the world inside the computer, the virtual battle she fights while Mai handles the real.

Mai tries to right herself behind the crates, her dead arm dragging, her rifle discarded. It's too late. She looks at Noor again, desperate for the right thing to say, one last right thing. The two have known each other a long time. They've been friends, they've laughed and fought, separated and reunited; whatever else they became, they were survivors first.

If Cal were there, she'd say, *You made the world better. But not everyone makes it to the promised land. Sometimes those who lead die on the last cliff, looking down into the new Eden.*

Noor presses a button, sealing the blast doors on as many floors as she can. Either John's inside the penthouse or he's not. There's nothing more she can do to help.

They wait, but the rush never comes. Noor stands, looks out past Mai toward the empty corridor, a space seconds before filled with gunfire. For a moment, the nexus goes quiet, the only sounds Mai's grunting breathing, the loud beeping of the distressed consoles at Noor's fingertips.

Then a drone gunship appears outside the nexus's outer

glass wall, hovering momentarily before it unloads its machine guns, all the electronics inside the nexus breaking apart into sparking explosions, Mai and Noor breaking too, bursting out of their skin, spraying blood and bone into the air, all they were made impossible to sort apart amid the flames.

SIXTY MINUTES TO GO. IN A LIVESTREAM BROADCAST WORLDWIDE, an inaudible explosion pops at the base of the Hoover Dam, just left of center. Twenty seconds later, a crack appears from the smoking crater, jaggedly climbing up the dam's facade until the concrete gives way. What's left of Lake Mead plummets through, forming a temporary waterfall reuniting the Colorado River with itself. Soon lights begin to brown out in Arizona's and Nevada's last inhabited areas. Every air conditioner reliant on Hoover Dam electricity hums discordantly, slowing to a last stop.

In the next minutes, the Oroville Dam explodes. Then the Dworshak. Then Glen Canyon. Then all the rest, dam after dam after dam blowing. The attacks unfold until every western waterway is loosed of human constraint, until whatever water remains can return to wilder courses, forever free.

CLOUDS OF CONCRETE DUST, BLOOD SPLATTER, SMATTERS OF metal flake, Cal and Julie climb through it all, firing their weapons in precise bursts, both women dirty, fatigued, still determined. By the thirtieth floor, the fighting grows more sporadic but also heavier: the soldiers farther up are better organized and better armed. Around the fortieth, someone fires two tear gas canisters at the landing Cal and Julie have occupied, the

gas chasing them upward; they return fire on the move, shooting through the pungent yellow smoke, hearing groans as their
bullets find unseen targets. They've been soldiering all their
adult lives; some of the people they're fighting today could be
their old comrades, making the best of the bad situation that is
the world. That doesn't mean Cal can cry off, doesn't mean Julie won't do what has to be done. You don't always choose your
battles, you don't always get to pick the right side, and if you
fight long enough you learn that being on the right side is too
often a temporary condition. Everything might change at any
moment, everything except the promises you made, the con-
tracts you signed, the pledges you made to serve and to fight.

By the time Cal and Julie reach the fiftieth floor, they need
the elevators to be reactivated, or else they'll have to climb
the entire needle to reach John and the clone he's hopefully
printed. Because whatever else happens, Cal needs to be there
at the end, to tell John what has to be done.

Fuck Eury Mirov, Cal will say. *Fuck everyone like her. They do
not care about us.* She'll say, *Isn't this place proof? This Farm, where
the only way to enter is to give up your citizenship, to volunteer to
be Eury's subject? Where you can be saved from the world the Eury
Mirovs made only if you enter another of their traps, another hier-
archy of power and subjugation? Where the purpose isn't to feed you
and house you but to make some better future, where there'll be all
the plants and animals Eury's world took from you?*

She'll say, *You and I were each given one body, one life, to do
with as we want. One body needing healthy food, clean water, safe
shelter. The essentials of life, none of which are guaranteed anymore
even if you work every minute you're breathing. There's not enough
effort left in the world to earn what used to be everyone's birthright.*

Every Volunteer has one body they have to beg Eury Mirov for

the right to keep alive. All she asks in return is their freedom, their
citizenship, their sovereignty, and their agency. All Eury Mirov asks,
all every Eury Mirov asks, is everything.

And while every Volunteer sacrifices to keep their one body alive,
to keep whole and safe the bodies of their loved ones, their fami-
*lies? Eury Mirov gets to have as many bodies as she wants—*at least
one new body already, if John's managed to print the clone he
promised—*and surely more will follow. Bodies as hungry and thirsty*
as yours. Bodies taking up space, bodies devouring resources, eating
the crops and drinking the water. Bodies breathing the air, bodies
pissing and shitting and wasting into the ground. The footprint of a
human multiplied endlessly so Eury Mirov can live as many lives as
she wants, now and in the future.

If Eury Mirov has found a way to live forever, we must not let her.

And if we cannot stop her, we must force her to take the rest of
us along.

As Cal and Julie exit the staircase into the fiftieth-floor administration offices, the lights go out; when the ambush begins, they fight in the dark, the blackness punctured by bright
flowers of gunfire, the stench of tear gas, the animal grunting of
the injured and dying, more armored security officers, a secretary cowering behind a reception desk, a slew of useless men in
expensive suits. After the fighting ends, they discover the prize
they've won is an unpowered elevator, the car stuck five floors
up, blocking access to the shaft.

On to the last narrow staircase then, nestled inside the needle's slim wall.

IN THE PENTHOUSE, JOHN WATCHES E-5 OPEN EURY'S LOCKS ONE AT
a time—the glow of the handprint scanner, the prick of the

DNA lock, the optical scan laser flicking back and forth across her face, E-5 saying *open* to unlatch the voice seal—and only now does he consider the mistake they've made, all these people torching the VAC fields and orchards, releasing the modified livestock and the bioprinted endangered species. It's Eury's mistake too: Why didn't she tell the world about Orpheus, why didn't she explain in time to stop this destruction? Wouldn't it have been a blow against the nihilism of the age, against the belief of so many that everything good was passing away, that nothing could be done to save the world they'd known and loved? What if she'd given the world the option to sacrifice even more, to offer up their present for a better future, even if everyone living now would never see it?

Human beings were not gods. They couldn't make a living world out of nothing. The future Pinatubo promised could only be made from the past, from the present Eury Mirov and Earthtrust were growing now, all over the world. You grew corn, you fed a cow, the cow died, you fed the cow to people—unless, with Orpheus, you recycled the cow, stored what it'd made from corn and water and sunlight for later, when conditions would be better.

If Pinatubo saved the future, then Orpheus could re-create the Garden, could reboot evolution from where it'd last failed, give the big apes and the ponderosa pines equal chance to succeed. That was the hope Eury offered.

But now John and Cal and the furious Volunteers are sealing all their fates. What could possibly happen afterward but more ruin? A starving populace, surrounded by wasted biomass. A dead animal could be scraped into the recycler vats, but the burned trees would be gone, their carbon added to the atmosphere instead of stored for after Pinatubo launched.

John understands the Volunteers' anger at the world they've inherited, the world they've been forced to inhabit. He'd been angry before too. He is angry now, although for years his anger had only seethed, rarely escaping. This is the one bomb John has planted that still hasn't detonated: the anger swelling in his chest, a pressure building inside the heavy cage of himself.

IF YOU HAVE TO CALL THE RESISTERS SOMETHING, CALL THEM VOL-unteers. Never terrorists, never freedom fighters. Let the Volunteer revolutionaries' existence be indistinguishable from the photogenic families eagerly presented in Earthtrust propaganda; make mention of their cause fade into the deluge of everyone praising or denouncing Earthtrust online or in the media, in the halls of what governments are left. All over the world, Earthtrust uses this same English word to denote the refugees forced into its Farms, those beneficiaries of a choice everyone knows is no choice; if Earthtrust was a country delocalized and distributed across continents and cultures and languages, then all these Volunteers are its disenfranchised heirs, stripped of their rights but ready to take back what they've lost, all the dignities and rights they shouldn't have had to give up.

Across the world, the Volunteers come together, fighting Earthtrust security and local militaries alike. In Indian Punjab, the Volunteers destroy an entire VAC, the first one lost today: its superorchards enflamed, its wheat and corn and rice burned and bulldozed and drained, its Tower struck by a succession of fertilizer bombs ferried in on solar-powered trucks, hitting the base of the Tower not all at once but in rapid sequence, creating a series of shock waves that shake the foundation apart. Other

Volunteers drive livestock from their enclosures, setting free cattle bigger than any ever seen before in that country or any other, cattle never intended to be eaten in India, allowed for a time to inherit the local earth. Loudspeakers implore the Volunteers to stop the destruction of their VAC, their home—but what is a home owned by another, how can they be convinced any of this is theirs once they've been forced to give up their citizenship, their rights and property?

Despite the provocation of armored soldiers on the ground and the drones above, not every Volunteer resists violently. Not even most. In some VACs, former refugees sit down in the tramways or beneath the spreading branches of the supertrees or alongside the livestock they raised or in the opulent lobbies of the Towers, spaces meant for anyone but them. Even in Ohio, some sit and wait and refuse. Work stoppages arise in Texas and Iowa, in France and Germany, in Argentina and Australia and Japan. Separated by language and location, by propaganda and systems of control, the Volunteers in one VAC can't know what the others are doing worldwide, but wherever they refuse to participate in the story Eury Mirov is telling, there they are united.

It isn't always possible to know what other story might be better for everyone. But it must always be possible to refuse to be a bit character in the wrong story someone else is telling, to refuse to do your part to enact the last chapter of a tale so destructive it's about to cost the world.

A refusal to take up arms against the living, a refusal to take up the implements of labor in service of any story of limitless production but only incremental progress: surely there will always be at least this choice, surely even at the end it will remain meaningful whenever someone makes it.

CAL AND JULIE EXIT THE LAST STAIRCASE THROUGH A HEAVY DOOR
unlocked by Noor in the security room before it was retaken.
Before Noor died, before Mai.

"Where are we?" asks Julie, swinging her light left to right,
the vaulted room they've entered only dimly lit, metal shield-
shades lowered over the tall angular windows to block out the
late sun.

Cal passes her rifle's light over the clear cube habitats set
atop marble plinths, then lowers her weapon. They're close now.
"The atrium," she says. "Eury's personal trophy room." The zoo
of living lasts, which should lead them to another staircase, this
one leading up to Eury's office, then a hatch that only opens
from above.

If John and E made it to the penthouse, the hatch will be
unlocked.

If not, not.

Cal and Julie advance side by side, passing through the central row between silent habitats. With the lights off and the windows shaded, the habitats are quiet, their inhabitants sleeping
or otherwise dormant—on one plinth's plaque Cal reads GALÁPA-
GOS TURTLE, on another she reads PEAK-BACKED TUATARA—but when
she passes her light over the surface of each habitat, the flashing glare makes a mirror: herself and Julie, reflected back. Once
she thinks she sees something else in the reflection, moving behind her, but when she turns there are only more habitats, the
ventilated first rows the only ones hosting anything living. The
farther they go, the more they find only the dioramas of Eury's
taxidermied lasts: the coyote and the fox and the bobcat, the
panther, the grizzly bear, arranged according to the dates each
species came here to reside forever in Eury's private collection.

"This is some creepy shit," says Cal. At the sound of her voice something in the habitat beside her slams itself against the glass, the trapped animal's voice screeching. Cal and Julie both stumble away, swinging their lights toward the habitat's glass. Again the glare, then a face surfacing through the reflection: the blackish-red head of a female Andean condor, its monstrous skull bald and sharp beaked, its face encircled by a ruffle of white feathers, its impossible wings spreading their crippled spans as it hops forward on gnarled, arthritic claws.

This beautiful bird, a harpy caged; Cal lowers her rifle, moves through the beam of Julie's light to put her hand against the glass. Seeing this bird taken captive is heartbreaking, but where else could it live? Its habitats vanished, covered over with air pollution sickening to raptors, to all the birds of prey already diminished by the poisons ingested by their prey, the polluted waste trapped in every carcass.

"Come on, Cal," says Julie. "We've got to go."

Cal takes her hand away from the glass, then puts it back. The condor no longer agitated, its face barely visible in the glare, its gaze deadly calm. And then the condor isn't looking at Cal anymore but at something else, rushing from behind her.

Cal spins to see a charging gray wolf pounce on Julie, Julie bellowing in surprise as she fires her rifle uselessly toward the ceiling, the bullets ricocheting back from a dozen angles. Cal yells Julie's name as she trains her own weapon on the animal, her breath slowing as she aims, her finger still evenly squeezing the trigger when the second wolf leaps from the room's dark recesses, its jaws opening to bare exactly the same teeth as the ones tearing into Julie's throat.

A three-bullet burst lifts the first wolf off Julie, too late; the second wolf knocks Cal to the unforgiving floor, her leg twisting, her weight pinning the bent limb beneath her. Her rifle falls, spinning away as the wolf's jaws snap at her face, its breath hot on the armored forearm she raises in defense. The wolf latches on, its teeth crushing the armor, sliding easily through the shirt beneath. Skin tears, bones break, there's blood and a scream, a scream Cal knows is hers but manages to divorce herself from enough to draw her printed knife from its belt sheath. A serrated blade of printed plastic, strong as steel: she reaches between the wolf's paws and puts the knife into its belly, pulls smoothly upward until the blade strikes the breastbone.

The rush of blood, the hot weight of loosed entrails dropping from the wolf's guts; Cal's a soldier, the instinct to gag happens only somewhere deep within her, some closed space where it can't move her body to action. She reverses her grip quickly, runs the knife back down the wolf, cutting against the first cut until the animal's jaws open, releasing her shattered wrist.

Cal pushes the dying wolf off her, then rolls over to check on Julie, who's already gone. The wolf gasps and gurgles, tongue limp in its panting mouth; it scratches its claws at the polished floor, tries in vain to stand, drags itself a bloody meter. A feebleness asserts itself. After its movements slow, Cal, who wanted only to save every living thing, kneels beside the wolf to pull her knife free, then to pet its heaving flank through its final heaves.

At Cal's touch, the wolf twists its head back toward her until she catches its gaze—a look, she thinks, that's not quite as inhuman as it should be. A ridiculous thought. After the wolf breathes its last—after its species once again becomes temporarily extinct—Cal reshoulders her backpack, leaves her rifle behind. She won't be able to use it with a broken wrist, will have to rely on the handgun holstered at her waist. She draws the pistol, holds it against her hip until her hand stops shaking, trying not to think about Julie dead, about the bodies of the two wolves flanking hers.

Cal's come so far, has only a little ways left to go: the staircase to Eury's penthouse office is no more than a dozen more meters away, at the far side of this mausoleum. She drags her injured leg, the knee already swelling; she tries her best to balance on this unsteady limb she knows won't finish bruising before the end comes.

Somewhere behind her, the female condor screeches farewell, its voice the last utterance of the last living animal Cal will ever hear.

CHAPMAN

Can Chapman know this will be the last year he and Nathaniel will plant together? Surely he senses the time draws near. Surely it's long been obvious theirs is a futile enterprise, one with no hope for remuneration or reward. Now all of Ohio is lost to them, the State settled and civilized everywhere and in no need of apple planters, except to populate the stories of the idle. The only lands they can plant are so far west of the Worth household Chapman knows they must soon decide to stay with the Worths forever or else forsake returning.

But he can't make this decision for Nathaniel.

Nathaniel, who barely speaks to him anymore.

Nathaniel, who spends his last winter slurring sentences, coughing up rosy phlegm.

As the snow melts, Chapman prepares their gear without a word. He divides their tools into two piles, one much smaller than the other. They've ruined innumerable hoes over the years, broken many gimlets and hatchets and knife blades. The only tool that's lasted the entirety of their apple planter careers is Chapman's leathern bag, its skin so pitted and scratched and worn it's impossible to believe it was ever an animal's. It's the one possession he treasures above all others, almost the only home he's had.

Engrossed in his work, Chapman doesn't hear Nathaniel approach, doesn't know he's there until he wordlessly touches Chapman's all-too-human shoulder.

"Brother," Chapman says, reaching up to take his brother's hand. "We don't have to go."

Chapman turns toward Nathaniel's beloved face, finds it momentarily untwisted with anger or drink but sagged with age, freckled and mottled by sun and wind. Chapman has been learning to be a man for years now, while alongside him Nathaniel has become partly an animal: his skin like leather, his hair and beard bright white fur, his ears and nostrils spilling more hair; his fingers yellowed, rheumatoid and tobacco stained, his cloudy fingernails sharp as talons.

"If we go," Nathaniel says, "I will give up the cider, I will get my health back, we will walk to the edge of the world if that's what it takes for us both to be free." An old gleam enters his eyes, as when he first talked about the manifest destiny of man, how this new continent would be made the kingdom of heaven on earth. "I don't want to die here, brother, drunk beneath a blanket. I don't want to die here wheezing, you beside me in a skin that isn't yours."

Chapman begins to object, but Nathaniel waves him off.

"I should never have brought you here. We could've kept going west. There will always be more frontier, more wilderness—

that is the one thing I believe this country will never lack.
Somewhere awaits us where you could've been what you are,
where we could've hurt no one, not even each other.

"I stole your life," Nathaniel says, quiet tears rolling down
his wrinkled cheeks, carving his canyoned face into deeper relief. "I stole your life and I am sorry."

Stoic Nathaniel, steady Chapman. Brothers still, brothers
forever.

Chapman takes his brother in his arms. They have never
embraced like this, or else it's been so many decades neither
can remember whatever childish hugs they might've shared.
"I took everything from you," Chapman says, "and never paid
my debt."

"West then," Nathaniel says, his grip surer than it has been
in years. "As far west as we can walk. To plant a place all our
own, from which no man might make me leave."

By June they've traveled farther southwest than they've ever
been, finding the land in far Indiana not nearly as dense with
forest or swamp as wild Ohio was. The brothers are quiet this
season, both given to their own reveries; later Chapman will
wish they had spoken more, but even at their most gregarious,
he and Nathaniel were often silent for days. Despite their recent
strife, they long ago said most of what they might say: they have
praised and blamed, accused and coddled, played and rejoiced
and celebrated. It's rarely possible for one to have a thought the
other doesn't know, everything revealed except for those Chapman holds back: what he saw in the ten years he spent in the
flicker, its other whens he still lacks the language to reveal; and
the first encounter with the witches and the singer, a story Nathaniel never quite believed. Even the day the giant trapper was

killed, even then Nathaniel couldn't have seen the wild women or the beasts they became, not as far back from the fight as he was, uselessly loading his musket.

Only now does Chapman realize Nathaniel must have thought it was Chapman who killed the giant trapper. For all these years he's believed his brother the faun was also his brother the murderer, capable of dismembering a man.

No wonder Nathaniel took to drinking.

Even without his faunish shape, Chapman remains a dowser for nurseries, able as ever to sense land primed to flourish. This year, he chooses a meadow enclosed in a curve of untouched forest, flat land dotted with only a few sturdy birches, bounded by a gentle stream burbling over smooth rocks. There's no reason to hurry: they will have to plow and till the meadow, but they don't have to cut many trees or remove many boulders. When the brothers finish one row of planting they pause at the nursery's far edge, resting overlong in the threshold of grass between the orchard to come and the first brambles and briars of the existing forest, all the life that lived here first.

They finish in the late afternoon of the twelfth day: all the seeds they brought west with them are almost exactly enough, buried now beneath the black dirt wild Indiana prepared for them, a gift of loam and humus, of dense soil ready to sprout whatever it's given.

Afterward, Nathaniel falls asleep in the grass with his felt hat over his sunburned face. Chapman waits until Nathaniel begins to snore, then undresses quietly, puddling his clothes in the shade before wandering away along the nearby stream, looking for a hidden place he might go alone to remake himself, as Nathaniel promised he could.

HOW MANY YEARS HAS IT BEEN SINCE CHAPMAN LAST WORE THE faun? A decade has been spent safely in civilized land, playing simple apple planter, earnest homesteader, no longer any wild creature. It's been years since he last dreamed of the witches, longer since he last heard the beheaded singer's song in the wind, long enough he sometimes pretends they're as much legend and myth as this Johnny Appleseed, who Chapman knows is no real person at all. It's been enough years he could almost choose to believe he was never a faun, instead making his memories of running free on powerful hooves into some hallucination or injury, something he made up to pass the infernal hours spent walking the frontier of this country, hours wasted planting thousands of apple seeds that brought exactly nothing, neither money nor magic. Perhaps the faunish days he remembers were just a fancy of youth like the stories Eliza Worth loves to tell, fairy tales and myths full of trickster shapeshifters and lost princes, capricious gods and clever girls and evil stepmothers, all transplanted to wild America from more civilized Germany and France and Greece.

But it wouldn't be true. He knows what he is, what he might be in any shape he appears.

His last transformation, on the day the witches murdered the wolf trapper, had been nearly effortless, masterfully controlled. Now he feels an uneasy sluggishness as he tries to reclaim his first shape from wherever or whenever it is he's stored it.

At first nothing happens. At first nothing happens in *waves*. The nothing rushes over him until Chapman's sure he's stuck, this plan to come west pursued to no avail, if its purpose was to let him be himself. He's dismayed but he can't give up. He persists, he insists, he pulls his body in, he folds his graying fallible human body in on itself, bending his shape until he feels the man squeezing its way back inside the faun, turning his skin inside out as it goes.

Immediately he realizes he's not the same faun he was, not exactly. Back in his fur, standing on his hooves, he feels the faun's age arrive not with the gradualness of lived life but with a sudden violence, his every physical deprivation a blow against the image he's held on to all these years: he lifts a hand and sees graying fur, sees how his claws are as yellowed by age as Nathaniel's fingernails; when he reaches up to grip his horns, his joints pop and complain.

Chapman curses. All the last years of his youth, wasted hidden inside the body of a man. He takes a few experimental steps on his hooves, then bounds a bit faster, leaping onto a series of mossy boulders, losing his balance as he misses a jump. The unfamiliarity of this aged body, its locomotion different from that of the one he's worn too many years. He crouches beside the stream's pool, lowering his face toward the wavering reflection dappled across the water's surface. He explores the crags of his cheeks, fingers probing ravines dug by time on the face he'd tucked away, wider and stranger than the face he wears as a man. The golden eyes are spaced farther apart, slanted in toward his broad nose, the nostrils flaring, his broad lips chapped and scowling. His whole horn at least remains the same shape as always, spiraled tight against the right side of his skull, gleaming white gold in the sunlight, but the broken one looks worse than ever, its keratin thinned, in danger of further cracking.

Stunned, Chapman strikes the surface of the stream's pool, splashes himself apart. He sits his trousered rump on a moss-covered stone, then startles when the stone gives beneath him. Not a stone at all, but a stump: sixteen inches high, a rough ball of old bark covered in another inch of moss. Chapman claws free a mossy strand, then digs into the softer wood below to find hidden veins flush with chlorophyll. He scans the surrounding trees, searching for an answer: How is this thwarted trunk alive? What is this unlikely persistence of life? Because it lives on by the gifts of its neighbors, their hidden roots tangled in its withering root ball, delivering doses of water and nutrients; the forest is a community of thriving life, and man will have to do worse than this to break its bonds. From this seat, Chapman hears deer walking the same paths he took to arrive in this place; he hears trout moving against the river's current, scales shuffling over rocks; if he concentrates he detects the gentle splash of skittering water bugs.

He remembers, all at once, a day twenty years ago, when he wandered the deep, uncut wild forests of the Territory, when for one afternoon—maybe the only afternoon like it in his life—he wanted nothing. Now he knows everything he saw that season is gone. Every singing bird nesting in the tallest trees, every lizard skittering over the granite boulders. The bear cub snuffling in the underbrush, the elk does he encountered at the salt lick, that sacred ground stuck through with mammoth fossils. The river gone, diverted. The salt lick drained with the swamp. Every movable rock removed, made into houses and forts, walls and fences; every tree cut to make way for fields or pastures, taken downriver to build some other settlement. The grasses burned, the flowering bushes pulled. Everything turned over to what pleases men, to fulfill what men desire.

Arrived in the future he foresaw that day, Chapman mourns the self-willed world he'd known then, a world where, in return for his not wanting anything, it for a time gave him everything it had. Here he is in some place still equally self-willed, where everything he sees claims its own way. Small god souls in everything: he'd nearly forgotten. He doesn't believe in the deity his brother worships, nor the one whose word Jasper Worth preaches, but he does believe in this: that every creature and every growing thing and every unique place might be its own small god.

He believes, but he hasn't always acted like he believes. He spent his whole life wanting something from the trees he planted, something magic could not offer, instead of accepting everything they gave. A life with a brother; a life outdoors under sun and moon, in fair weather and foul; a life where they always had exactly as much as they needed and no more. It could have been enough, if only they'd ceased their wanting.

And isn't it too late now for these thoughts?

Isn't he only an old faun, an old and stupid faun still allowed to do too much harm?

If he stays in this shape, the witches will come. After the vision he saw in the flicker, the first night he met them, he'd thought they wanted to punish him for something done in a past life, something out of a story. But when he saw what they did to the trapper, he also understood what the witches would soon do to prevent the future men had chosen from manifesting: the settlements they would undo by violence and disease, the livestock slaughtered and the crops withered. A warning, and not only to him.

The witches are not winning, if winning means holding back the settlers' march. But still he could have listened better, still he might've been turned from his path. Now that he's returned to this shape inside which there can be no hiding, he thinks they will come to find him. And when they appear, surely it won't be only to tell him one more time what they've already told him plenty of times before.

BACK IN THE NEW NURSERY, NATHANIEL SITS ATOP THE BROADEST of the nursery's fresh stumps, surrounded by yesterday's sawdust. Nathaniel worn down to bones, Nathaniel old and emptied out, Nathaniel smiling and joyous and more present, this last passage through the country his first sober journey in years, the first happy one in longer. Now all bitterness is absent, at least for the hour: for a decade Chapman and Nathaniel have worked man beside man, but as Chapman returns in the shape he was born in, Nathaniel beams at the sight.

"Brother," Nathaniel says. "I missed you, brother." His voice is gravelly, an old man's voice; he is an old man speaking with the same affection as the fifteen-year-old boy who saved infant Chapman, who gifted that infant their father's name, who designed this whole apple-planting folly so his uncivilized sibling could have some way to live.

"And I you, brother," says Chapman, and as always the word *brother*—this word they have said to each other a thousand thousand times, a word as abundant as the many seeds they've planted—the word *brother* forces his heart into faster movement. There's so much Chapman hasn't had, but he has had a brother. A brother is enough. A brother is a magnificent thing, a gift given and a gift returned in kind, wherever one brother brothers the other.

Nathaniel keeps his seat on the sawn trunk, his elderly legs kicking childishly against the wood. Chapman sets about building their fire, bounding back to the stream for a potful of cool, clean water, a handful of wild carrots spied growing nearby. He makes a simple broth—vegetables and salt and river water—he silently brings it to a boil while the world speaks with a gentle breeze rustling the trees, with birds who cry out warnings about the faun and the man in their midst, their calls beautiful despite their alarm.

Chapman pours the broth into their battered and dented tin cups, then joins Nathaniel upon his stump. There isn't enough room to be beside each other, so they sit back to back, each sipping from his cup, each smoking his pipe. Chapman hears Nathaniel's booted heels tapping the trunk on one side; Nathaniel listens to the softer tap of Chapman's hooves doing the same. Chapman's taller than Nathaniel, at least as a faun; his older brother leans back his heavy head, resting it between Chapman's bare shoulder blades.

The sun sets, darkness falls, the wind picks up, blowing newly, easily, across the cleared space of the nursery. The brothers shiver back to back, they shiver their flesh against each other's skin. Chapman takes his pipe from his mouth, lets it go cool in his hand. He closes his eyes, listens. For this moment, he is just Chapman, just one faun alive in this one unique moment with his brother, both of them alive in this hour and alive in the next and alive in the one after—until, in some other after, it's only Chapman who is alive, asleep and dreaming, so that it isn't until he awakes in the predawn darkness with his brother's cold weight against him that he realizes Nathaniel has passed in the night.

Chapman buries his brother beside the sawn trunk they shared, digging up rows to make Nathaniel a grave, then replanting the closed ground with the leathern bag's last handful of seeds. The trees here will grow from Nathaniel's body, each tree expressing whatever attributes it carries in its seed, the endless randomization of an ungrafted apple tree. In death, what was Nathaniel will continue the brothers' work, not across the nation coming into being but here in this one unique place, a place exactly unlike every other.

By the time the task is done, the sun is rising. Threshold time, doorway time, the liminal space, the light of the rising sun limning living Chapman. He huffs, drops his head, waits for what tears will come. He's been a man so long his restored faunness surprises him every time he sees it: the furred legs, the black hooves. Whatever sadness Chapman feels, the emotion lasts exactly until he hears the song, its sound robbing him of his grief: the beheaded singer, his blasted funeral dirge, his elegy made physical pain.

Chapman raises his horned head, snorts in anger.

They're here.

JOHN

Where is Eury Mirov while her empire burns? First Beijing, where, after nearly three days of silent captive acquiescence, she begins speaking again. In flawless Chinese, she convinces the military police standing guard to free her from the Zhongnanhai cell where she's been held since the interruption of her speech. Upon her release, she's taken to the office of the general secretary, where without preamble or apology she begins pressuring him to send his troops into the Sichuan VAC to stabilize the uprising there, and to do it fast, before the terrorists, as she calls them, breach the Tower. It's the Tower Eury wants protected, more than the land, more than the livestock or the crops or the infrastructure the Communist Party's funded.

"Everything else can be rebuilt or replanted or regrown," she tells the general secretary. "But the Towers have to last the day."

The general secretary doesn't share Eury's motivations: he reminds her of his security council veto of Pinatubo. Any setback there is a positive. "You have your own soldiers," he says, but Eury presses for assistance: the resistance is too sudden, too expertly dispersed. The general secretary waves a hand, gives in. China needs the VAC to feed its cities, will acquiesce to keep the population from starving, from revolting again. Better they fight Earthtrust than Beijing.

Reunited with her China-based security team, Eury flies for Brussels. Midflight, she appears in Syracuse, where she screams for the president to mobilize the National Guard, the army, whatever he can. But the Farm—and all the Sacrifice Zone, and all the Midwest between the Farm and St. Louis—is completely under Earthtrust's administration: it's her soldiers who will have to fight, he says, not his. They are, as always, speaking alone. Eury doesn't negotiate in front of others, never subjects her demands to public scrutiny. This rung's security detail waits outside, the president's Secret Service escort standing guard beside them.

In the cheap replica of the Oval Office, Eury slaps the American president across the face. It doesn't change his mind, but there's nothing he can do to punish her. "Then your people will starve," she says, all the while thinking, *If John were here, he would object: Are the Americans not her people too?*

Perhaps not, not anymore.

An hour later, in Moscow, the Russians give her everything she asks for, but only if she agrees to pull Earthtrust out of Ukraine. She picks up a phone, gives the order. By nightfall, the Ukraine VAC will be completely dark. Better one country starves than every country. Besides, she doesn't need every VAC for Pinatubo to succeed. Only most of them.

By the time her armored town car reaches the new government-only airport in Syracuse—by the time a similar car is parking on the runway at Domodedovo—Eury is back aboard her near-empty jet, now beginning its descent into Brussels, where the European Union parliamentarians loyal to her wait for instructions.

For at least a little longer, she needs these allies. From the sky over Brussels, she can see the fires below, the European Quarter besieged, the automated factories bombed at the outskirts of the city, other crucial infrastructure destroyed. Beijing, Moscow, Syracuse, Brussels, all attacked in a matter of hours; the entire world is on fire hours before she plans to save the world from burning. A futile gesture. The only thing these terrorists are doing is increasing the difficulty of what must be done, what Eury will ensure is done, no matter what. On the plane's satellite phone, she berates her commanders, speaking into all their earpieces at once. "The biomass," she howls. "Stop the burning, recover the stock, keep the Towers safe."

If the Towers blow, if the tanks beneath them explode, the future she dreams of is doomed. But for now there's little else Eury can do herself but wait for Pinatubo to launch.

Separated by a thousand miles, Eury and John think more or less the same thoughts. They think: Not to act is still acting. You cannot win by refusing to play. Even if you play, you will likely lose. So you don't play along, but you do act. You act, not knowing if what you choose is right. The past is unchangeable, the future unknown. You act, making the best choice you can in the present, the moment that is passing, that is now past.

Did you act while you could?

This close to the end, you might not get to know if you did the right thing.

A moment passes, a moment passes, a moment passes.

In how many of these fleeting moments did you do nothing?

THE HATCH TO THE ATRIUM IS CLEVERLY CONCEALED: DESPITE HAV-
ing descended through it with Eury on his first visit to the penthouse, John rediscovers it only once Cal's fist begins pounding
from below. Standing above the sound, he squeezes his fist to
switch to Eury's profile, then watches as a square of the office's
wood floor lifts free.

John smiles as the hatch lifts, but his cheer fades when he
sees Cal's bloodied face, when he realizes Julie isn't following
behind. He offers Cal a hand, but she waves him off with her pistol. "The stairs go all the way to the top," she says. "Just back up."

Cal emerges slowly, wincing whenever she steps on her sore
leg, holding her broken wrist to her stomach, clenching her pistol in her other hand. She's covered in blood, hers and others',
her clothes sweat soaked and dusty, reeking of tear gas. There's
a story here John wants to hear, but he knows there's no time:
even as John's querying Julie's fate, he's already squeezing his
fist. With the purple light unlit, only the orange still steadily
glows. He waves off Cal's answer. How much death has Cal seen
today? How much has she caused? What they've come here to
do is impossible to fully apprehend: you can say *the stratosphere*,
but there's no way to experience it; you can discuss geoengineering forever without forming any emotional attachment.
But Julie's death, Noor's death, Mai's death, those are events local enough for John to feel, as are the other deaths they caused,
the men and women who died trying to keep them from reaching this room before Pinatubo launches.

"This way," he says, his face filthy, his mind tired but wholly engaged. "Less than ten minutes left."

Cal follows him through the opulent office—all the organic finery, she thinks, this old growth made into a desk, the finest wood floors, the finest leathers, everything the best of the end of the real, while the Volunteers live in concrete cubes, wearing plastic clothes—and then John and Cal enter the launch chamber together, the more austere environment packed with computer consoles, dozens of telescreens showing the status of the other VACs, the myriad Pinatubo injection sites spread across the world. In all the other places under attack, everywhere the Volunteers rise up, that resistance, Cal sees, is already being suppressed.

Cal sets her pistol down on the ledge of one of the consoles, then snatches it up again when she sees E-5 standing expressionless in the center of the room, dressed exactly as Eury Mirov last appeared. How many times has she imagined raising her pistol to this woman's head, ready to end her for what she did to Cal's country, to Cal's home, to the people and places and beings Cal loved, even the places she'd only dreamed of, the distant beauties of the world, the remote wonders she knew she'd never see, that she'd loved anyway?

It's not all Eury Mirov's fault. The problem is bigger than any one person, any one company or government: the problem belongs to every last person; until it's solved everyone remains complicit, even if they resist.

Cal knows all this. But what she would've given to have had someone to punish.

"You," Cal sneers, her face twisting, the snarl wrenching her bruises. She gestures with the pistol, stepping toward E—E recoils, alarmed—then puts the pistol down again. "I'm sorry," she says. "I know you're not her."

But does she? Because despite this clone's blankness, when she smiles it's with Eury's winning smile, when she speaks it's in Eury's hypnotically charismatic voice: "Only me," she says. "I'm only me."

"Eight minutes to go," John says, pulling Cal's attention away from E by gesturing for her to join him at the command console. "But there's a problem."

"Where are we at?" Cal asks, stepping to John's side. The displays are swimming with numbers, video feeds, scrolls of code she can't read. Warning lights flash from a dozen screens. "What's next?"

"That's just it," he says. "I can't stop it. There's no kill switch. When Eury started the countdown three days ago, she'd already ensured it would happen. Short of blowing this control room—and probably every other, in every Tower—there's no preventing the launch." John lowers his gaze, shuffles his feet. "I'm sorry, Cal. I wanted it to be different."

Cal lifts John's face with her one good hand. Her grip leaves a mark, smearing dust and blood across his chin. "Old goat," she says, offering him the crooked smile she knows he loves. "You've done everything exactly right. I don't want you to stop it. I want you to make it better."

At the end of the world, an argument ensues. It begins with Cal explaining what she wants John to do, what only he can do in the time they have remaining. Eury's plan is to pause the warming of the planet long enough to buy Earthtrust and the other megacorporations and the last standing governments time to supposedly put in real reforms, to agree upon a way to reverse emissions, to stop carbon release and implement its capture.

"More time," Cal spits. "For what? More efficiency? More conservation? More *sustainability*?" No increase in efficiency, she says, has ever resulted in a true decrease in total emissions; instead the more we saved, the more we used. "The one choice we never make is to leave the oil in the ground, to let the trees grow uncut, to let the water slosh in its aquifers. Once we have the capacity to use a resource, we use it all. We grow, whatever the cost. All one energy-efficient, water-conserving city means is that another city can be built. There is no such thing as sustainability as long as unlimited growth is the end goal. I say it's time to stop growing. I say it's time to force a contraction. Whatever humanity does next, it must never again be allowed to grow."

Fifty years ago, Cal argues, there was a series of red lines that couldn't be crossed, any number of points of no return after which civilization as we knew it would be doomed. But we crossed every one. We didn't even slow down. The only thing lowering carbon emissions now is that so many people are dead from drought and disease, from the horrors of cities drowned or burned or shaken apart or otherwise made uninhabitable, from war and closed borders.

What if there was an alternative, Cal says. What if they forced Eury's hand? "Give her twenty-five years, John," says Cal. "Give us twenty-five years. No more solutions delayed, promised by the end of next century. No more by 2150 the sea levels will be this and that height if we do nothing. No more ice deferred, no more pretending the present must be sacrificed for a distant better future never arriving. Make the present the last human world, unless we change everything about how we live, unless we do it together. We can't keep pretending there's nothing to do. We act or we do not."

John went west to walk away, because he wanted to withdraw from the world; he came back because he hoped there might be a way to save it, if only he could put a hand on some truer lever of power. This is the room with the lever; this is his hand, poised atop it. All he has to do is decide whether to pull.

If he does nothing, Eury gets her way. Choosing nothing is a choice too.

The launch can't be stopped, but it can be subverted, just this once, from here, right now. John stands with his back to Cal, his hands floating over the main console's keyboard, his gaze flitting from screen to screen, each monitor depicting one of the Towers waiting to send up its nanoswarms as fast as their production facilities can print them, all working from the final designs he uploaded late last night. He wishes he had more time but more time is not coming. There are exactly three minutes left, then there's less. Always less. Every noncommittal breath, every vacillating utterance, every frustrated gesture, every wavering thought: the only result of inaction is less time.

No matter what you do, there will never be more time left to act than there is now.

"You lied to me," John says. He turns toward Cal, toward E-5 standing beside her. "You said we could stop Earthtrust, that in doing so we'd save the world. Now you want me to end it."

"With or without you, this world ends," Cal says. "But you can choose how. You can choose not to let anyone escape the common fate: either we all save each other, or else no one gets saved."

If John's going to change the nanoswarm parameters, there

isn't much time left. Once Pinatubo is launched, the strato-spheric nanoswarm will continue to refine itself without out-side interference, all its decisions made by the hive mind above the clouds. Whatever he does or doesn't do next locks human-ity into the future he chooses. It'd be easy enough to reprogram the nanoswarms to do what Cal asks, easy enough to hide what he's done until it's too late to stop it. Initially the effect would seem the same as in Eury's plan, but then would come a rapid thickening of the solar-blocking layer, set to commence after a mere quarter century, with only a total global carbon draw-down able to prevent the worst outcome.

And if the world isn't ready, if we won't or can't work to-gether, if humanity does nothing to save itself in the next twenty-five years?

Then the nanoswarms will block enough solar radiation to trigger a global ice age capable of wiping humanity off the planet's surface, summoning new glaciers to reset the earth for however many centuries it takes for the man-made greenhouse gases already trapped in the atmosphere to dissipate.

"Always," Cal says, "there will be life, no matter what we choose. All we're discussing is whose lives get saved, all we're deciding is how good those lives will be. Human or nonhuman, animal or plant, it doesn't matter to Eury Mirov. She guarantees only the steady diminishment of the shared world, only the suffering of the many until the planet is ready to be given to the few. I say abundance or nothingness, abundance or noth-ingness for all."

Two minutes.

Then a little less.

John curses, John plants his fists against his eyes and pushes until he sees stars.

The choice is his. Ten billion people alive on the earth, and only he can decide.

In his mind, in the starry flicker behind his fists, he grips the lever he's always imagined.

He chooses.

He pulls the lever all the way down.

CHAPMAN

The witches arrive at sunrise. Now here again are their inhuman voices, rolling fog and growing moss, the cracking of eggshells, the wet speech of aquifers collapsing, the scraping of rock on rock like the gnashing of teeth, the crackling lashing of tectonic tongues. Even as Chapman's fear threatens to paralyze him, pity wells in his heart at the reduced creatures the witches have become: in the myth, they were regal and grave, beautiful beyond words; twenty years ago they were entrancing even at their most terrifying, their abundant bodies attractive in their fleshy thickness, their feral faces muddied and bloodied but beguiling too; now all three have become gaunt and drawn, their old voluptuousness sagged into want and wreck.

Despite whatever kinship they might share, Chapman has never understood the complaints of their inhuman voices. He wishes he could, but being a man has cost him almost all of being an animal. If only he hadn't had Nathaniel, if only he hadn't plowed the Territory under in search of his Tree, if only the witches had come to him earlier, before he was Chapman, maybe then the unnamed faun and the nameless witches could have been wild together, wildness incarnate.

"I want to understand you," he says, speaking truthfully. "I want to know what you want.

"I want to help you, but you killed my brother," he says, and this too is true. They've accused Chapman before; now he accuses them, but as he speaks he doubts.

Only the singer they bear with them always has not been further wounded by linear time. His face remains the same sallow shape, its features just as sunken into cheeks pancaked with dust or makeup; his voice rises and falls in the same sonorous drone Chapman's heard in so many dreams. As his song fills the air, Chapman and Nathaniel's last nursery begins to shift, the planted soil shimmering then flickering, the dirt becoming grass becoming gravel, then blacktop, then asphalt, then every surface appearing at once, all together making a rippling band of changeable earth upon which the witches paw their clawed and taloned feet, still making their last accusations in overlapping cries of fog and moss and shell.

"No more future," Chapman says, covering his ears against the battering waves of song. "Shut him up and we'll talk."

He knows the witches won't be women for long, that what they are is never exactly *women*. Already their shapes churn and warp. The witch holding the beheaded singer finishes her shift first, abandoning her passenger to the dirt as her hands vanish, his singing unceasing even though his face is pressed against the tilled earth: the vulture the witch becomes takes to the air on wings missing too many feathers, its flight made difficult despite its impressive flapping; then the grizzly bear with its threadbare fur appears, its enormous bones straining sharply at its stretched skin; and finally the panther, slinking close to the ground, a once graceful predator now stumbling side to side, its tail dragging in the dirt as its transformation finishes, the witch inside the panther struggling to find her footing.

Chapman is half man and half animal, all his life there has been danger in thresholds, in in-betweens: the twilight hour of dusk and dawn, the faded but not gone dribble of the last dream before waking, this just-planted nursery, where no seed has yet sprouted, neither settled nor wild. Now, as the sun fully breaches the eastern horizon, the present collapses, the future arrives, the flicker *flickers*. At once the witches cross over from the wild forest into the nursery, the bear charging first, bounding across the nursery even faster than Chapman expected, then rearing up on its hind legs to swing a clawed paw at Chapman's horned head. Chapman ducks but too slowly, his present body divorced from the preternatural speed he once enjoyed, the paddle of the bear's paw smacking his unbroken horn, spinning him around on his hooves. As he spins, he lashes out with his own claws, raking them across the bear's softer underbelly. It's not a deep wound, he sees, only a slim new hurt—but as the bear's body moves past he smells all the other hurts the bear already suffers, the traumas carried in its rotten flesh, its sloughing fur.

He expects the panther to make its pass next, but it's the vulture who comes, diving with outstretched talons for Chapman's eyes; he turns his face aside, the talons ribboning one cheek before he catches one of the vulture's incredible wings, his hands tearing and twisting. Feathers snap free, hollow bones break, the vulture's momentum carries it spiraling away, its crimson head squawking, its sharp beak snapping around the furious wobble of its darting tongue. Now comes the panther's expected charge, the lean black shape leaping across the tilled earth, each bound faster, more graceful.

Of the witch-beasts, the panther is the least injured, the most dangerous; Chapman swipes blood from his torn cheek and squares his body against it. He's spent ten years hiding from these women, these beasts, from whatever else they might be. By the singer's song they'd shown him where they'd come from, the same story from which he'd emerged: like him, they've shaken off the myth of their birth; unlike him they've become protectors of the land, fates no longer, now only furies, whose anger is provoked by every clear-cut, every burn, every dammed river or diverted stream, every livestock species treasured by man, every invasive pest accidentally introduced that wiped out something uniquely native, every destroyer of whatever small gods lived and thrived in any particular place. Even if he'd cleared no ground and planted no trees, Chapman couldn't have ended his complicity, could not have exited the story inside which he and Nathaniel had lived, not as long as he lived a life dependent on all this human destruction, not as long as he chose his brother over the world.

The panther is faster than he expects. He misses his dodge and the beast bowls him over, digging its claws into his bare shoulders—but Chapman's the equal now of this witch in cat's clothing, her great shape not broken by the damage men have done but injured enough to give him a chance. The panther pushes its claws into Chapman, but the faun is clawed too, his whole horn and sharp teeth equally dangerous. The great cat screeches, leaps away; now the bear circles in one direction, the panther in the other. Chapman turns at the center of their stalking, trying to keep both beasts in view, while the broken-winged vulture hops at the melee's outer orbit, screeching its complaint, snapping its beak uselessly in his direction.

"I'm no killer," Chapman argues, "I'm no killer," he says again, but it is only for men that he's stayed his hand. What about all else that's gone from the Territory, from the State, vanished at his hand, his brother's, all the others like them? It wasn't the witches who cut down thousands of trees, who displaced untold bird's nests, who unearthed countless dens and burrows. It wasn't the witches who plowed every inch of land they could, wasn't the witches who bragged of planting horizon-busting orchards, who dreamed of apple trees bred double or triple their size, the great weight of ever-brighter, ever-sweeter globes of apples bending low every crooked branch.

Didn't man have a right to till the ground, to plant his fields, to make a living for his family? Yes. But itinerant Chapman, made the legend Appleseed, who yearly converted more of the Territory into what humans wanted it to be than any other—surely he was no mere man.

Long-lived as a faun might be, this Appleseed might endeavor to take more than his share, might plow and plant and reap more than one life, all of it serving only his selfish desires, his useless story of the Tree that never was.

He's thinking when he should be fighting. Now the grizzly roars, the wedge of its battered head leading the muscled hump of its shoulders as it wheels toward Chapman, who tries again to plead his ridiculous innocence: "I'm no killer," he says, denying his complicity for the third time, refuting the witches' vengeance even as he sets his hooves, ready to meet the bear's attack with equal force. He drops his head, hammers his good horn against the bear's temple hard enough to stagger it; he staggers too, stumbles a step before he recovers. He feints toward the bear to bait the panther, then leaps away from its pounce, letting the two beasts knock each other to the torn ground. On the other side of the nursery, the vulture screeches, hopping crooked with its broken wing, flickering back into its witching shape, the woman who is not a woman appearing in a series of stuttering images, some vulture, some dangerously neither bird nor woman, then a woman with the witch's face, wearing the features of the bird: the sharp nose, the beaded eyes, her ears pinned to the sides of her head, her raptor's tongue too small between her human teeth.

Broken arm flopping behind her, the half-woman, half-vulture witch screeches after Chapman, who's running hard now, risking everything in the hope of reaching the nursery's edge before he's caught. As the witches took their animal forms, they'd dropped the singer facedown in the dirt at the tree line; now it's Chapman who rescues him, lifting the singer by his topknot, holding the half-rotted head like a lantern as he spins toward the pursuing bird-witch. As he turns, he slides the fingers of his free hand into the singer's neck, working the throat open, recoiling at the waxy stuckness of the dead flesh even as he widens the throat: the singer's voice rises in volume, its terrible beauty magnified, its awful screeching louder than ever before.

Chapman has seen how the song finds the future in the flicker and brings it back: he'd seen the frozen world when the trapper was killed, the country of poured rock at the abandoned cabin all those years before. He remembers the visions the singer gave him decades ago, of the nymph in the dale, the niece they said the faun killed in a life Chapman can't remember. She was the witches' niece too, when they were sometimes fates and not just furies; she had been the one beautiful truth at the center of their world, the purest spirit of the woods, joined in marriage for only a single day to the singer whose head Chapman holds, who'd been the best of that world's men.

When the faun who lived in the myth caused the nymph's death, his greed broke the union of man and tree, the covenant between humans and the world. But this story didn't have to be that story. Surely anything but that inevitability.

Surely there is a choice, even now, if only Chapman could see it to take it.

The song pummels the bird-witch with waves of sound, its battering aging her terribly: Chapman sees her again become simultaneous, her body appearing at every age she ever was, ages making no sense for a shapeshifter, a woman who is a beast, a beast who is a woman, a beast and a woman who are avatars of an idea, expressions of savage force. All magic is more fragile than anyone ever imagines, even what's seemingly immortal. The bird-witch ages into who she should have become only many years from now, after the human conquest of the world has completed its diminishments: her skin sags, her joints crumple, her hair wisps and blows away, yellow teeth drop from snarling lips. Everything the witch was collapses at once to fertilize the earth of the nursery, the planted orchard-to-be already sprouting, buried Nathaniel and the decomposing bird-witch together feeding the accelerated fecundity of this patch of earth, its transformation sped by the song.

With equal parts wonder and horror, Chapman turns the head on the bounding panther, its yellow eyes blazing, its remaining claws churning the earth with every song-staggered step; he aims it at the roaring grizzly, the sound ripping the bear's hackles free in graying banners, fur lifting like sod from the rotted surface of the bear: one by one, the witches come apart, bodies once unbound by time becoming flesh dissolving, returning to the earth. During their dissolution, in the nursery something like ten years passes at once, the time lapse local, the singer's voice powerful as ever, ready to generate possible futures, ready to choose one and make it true: *More life*, Chapman thinks, as the song rises, *more life*, he cries as trees just planted, trees that should need ten years to grow, *grow now*, their sprouts unfurling, each seedling rising jerkily: seedlings becoming saplings, saplings becoming trees unfolding atop Nathaniel's grave, their roots eating his flesh and drinking his blood and ferrying some of who he was back up into the living world as the trees' sudden branches bloom, as their blooms turn to fruit, as the apples ripen upon their stems.

After the flicker fades, Chapman walks the orchard, the singer's head still dangling from his right hand. With his left, he picks an apple, sticks it between his sharp teeth, bites down.

What idiotic hope prompts that bite? What does he expect to find, at long last?

Something magical, something life-changing: the promised fruit of the Tree of Forgetting, a miracle grown from the end of the witches and from the body of his brother, planted here in the last nursery he'll ever sow.

Instead the apple he chooses is as bitter as any other, unsuitable for anything but cider, its fruit half wood and hardly any sugar. But maybe now wood is enough. With his free hand, Chapman pries open the singer's mouth, then shoves the oaky density of the bitten apple in past his half-rotted teeth, choking the singer on all its leathery skin, its tasteless flesh, its stony core. This is apple as stopper, as gag, not enough to keep the singer from singing but capable of dulling his song, making it a manageable trickle of revelation, its prophecy unspooling only at the normal human pace, its next future always due to arrive exactly one second after the present, fast enough.

JOHN

A keening sounds. A moment later, Eury Mirov arrives at the top of the Tower's needle, freshly installed in the recently docile body of E-4, her Ohio-based rung positioned safely behind the soldiers attempting to breach the penthouse. She stretches, loosening a stiff muscle found waiting for her in her new neck—unless the ache needing soothing is just a tickle of remainder, a leftover need of the old body expressing itself in the new. It doesn't matter, she knows. This body or that body, all of them are hers, all their feelings and thoughts are her.

"Five minutes to go," Eury says, immediately assuming command of the operation. "Let's get this door open already."

She paces while the soldiers continue prying at the blast doors, their mechanism permanently sealed when the security nexus exploded, a safeguard meant to keep Eury safely inside, not trap her outside. The commander of her local bodyguard affirms Eury's orders, her voice slightly garbled by her helmet's face shield; Eury waves off the apology that follows, for the miscalculation of attacking the nexus. Mistakes have been made, by her as much as anyone else. She knows the soldiers are trying their best, first with the thundering battering ram, then with an unwieldly two-person laser saw. The impressive door resists their efforts, the laser throwing off heat and sparks but barely scratching its nearly impenetrable surface, this last line of defense in Eury's fortress holding exactly as it was designed to do.

Still Eury impatiently stalks the small anteroom. It's not her soldiers' fault they can't breach her office, these loyal men and women who've followed her for years, dressed again in their heavy matte black armor, never before needed on the Farm. Armor was for the war, armor was for the West. The Farm had been meant to be home; now once again it seemed the frontier.

"Do we at least have a visual?" she asks, interrupting a discussion of other tactics for breaching the penthouse, then the Pinatubo launch chamber: rappelling in from a helicopter could work, but it would be difficult to avoid wrecking the equipment inside; if their only goal was to take out the terrorists, an attack drone could deliver a rocket or a machine-gun burst, but heavy weaponry would again damage the control room, a disaster this close to launch.

"Without the nexus, we can't access your office cameras, but we're flying a surveillance drone around," the commander says, knocking on the touchscreen embedded in her gauntlet cuff. "Should be in range any second now."

A matter of time then. The launch can be disrupted but it cannot be stopped. In four minutes, the many Towers will open their needles, releasing their nanoswarms; once airborne, the swarm from the Ohio VAC will deliver its instructions to the global hive mind.

Stupid, treacherous John. But as long as the swarms work, he's done his part. And Eury is sure they will, because everything John has ever invented has worked. Everything Eury has is part John's, everything except the Loom. So much of the rest of Earthtrust is built on his ideas and his inventions, even the nanobots about to repair the world. Why can't he accept that all this is what she thought he wanted, what she wanted to make with him, for him?

"Director," the commander says. "Come look at this." As she offers Eury her wrist-mounted screen, an explosion at the Tower's base shakes the high antechamber. The screen jostles as the commander adjusts her footing, but Eury grabs her wrist, pulls the half-glimpsed image close: John stands at the launch controls, working furiously, while his terrorist girlfriend scans the penthouse windows, her eyes tracking the drone's horizontal hover. Eury watches as the woman staggers, then catches a falling third figure in her arms, as a second explosion rocks the needle: another Eury Mirov, saved from the aftershock.

"Fucking hell," Eury says, already peeling the long black glove from her right wrist. She squeezes her thumb against her bare palm until the usual row of lights winks on beneath the skin at the back of her hand, all the indicators white except the blue-blinking fourth, no longer the last in line, as it should be.

So now there are five, she thinks. *Now there are five of me.*

Now there is John, half turned from the console, frozen in place, looking over his shoulder at the newest E, held in the arms of his other woman. John as indecisive as ever, as unwilling to choose. Eury's raw fury never lasts; already it's going cold, calculated. When had this happened? Sometime within the last dozen distracting hours. There were no safeguards on the Loom, no alarms or alerts sent when it was activated. Why should there be, when no one could enter the room but her? She knew she shouldn't have shown John the Loom but couldn't help herself; somehow he had hacked and spoofed her pebble, copying her passcodes to gain entry, then discovered the code name she'd given her blueprint. He'd understood what else the Loom could do, then used it against her. If he knows this much, then he might also understand the last step of her plan, the part she hadn't told him: it isn't only the animals and the plants the Loom will reprint, repopulate. If worse comes to worst, Eury will blueprint the human race before it goes extinct; then, when it is safe, she will put everyone back. Starting with herself.

It's okay, she thinks. *John, I have chosen for you before. I can choose for you again.*

Eury squeezes her hand again. There's never a long delay between bodies, but nothing is instantaneous. A snatch of keening drone, followed by the flickering, a slight blinking pause of barely a second, before she comes loose from her flesh, and then every single time the same awe: *I am the only person who's ever experienced this. The soul, freed from the body, free to inhabit another—isn't that immortality enough?*

Humankind had dreamed of this since the beginning, in paintings in the caves, in the first stirrings of myth and religion. Now Eury has made the dream real. Sometimes she wishes she could stay in the flicker forever, living on as a mind safely wanting nothing, only floating, floating—but then always there's the next body, calling her back to the world.

"SHE'S FINE, JOHN," CAL SAYS, TRYING NOT TO SNEER AT JOHN'S concern for the Eury clone, nearly fallen to the floor in the aftershock of the second bomb blast. "Get back to work."

"Nothing left to do. It's over. I did it." His face is closed, his expression unreadable. "Ninety seconds to go."

"We did it," Cal says, triumphant, relieved. She stands E back on her feet, then steps away to rejoin John at the console, wanting to be at his side for the launch. But as she slides by E, she sees—what exactly?

E blinking a bit too fast, maybe her breathing momentarily changing pace. Nothing, really. Just a little bit of shock, Cal thinks—and then she doesn't think much of anything ever again: Eury smiles cruelly as she grabs the pistol off the console's ledge, her expression hardening as she quickly aims the weapon and pulls the trigger, shooting Cal at nearly point-blank range.

"You bitch," Eury says, standing over Cal's already crumpled body, watching her gurgle blood through a hole low in her throat. Cal's chest is heaving, her eyes wide, one hand scratching at her gushing wound while the other digs inside her backpack, its contents half spilled beside her; already her strength is failing, her movements slowing. "You killed my dogs," Eury accuses, hot tears forming in the corners of her eyes at the remembered sight of Cal raising her rifle to shoot the second Ghost, a scene Eury had streamed from the first Ghost's retinal display moments before flickering into E-4. "You killed my dogs and all I could do was watch."

She can print another Ghost but it won't be the same, she'll have to start over, training the new wolf again from scratch. *If I live through this*, she thinks, *it's time to invent better backups.*

John squeezes his eyes shut at the gunshot, his hands

paused above the keyboard; behind his thumb, an unwatched orange light flares then goes out forever. "Eury," he says, his voice choked. He raises his hands in surrender, his eyes flicking between Cal, fallen at Eury's feet, one hand awkwardly buried inside her pack, and Cal's pistol, held in Eury's right hand. "I didn't know—" How had she inhabited E-5? He'd missed something crucial and it had cost Cal her life: E wasn't a clone but a *vessel*. He waits for his anger and grief to rise, but for now he only feels numb; he fights to keep his voice as even as he can. "You didn't have to kill Cal, Eury. Not now, not anymore." Less than a minute to go. He has only to delay her.

"She wouldn't have done the same to me if she could?" Eury steps over Cal, raising the handgun again. "You can't stop the launch, John. You and your friends have made everything worse, for *nothing*. Haven't you learned anything? Every remaining resource is precious, every bit of biomass we can gather is necessary for us to survive." She gestures to the windows, the black smoke rising from the flaming Farm. "That's the future burning. Suffering today, absence tomorrow. All because of you."

John follows her gaze in time to watch the Earthtrust drone make another pass. He says, "There was no grand plan, Eury, no conspiracy. These are ordinary people, rising up. Wanting a say in their own destiny."

Eury shakes her head. "They're not ready, John. Always a necessary few lead, by election or by force. I am leading now, doing what cannot wait for a vote."

"Okay, Eury. Okay." It doesn't matter who's right, not anymore. The choice is made.

Eury's expression clouds. He's too calm, too accommodating. "What did you do? John, what have you done?" She casts the gun aside, rushes forward to the command console. He stumbles when she pushes him out of the way, then moves to Cal's side, slumping to the ground to take her in his arms. Behind him, Eury desperately tries to see the changes John's made to her code, but before she can even touch the keyboard the launch commences.

In these last moments, John remembers the bees he raised on his farm, plus all the other real bees he's known: a species extinct, but maybe not forever. He pulls Cal's body against his own, wishing there'd been time to save her; as her arm slides free of her backpack, he hears a sharp ticking, the clicking sound steady at first, then speeding faster. He freezes: in Cal's opening fist, John sees the bomb with which she'd planned to kill Eury Mirov, or at least destroy this launch chamber: a perfect globe the size of an apple, a bloodied clump of illegally printed plastic explosive, its detonator shoved through its meat.

The bomb's short countdown completes as the first bright nanoswarms rise from the Tower's needle, and also from the VAC outside Berlin, where the winters were once thought over forever, and from the Tower erected in the Burgundy region of France, where there is now only one variety of grape, grown only on Earthtrust's farms. Swarms rise in Doukkala, in Overberg, in West Bengal and Sichuan, in Singapore-controlled Kedah, in the Mekong and Chao Phraya Deltas, in Beauce and eastern Ireland and Andalusia, in Ukraine and Brazil, in Argentina and in what remains of Patagonia: all over the world, Eury Mirov's Towers simultaneously send forth the same nanoswarms.

Goodbye to blue skies forever, goodbye to that particular phenomenal beauty no one now living will ever see again, because in less than three days the sky everywhere will be bright white on even the clearest days.

THE WEAKENED BLAST DOORS BUCKLE INWARD, ARMORED EARTH-
trust soldiers breaching the torn seam in a rush; by the time
Eury sees the bomb in Cal's hand, there's no time to warn
her charging soldiers. She squeezes her fist, and the keening song fills her head, radiating outward from the port implanted in her neck; she transfers out of the launch chamber
and into the flickering in-between, momentarily floating as
she's beamed rung to rung, landing first a dozen meters away,
back in the body left behind the charging soldiers, their commander barking orders as the bomb explodes, bursting the
high windows, sending a storm of shrapnel blasting through
Eury's office.

Eury whips her cloak around her, feels the worst of the
shrapnel slide around its shielding shape. Even so, she's cut in a
dozen places, although nowhere critical. She wipes blood from
her face, sends the wetness splatting to the floor with a flick of
her hand.

It doesn't matter how hurt she is, as long as this body doesn't
die while she's inside it.

"I want him *alive*," Eury commands, her fury rising. "I want
him *scanned*."

She clenches her fist, sees that once again there are only
four lights there, E-5 having been obliterated in the blast. If
John's dead, he's dead. But if he lives, she needs to know what
it is he did to Pinatubo, how he planned to steal her triumph
from her. Did his plan succeed? All she knows is that the nanoswarms continue to rise from this Tower exactly as planned,
and presumably from all the others. She turns on her heel, already walking away when she hears John's screams rise above
the din inside her shattered office. Her bodyguards follow her

to the reactivated elevator, ready to escort this body wherever she wants it next, to keep it safe for her eventual return.

A moment later, Eury flickers to Brussels, where there are allies to calm; then back to Syracuse, where the American president must be kept in his place. Hours later, when the situation's stabilized, Eury leaves her Syracuse-based bodyguards and staff behind, flickering to the genetic repository built inside Yucca Mountain, a facility once too close to Las Vegas for any Nevada senator to allow in the nuclear material the facility was built to store. Her office there is much like the Farm's bombed penthouse, only this time built a thousand meters deep instead of a thousand meters high.

Eury walks the empty halls of her facility, halls that won't be empty long. Decades ago, nuclear waste tankers had been scheduled to arrive here, their radioactive cargo meant to be sequestered under the earth for ten thousand years. Now other tankers will come, bearing all the biomass scraped and extracted and refined in the Western Sacrifice Zone.

In the Yucca Mountain Loom, Eury requests a blueprint from Ohio, one that isn't yet ready. While she waits for the transmission to arrive, she prints herself a new wolf, another Ghost exactly like the last. Afterward, the animal sits beside her, panting gently. She reaches out, scratches it behind the ears, the wolf pushing its head against Eury's hand, greedy for more.

Eury smiles. It'll take some time before the wolf truly becomes her Ghost again, but Eury has nothing but time. Not unlimited time, not endless time. But more time than most, more time than anyone else has.

Later, in the mountain facility's secret heart, Eury approaches a glass tube the height of a man, filled with viscous pink recycling fluid, a substance that dissolves everything it touches, everything except what floats in this particular vessel. A series of microphones circle the tube's circumference, set flush against the glass to record the voice captured inside the roiling acid.

Eury steps close, puts her hand against the glass—warm to the touch, heated by the liquid within—and peers into the pink.

At first she sees nothing except the swirling churn of the liquid, but just as she's about to give up, a shape bangs against the tube's wall, bobbing in the sludge.

Eury starts. A stream of bubbles churns upward through the dense pink, the source changing depth in the liquid without again coming near the glass.

The bubbles are evidence of an unheard voice breathing. A voice speaking. A voice *singing*. The microphones are always recording, but the room remains quiet except for the static hum of the equipment, all the noise inside the tube muted by the singer's soundproof prison.

Eury relaxes, ever so slightly—and then the singing thing presses up against the glass.

IN EURY'S PENTHOUSE, THE EXPLOSION UPROOTS JOHN'S LEGS EVEN as it throws the rest of him free, screaming as everything below the knees vanishes in a burst of viscera. Cal's body disappears in the same instant, ripped from his arms by the blast: he'd accidentally gotten her killed, now she'd nearly done the same to him. Sudden blood loss and traumatic shock ensure he loses consciousness almost before what's left of him hits the burning floor; when he wakes, it's to discover the limits of the only salvation Eury can offer.

In the final moments of this life, as John's dying body is laid inside the recycler tube, he learns that the Loom's scanning process is crudely medieval, despite its technological marvels. Unavoidably destructive, the recycler's scanner is what killed the last bison, the last wolf, the last of every species collected by Earthtrust at Eury's command, the method of the promised resurrection also the final tool of mass extinction.

The pink sludge falls from the ceiling of the recycler chamber, the liquid brightly coating what remains of John, his nerves blazing hot then burning out, every inch of him acid-drenched, melting fast, inside and out. He tries to scream, but his face is already coming apart; his mouth fills with the sludge, he drowns as he dissolves.

Eury Mirov, the one John had known since childhood, has been dead for two years.

Eury is already dead, but now Eury might also never die. Hours later, beneath Yucca Mountain, she looks down at John lying loomsick and legless in his hospital bed, recovering in a brightly lit ward Eury imagines will one day be filled with freshly printed human beings, new Volunteers ready to reclaim a planet. She rests a cool hand on John's burning forehead, touches his stubbled cheek, feels the scratch of the same five o'clock shadow he was wearing when he died. He's sleeping, dreaming, battered by the torturous process of being born again, printed alive. She runs her fingers across the rough skin capping his knees, the best she could do on short notice. Always there is so much waste, so much unnecessary brutality and pain, she thinks, looking down at her new wolf, sitting patiently at her feet, panting happily, expectantly.

Eury smiles, proud as ever of her Loom: at a glance, there really is no telling this wolf from the last one.

Despite his missing legs, this John's not so different either.

Eury kneels, takes the wolf's face in her hands, the wolf becoming deliriously happy at her touch, exactly as Eury designed it to be. She says, "What are we going to do now, Ghost? What kind of body will our next John want, to wear in the world to come?"

C-433

The first figure lopes ahead of the other: a green blur on four legs, it zigzags across the earth, pressing its glowing nose to the snow. C's weary brain sets to work studying it, dredging up the map room words, the binder pages he memorized: *Canis lupus*, he thinks after a moment, although he knows that's not quite right, that the binder had read GRAY WOLF instead.

The second figure is easier to name. The second figure, C knows, is a woman. Her face is uncovered except for a swirl of long dark hair; her blazing eyes are intensely brighter than any other part of her, brighter even than her pale green skin glowing the same color as her thin gown, an article of clothing that would be insufficient for the freezing weather if it were real cloth, if the skin beneath it were real skin.

C shivers, gooseflesh growing wherever it can still grow.

"Ghosts," he says, remembering the word *ghost* only as it escapes his mouth: the ghost of a woman not dressed for the freezing temperatures, drifting through the blowing snow; the ghost of a wolf leading her toward the bubble, hovering where it stalled before the one functional machine-gun nest.

C thrusts his body forward, the hoof leading the trunk, the flesh dragging the tree. At the glass, he unfolds his paw against the bubble's steamy curve, watches his breath fogging the surface. The woman and the wolf keep coming, her steps leaving no footprints, although the blowing snowfall behind her eddies in her wake. As she approaches, O becomes agitated too, his voice setting C's skin to new achings: his teeth chatter, his bark quavers, the flowers shut their petals as the beetles scurry for cover.

The ghost-woman pauses, cocking her head in surprise at C's appearance, then lifts up on her toes—only now does he notice she's barefoot—before floating into the air, rising until she's level with him, their faces barely separated by the glass. With one pale hand, she reaches out to where his shaking paw rests, placing her human hand opposite his furred fingers.

"You're here," she says, but C barely hears her, enraptured as he is with her face, the first other face he thinks he's seen. Below her floating feet, the ghost-wolf barks, while O's voice screeches on, moaning between the usual dirge and the rarer sustaining hymn C heard during the night among the monoliths, when the melody set the beetles to flying.

"You're here," she repeats, "and you brought him too."

The ghost shakes her head, snow falling uninterrupted through her body except where some flake hits an obstruction invisible to C but hot enough to sizzle the precipitation, transforming the snowflake to a puff of steam. Tens of thousands of nanomachines, he sees, a hive mind swarm making a body for a digitized consciousness. How deeply buried is the remainder that offers this explanation, how long ago were the memories made that enable the guess? Certainly nothing like this swarm ever existed in the crawler.

"Who are you?" C asks, his rusty voice echoing inside the bubble. "How do you know who I am?" *Him too.* "And O? How do you know O?"

"Is that what you call him?" the ghost asks, surprise flashing briefly across her face. "O, then. And you are?"

"C," he wheezes. "My name is C."

The ghost-swarm floats closer, her body curling to match the bubble's curve; she makes herself a parenthesis of a person, a wraith pressed against photovoltaic glass. "I no longer have only one name," she says. "But you, C, can call me E."

C starts and jerks away, overreacting, he thinks, recoiling backward into the wail of O's grief, stumbling to the bubble's floor with a wooden, fleshy *thunk.* He hears the wood snapping around him, he fears he'll fall unconscious but does not. He pushes himself upright, first to his good knee, then back onto the support of his tree side, cracked and bleeding sap and shedding flaking bark. By the time he rises, E is already floating into the bubble, the craft's door having opened without C's giving the command, her shifting, swarming visage beautiful and terrible, her beauty equally as terrible as O's voice.

With her swarm so close C can hear its buzzing, E says, "I can't believe you're here. I waited so long for you to return, but I never expected you to come back like this." But she's not only looking at his woody growth, at the many beetles covering his branches. She's also tilting her head, listening to O's insane voice, its mad song of unbearable grief.

When E smiles, it's the kindest sight C-433 has ever seen. She waves a hand, summoning the craft's console into solidity, then blinks through a silent series of commands. The console's surface swims, brings up previously undiscovered configurations of controls, data screens, and haptic buttons. E reaches out a hand, its dim green glow brightening and solidifying as the rest of her body wanes, the ghost-swarm adjusting its composition to give her gesture corporeality, physical heft. She presses a button on the console, she says the word *pause,* the same word etched on the button.

Immediately, O stops singing.

This is how the final remainder of this O dies, a death long delayed, denied even longer than C's.

E, hesitating, then pressing STOP.

E, stopping herself, almost.

E, with sudden finality, pressing DELETE.

THE WIND SHIFTS, THE SNOW SLOWS. NOW BLACK MOUNTAIN AP-pears, its entrance not far past the machine-gun nests: a massive black steel door set in a rock face blasted flat, large enough to launch the crawlers once meant to remake the world. The door rises slowly, lifting with a groan of rusting gears and falling dirt to reveal an unlit void within, a cracked blacktop road descending into the facility's underbelly. Piloting the barely recharged bubble, C follows E's ghost-swarm inside, her incorporeal wolf bounding alongside the floating woman. The white sky vanishes as the craft crosses over the threshold into the dark maw of the earth, the outside light falling off until all he can see is E's green glow drifting in the bubble's lamp beam, insufficient to illuminate the deep dark of the tunnel.

"This way," says E, gesturing C onward. "A little farther in and we can close the gate."

Only after the door is fully shut does C see the other figures waiting for him inside the tunnel: a half-dozen humanoids climb the road's slope, their bent bodies half his height, their steps shuffling. The creatures hunch toward the edges of the bubble's lamp beam, where they shield their faces with pale forearms, exposing bleach-white skin covered in silvery fur. They whine, unsure before the brightness, until E says, "C, shut off your light. It's hurting their eyes."

Once only the rows of dim roadside lights remain, the creatures come on more steadily, eyes glittering milkily, naked bodies roped with muscle, powerful arms ending in surprisingly slender hands. The creatures are humanoid but surely not human. Anything but that. Surely this cannot be what being human means.

"What are they?" C asks, broadcasting his voice through the bubble's glass.

The ghost-swarm explains, her voice matter of fact, slightly bored: dwarves bioengineered by E, derived from humans but heavily modified for increased physical strength and resilience, diminished intelligence and agency. Genderless, sterile, printed without reproductive organs, each given an allergy to sunlight: if they ever left the Mountain, they'd go into anaphylactic shock in minutes.

"Don't be alarmed," E says, answering a question C hasn't asked. "Whatever's next won't come from them. They're only my hands, the many bodies I need to maintain the Mountain's machinery, to protect the equipment we'll need to reseed the earth." She speaks in the language of the map room binders, of the life he'd abandoned atop the Ice. E's body dims, her face solidifies and brightens as she turns toward him. She gestures toward the bubble, her motion trailing green tracers. "Are you ready to leave that thing behind? You won't need it anymore, where we're going."

C gasps, struggles to draw enough breath to speak. "Where are you taking me?"

"Home," E says. "You've been gone a long time."

The fleshy dwarves crowd the bubble, one of the creatures dragging a dingy yellow sledge, his shoulders harnessed to its traces. Despite their reduced stature, the dwarves easily lift C's ungainly woody body, ferrying his dense shape out of the bubble, his tree half having long outgrown his flesh's capacity to carry it: in the bubble, he slept his last few nights leaning against the trunk of his left leg. Now, supine on the sledge, the tree's engorged weight further burdens his already struggling lungs.

E communicates with the dwarves by clicks and whistles, barked monosyllabic commands. C tries to complain about the painful way they've strapped him down, but one look into the dwarves' blank moony eyes is enough to stop his struggling. The dwarf in the traces rolls its shoulders and stamps its feet, just toeless slabs of thick muscle. When it stamps again, C shudders, the slightest hint of ancient memory washing over him: not of stamping *beneath* a mountain, but *atop* one, in the moment before beginning a descent not into the endless dark but into a blossoming morning, into endless unbroken abundance.

A false memory, he knows, because in it the sky had been blue, an obvious error of his exhausted mind.

The dwarves take turns dragging the sledge through the

dark, bouncing it over the undermountain road's split concrete. The two ghost-swarms flank the sledge, one on each side, their shapes sometimes drifting over and around C: a cloud that is a woman, a cloud that is a wolf, a cloud that could, he thinks, take many other shapes, if she wanted. He feels a beetle crawl across his lips and shudders, then closes his good eye. For a time the quiet stays quiet and the dark gets darker as they progress toward the truer entrance into Black Mountain, an elevator large enough for a revolving stretch of rail bearing a squat two-car tram: one car for passengers, one for cargo.

E floats across the platform, clicking out orders; the dwarves lift C as a team, creature and tree and sledge all loaded onto the flatbed car in a crashing heap. Strapped down twice—once to the sledge, once to the tramcar—C will be able to see only what his free eye can spy passing the tram's right side. "We're ready," E says, then issues a series of voiceless clicks. The dwarves pile into the passenger car, jostling each other's rude bodies for space, or else hanging off the edge of the tram. One of the dwarves sets the elevator in motion, all its controls physical, the tram's console bleeping as the elevator begins its creaking descent, rust flaking off exposed cables and machinery.

E floats downward alongside C, keeping her insubstantial feet above the surface of the falling platform, the wolf prowling beside her, occasionally barking or growling at the unperturbed dwarves. How long is it before they arrive at the bottom of the shaft? How far do they have left to go once the tram leaves the elevator platform, its electric motor powering it quickly along rickety steel rails, through looping systems of claustrophobic tunnels? It's impossible for C to judge. E's floating voice narrates the tram's movements as they enter a cavernous hangar housing a dozen crawlers, plus empty docking bays for the other dozen already sent to the surface. Dual fuel lines snake into the bowels of every waiting crawler, one for gasoline and one for biomass: the Mountain's biomass tanks, E explains, lie even farther below, down in the deepest of the deep.

They pass through more tightly twisting tunnels, then into a sprawling archive, the great room patrolled by drones opening and closing deep shelves.

"Seed repositories, being inspected for rot and ruin," E says. "Everything we could save, everything we could gather. Millions of crop samples, two billion seeds in all, the result of thirteen thousand years of human agriculture. There's more than one way to put back the world."

But some of the archives have toppled, their bases cracked; E recounts unexpected seismic activity, water damage, breakdowns in the temperature regulation systems. "It was so hard," she says, "when I was the only one awake." Now the tunnel narrows, no wider than the boring machine that dug it, the dwarves chittering, circling the tram, trading seats for handholds, their bodies restless, their inane chatter incessant. E stops to click commands, then loses the grip of her story. Her speech trails off, doubles back, argues with itself in other voices C can't understand, speaking languages he doesn't understand: English and German, French and Russian, Mandarin and Pashto, Navajo and Mojave—the monolith languages, chosen to ward others from this Black Mountain, beneath which was never stored any present danger, only an endangered future.

C jerks his head, tries to find E in the dark. Above him floats her woman's shape, following the tram but not tethered to it; then there's the glowing suggestion of the wolf, panting beside him; then only a shapeless cloud, the cloud speaking in the same voice as the woman or else barking like the wolf. His vision blurs, the tram ride lulling him nearly to sleep before a sudden stop or steep turn jolts him awake. Countless hallways and corridors shoot off the tunnel, countless shafts lead between floors; other chambers are hidden behind enormous blast doors. As the tram rolls on, C sees many more dwarves working at various labors: digging with jackhammers and shovels, clearing rubble; welding new supports to replace bent girders, dragging lengths of tubing or wiring between gasping water pumps and sparking power conduits.

How much more biomass does E have stored beneath the Mountain? What have the dwarves cost her, how much have they taken from her stock? To keep the machinery running, she'd had to print new life; but every life she prints means it matters less and less if the machinery runs. "If we arrive at the promised future with nothing left of the past we've preserved," she asks, in a sad voice C thinks isn't quite hers, "then does it matter that we arrive? What good is the earth reset if nothing living survives?"

At the main habitat's platform, the dwarves separate the sledge from the tram, then C from the sledge, transferring him to a waiting gurney, its metal frame groaning under his weight, the weight of the tree. The dwarves rush him through narrow hallways showing their age, bright paint stripping from yellowing concrete; heavy hatches separate corridors marked with a designation system C can't comprehend. As they arrive at the habitat's hospital ward, he remembers his first days in the crawler, his body sick from the Loom—days he spent curled shaking in the nest of rotten blankets in one of the trashed rooms. After he left that place, he'd pretended he wasn't seeking Black Mountain to save himself—he'd told himself it would be enough to save the tree—but as the dwarves lift him from the gurney into a hospital bed, he knows he wants to live too.

His room is no less dilapidated than the rest of the facility, its walls flaking, the bed's mattress collapsed with age. IV stands and various monitors are wheeled into the room, plus a pair of ultraviolet sunlamps ready to be activated after the dwarves depart. The dwarves work without instruction, poking needles through the flesh of C's free arm, securing an ill-fitting oxygen mask over his face, the mask not made for what his mouth has become.

Now E materializes again, her body more solid, the wolf subsumed into the woman. "There's something I need you to give me," she says.

What, C rasps, his voice barely audible, his body starving and worn, desperately in need of rest and care.

E doesn't immediately answer. Instead she waves over one of the dwarves, this one thinner and taller, or maybe only less hunched. In his hands, the dwarf carries a pair of rubber-handled shears, the rubber the same bright orange as the knife C used to prune his tree.

"Just a cutting," E says, "so we can learn what you've become."

C screams his protest, but his flattened lungs empty fast. Other dwarves rush the bed, piling atop him, pinning his bucking body to the sheets as the lean dwarf steps forward. When the dwarf places the shears against the base of one of C's branches, C ceases his struggling, nearly sick with relief. He'd misunderstood, had thought she'd meant to cut *him*, to take some of his own flesh: a finger, a hoof, or a horn.

But the tree is him too. When the shears cut through the base of one flowering branch, the pain is immediate, extraordinary, impossible to soothe. E doesn't even try. She waits, floating, morphing shapes and densities until C wears himself out, the furred half of his face streaked with salty tears.

"I need you to understand," she says, her color stuttering, green going gray, green going blue: a command is being sent. "C, I want you to remember that all this was something you chose."

IN THE MORNING, A MAN ENTERS C'S OTHERWISE UNOCCUPIED room, propelling himself in a wheelchair to the side of the bed. The man's hair is wet, his expression bemused, his legs amputated above the knees. A smell C knows well follows him: he's fresh from the Loom, despite his obvious injury. C gulps repeatedly under his oxygen mask, his good eye rolls in its woody socket as he tries to take in as much of the man as he can. His head and shoulders are all that's visible above the bedside rail, but it's enough.

The man's face is stained with yellow bruises, dark and tanned, because when he was scanned he was dark and tanned, bruised, sunburned.

Sunburned. A danger from another time.

C understands, even across the many years, the many bodies that have passed since he last saw this face. This man wears the face he wore long before the bark took it; he's who C would be without horns, without blue fur threaded through his skin, without claws or hooves. His breathing accelerates as a fresh panic rises; his heart pumps bloody sap through the tree's cracks, its bark healing slower than flesh. He feels the beetles fleeing his anxious fear, all of them burrowing into the bedsheets or else taking flight, buzzing loudly as they fail to escape the room.

"It's okay," the man says, reaching through the bedrail to touch C's arm, his hand seeking C's skin wherever it's still skin. "No need to be afraid." He laughs, a low rueful sound. "Here you are again. But why should I be surprised? We never could stay away from her." He takes C's hand, their hands identical in size and shape, one hairy knuckled, one blue furred and clawed. The man who is and isn't C says, "She wanted to tell you our story herself, but I don't think she remembers it all anymore. It's been too long, she's been awake too many years. I don't know when she became the swarm, when she made those things serving her. I have some idea what both of those decisions have cost, might have stopped her from making them, if I could have. But how can I be angry with her now, when I'm here too, looking at you, looking at this?"

Releasing his grip, the man holds his hand out palm up, waiting patiently for one of the beetles on C's trunk to fly to him. An expression C can't name crosses the man's face as one does, its bright body circling the man's palm, then crossing onto the hand's hairy back as the man turns it, adjusting to keep the beetle upright until it loses interest and flies away.

"I never thought I'd see a bee again," he says, smiling, his eyes kind but sad. "I didn't know I was still hoping I would." After his smile fades, his hand finds C's again. "When I finish, E will want you to make a decision," he says. "Even though you're me, I promise you whatever choice you make will be yours alone."

CHAPMAN

Chapman chooses. He considers going farther west, across Indiana and Illinois, across the greater plains, into other Territories not yet fully settled. Somewhere there awaits the Mississippi, the great river he's never seen but whose tributaries and watershed he's spent his life working; beyond it he hears there are mountains far greater than the Alleghenies he knows so well. He has heard tales of creeping glaciers to the north, parched deserts to the south, and somewhere beyond them all, there is the verdant promise of California and the unfathomable depths of the Pacific, visions Chapman can hardly imagine. For now, almost everything west of him remains frontier, wild enough spaces where a faun might yet roam, unseen and free in this vast America.

Holding the singer's head by its topknot of hair, Chapman surveys his last orchard, grown from seed in ten flickering years, years that took only a few moments of his own time: trees growing bitter fruits, spitter apples; each tree a miracle, part brother, part witch, utterly itself.

If he goes west, no matter what else happens, he will not live forever.

If he goes east, he'll still die, but he might not have to die alone.

Without Nathaniel, Chapman will never plant again, because the planting has already served its truest purpose: not to make the brothers rich, but to keep them *brothers*. Now that this brotherhood is ended, he abandons his tools, then begins making his lonely way east, toward the only other fellowship he's known. At the last moment he decides to bring the singer with him, the singer's song the last of the true magic he's seen. With the core of the song-grown apple still gagging the head, reducing its drone to a muted retching, the settled landscape Chapman crosses doesn't flicker much, but nightly he hears in the singer's leaking sound stuttering dreams of futures to come, poured roads cutting black paths across blighted treeless landscapes, then dryer lands, the ground everywhere cracked clay; he wakes to the loud shake of explosions breaking open the mountains, to the roar of machines stripping the surface of the earth, to white masts being fitted with white blades, somehow farms too, farming the wind.

Chapman's passage is slow. He travels the starlit nights, trotting through wood and field with the singer's hair clenched in his fist; he hides during the day, sleeping fitfully in shaded copses, his hands clenched over the apple-filled mouth. All the way across Ohio, he lies to himself, boasting to himself that he won't ever again take the man's shape, even if it might speed his passage, even if it might buy him a home: either he'll make it safely back to Splitlip Creek or he won't; either the Worths will accept him as he is, or else he'll flee their home forever.

Soon it's August again, the air buzzing with black flies, mosquitos, grasshoppers the length of his fingers, locusts the same color as his claws. Everywhere Chapman roams, Ohio's planted lands burst with tall corn and wheat and barley tilting listlessly; the branches of apple and pear trees bend low with heavy fruit. Every crop is healthy and high; there are so many bountiful signs of the human world's confident flourishing.

Ten miles from the Worth homestead, the singer renews his squirming in Chapman's grip, moaning around the apple stuck in his craw. His song insists against his gag: Chapman pauses, then steps through its flicker into one possible future. He stands between two monstrous rows of apple trees, the black of their bark absolute, their fruit the biggest he's ever seen, gold and red and bright green globes of fruit. At the center of the orchard, he watches a gleaming tower climb floor by floor into the sky, his imagination balking at the structure, surely taller than the castles in Eliza Worth's stories.

"No," he says, addressing the singer. "This cannot be what will be."

But what can the singer say?

Nothing, with the apple stuck in his mouth; nothing ever, even if it were removed.

The singer does not speak. He *sings*.

The faint song changes, the ripple reverses, the flicker steadies: where the bright tower rose, the Worth house now stands.

Chapman hesitates. Here is the lamplit house, here is the orchard of apple trees that's all that stands between him and the family he has learned to love, the family with whom Chapman doesn't know if he belongs without his brother to grant him passage, without his human shape to ease his entry. He raises his hands, watches them morph, each transformation part of his unmade decision: he sees his pale hands as a man, then the darker hands of a faun, covered in graying fur; he passes one clawless hand across a hornless forehead even as the clawed other reaches for his whole horn. He stamps a hoof, he stomps a foot; he's warm within his barked skin and furred flanks, he shivers in naked flesh.

The sun sets. As night falls, Chapman watches the Worths through their windows: Grace playing her fiddle, Jasper reading his holy books, young Eliza beautiful and lovely. After the family extinguishes their lamps, he stalks past the pigs and the goats, his cloven brothers and sisters, all the mute domestics. Never has he thought them kin; always he's identified with men instead of beasts—as if a man cannot be made a product too, denied his agency; as if his sovereign flesh cannot be bought and broken and put to use.

In the orchard, Chapman crouches over his hooves—hooves sometimes feet—and he uses his hands—hands sometimes clawed—to dig a hole. The orchard is well established, over two decades old now: he has to tear up the grass, rip the sod, claw the rooted, wormy soil below, digging and digging while the leaking singer's voice keeps his shape turning.

In the end it's not so much hole, just deep enough for a head.

Chapman puts the singer in, the singer's head made a seed, his mouth still choked with the apple core, trying desperately to sing as Chapman drops a first handful of earth across its forehead.

"Whatever I did to you in some other life," Chapman whispers, "I wish I hadn't."

The singer doesn't respond to this apology, only continues to try to sing around the apple core. Chapman covers the head with dirt, packs down the soil. Afterward, his hooves are steadily hooves, his fur stops receding and reseeding; he can still hear the singer's voice, but just barely—and then mercifully not at all. Still, he wonders what might grow from what he's planted, here behind the Worth household, here at the center of the first nursery he and Nathaniel seeded in that last easy season many years ago, before their brotherhood was broken for the first time. Will the singer's song change this place's potential, as it changed the future of so many others?

"If I cannot gain entry to the Worths' as I am now," Chapman whispers, "then maybe someday I can find some other way."

Above his head, an apple breaks its stem; he catches it easily in one gray-furred paw. He rolls the fruit over, considers its deep golden color, its skin only slightly speckled. Lifting it, he snuffs in its heady ripe scent but doesn't yet bite the flesh. How many apples has he tasted already? Not as many as he's planted, not as many as have grown from his labors, but many, many apples. Once he thought one would save him, as if he were the first man in the Garden, or else a boy safe in a story. Trees of Knowledge, Trees of Life and Death, Trees of Forgetting: even in the holiest stories men tell, trees are never allowed to be only trees, they must be temptation or salvation, they must serve as sustenance and instruction and redemption.

This time Chapman doesn't even eat the apple; instead he digs into it with his thumbs, forcing his fingers past the skin. Scraping out the flesh from under clogged claws, he refuses any expectations of color, refuses the smells he knows, refuses every memory the apple offers. He wants nothing but to be here, to be present and then, afterward, to go on, to let the phenomenal present become the unregretted past. Sweet juice streams down his hands, mats sticky his fur; his skin itches, the ground collects golden fallen peels, chunks of moon flesh. Reaching the wooden part, he forgets its name; beyond it, he forgets not just the apple, but also himself, becoming nothing and no one—but when at last the spell breaks, Chapman looks up from the grave he's dug, decorated with all the discards of an apple reduced past its parts, to find Eliza Worth standing between the orchard and the house, her mouth widening in horror, readying a terrified scream.

Haloed in moonlight, the faun rises slowly, standing almost a foot taller than he is as a man. His gray fur rolls lush from his abdomen to his hooves, his denser winter coat already coming in; his skin is dark brown, tanned leather-bark, everywhere unblemished except for the scar over his breast where his brother's musket ball pierced his chest. He shakes out his hair, swings his horns. As a faun, his craggy face is wider, his mouth is elongated into a snout, his eyes are gold instead of gray, but it is *his* face, Chapman's face, the face Eliza's known.

For the last time, this is the faun entire, the faun no longer pretending.

Eliza Worth is a creature of story too, made of the fairy tales she loves, the myths read and recited until they're almost her own memories. Chapman is something like her uncle, and in the stories she loves it's not uncommon for an uncle to transform, to appear in more than one shape, to wear multiple skins. But in reality the moment is too unexpected, the faun in the family orchard too uncanny an encounter for such a rational thought.

Instead of recognizing the Chapman she's known, his kind

features barely submerged beneath this creature's face, Eliza releases her scream, startling the faun into involuntarily moaning a monstrous reply, the distressed cry of the dumb beast
whose shape he most resembles.

Still screaming, Eliza turns, picking up the edge of her
nightgown to run barefoot back toward the house. Chapman
immediately hears new movement from inside: Jasper and
Grace, waking up to the sound of their daughter's terror. He
cannot stay, not as the faun; he must flicker or flee. He tries
to change back to the shape Eliza and her parents know best,
ready to brush off what she'll say she saw as imaginative fancy,
as walking nightmare.

But now the flicker doesn't come.

Groaning in distressed disbelief, Chapman grabs his horns,
the one horn whole, the other broken where, as a lonely child,
he'd tried to remove it, to become like any other boy, to be like
his beloved brother.

As a child, he'd failed to commit to such magic. This time
must be different.

Beside the orchard is the Worths' barn, stained red with lin-
seed oil and rust. Inside are Jasper's tools, including a handsaw
kept sharp as all Jasper's saws always are. Chapman does the
broken horn first, guesses its weakened shell will be the easier
to cut. When the horn begins to flop away from the skull, he
grips the hollow shape: with a tearing zip of ripping skin, it
snaps free, leaving behind a bleeding wound, a raw circle of
intense pain. Chapman moans lowly, he bites the meat of his
hand to mute his voice. From the house, he hears the slamming
of the cabin's door, then Jasper's heavy footfalls on the wooden
porch, advancing cautiously toward the barn. Chapman's sec-

ond horn is whole, undamaged by age. He sets the saw against its base, he grinds his sharp teeth as the blade slips once, twice across the scalp; at last it finds its purchase, crosscut teeth digging into stubborn keratin. When Chapman snaps this second horn, he screams again—but when this pain recedes, the last of the flicker fades with it, helping him one more time as it goes, taking from him what he asked it to take.

Soon he will be only the man Chapman, living in this where, this when.

But not soon enough.

The unhorned faun bursts through the barn doors, knocking aside a stealthily approaching Jasper, the man stumbling, his rifle spilling from his grip. Blood streaming from his forehead, Chapman flinches from his friend's visible fear; he raises his hands, retreating, trying to call out his own name even as pain and fear rob him of speech, his snoutish mouth instead pleading frightened nonsense as Jasper scrambles to his feet, as he raises his recovered musket.

This is gentle Jasper, brave Jasper, who many years ago went looking for the creatures who killed his goat, while all the while this other monster hid inside his home, safe beneath his roof. He aims his rifle but at the last second twitches the barrel upward, so that even at close range his bullet misses; Chapman doesn't need a second warning. He flees from his friend, from this sweet family and their once welcoming home, the only human place he ever felt welcome, the one place in this State he helped make he'll ever miss.

By the time Jasper realizes why he jerked his musket into the air, by the time he understands who it was he almost killed, his strange but beloved friend Chapman will already be many miles away, running as far west as his hooves will carry him, running until his hooves vanish and his legs for the last time become human legs.

FAUNISH DAYS ARE ENDED BUT CHAPMAN'S LIFE GOES ON. NOT FOR-ever but for some years. He will never return to the Worths, not in this life; he will wish until his dying day that there had been some way to become an honest member of that family he'd known and loved. Everywhere he wanders next, he wears a wide-brimmed felt hat, not to hide his face but to cover his scars; for the rest of his life, he goes shoeless everywhere, his feet toughened by now to rough leather; he carries a walking stick but his leathern bag is gone, left in the faraway orchard where Nathaniel is buried.

Halfway across Ohio or Indiana or on his way to points beyond, in a pleasant town whose name he never learns, Chapman hears new calls of *Appleseed, Appleseed.*

He turns, guilty and ashamed, afraid of being caught—but by whom? For what?

The speaker is some young farmer come into town for supplies, a man who recognizes Chapman from the folk tales sprung up around him. "Is that you, Appleseed?" the man asks, hat in hand, his earnest curiosity burning.

Chapman could say yes. Chapman could say no. Either would be true: he is and isn't his legend. But if he says yes, the man might take him with him. If he says yes, the man might introduce him to his kin, might invite him to his table. The man's wife might cut him a slice of apple pie, pour him a glass of apple cider, sharing the fruits of trees planted nearby by Chapman or Nathaniel, trees making the family's land a farm, making their farm a home.

"Appleseed, is that you?" the man asks again, nervously jumbling the question's order.

Lonely Chapman smiles. He accepts this story or else he doesn't.

No matter what story he chooses, surely the man Chapman one day forgets enough to make himself believe he's earned it.

JOHN-X

This is the story you've forgotten, yours and mine, ours and hers.

In this story, the world didn't end only once. The world I was born into ended when the sky turned white; afterward, another began. This new world ended too, exactly on schedule twenty-five years later, when the endless snowfalls started, when the rivers and lakes and even much of the oceans froze solid, when suddenly everywhere we traveled there was more snow every day, ice where there hadn't been ice in thousands of years. All over the world new glaciers began their rapid accumulation, their great weight pulverizing the land, buckling the earth's crust, reshaping the continents, sending them drifting in new directions at new speeds.

It all happened so fast. Before Pinatubo, the world had spent fifty years preparing for drought. We gave ourselves twenty-five years to prepare for ice instead, but it wasn't enough.

And so the world I knew ended then ended again.

But ours wasn't even the first end of the world. Not if *end of the world* means *cataclysm*, not if *cataclysm* means a violence after which nothing is the same. The industrial revolution was a cataclysm. Before that, the colonization of the Americas, of Africa, the genocides and environmental devastation that followed. Then, later, the invention and weaponization of the internet, the coming of big data and inescapable surveillance.

Not every cataclysm was immediately global; they were never so quick as we imagined.

You and me and the one you call E, what we've become and what we've made—her weird dwarves, your tree and your grass and your insects—we're all that's left, as far as we know, at least on this continent. The last gasps of the human, rememberers of the world humans knew.

It's not much. It's more than there might've been, if we'd done nothing.

The first time E printed me—back when she was only Eury, back when it was me in a hospital bed instead of you, me without legs for the first time—she asked me, *Do you still want to save the world?*

Taking my hand, she said, *Then promise you'll stay through its end*.

I promised. I owed her. She'd designed one end of the world. I'd forced another. Together, we fought to prepare for what would happen next, but nothing we did was enough. As Pinatubo progressed, governments collapsed, new orders emerged, prevailed for a time, collapsed again. Other players tried to force other outcomes. There were mass migrations, civilians fleeing new wars erupting on every continent. The weather grew entirely unpredictable, with the reduction of ultraviolet radiation and the worldwide snowfall setting off cascades of irreversible insect death, whole ecosystems crumbling as plants became unable to propagate without pollinators or human intervention, aid we were too busy to provide. The catastrophic extinctions of the early twenty-first century were nothing compared with what followed: once enough plant cover died, the end of the animals didn't take long. It wasn't any better under the ocean, where insufficient sun meant a lack of phytoplankton to feed the bottom of the food chain.

The end of the world. I keep saying it like it was one moment, but the end went on and on.

I keep saying *the world ended*, but the world will always be here.

In place of *world*, I should say *story*.

Our story ended, but no story has ever ended so definitively another could not be told.

Humanity's lasted a quarter of a million years, our civilization's a mere ten thousand. Not long, in geological time. But when we went, we took so much else with us.

Whatever life flourishes next—maybe this new tree you've brought back with you—I can only imagine it stands a better chance without us.

WE HAD TWENTY-FIVE YEARS TO FIND A SOLUTION. IF EVERY GOVernment had worked together, if Earthtrust and every other megacorp had done the same, if people everywhere had been united instead of divided, maybe we could've been prepared by the time the long winter began. But mostly Eury and I and everyone like us kept making the same mistakes, wanting to rule the world instead of living in it. There were systemic problems—unchecked capitalism, unregulated extractive industries, the fossil fuel economy—but the solutions to those problems weren't solvable at the scale of Pinatubo. We kept trying to fix the entire planet at once instead of tending to the many individual places where people might live well, where nonhuman life had once flourished. What we needed wasn't the flipping of one global switch but instead a million small efforts, emplaced in localities, rooted in the specific land and water and air of the particular places where people lived. If we'd used Earthtrust's technologies and the land it had seized to empower people to rebuild places they knew and loved, how might our story have ended differently? We could've taken down the fences, undone private property in favor of public ownership and shared commons, could've used the sovereignty Eury had wrested from governments all over the globe to give people the chance to discover new ways of dwelling, instead of trying to preserve the one way of life almost everyone was by then living, a way that had already failed.

We made our mistakes not once but over and over. Together, Eury and I kept Earthtrust's farms going, but eventually we chose to reserve the biomass we produced for the future, even if it meant more people would starve in the now; afterward our facilities became targets for rival corporations, unsteady governments, would-be revolutionaries. Earthtrust fractured: dissent in the ranks rose, exacerbated by the difficulties of coordinating the company's efforts at scale. Eury and I retreated beneath the Mountain, but as long as we had other bodies on the outside— and as long as our satellite network held—we could bounce our consciousnesses rung to rung, body to body, still trying to lead in person. But inhabiting our outside rungs required risks we eventually decided we couldn't afford: one of E's bodies was taken hostage by a security team gone rogue, then held for ransom; one of mine had its rung hacked with a virus designed to wipe out the servers here when I flickered back.

After I isolated the virus and destroyed the infected body, I decided to stop leaving the Mountain. Instead of going out, I developed the crawlers, mobile laboratories equipped with Looms, each a self-sustaining community ready to repopulate the world. The bubblecraft came later: we built dozens but only a few ever worked. By the time they did, our geoengineering had rendered solar power so ineffective we mothballed the bubbles as tech for the next age, for its new sunshine; meanwhile the crawlers could run on fossil fuels, while we waited for the sun to regain its strength. The irony wasn't lost on us, as we built a nuclear reactor beneath the Mountain, as we stashed the reserve of oil we knew we'd need while we waited for the sky to change back to blue.

The sky is still white, E says, so we know the nanoswarms remain active, even though we no longer have any way to communicate with them. But if you crossed the country on solar alone, that means they've started to draw down the sulfate layer. Your journey wouldn't have been possible when I was last awake. Wherever you crashed your crawler, you were until recently truly stuck. And maybe that's why you deleted us from your memories: What was the point of remembering this place, if you thought you'd never return, never see Eury again?

Or maybe you didn't delete us. Maybe it's just that the world where your memories were made no longer existed. As that reality went, maybe the knowledge needed to live in it faded too.

Your centuries of nothing but icy flatness, of loneliness sprawling in every direction? Maybe there's so little left of who you were when you were me because that world didn't need who'd been in ours.

Eury tried to leave once too. She'd designed a city-sized generation ship, one ready to print colonists from onboard biomass once the ship's computer found a suitable home. Built in low-earth orbit, it was to be supplied by tanker vessels capable of rising through the nanoswarm cloud, but right before we began sending up stock, there was an accident or an attack: the spaceport was always a target for terrorists who wanted us earthbound, who wanted us to save the only home we'd been given. Whatever happened, the tankers exploded on the launchpad, the fires engulfing the command center, buckling the on-site array of biomass tanks.

After that loss, we couldn't bear to risk so much again, even if there'd been time to rebuild the spaceport. The ship's still up there, though. During the clearest nights spent in your bubble, you might've looked up and seen its central spire, the ark's habitat rings spinning perpetually. Even now it's the brightest star in the sky, one of the few whose light is capable of penetrating the nanoswarm layer, a dully burning reminder of a second chance we'll never reach.

In the end, the terrorists got what they wanted. Earth would be our only home. We would thrive here or nowhere. We continued our extraction up until the moment we sealed the Mountain, almost twenty-five years to the day after Pinatubo. We brought with us the biomass of every tree the VACs could grow, every field of soy and corn, every uneaten head of livestock. Dronedozers scraped the freezing ground, collecting topsoil to be sifted for its grubs and beetles and worms, its rotten roots and collapsed fungal networks. We tried not to leave anything, but always there was so much waste, so much we couldn't harvest before it was too late.

At the same time, we set about collecting as much of humanity as we could. Before Pinatubo, Earthtrust had built VACs in dozens of countries, where its first Volunteers became farmers, ranchers, and manual laborers; now some would become terranauts and time travelers, sacrificing their bodies in one time so they might be reborn in another. But we couldn't force anyone to participate, because we never discovered a way to scan without destruction: to Volunteer, you had to choose to die; all we could offer in return was the promise you'd live again in a better world. In time, we'd terraform our planet into the world of our grandparents, their grandparents' parents. We'd put back the plants they'd grown, the animals they'd loved. This time around we'd be better stewards of the garden we'd been given.

Always we refused to admit the deeper truth: there was no garden to go back to. No matter how exact we made our copy, the world would never again take exactly the same root.

There was so much loss, so much destruction. But nothing we did stopped life from happening. Nothing we could do ever will. Surely life waits frozen in the ice, surely it squirms from the steam vents at the bottom of the ocean, crawls from the depths of caves and hunts the deep aquifers.

We act or don't act. But even if we do nothing, there will be more life.

You're proof of that, C. So is this creature you became, your black tree and your purple grass, the *bees* you keep calling *beetles*, that maybe are beetles now—why not? What does it matter anymore what I'd call anything?

The important thing is this: you've brought us a new addition to creation, grown from human soil.

E will try to take it from you. I want you to set it free.

UNDERGROUND, INNUMERABLE GENERATIONS OF OURSELVES came and went, over years, decades, whole centuries. Eury had learned how to back up the mind, how to make sure everything we learned each life cycle could be stored in the rung and passed on. Our knowledge increased, our memories compounded with all a person can learn in two lifetimes, in five, in ten, in fifty or one hundred. Some lives were mere weeks long, both of us succumbing to more frequent accidents as Black Mountain became more difficult to maintain: when the glaciers started their passage across the country, crushing the surface of the earth to gravel, their weight caused an age of constant seismic activity, tectonic slippages and plate fractures.

We got lucky: the Mountain buckled but it didn't break.

Eury had developed the Loom herself, most of its workings detailed only in her thoughts, but the rung was an Earthtrust invention, refined by teams who kept the usual documentation, lab notebooks and meeting minutes and slide presentations. One lifetime, I did nothing but study their ephemera: How did the Loom work in concert with the rungs? And what did the song Eury recorded have to do with it? How did its keening drone make it possible for us to keep transferring consciousness body to body, rung to rung? Earthtrust's best researchers never figured it out, but Eury showed me where it came from, or said she did. This was years after we'd sealed ourselves into the Mountain. By then there was nothing left of the person Eury said had been suspended in recycling fluid for decades. The fluid was cloudy, fouled. All that I saw in it were floating scraps of what might have been skin, stubs of what might have been teeth or bone. I remember how she screamed to see it. It'd been a long time since she'd entered that dusty room. I thought she'd been about to tell me a story, but after she stopped screaming she refused to explain. Whatever I saw in that microphone-studded tube wasn't what she'd been expecting to show me.

The first time Eury printed me, she left me as I'd been scanned, my bomb-blasted legs ending at the knees, printed with clean caps of skin completely unlike the gnarled scar tissue they would've grown if I'd lived without being forced into the recycler. Sometimes later I had legs, sometimes not. I wasn't sure which version of me was more real, the one that walked or the one that rolled. By then the Loom's keening was impossible to shake. It gets stuck, doesn't it, looping inside the mind? The brain's architecture wasn't made for the lives we've led; some of our memories are hundreds of years old, the leftovers of different lives lived in different bodies, hard to remember.

Eury was thirty-eight when she was scanned. Ten years into every cycle, she went through menopause again, the clock of her body reliable even in its deprivations. A dozen times, fifty times, a hundred. We both lived through the fullness of cancer only once, bearing the chemotherapies and the radiation treatments before dying anyway. To save biomass, we knew anything bearable should be borne, but we were not saints. When we suffered, we healed our suffering the most reliable way we knew: we started over. Every time we rebooted ourselves we made the future smaller. But the world above was still frozen solid beneath a white sky. It was easy to believe we'd find a solution before the time came to enact it. It was easy to tell ourselves the future we planned to make for everyone else depended on our own survival. And so we reset ourselves in the only bodies we had, bodies thirty-eight and forty years old each time they were born, bodies immediately beginning again to age and to fail.

We'd planned for mission critical personnel to be printed as needed to do maintenance, to study the conditions in the outside world, to generate predictions Eury and I weren't qualified to make. But we had to stop bringing them back almost immediately after the closing of the Mountain. Whenever we spun someone up, we explained how much time had passed since they'd last lived, detailed the current conditions. Then we'd ask them to flush a clogged water pump or repair the air filtration system, to debug some software error or rebuild a server rack. No one ever said no, but some of the Volunteers delayed. They knew what we would ask of them afterward: to willingly step into the recycler and return to the biomass.

Most of the time, we could convince the Volunteers to go peacefully. But the recycler wasn't painless. Some Volunteers came back screaming, their minds as they'd been at the moment of their deaths, recorded as we'd destructively scanned them.

Those Volunteers did not go easily.

The first time Eury shot a Volunteer, it seemed the sound of her sidearm's discharge reverberated for days. Together we scrubbed and scrubbed, but the blood stained the concrete.

The spot took years to fade but eventually it did.

We became more careful. We didn't want to spook the Volunteers. Better to force them into the recycler without spilling more blood, because spilled blood was waste, and the first rule was to never waste anything. Then one day Eury presented me with a new solution. We could keep printing the expertise we needed, with all the frustrations and danger other people brought—or she could simply download what she needed from the backups, adding their expertise directly to her rung.

I objected. It wasn't what we'd promised. It was, explicitly, a violation of what we'd said we'd do. *But it's for the greater good,* Eury said. Printing a scientist would use up irreplaceable bio-mass, then that person would for a time consume food and water, precious air pumped in from the frozen surface. When we didn't need them anymore, they wouldn't want to recycle themselves, while we wouldn't want to have to force them.

All I have to do, Eury said, *is make sure each new personality remains subservient to my own*—and as soon as she said this I knew she'd already done it, was convincing me only after the fact.

Once she started, she couldn't stop. There was too much to know, too many skills she didn't have. She became a conqueror again, ruling over a collective of the minds we'd scanned, imprisoning them inside her skull. I confronted her, we fought. But it was impossible to win an argument with her: soon a thousand philosophies were at her command, thousands of minds. How she was able to integrate them all, I'll never know. I was too busy fighting to contain my own many selves, the remainders of all the lives I'd lived beneath the Mountain.

I—me and you, me and all the others who came between us—struggled from the first not to go mad from living alongside so many other versions of ourselves. Eury didn't have the same problem, not for a long time. Of course not. In any contest of wills, she was always the strongest.

I gave in, accepted her crimes. The Mountain had become a microcosm of the world we'd lost: we'd harvested as much as we could but it wasn't enough, not if we consumed more than we replaced. We did not stop consuming. Sooner or later the batteries below the Mountain would fail. We knew this. Sooner or later every storage medium would disintegrate. We knew this too. There could never be enough backups, never enough redundancies. We had printers that could print more printers, but even their feed materials would eventually be exhausted. The servers holding the scanned humans would one day fail, but Eury had become a storage medium too, her rung a backup of every mind we'd saved. She held the expertise of countless disciplines, she knew a hundred languages fluently, often sliding between them as she spoke, some thoughts better expressed in one than in another. We began to have trouble communicating. Whatever she'd become wasn't what used to be meant by *a person*. She asked me to join her in becoming whatever it was she'd become, but I didn't need more voices echoing inside my skull than I already had.

I told her I didn't want what she wanted—but there was something else I'd begun to believe my body might be made to carry.

I could only add so much per cycle. The genomes couldn't be loaded wirelessly, like the personalities crowded into E's rung. But every time I prepared myself for the recycler, I had the Loom splice in more foreign DNA, replacing unexpressed, unused parts of my genome. It was simple enough to take some of that useless material out, then put in the genetic code for a black bear, a raccoon, domesticated corn, the apple tree. We had thousands and thousands of scans, some for animals I'd never heard of before they went extinct, uncounted varieties of plants we'd never remember were missing if we decided not to put them back into the world. There was only so much unused space in my original genome, but with each new addition my genetic capacity expanded—and then the next time I cycled out, I spliced some other creature into the blank spaces in whatever code I'd added last.

The matryoshka method, I joked to Eury, who didn't find it funny.

She might have, if I hadn't said it so often, every time I was recycled and reprinted.

She might have, if she hadn't guessed what I was preparing to do. She knew before I did that after I made my genome into a genetic repository exactly as complete as the one in our computer, I'd try to leave. Centuries of homesickness, of wanting to be anywhere but buried beneath the weight of the world. She didn't want me to leave, or at least she didn't want to be alone. I didn't want to be alone either, but I didn't think I could stay.

One of the last years we spent together, I found Eury in the auditorium built to one day welcome our Volunteers back to the restored world. The auditorium was dilapidated by then, crumbling like so much else. She sat on the edge of the buckling stage, kicking bare feet against the plastic boards, but she wasn't alone: she'd spun up the tiniest yellow warbler, a little bright-beaked thing, its flash of color breaking up the dull monotony of the fading facility.

We'd long since agreed she wouldn't print any more wolves, all of them so unhappy underground, never lasting long enough to be worth the mass. But this bird, flitting through the vacant echoing air, singing the prettiest tune you ever heard? It was a gift. It was against the rules but the rules were ours. It was against the rules but we'd lived dozens of lifetimes by then, all spent in a cavernous underworld bereft of what made life worth living.

We let the bird stay but it was lonely too. We trapped it in the auditorium so it wouldn't vanish into the rest of the facility; all we had to feed it was the same nutrient gruel we ate ourselves. The bird lived a year, maybe two. But after the first few weeks it never sang again. Then it died and went back into the recycler, making only the smallest, saddest puff of paste.

Soon after that, when the time came for me to leave, Eury didn't try to stop me. Maybe she knew our choices had separated us. Maybe she wasn't herself enough to care. By then, she'd integrated all the human consciousnesses we possessed. There was no more romance in us but we might as well have been married, we who'd ruled this underworld together for untold numbers of years. When the centuries-long snowstorm outside the Mountain stopped—when it seemed we'd weathered the worst of what we'd made—then we divorced. Together, we printed a dozen copies of the me you used to be, each ready to command a crawler stocked with enough biomass to begin the terraforming experiment wherever the continent was ready; each of us was spliced with so much DNA that if local storage failed it might be possible to reverse engineer an entire biosphere from what we carried inside our blood, kept safe at the center of our every cell.

It's easy to cast Eury as the villain of our story, but tell me: Which of us was the greediest? The woman who wanted to be humanity? Or the man who tried to become the world?

My crawlers left one after another, each of us headed to different regions by whatever route might be possible; once there, each of you would bunker down, recycling yourselves to wait out the ice age, letting the crawler's Loom reprint you every fifty years to check conditions.

Eury says only one other crawler ever returned, arriving under someone else's command, manned by reprinted personnel who'd mutinied before journeying here to seize the safety they thought the Mountain hid. You saw the machine-gun nests outside: we weren't unprepared for that eventuality. Eury sympathized but she couldn't let them enter. Before she fired, she tried to explain how they'd been printed from scans stored inside the Mountain.

It wasn't murder, Eury said, because inside the Mountain weren't they still alive?

After all the crawlers had left, I made Eury promise not to reprint me. She agreed, but as I stepped into the recycler for the last time, ready to be finished with this subterranean life, she offhandedly recounted a dream I'd had a long time ago, something I was sure I'd never shared. I screamed inside the recycler, furious to learn she'd downloaded me too, that she'd already added my life to her rung, already had all my many lives snug inside her head.

It was a long time ago now, I know. And despite her promise, I'm glad I'm here to meet you, to see Eury one more time.

Whatever her flaws, whatever her mistakes, she really did intend to save the world.

Even now, I know she believes it's possible.

As for us, well, when you left you were me, exactly as you see me now, plus two good legs tacked on to make surface life easier. I don't know how you became this astonishing creature instead. Was it an accident caused by trying to stretch your biomass, or did some version of you mean for this to happen? Do you feel any guilt for the mission you abandoned, for all the potential life in the crawler that you never brought back? Do you somewhere in you still carry the remorse I felt at my many mistakes, my unending hubris, how always I convinced myself I was on the side of the righteous, even after it was clear we'd doomed the world, even knowing it was the decision I made that chose the way the world would end?

Now, at this cycle's end, do you still crave forgiveness or forgetfulness, as I do?

What would you give to get it? Would you give your life?

Would you give our last life, always the only one that really counts?

C-433

You won't survive the operation," E explains, returning at the end of John's story to hover beside his wheelchair, all of her a mere bot-wisp except for her face and a stretch of disembodied neck, her right hand resting on John's shoulder. "You'll die, but the tree will live," she says, her swarm's glow throbbing in a comfortingly rhythmic pattern. "The tree, its beetles, whatever else should grow after the tree no longer grows in you."

"You can't—" C's voice rasps, breaks. The tree's pressure on his chest is heavier than ever. "You can't scan the tree without destroying it."

E's ghost-swarm swirls angrily, flashes red.

John says, "You told me to tell him the truth. I told him. There's no scanning without destruction. If you recycle C, the tree dies. If you cut away the tree, C dies. If you cut the tree from C, then scan the tree, they both die. Maybe you can print another. Maybe you can't." John spins his wheelchair, the ghost-swarm fluttering out of his way. "Think of all your lasts, E. We told ourselves it was worth it to make each species extinct sooner, because later we would bring them back. But we haven't. They would've died anyway, I know. But we didn't have to rush them from the world."

"We saved them," E says petulantly. "They're all still here. We can make them live again, exactly as they were. Just as soon as we put the world back the way it was."

John shakes his head. "Help C live, E. Help his tree as it is, not as you want it to be." John turns to C, C struggling to breathe, C struggling to stay in the scene, to be a part of the conversation deciding his fate. "You have to choose: this one life you have been given, the life of C-433, the creature who grew a tree. If that's what you want, we'll help you live the best you can. Surely there's some way of easing your pain, of making it easier for you and the tree to share this one body. Or we can cut the tree free from you, save it and whatever might grow from it until the time it can be planted on the surface. But if we do—"

E interrupts, her ghost-swarm swirling around John's chair, enveloping him in her glow. "Freed from you," she says, "the tree can be studied, scanned, its fruit replanted, its branches grafted onto root stocks printed from our data banks. If this tree evolved *inside* you—generation after generation, the DNA shifting inside the hollow spaces of your own genome—now it can evolve on the outside. A tree made not for the world that was but the world as it is. This is the gift you've brought us: an ecosystem in miniature, primed for the future we made."

It isn't only the tree they want. There is the purple grass, clumped and mossy in the bark's cracks; there are the buzzing beetles that John calls *bees*, feeding at the flowers' nectar, nesting in new cysts swelling beneath C's skin, ridging the flesh along the bark's edges.

C is no longer the creature he'd been born. But what he's become is not only a tree.

"You will be the seed," E says. "The seed from which the new world grows. We can back up your mind before we take your body. We can give you your own swarm, like mine. No more pain or suffering. No more crawling into the recycler, no more waking loomsick and starving and lesser. This is your chance to live forever. I took it when it was my turn. You, when you were John, refused to entertain such ideas. Be better than you were. Show me you learned something in all these centuries. Show me you've got the will to win.

"Say yes," she says. "John, tell him to say yes."

John leans in, again taking C's gnarled hand in his own. Their palms are exactly the same size, their fingers exactly the same length. John moves his head as close to C's free ear as possible. C can barely see John's gray eyes, can barely hear him whisper a single word.

Run, John whispers.

Louder, he says, "She promised the choice would be yours, not hers."

Run. C hears it again, but this time the man's lips aren't moving. Maybe it's what he imagines wheelchair-confined, recycler-bound John wishes.

Run, C hears a third time, *or else fight*—and this time he knows the voice is inside his rung, speaking from the same place the remainder's voice once originated—and contained inside the imperative is a simple program, a wirelessly transmitted gift of a couple hundred lines of code, a worm C understands he could pass on to someone else with a squeeze of his one good fist, the same hand John releases before turning from C's bed to push his wheelchair out of the room, back toward the recycler and the dreamless sleep of the unprinted.

AT FIRST E DOESN'T PRESSURE HIM. SHE LEAVES HIM ALONE, KEEPS the dwarves away. Time passes, but C can't tell how much in the perpetual red glow of the hospital lights. He clocks time there in the sunless facility only by the continued advance of the bark crossing his body, by the appearance of another generation of beetles. He knows it's foolish, but he can't stop hearing John's voice, hearing his own voice as it sounds from John's body: *Run*, he'd told himself, but how can he run when he hasn't walked in days, when he hasn't left this bed since the dwarves lifted him into it?

Except he's stronger than he's let on. He's been resting, intravenously fed and hydrated, breathing filtered air, soaking up the rays of the UV lamps E instructed her dwarves to install, beaming radiation at his leaves: the weak sunlight outside was barely enough for photosynthesis, so the tree had no choice but to feed on his flesh, on nutrients soaked up from the paste he swallowed twice a day. Now the tree feeds itself, its leaves brightening, the pulp of its bark swelling thanks to the limitless nutrients from the IV, the limitless sunlight of the lamps. Now it's C who eats from the tree, healing even as the bark buries him beneath its burden. Every day, the tree of him is more immense, but perhaps it isn't a tree overtaking a body. Perhaps it's just him giving up one shape to become another. Perhaps he, last in a line of monstrous creatures, is merely the first in this other species, the faun who became a tree.

No matter what he told E before, he no longer wants to leave the tree behind. Not if it means he'll die. Not if it means he'll live on only as a ghost.

Because to live without a body is not to live.

C wraps his good hand around the breathing tube snaked into his trachea, then pulls. A long gagging slowly reverses. He tries to tear the IVs from his elbow, too difficult with only the same hand free: he raises the tubing to his mouth, chews through it with his remaining teeth.

In one corner of the room, a previously unnoticed red light begins blinking steadily.

C leaves the bed with a dense *thud*, landing on the creaking, cracking trunk of the tree, his left leg vanished into its wood. With his hoofed foot leading, he drags the meat of him to the doorway, something of the tree breaking with every step.

No tree was ever made to walk—but surely the faun was designed to run.

And so the last faun runs, dragging the tree behind him. The dimly lit corridor offers no clues for which way to go, the hospital ward as silent and empty as the rest of the habitat; all C can do is move one heaving lunge at a time. His body is unwieldly, his movements slow and fraught; he can't turn his cracking bulk without cost—and when he hears a sound behind him, he knows what it is without looking: E's ghost-swarm, divided again into the woman and the wolf.

"You're making a mistake," E says, steadily closing the distance between them. "You're making everything worse than it has to be."

Let me go, C wants to say, but every word would cost him a step, every utterance a gesture. He plunges forward, the tree dragging behind the flesh.

He knows he won't escape. But better to die on his feet, on his hooves, within his tree.

Better than on his back, waiting for the dwarves to carve him up.

The corridor is barely lit, the way ahead darker than the way behind. E's green glow follows faster than C can move, but there isn't enough of her to stop him, her swarm worn thin. He stomps on. The end of the corridor approaches, a closed hatch blocking the way forward. What lies beyond—another hallway like this one, corridors leading to more corridors?

"Stop," E says, her glow passing him, her face turning to float before his, her swarm backpedaling without touching the ground. "John, stop this."

But he's not John, won't follow orders like John would have.

"I don't want to die," C says, gasping out the words, unable to avoid the mistake. Each word a step lost, a diminishment of the possible moves left to him.

"You won't die," she says, her shape shattering. "You'll live on, safe in your own swarm. Inside me are all the voices of man and woman and child, every Volunteer who trusted me to get them to the future. All those promises, thinning but not gone: Are we not there, in the future? In the swarm, I hear every voice simultaneously, we share everything equally."

C doesn't remember who E was but he recognizes what's left of her will. He trudges onward, stubborn to the last. E's swarm becomes hundreds of mites, beetles, and bees, here and there something naming itself a *worm*: they land on C's face, his neck, his branches, go scurrying through his leaves. Her face is reduced to a glowing jawbone, a suggestion of lips parting, teeth and tongue visible, the rest of the skull vanished. "You are not your body," she says. "When you're out of your rung, you won't be alone anymore. All of you, all the different selves you were, the lives you lived, they'll be distinct voices, one bot for every you there ever was. Together we'll be so many people, we can be all of humanity together."

You are not your body, E says, but C doesn't believe her. He isn't only part creature, part tree; he's flesh and blood, plastic and steel. Outside of this body, who would he be? A ghost who remembers being a man, a creature, a tree, a beetle or a bee? He tries to shake his head but it barely moves, his neck stiffened by a new wooden protrusion poking against his trachea, straining his speech.

"No," he says, his good knee weakening, threatening to tumble him to the floor. "No," his voice flattening into despair. The tree he tried to save, the tree he brought E? He believes it's what she hoped for too, all these years. What she's been waiting for. What everyone inside her has been waiting to see, *new life.* So why can't she see what he sees? Why can't she let it alone, let it live as it wants, planted in his flesh?

E says, "You can't escape. Your flight ends the moment I will it. This vain attempt, is it for you or for the tree? C, the tree will survive better without you."

He tries to speak but cannot: *I am the ground the tree lives in,* he wants to say. *I am the only earth the tree knows, and I do not want to let it go.*

But now he asks himself: *What does the tree want?*

Only the tree is him. He might as well ask: *What do I want?*

But he's never truly known the answer to that question. Not in any of his many lives.

E's swarm lifts off C's body to re-form a mouth already clicking and whistling. The dwarves climb out of the grates in the floors, out of hatches into tunnels leading to nowhere C has ever seen. Within seconds they're bounding on all fours, running on their knuckles to leap atop him. He struggles, but only with the half of him that's flesh, resisting now with curled fist and flailing hoof. He punches at one dwarf, he kicks another, but it's not enough. The dwarves pile on, their naked weight overwhelming his waning strength, dragging him down, the tree breaking against the concrete, the sludgy red blood-sap leaking, the blinding pain of bark flush with nerves breaking apart. In one of the dwarf's gnarled hands, C sees a branch, strained and almost snapped—and on the branch, he sees something new, something he didn't know was there: the first unripe fruit his tree has ever grown.

He moans, he bucks and squirms, he stops, gives in, gives up.

WHEN C WAKES FROM THE DWARVES' SURGERY HE IS HALF MACHINE, or more than half, his mind at home in the less than half of who he was that's flesh: the remaining arm, the leg, the hoof, the ruined torso covered in bandages, threaded with tubes and wires; the bark of him removed and replaced with a printed shell stapled to the skull, his swelling brain pushing at its unaccommodating cages, one bone and one plastic, both prisons of apparently unending pain.

The tree is cut from his body, but not gone. All this time he'd misunderstood, had thought the tree had been something separate, something growing out of him, not a new part of him that's also him.

Now C is the human-enough creature strapped to the bed, flesh riddled with machinery, dying, a body being prepped for the scanner.

Now he is the tree, floating in its new habitat, its bloody

roots replanted in chemical soil, a bed of prepared dirt and biomass.

He hears the scuttling of beetle legs against a glass jar, knows their legs are his legs; he feels a rush of recycled air moving through his mossy blades of purple grass, replanted all around the tree's severed trunk.

The next morning, he watches E's green glow circle the tree, her shape nearly incorporeal, all her swarm summoned to substantiate a hand with which to pick a single fruit, ripened overnight upon the tree C once was, still is.

C knows when E leaves the chamber where the dwarves have planted the tree; he waits for her to float into the operating theater, her form reduced to a hand holding something almost an apple. In its chamber, the tree grieves its missing fruit; in doing so it learns absence, a letting go, an end to the joy of how when the apple was connected to its branch it was both tree and not tree, a future connected to the present by the slimmest of stems. Now the fruit is set apart: the apple darkest red, its glowing skin soft velvet; its stem thorned, the thorns spiraled into tight horns; its stem leafed, E bearing two of C's leaves back to him.

In the recovery room, E puts the apple in C's only hand, closing his furred fingers around the fuzzy fruit, his claws gently denting the apple's skin.

E's shape shimmers, the hand evaporating as the body and face solidify. Floating beside his bed, amid the hums and beeps of his life support machines, she says, "Let me tell you a story." Her buzzing weight shifts nearer, a shape almost a woman's, her voice tickling his one remaining ear. "In the Garden," she says, "there were many trees, but only one Tree. And on this Tree there grew an apple just like this one. There was an apple in the Garden, and there was a creature, a creature like you. The creature had been forbidden to eat the apple, but by whom, for what reason? Perhaps the price of eating the apple was the creature's death; perhaps it was the doom of his world. But maybe none of those prohibitions lasted. Maybe one day the creature found himself past the end of the story into which he'd been born. Maybe all the gods who made the rules, all who'd watched and judged the creature, maybe all those gods were gone. Maybe now the creature was free to eat whatever it wanted. And so the creature—the creature who is also a man—makes a choice. Afterward, no matter what happens, surely the world doesn't end. The world lives, even if the creature, last of his kind, even if by making his choice he comes to die."

E takes the fruit from C's weakening hand before it falls to the floor. "You choose," she says, lifting the fruit to his mouth. "Choose," she says, forcing it against his lips, its rough hairs tickling what's left of his bristly beard.

C chooses. He squeezes his empty fist weakly, just enough to send John's recovered virus surging out of his rung and into the air to infect E's swarm, the program entering her bots through a backdoor designed centuries ago, a security flaw never patched in any new design. This is the sure end of human intelligence, an ending delayed only until the bots that make up E's last body fade and fail: never again will she be able to transfer her consciousness to another swarm, another body. When the virus finishes its undetected upload, her face flashes then temporarily goes dark; after her glow returns, she smiles her wolfish smile, that once famous grin made momentarily uncertain. Nervously, she offers the apple ever more persistently against C's mouth, pressing its fur against his teeth.

"Choose," E insists—but C already has—"Choose," she thunders—and in the end, C eats the apple—

Or else he doesn't.

Either way, at the center of the apple, he worries he's the worm.

———

See the great Tree, kept sequestered beneath the Mountain only until the weather above shifts and the great snows slow, until the ground beyond the gate can be properly prepared, its crust broken and tilled, irrigated and fed nutrients collected long ago. All this costs precious time, but the Tree might live a thousand years, it might live five thousand years or ten—surely the Tree will live as long as it's needed. After its final planting, it ages onward unmolested and untended, freed at last to become whatever it will, in soil nourished by rainwater and snowmelt, its thorned boughs lifting its leaves toward the brightening sun; decade by decade it grows into a massive tower of crooked black branches budding ever more feathery blossoms, producing ever more bountiful harvests of glowing red-furred fruit softly illuminating the many seedlings and saplings soon growing among the columnar monoliths and the sharp black obelisks, all those old warnings slowly being undone by the Tree's creeping suckers, by its bloody roots digging down, breaking bedrock, churning dead clay into future soil.

Bright beetles buzz by on the fragrant breezes above the Tree's flowers, building waxy hives and papery nests in the hollows of its trunks; later generations give up their wings, preferring to crawl through the spreading purple-grass prairie or to dig beneath the Tree's roots, spawning new species to evolve into every empty niche. Every passing year the sky above turns a bluer shade of blue, and on the brightest summer days the melting mountain snowpack sends clean cold water coursing down the slopes to carve new spillways and new pools, to replenish dried-up lakes and ancient aquifers.

The gate leading underground is left gaping, its black maw leading into a past from which a final few machines emerge, tilling ever wider spirals of desert ahead of the coming monsoon rains. As late as a century after the Tree is planted before the Mountain, two pale green ghosts sometimes still move among its offspring, at last wanting nothing from them. One ghost is horned and hooved, planting his steps while the other floats, her bare feet trailing beneath the hem of her gossamer dress, pretend fabric wavering in the real wind; this green-glowing faun and brightly lit nymph are two minds sharing the same swarm, pausing often to listen to the droning keening that leaks from the monoliths, a voice once believed to be able to sing many futures into being, including this new hope the ghosts begrudgingly accept was never meant for them.

Finally every digging machine runs down, every monolith crumbles, dismantled by the Tree and its offspring. When the last monolith goes, the song stops. In the quiet that follows the ghosts fade and flicker out too, their voices vanishing one bot at a time, until there's only the sweet wind breathing through the leaves of the many young trees, only the buzzings of the abundance of beetles they support and the rustling of new species of grasses in their shade; and sometime after that last hour of the ghosts there follows the unwitnessed clamor and glory of the Tree's apples thumping to the ground one after another, more furred apples than ever before rolling through purple-blooded grass, each bright-gleaming fruit full of seeds, each seed flush with potential, carrying within it all the many trees and not trees coming next, enough living variety to one day spawn a newly sprawling splendor, a beginning born of a forgetting, not an orchard of human want but a forest set free, a forest endlessly desiring to plant itself a world.

ACKNOWLEDGMENTS

Thank you to my editor, Katherine Nintzel, whose keen talent improved this novel in innumerable ways; to Eliza Rosenberry, Molly Gendell, Nancy Tan, Angela Boutin, Ploy Siripant, and everyone else I've had the pleasure of working with at Custom House; and to my agent, Kirby Kim, whose constant championing of my work has made so much possible.

Thank you to all my friends who aided my writing here, with special thanks to Anne Valente, Joseph Scapellato, and Gregory Howard, for their sustaining long-distance conversations; to Amber Sparks, for being my first reader and for her invaluable encouragement; to Travis Franks, for his counsel, especially on issues of settler colonialism; to Mark Doten, for celebrating with me in the hours after I finished writing the first draft of this book and for all his wisdom over the past decade; and to Ron Broglio and Jeffrey Cohen, for so much, including our regular Wednesday afternoons at Tops, where so many invaluable conversations were had.

Thank you to the Vermont Studio Center, where I wrote much of this novel's last act in what will likely be the most intense week of writing I'll ever experience. Thank you to all my students and colleagues at Arizona State University, especially those in my two novel writing classes; Ed Finn and Joey Escrich at the Center for Science and the Imagination; and Leah Newsom, who co-taught a crucial class on climate fiction and eco-fabulism with me. Thank you to Bradford Morrow at *Conjunctions* and Kaj Tanaka at *Gulf Coast*, for generously publishing excerpts from *Appleseed* while it was still in progress.

Thank you most of all to my wife, Jessica, for her unequaled love and support, and for her great affection for nature, expressed in her photography, her volunteering and advocacy work, and her continuing education as a naturalist and a birder. I'm so lucky to be a witness to her care for our wild places and for everything that inhabits them, and to spend countless hours alongside her exploring and enjoying the natural world we both love.

Appleseed, like all novels, owes innumerable debts to the books and writings of others. For instance, one moment in Chapman's final chapter is a retelling of Jack Gilbert's poem "Hunger"; earlier, a settler Chapman meets gives a speech adapted from a passage in R. Douglas Hurt's *The Ohio Frontier*. The author John quotes but can't quite remember is Wendell Berry, whose *The Unsettling of America* was a major influence; similarly, Naomi Klein's *The Shock Doctrine* provided the framework I needed for designing that timeline's political upheaval. The obstacles C-433 faces in his final approach to Black Mountain were inspired by the Sandia National Laboratories report titled "Expert Judgment on Markers to Deter Inadvertent Human Intrusion into the Waste Isolation Pilot Plant," authored by Kathleen M. Trauth, Stephen C. Hora, and Robert V. Guzowski. Finally, thanks to Michael Pollan, whose recounting of the legend of Johnny Appleseed in his *The Botany of Desire* provided the imaginative spark that set me down the path of this novel.

About the author

Read on

Insights,
Interviews
& More . . .

Meet Matt Bell

Jessica Bell

MATT BELL is the author of the novels *Scrapper* and *In the House Upon the Dirt Between the Lake and the Woods* as well as the short-story collection *A Tree or a Person or a Wall*, a nonfiction book about the classic video game *Baldur's Gate II*, and several other titles. His most recent book is *Refuse to Be Done*, a guide to novel writing, rewriting, and revision. His writing has appeared in *The New York Times Book Review, Esquire, Fairy Tale Review, American Short Fiction, Orion*, and many other publications. A native of Michigan, Bell teaches creative writing at Arizona State University. ❧

"The Monstrous Birth"

"The Monstrous Birth" was originally published in Gulf Coast.

This short story was originally written as a backstory chapter in *Appleseed,* but even before I'd finished it, I knew it probably wouldn't be included in the novel. Still, I liked it on its own merits, and so I'm glad to include it as a short story here for readers wanting a little more Chapman. It tells of events that in the novel proper are sketched out in only a few scattered sentences, detailing Chapman's birth to human parents in 1770s Massachusetts. But what happens here isn't quite the same as what's explained elsewhere, in part because *Gulf Coast* editor Kaj Tanaka wisely pushed me to give this version an ending that could stand on its own, without a need for the rest of *Appleseed.* Because of those changes, the birth story related here is perhaps best thought of as a retelling of my Chapman's origin, in the same way that my Chapman is a retelling of the historical John Chapman/Johnny Appleseed.

LONGMEADOW, MASSACHUSETTS, 1774

Now the long-awaited hour arrives, now the baby kicks and kicks, Elizabeth grunting at each blow, the baby's foot a hammer lashing out from within her ▶

swollen flesh. She puts a calloused hand atop her belly and feels the hard sharpness of her nearly born child's foot striking her palm once, twice, three times—and on the third strike she grabs at her taut skin, squeezing the pressing shape of the tiny foot: not for the first time, she catches something firm and angular pressed hard against her skin, rising from deep within.

Her hand holds the painful angle—*What,* she thinks, *is this child within me?*—and then she releases the foot, watches its wriggling shape sink back beneath skin and muscle and membrane.

Freed from her grasp, the baby immediately kicks again, once, twice, the blows arrhythmic and sharp, and Elizabeth thinks: *Not a hammer. An anvil.* And not that either.

She is a farmer's daughter from a line of farmers' daughters. She thinks, *I am giving birth to a beast,* knowing another version of herself—Elizabeth who is not pregnant—would think this ridiculous. But Elizabeth who is pregnant has come full to term and such thoughts are common now, all the ways her steady brain struggles to keep up with her changeable body, stretched anew to accommodate this last child.

The autumn breeze stirs the cabin's air, singing through the room's shutters, left open to let in the day's light, the afternoon sun that today burnishes the family's possessions into brightest gold. In the yard, her husband swings his axe over and over again, splitting another cord of firewood, and inside the house the blows from within Elizabeth's belly begin to keep similar time—*left foot right foot,* she thinks, *left foot right foot left hoof*—until she cries out loud enough that her husband pauses his work.

The kicking stops too, and Elizabeth bites the meat of her thumb to still her voice, to keep from crying out too early for her husband's help. He isn't an especially attentive father—even her son Nathaniel gets only the attention required to instruct him in his chores, in the ways of plowing and planting, animal husbandry and the butchering of meat—but Elizabeth believes her husband is a good man, a solid man not given to squeamishness or despair. His love goes, as Elizabeth supposes he thinks it must, to the land where they have built this home: to its fields, which only recently have finally been cleared of their unsightly stumps and boulders;

to their small herd of cows and goats, animals he knows better than he knows any of his children.

A moment later, the sound of chopping resumes, and with it the painful kicking, that strange foot once again pounding the skin in time with her husband's axe blows. Elizabeth knows what she sees and feels but she's not sure what exactly it is she's about to free from her body. For weeks, she has thought of saying to her husband, "Our baby is an animal," but she knows he will not believe her, that he would only look at her with the flat blank stare he reserves for when she's being too fanciful, making herself ridiculous in his eyes.

But her husband has not put his hand against her belly. He has not felt the foot as she has, has not felt the hoof pressed hot against the inside of her skin.

A galloping, Elizabeth thinks, almost laughing aloud. *A beast of the fields, ready to be loosed from the pen of my body.*

Elizabeth awoke this morning prepared to wait, but by midafternoon it's obvious her labor is progressing faster than expected. The kicking feet continue their pummeling, and she realizes her baby isn't coming sometime later this day but right now. As her thoughts linger over the word *beast,* she feels him begin to move anew, falling fast through the heat of her body, his dense shape dropping sharp and urgent, his imminent arrival announcing itself with a fresh blast of such violent pain that Elizabeth barely has time to call out for her husband before she weakens almost past the point of speech: *Chapman,* she cries, thrusting herself against the posts of a window frame at the back of the house, *Chapman Chapman,* Elizabeth screams, Elizabeth who from the first has always called her husband affectionately by his last name, *Chapman Chapman Chapman,* the name she was so glad to take after her first husband died, leaving her and her Nathaniel abandoned and alone and without sure prospects upon what was then the very edge of this American frontier.

AT THE CHOPPING BLOCK, Chapman hears the distant alarm in Elizabeth's voice and comes running. Finding his pale and slender wife staggering wall to wall down the skinny hallway of the tiny ▶

clapboard house, Chapman leans his axe against the doorframe, then takes Elizabeth in his arms and carries her into the bedroom, lays her on the bed where all their four daughters have been conceived and borne and birthed. Seeing Elizabeth's body contorting in the reddening bedsheets he thinks of how lucky he is that his children are off playing together outdoors, so that this sight will not be the last memory they have of their mother—for as soon as Chapman sees Elizabeth's labor pains he's sure she's going to die.

"Elizabeth," Chapman says, speaking around an anger he cannot swallow, "tell me what to do and I will do it."

Chapman is rarely tender, never subservient, and the acquiescent tone in his voice scares Elizabeth more than any amount of bloody pain. She's scared but she has resolved to greet this child whose clawed fingernails and sharp hooves she has felt scratching at her for months. He's coming fast, hurrying to meet her. The baby is coming now, and as Elizabeth moves her hands over her heaving belly she realizes he's also coming turned, breech, like her second daughter had.

"Do you remember," Elizabeth says, her voice an insistent rasp, "when Lucy was born? Do you remember, dear Chapman?"

Chapman remembers. How the midwife was able to reach inside Elizabeth, to turn the baby. Chapman is no midwife, but he's seen a calf born breech, has tugged a turned goat kid from the body of a straining doe. His wife isn't a cow or a goat and he's no midwife, but he kneels between her splayed legs, he hesitates only a moment when she cries out again, her feet juddering the cedar bed frame, her swollen toes curled in pain. Chapman takes a deep breath. He enters her hesitantly, his fingers questing for the baby's bottom he expects, but when they touch the stuck child he pulls back, confused.

He says, "Elizabeth, there's something wrong with the baby."

"No," she says, whispering through clenched teeth. "Not wrong. Different."

Elizabeth howls and grunts and her body heaves and Chapman reaches in again and what he finds isn't only the baby's body but also the slick membrane of a caul, something he knows only from goats—is there anything about the bodies of women that

Chapman did not learn first from his livestock?—and within the tearing caul he feels something else, kicking and scratching its way through the membrane: the two cloven hooves attached to two furry legs, impossible limbs struggling their way free of his wife's body and the amnion that encloses them.

Now, at least, Chapman knows what to do. He wraps one strong hand around the two tiny hooves, the branch-like legs, the caul sliding slimily between him and the child, and then he pulls.

In goats, Chapman thinks insanely, *the caul breaks when the kid falls to the ground.*

Elizabeth moans as the baby begins to move again but Chapman does not pause his pulling. It must be done all at once, he must get this child out of his wife, then out of the caul so it can breathe. Chapman's own breath grows ragged as he tugs evenly at the two hooves held crisscrossed in his right hand, the caul a wet greasiness caught between him and the task. The legs come free—furred and bony below the knees, the hair thickening over chunky baby fat thighs—then Chapman sees a mass of black fur over narrow hips—*a boy,* he thinks when he spies the genitals, *my promised son,* the thought both maniacal and grieving—and now the rest of the caul slips, ripping beneath Chapman's scrabbling fingers, now the belly and torso of the baby as ordinarily human as other child's he has ever seen, and somehow this is worse than if the entire child had been born a goat—and then the head comes free of Elizabeth's body—the head momentarily obscured by the last of the caul hanging over his crown, the caul soon wiped away—a head covered by wet black hair almost but not quite thick enough to hide his son's two tiny horns, sharp buds curving upward from the temples.

Lifting his son in his hands, Chapman screams, something he has not, he's almost positive, ever done before in his long and stoic life.

When the sound stops, Chapman is standing before his wife, holding their child—a child half-covered in fur, a child horned and hooved, a child crying out its first needs into the air, still attached to its mother by its umbilical cord—and Elizabeth is smiling, delirious, reaching out with trembling arms.

Elizabeth says, "Chapman, give me my son," and Chapman ▶

looks down at the baby and realizes he cannot, will not give this *thing* to his wife.

"No," he says. "Whatever this is, this is no child of ours."

"Please, Chapman," she says, her eyes lidded, her voice barely a whisper. The bed rent and ruined. The air in the bedroom thick with sweat and iron. "Please."

"No," Chapman says, "this child is a devil, a curse"—but if Elizabeth asks again, he knows he will have to say yes, because never before has he denied his much-loved wife anything three times.

She does not ask again. And in the silence that follows Chapman is free to do what he wants, what later he will know he planned from the second his hand touched the hard angles of his son's cloven feet.

THE CHAPMAN HOME IS at the far edge of Longmeadow, and between Chapman's house and the nearest neighbor's there are still virgin stands of uncut wood, plus a deep sandy ravine carving its stubborn way through the otherwise reshaped landscape, its sides steep and its bottom nearly unplantable swampland. Thanks to the woods and the ravine, the Chapman homestead is private enough, secluded enough, that Chapman does not hesitate as he walks out of the house with the horned child squalling in his arms, he does not wrap the child in anything more concealing than a blanket before crossing his fields and pasture for the western woods beyond.

At first Chapman seems to wander, his route through the dark woods rarely straight, but despite his angry haste he has a sure destination in mind: a small clearing in the woods, an orchard of wild apple trees he visited long ago and never again since. The ground crackles with fallen leaves and dry pine straw, but there is a springy moistness under Chapman's steps, the densely nutritious humus of a thousand years of abundance and decay that undergirds this wild edge of the Massachusetts colony. A man unfamiliar with the landscape could easily become lost, but for Chapman there are trails to seek, narrow paths through the brambles left by the playing of his children, by the passage of larger mammals from bedding to food to water and back again.

When he first set out, he wasn't exactly sure the orchard he sought was a real place, that his memory of the abandoned trees was not the memory of a dream—

But then, with unlikely ease, he finds he's already there.

The orchard is small, a stand of a dozen irregularly planted apple trees clumped too close together, the untended ground between overgrown with native grasses and scrubs. The apple trees themselves are unruly and untrimmed, branches heavy with spotted fruit, trunks flush with sucker roots stretching out in every direction. No decent farmer would stand his trees looking so untamed, but Chapman knows this orchard is no longer any inhabited place, just a past settler's failure gone wild again.

There is something else about it, something unimaginative Chapman does not have the language to describe, although it's this quality that attracted him here today. How the earth here seems less solid, less real than the woods that surround the orchard. How the trees, leaves dancing in the breeze, seem also to *flicker,* a word uncommon enough in this time that it's possible Chapman might not know its shape or its sound.

Whether he could name it or not, this flicker is why Chapman is here. A strange place for a strange deed.

Chapman steps to the center of the circle of trees. He holds his monstrous son roughly, thankful for the blanket tight around its horrible legs, its mother-murdering hooves still trying to kick. He looks down upon the unlikely face, its budding horns, its long mouth open still but fallen silent, its gray eyes set too far apart below the wide forehead, their orbs unfocused and searching.

Searching for what? A mother? A father? It will find neither, not here.

"Whatever you are," Chapman says, "you will be no son of mine."

Chapman lays his hand on the haft of his knife, returned to his belt after cutting the child's umbilical cord. He has made this decision before; he has killed calves or lambs born wrong or runtish without a second thought, the act no crime but only a part of farming, of decent husbandry. It should be easy to do the deed here, out of sight of any other man. ▶

"The Monstrous Birth" *(continued)*

Chapman grows frustrated that it is not.

Chapman lets his slow mind tumble toward its decision, pushes away the questionable, quarreling logic of his doubts—*if the child is a devil, it is not all devil; if it is a son of mine, it is not all my son*—and decides that if he cannot kill the child, he can still be sure it does not live.

Setting the child down on the grassy orchard ground, Chapman unswaddles its horrible body. He gently lifts its squalling weight and slides the blanket out from underneath, letting the creature fall naked upon the rough grass and the fallen leaves. The blanket is something beautiful Elizabeth made, born of her hands, but despite this child's birth from her body, Chapman has convinced himself the baby is something other: a mistake, a curse, a punishment. For years, he's prayed for the growth of his family, for an increase in the numbers of his small herd of livestock. Here on the grass before him might be one answer to his two questions, but what good man should be forced to accept such a bedeviled reply, even from God?

Chapman watches the child's naked movements, its hooves scraping lightly at the chilled earth, its mouth quietly hungry and grasping. It is dusk, it is autumn in New England, the day's heat has vanished, the air already darker and colder than when he set out. Chapman tells himself that the night is full of dangers, that even tomorrow there might be little sign this child ever lived. All that might be left will seem the remains of a lost goat carried off by wolves, broken bones and inedible hooves, evidence anyone else might believe once belonged to some Longmeadow farmer's flock.

Evidence of a struggle, sure, but not evidence of an infanticide, because whatever remains might be nothing anyone would recognize as a child.

Chapman speaks the only words he will ever address to this son of his, this son that belongs to him no matter how he denies its parentage: "I cannot promise you will not suffer, but I hope you will not suffer long."

Good enough for Chapman, who believes he's lost so much today that this last loss fails to register. When he turns his back on his final child, he feels nearly nothing, because already his heart is exhausted, grieving the woman he has quietly loved instead of this devil child whose face he will never see again, he hopes—he hopes, he cannot believe he can still hope and yet here he is, hoping, hoping as he turns and walks away, hoping for the unwanted child's ending to be quick and final and forgotten.

Now THE HORNED CHILD barks in a worldless language, cries out his lonely complaints into the falling dusk. Choking on his own spit, he clears his throat and begins to cry again; he struggles unswaddled against the cold, his bare brown chest left exposed, although his furred legs are no more naked than those of any other woodland babe. No human comes but other creatures are called to gather around the edge of the wild orchard: first a rust-furred fox appears near the tree line, then a pair of barely grown female coyotes slink into the shadows falling on the orchard's other side. A raven taller than a human toddler claims the crown of the tree nearest the baby and caws away an opportunistic vulture circling overhead. A bobcat climbs a rock still warm from the afternoon sun, upon which it might stretch and yawn, feigning boredom but anything but bored.

The baby comprehends little of this, sees almost nothing with his slowly opening eyes. He kicks his hooves and arches his back and balls his dumb fists. He cries until his golden cheeks turn blue, his tiny white nubs of horn nearly glowing against the bruising color of his too-wide face. Around him, more beasts gather: a jackrabbit sitting tall on its huge haunches, a white-tailed deer and her fawn browsing nose-down in nearby thistles. The raven holds court over the treetops but other birds join her, jays and starlings sharing an apple branch, and overhead circling diving sparrows practice their acrobatics. At dusk, an owl joins the raven, the two birds jostling vocally for command of the scene. The animals gather but they do not approach the furry babe, all of them keeping their distance except one, the last to arrive: through the pooling dark beneath the apple trees, a timber rattlesnake slinks silently toward the child, its dark scales barely rustling the low grass, its quick-flickering tongue steering the way.

Most of the rattlesnake's kind are brown or copper, their long shapes banded with black rings, but this one is dark end to end, ▶

its scales black on black, with only the tiniest variations visible in the moonlight. And then only if one knows how to look, how to see the nearly invisible snake undulating across the orchard earth.

But with all eyes on the child, no one is looking for the snake.

Now it approaches the child unnoticed by the owl, who might have swooped from its perch to snatch it by the neck, carrying it high into the night sky.

It goes unnoticed by the raven, who might likewise have flexed its talons around its scales, or by the white-tailed doe, who like all hooved animals hates snakes and could have attempted to stamp the rattler to death.

It goes unnoticed by the bobcat, who might have hissed at its coming, and by the fox and coyotes, who prey on snakes but never one of this size.

The rattler slithers ever closer, its scales scratching through the grass, skittering over rock and dirt and branch with the same slow ease. It is so very close now, its head a body's length away from this seemingly defenseless child, a babe abandoned and alone, obliviously crying itself sick, its wild eyes too young to focus.

The rattlesnake slides close, its undulations tightening, its speed increasing, until slowly it coils in on itself in the shaded grass, rising to strike.

Its fangs glinting in the moonlight. Its jaws unhinging above the baby's neck.

The rattlesnake rears back its head, its gaze the dull and unthinking and dangerously blank expression of any reptilian predator, a snake always only a snake and nothing more besides—but its strike is met from below by a matching blow, the child's clawed hand catching the snake's neck with an unexpected, uncanny dexterity.

The child, born this day but hardly helpless, closes his tiny, furred fist around the rattlesnake's black throat, his grip strong beneath the snapping fangs and flickering tongue. The snake writhes and tries to flee, it furiously thrashes its body, swinging its great black length through the grass and against the child's strange shape, but the crush of the child's grip does not open.

The child cannot yet stand, but he will soon enough. Already he has enough control to plant his hooves into the dense dark soil, instinctually seeking leverage. He arcs his back and pulls the rattlesnake against his chest, one hand still around the snake's throat, the other clutching its flailing body close in a deadly first embrace. The snake's entire body is become tail, a tail whipping and lashing in long strokes of mindless anger, its rattle rattling with desperate alarm. But everywhere this child is not covered in fur he is covered in thick tough skin, he is a creature of hoof and horn, of leather, bark, and stone—and whatever he is, whatever name you might call this creature so new to this American continent, surely whatever he is was never meant to be any simple snake's prey.

Surely this miraculous child was not meant for such an end.

WHO OR WHAT HAD sent the rattlesnake? No one, nothing. It was only a snake, a symbol of nothing, self-willed and hungry, closing in on some new prey. Now it dies; dies suffocating, as the baby lets slip an awful inhuman giggle. The giggle becomes full-throated laughter, a *bray*, a sound so incongruously joyous it almost makes the child adorable, despite his unfathomable oddness. Without releasing the dead snake, he begins to kick his hooves in a steady trotting rhythm, digging into the earth to turn himself over. For just a moment, he's on his hands and knees, ready to crawl, and then he's already standing on his two unsteady legs, an event so joyous he lets out a triumphant cry, a cry whose barking sound causes every apple on every branch of every tree in the rewilded orchard to break loose from its stem, apples of every color and condition falling suddenly to the ground in a cascade of wet and weighty thumps.

The animals standing watch are used to the violence of predation and escape, but not this creature's strange laughter nor the sudden plummet of so many apples. Startled, they scatter, the bobcat leaping from its rock, the doe jumping with white tail flashing back into deeper woods, the birds fluttering into flight, all except the raven, which keeps its perch and only caws all the louder once the owl and the jays and starlings and sparrows take wing. The animals flee quickly, and the child follows: having taken his first step only a moment before, he's soon standing, ▶

weaving hoof to hoof at the edge of the small orchard, staring up at the moon rising above the western lip of the forest.

The child drapes the dead length of the giant black rattlesnake around his thin but sturdy neck, he drags the snake's broken length behind his prancing steps. With one hand, he secures the fanged head by its neck; with the other, he clutches a battered and bruised apple, gathered from among the many fruits fallen to the scuffed earth of this wild orchard. So recently born, he is already teething, sharp white teeth poking through bloody pink gums: the child is hungry and if there is no one to nurse him, then he must make what he needs to feed himself.

There is blood on the child's face but it's the child's own blood, dripping from his burst gums. He lifts his apple up before the moon to study it in the light, turning it this way and that with his small, clawed hand.

The apple is a particularly misshapen fruit, worm-spotted and browning, but the baby is so hungry. He sticks the apple between the raw needles of his new teeth. He bites down. His teeth ache but still he squeals with delight at the apple's taste, at its juices running down his long face and onto his fleshy torso, sticky clear juice rivuleting down what on any other baby you might call a tummy, but not on this one, his belly fuzzed as it is with fur that falls down over the baby's narrow hips, his shriveled genitals, his goatish legs.

The baby bites through the apple's skin again, he tastes the apple and he tastes his own blood and then he giggles again.

The suddenly agile kid giggles terribly, and then he runs off into the western woods, dragging his snakeskin and carrying the remains of his apple toward what he will learn to call the American frontier, a land already filling with industrious men but that for a little longer might still house other creatures as divinely wild as himself, a land where he might grow up as not quite man nor animal, only himself, a species of one, undomesticated and free, at least until he reaches the age at which he begins his life's work.

Watch the child flee the death his father intended him, but know as he goes west the hint of his future life he tasted in that first apple, taste made destiny: how for the child every apple skin will contain a world of flavor and texture, flesh and core and seeds; how every such world will tell the man the child will become its own unique story of sunlight and soil, water and rain, and the passage of time; how likewise for every creature born there must be one best tale waiting to be lived, one best tale waiting to be chosen, like a fruit wanting to be plucked from any good seed-grown tree, a fruit offering an experience normally never to be exactly repeated—but given an infinite number of apple trees, surely even the wildest fruit *could* occur more than once.

Surely, given enough chances, every good thing would have to come again.

Surely some stories, no matter how known, can be told as many times as it takes to get them right, if only you plant enough seeds.

This horned child, fleeing the edge of the settled world, headed west on new hooves? One day he will try to plant them all. ∽